STEPHANIE CHONG

"Chong delivers a wicked tale of a sexy guardian angel
battling for a not-so-lost demon's soul."
—*New York Times* bestselling author Caridad Piñeiro

"Stephanie Chong taps into a delicious fantasy
older than time, spinning it masterfully into a sexy,
moving tale that feels fresh and new.
I am sincerely her newest fan."
—*New York Times* bestselling author Maggie Shayne

"Mix a spirited angel with a sexy demon,
and you get one heavenly read!"
—*New York Times* bestselling author Kerrelyn Sparks

Watch for the next book
in the Company of Angels series
coming from Stephanie Chong and MIRA Books.
THE DEMONESS OF WAKING DREAMS
will be available in fine bookstores everywhere
in Spring 2012.

WHERE DEMONS FEAR TO TREAD

STEPHANIE CHONG

MIRA®

ISBN-13: 978-0-7783-1247-5

Recycling programs for this product may not exist in your area.

WHERE DEMONS FEAR TO TREAD

For questions and comments about the quality of this book please contact us at Customer_eCare@Harlequin.ca.

www.MIRABooks.com

Printed in U.S.A.

To Ed, my beloved husband,
my very own demon lover turned guardian angel.

Prologue

Nobody understood the fine art of poison like Luciana Rossetti.

After two hundred years, the mysteries of deadly plants, of animal extracts and lethal bacteria had long since surrendered their secrets to Luciana's subtle hand. Adder venom or anthrax, belladonna or botulinum, she loved them all. Took pleasure in the unique properties of every toxin. Her pale green eyes glittered, fixed on the vial she held now, the liquid inside it deceptively dull beneath the crystal chandeliers cascading from the vaulted ceiling overhead.

A tiny glass vial whose contents looked as guiltless as holy water.

Colorless. Odorless. Tasteless.

Perfection.

But this little vial held not a blessing, but a curse. A curse only a demon could dream up. A curse that could send another of her kind straight back to hell.

"What's in your newest concoction, my love?"

Her lover's voice broke her reverie. His fingers slid through her sable curls, his lips brushed against the exposed skin of her neck. What feathered down her body was not a shiver of pleasure, but anticipation of something darker.

"Something splendid, *mio caro*," she said, her voice sweet and smooth.

Luciana knew better than to disclose the little vial's exact contents, even to Corbin. Especially not to Corbin. In the three months of their affiliation, she had learned that he was not a creature to be toyed with. Nor was he to be trusted. His clean-cut Nordic masculinity could have featured in an ad campaign for yachting or polo. But in his amber-colored eyes, cruelty lit like a flash of lightning, that quick and that powerful.

Every demon in his employ, within this hotel and in all his others, respected and feared him. As an Arch-demon deserved to be respected and feared.

For Luciana, the benefits of taking Corbin as a lover outweighed the considerable risks. He was the fastest way to get what she wanted.

Revenge.

He pulled her toward the sofa, and she clutched the little vial in the palm of her hand as they sank together into the sumptuous velvet. His amber eyes regarded her, a lion's gaze settling on a prime bit of prey. She steeled herself to look back squarely. *That, or be eaten alive.*

With a blink, his intensity dissipated. He released her suddenly. "Let's test it out."

"Is there a dog somewhere in the hotel?" she asked.

"Hell, no. There's a bellboy who might be able to help us out." From an elegant little side table, he picked up a phone and said, "Send up the one who broke the vase."

When the bellboy arrived, Luciana almost felt sorry for him, a frail little excuse for a demon, who flinched visibly at Corbin's strong handshake.

So fragile, he's practically human, she thought.

"Are you aware that the vase you broke dated back to the Ming Dynasty?" Corbin said calmly.

The boy coughed. "No, sir. I didn't realize. I apologize."

Corbin let out a heavy sigh. "Sit down. Have a drink with us while we decide what is to be done. I've just decanted a vintage merlot I think we'll all enjoy." He gestured to Luciana. "Will you do the honors, my dear?"

While the young man took a seat in a leather chair, Luciana turned her back to them and poured three glasses of wine. Corbin distracted him with mindless talk as she meted out a few drops from the vial into the first glass. She watched, fascinated as it dissolved into the blood-red liquid. Seamless. Deadly. That glass, she handed to the boy.

"Please. Drink," said the Archdemon. She served Corbin a glass, and he swirled the wine, observing its color and its legs before inhaling its scent. He swallowed, and a smile of immense satisfaction crossed his face.

Luciana sipped her own wine, the dark notes of oak and plum sliding down her throat, loosening the wire-tight stretch of her nerves.

Finally, the boy took a small gulp that sent his Adam's apple up and down in an awkward little dance. "I know the vase must have been expensive, sir. I'm very sorry. I'll pay for it somehow."

"You could never," said Corbin. "It was priceless. Worth a hundred times your yearly salary. It would take you a century to pay for it. I don't think I'm willing to wait that long. Indeed, one might even say the vase was worth more than you are. The question of repayment is nil."

"There must be some way," said the boy. Worry creased his face. He swallowed once, touching a spot in the center of his neck. Then he cleared his throat. And again. The sound was awful even to Luciana's ears, the noise of death rattling up his windpipe as he began to choke.

He fell on the floor, twisting and convulsing. Luciana braced herself against reacting to his feebleness. If Corbin scented weakness in her, he would destroy her, too. But she was not weak. Weakness was something she had let go of two hundred years ago. When she'd let go of her own human life.

The twitching finally stopped. The boy lay on the floor, so still that his quietness seemed to create a vacuum in the room, a black hole of stillness. She did not look. She had seen corpses before, more than she cared to remember, although mostly human ones. The demon body had all the physical characteristics of the human one, but was virtually indestructible. Yet, as she had just proven, not altogether immortal. It was the *soul* that could never be destroyed. The soul of this boy would go back to where Corbin had found it.

Back to hell.

Corbin swirled his glass again. "So he was useful,

after all. Poison is such an antiquated means of disposal, but it produces some interesting results."

She inclined her head and smiled, accepting the compliment.

"This wine has such a lovely bouquet. Complex, yet subtle," he said, returning her smile. "I so love a woman who appreciates the finer things in life."

She tucked the vial into a silk sachet and then into her handbag. The poison had worked on a low-ranking demon. But its intended victim was a hundred times stronger.

Corbin caught her gaze, perhaps wondering if *he* were the intended victim. In that moment, she wondered how much he guessed. Whether he sensed that she was using him as a means to an end. But then he said, "If it can kill a demon, perhaps it could be useful in dealing with the Company of Angels. They've been causing trouble for me lately. Like sewer rats."

Luciana resisted the urge to roll her eyes.

Corbin was obsessed with the Company, a group of Guardians, whose vast network stretched around the globe. They worked in units of a few dozen individuals each, more united than anything demons had ever managed to organize. By their nature, demons were highly divisive, argumentative and generally incapable of co-operation. Unless driven by a dictator. Like Corbin.

"Why don't you just obliterate the Company outright?" she suggested, masking her disinterest. Luciana couldn't care less about angels. It was a demon she wanted to kill. One demon in particular.

"There are rules in the battle between angels and

demons," he said, frowning deeply. "Rules that must be honored. Rules that must not be broken."

"Rules can be bent."

His frown eased. "Your talents are wasted as a rogue demon, my dear. You may have your independence, but you don't have the support of a critical mass backing you. Consider joining my organization in a formal capacity."

"Perhaps one day, *mio caro*," she said.

The day hell freezes over. She would sooner poison herself and return to hell than join Corbin's demon mafia, under his control. Once she had finished what she had come here to accomplish, she would leave immediately, return to her home half a world away. *Back to Venice.*

And she did not plan on seeing Corbin again.

Now, he caught her by the waist, kissed her deeply. He whispered against her skin the perverse things he would do to her, the odd ways he had of pleasuring a woman, torturous yet strangely arousing all at once. It was difficult to say that she actually disliked having sex with him. Perhaps if the circumstances had been different, she would have let herself enjoy it. But they were not. She kissed him back and let her hands wander down his hard body, encouraging him. Letting the flush of his lust sweep away his suspicion.

To Luciana, Corbin was the lesser of two evils. She was far more concerned with his friend and business partner. Julian Ascher, the man who had ruined her life. Who had corrupted her innocence, had seduced her and then betrayed her. Who had left her no choice but to survive the only way she knew how. By harnessing the darkness within herself.

Now, the time of vengeance was approaching.

Revenge was a dish best served cold. Luciana's had been chilling for over two centuries, frozen into solid hatred, hard as ice, a dish she would shove down Julian's throat with the greatest of pleasure.

Chapter One

West Hollywood, Los Angeles

Devil's Paradise was the hottest place to party on a Saturday night in the City of Angels. The perfect venue for temptation. The ideal setting for sin. And it was all his.

Julian Ascher surveyed his nightclub from a glassed-in observation tower two stories above the dance floor. Below, a sea of nubile bodies writhed to the booming bass of the music. Sweat and pheromones mingled in the air. A legion of bartenders worked behind the bars of polished white terrazzo marble, pouring rivers of cocktails, beer and shots.

Most nights, Julian was content to stand up here, watching. But tonight, he was restless. Deep in his gut, a tension was building. He needed something to relieve that tension.

Preferably something soft and feminine.

He swung open the tower door. A blast of music and the heat from hundreds of bodies hit him, blaring into his pores as he descended the metal staircase to the main floor. The crowd parted, sensing his power as he strode through the club, past upturned, admiring faces.

Regulars reached out to shake his hand—a drunken football hero here, an underage starlet there.

A few women tried to engage him in conversation; he disengaged them easily and continued on his path. It was a hobby of his to destroy beautiful women. He found a great deal of gratification in ruining the sublime. But he had very particular tastes, and none of the females here tonight suited him. Disappointed, he wandered onward.

"Julian, over here!" the club's general manager shouted, trying to flag him down.

"Not now," he called back without stopping. He roamed through the mass of beautiful people who flocked here like butterflies drawn to a pool of nectar. As an Archdemon, Julian had been responsible for the corruption of *thousands* of souls. His chain of nightclubs stretched across the country. It had come to fruition after two hundred years of studying humans in their greatest moments of weakness and desperation, of fantasy and desire. And Julian, the owner of this empire of iniquity, had become a connoisseur of pleasure.

At the beginning, it wasn't so simple. As a fledgling demon, he'd had his share of battles over souls that he frequently lost. But now, after these two centuries, it was all becoming a little bit too easy. These days, when Julian fought for a soul, he always won.

His latest venture, Devil's Ecstasy, would open in Vegas at the end of the month. Housed in fellow Archdemon Corbin Ranulfson's spectacular Hotel Lussuria, the newest nightclub would be Julian's pièce de résistance. A guaranteed success.

So why wasn't he satisfied?

He swept his way through the crowd and into the VIP lounge. On the white leather furniture, couples necked and threesomes groped in plain sight. In one corner, a popular young Hollywood actor was snorting lines of coke off a call girl's exposed ass. Around him, clubgoers stared.

"Keep him happy," Julian said to one of his staff members. "Make sure he's well supplied tonight."

Julian's jaded gaze surveyed the scene, utterly indifferent to the lascivious behavior he saw around him. The same lecherous acts he saw every night that the club was open for business. Nothing here remotely excited him.

Sunk in utter apathy, Julian turned, ready to head back toward his observation post.

Then he saw her.

In the periphery of his vision, she shimmered like gold in a muddy riverbank. He blinked, unsure if what he'd seen was a trick of the light. When he turned his head to look again, there she stood.

She was dressed for a day at the beach, not for a night at the temple of sin. Her simple yellow sundress showcased toned arms and lithe curves. Blond hair curled in waves down her back. The structure of her face was classical perfection, her beauty so striking that it caught his eye even from a distance. Other men saw her, too. They circled like sharks scenting blood in the water. Was she searching for a lost friend? A lover?

As he stared, salivating, she looked up, as though she could read his thoughts across the noise and the crush of the VIP lounge. She gazed straight into his eyes.

From thirty feet away, it was a direct challenge. Then she turned and disappeared.

Somewhere deep inside him, the hunter's instinct engaged.

He tracked her through the crowd, glimpsing her blond hair, the exposed flesh of her shoulder as she wove deeper into the throng. The beat of the music pounded through his veins like an amphetamine high, spurring him on. He pushed his way toward her, oblivious to manners.

When she was within reaching distance, he closed his fingers around her arm. It was like stroking a newborn's cheek, her skin was so soft. The silk-covered steel of her biceps flexed beneath his tightening grip. Desire surged through his fingertips and landed straight in his groin. She stopped dead at his touch, swung to face him. From a distance, she was beautiful. Up close, she was divine.

His gaze drifted over her high cheekbones, her lush lips, her wide and trusting eyes. The innocence he saw in those eyes had nothing to do with guilelessness, and everything to do with faith. Faith in the untainted goodness of humankind. He wanted to devour her. To sink into her, to make himself a part of her and never let her go.

As he gripped her arm, time hung suspended. All noise stopped. Into that silence broke the rustling of feathers, the flare of a wingspan unfolding. The realization sent a jolt of energy reeling through his body—she was an angel. A Guardian, the lowest rank of celestial beings, responsible for the earthly care of humanity.

Why he was so surprised, he didn't know. He'd

encountered angels many times before, had battled with them often. But never were they foolish enough to set foot in his nightclubs. What was she doing here, in his domain?

He blinked. Around them, the club whirled back into action, the pounding bass of the dance music flooded back into his bones. She twisted, trying to disengage herself. He tightened his grip, unwilling to let go.

Whatever her reasons, she, in her innocent little sundress, with her laughable belief in the goodness of the human race, had entered Devil's Paradise.

And she was on *his* territory now.

What stopped Serena St. Clair was a mere brush of fingertips against her bare upper arm. The touch of a lover. A caress so gentle, so reverent and yet so sensual that it sent pleasure skimming over the surface of her skin. It washed over her entirely and set the most secret places of her body singing. Even in the hot crush of the nightclub, the sensation was so intense it stopped her cold.

When she turned, she found herself looking into the face of a god. Angular planes chiseled to a perfect symmetry that only a divine hand could have wrought. But his eyes were pure sin. There was no goodness in that gaze, only naked desire. He towered over her, his athlete's build draped in a perfectly cut suit, a dress shirt open at the throat. Armani, if she had to guess. His dark hair was artfully tousled, a casualness that contradicted the intensity of his gaze.

"Welcome to Devil's Paradise. I'm Julian Ascher."

His voice, low and deep, seemed to vibrate in her bones.

For a moment, she stood stunned. Then she reminded herself to breathe. Squeezing her eyes shut, she directed a burst of energy into his mind, a bright light that would override his willpower and wipe his memory clean of her. She waited for him to stumble away and release her, leaving her free to complete her assignment.

To find the human she was assigned to guard. And get the hell out of here.

Except Julian Ascher didn't move. A flicker of annoyance rippled across the surface of his casual facade. Then his perfect composure smoothed back into place. A single word reverberated in her mind and swirled in her gut.

Demon.

Somewhere deep inside her, a voice whispered: *Run.*

Arielle, her supervisor, had hammered an elementary principle into every trainee at the Company of Angels. *If you encounter a demon more powerful than you, get out immediately.*

Serena had completed her Company training with flying colors. But now she stood rooted to the spot, unable to move. Julian's fingers still curled around her upper arm. Yet, it wasn't the physical contact that held her immobilized. Panic flooded into her bloodstream, its chemical flush paralyzing her.

"Don't try that little trick again," he said mildly. "It may work on humans, but it won't work on me. Come, I'd like to speak with you in private."

"Sorry. I'm meeting a friend here," she said.

Nick Ramirez. Her Assignee, not exactly a friend. Nick was in here somewhere, so close she could sense him. She had to find him, to stop his path of self-destruction.

The Company was counting on her. The task was simple enough. An assignment fit for a fledgling angel like herself. Or it should have been. But this demon was in her way. This dangerously handsome demon, with the promise of pleasure glinting in his eyes.

"It wasn't a question," Julian said.

"I said I didn't want to."

Angels aren't supposed to lie, she knew. In truth, she wanted him. Like she'd never wanted a man before. With a desire that came up from the depths of her, rising through her body to set her skin on fire. She wanted to feel the drag of those fingertips over every heated curve of her. Wanted his molten voice to flow over her and melt her.

Incarnated in a physical body, she still felt all the sensations and emotions that came along with being a part of the material world. And right now, she felt those feelings so strongly that they threatened to sweep her away. In his grasp, she trembled. She knew instinctively that if she let him, this man would destroy her.

She squirmed; his fingers tightened.

"Any further attempts at resistance will only serve to annoy me and put you in danger," he told her. "When you crossed over the threshold of that front door, you came into *my* nightclub. Here, you'll abide by *my* rules."

His tone was so banal he might have been inviting

her to tea. But as his fingers flexed on her arm, she did not doubt the power behind his words.

Julian led her through the crowd, keeping his grip on her. She resisted yet again, hauling her weight backward and grabbing on to a carved railing as an anchor. But her flimsy sandals had no traction on the hardwood floor, and he overpowered her with a single tug.

Through a set of doors, the noise receded as they passed into the bowels of the club. He guided her down a hallway and into his office. It was a slick, modern space, the clean lines of the dark red leather and polished wood furnishings she would have expected in an upscale advertising agency rather than a demon's lair. He shut the door and clicked the lock shut before he released her arm.

"Champagne?" He motioned to a bottle chilling in an elaborate silver bucket. Then he gestured toward a collection of wine bottles that lined half a wall. "Or perhaps you'd prefer a glass of something else?"

"I'm not exactly here to socialize."

In this light, she could see the color of his eyes. Deep blue, shot through with green and gold. Lucid and beautiful, but their intensity sent a shiver through her. She forced herself to breathe slowly, trying to calm her wild heartbeat.

"Spoilsport. How about an apple, then?" he said, picking one out of a bowl that sat on his desk. He held the shiny red orb an inch away from her lips. "Have a bite."

She turned her head away slightly. The beating of her heart was so intense she wondered if he could hear it. If he could see its tremor shaking her body. "No, thanks."

"Suit yourself, if you want to be superstitious. You don't believe that old wives' tale, do you? Eve and that business about the tree…it's all just a product of an overactive imagination. What could be more innocent than a piece of fruit?"

He bit into the apple, his teeth sinking into its flesh with a crisp sound of tearing. His eyes closed, and a look of pure bliss settled over his perfect features as he swallowed. He set the fruit down on his desk.

"Now, why don't you tell me what a girl like you is doing in a place like this?"

"I told you," she said stubbornly, "I'm meeting a friend."

"Fine, if you want to play that game. He must be a good friend, this man you're looking for. What did you say his name was?"

"I didn't."

"Too bad. If I knew who he was, perhaps I could help you. Otherwise, I guess we'll just have to wait here all night. Your friend will wonder what happened to you."

He picked up the apple, took another bite out of it. She watched as he licked its juice from his lips. "And you and I will have to find some way to amuse ourselves," he said, leaning toward her.

She took a little step backward. Hesitated.

I could keep you here forever, his eyes told her. *Just give me an excuse.*

She swallowed, glanced toward the door. After a long pause, she said, "It's Nick Ramirez."

Recognition sparked in those beautiful eyes of his. "Ah, yes, Nick. Hollywood's flavor of the week. I just saw him a moment ago, but I don't think he needs your help. He seems to have made other friends here. Female friends, if you catch my drift."

One corner of Julian's beautiful mouth quirked upward.

Serena's lips pressed into a flat line.

She knew exactly what he meant. Nick's fondness for female companionship—*paid* female companionship—was no secret. Under Serena's guidance as his yoga teacher and Guardian, he'd begun to show some improvement. It had only been three weeks, but he had already started to curtail the illegal substances, had tamed the wild partying. She hadn't anticipated a setback like this.

"Jealous, are we? Is he your lover?" Julian asked.

Heat rushed into her face. "That's none of your business."

He leaned back against his desk, crossed his arms. "So he's not. I'd wager you don't have a lover. An assignment then, I'd guess. How badly do you want to get him out of here?"

"What do you mean?"

"Perhaps we could arrange a trade. What do you think you could offer me?" His eyes scanned her body.

With trembling fingers, she fished her wallet out of her purse, began to leaf through its contents. "I have fifty dollars. I know it's not much, but…"

He chuckled. "Refreshing. I'm genuinely amused." He drew closer. "Sweetheart, it's not money I was thinking of."

"I don't have anything else to offer. I'm just a yoga teacher." She remained still as he circled around her.

"You may be trying to pass yourself off as such. I think we both know better. Let's discuss *that* in a moment. But since you insist that you're *just* a yoga teacher..." She could feel his hot gaze running the length of her. He completed his turn in front of her. "Would you say your body is your temple?"

She nodded once, almost imperceptibly, afraid to move.

"Then let me come in and worship."

One of his hands slid around her waist, the other into the hair at the nape of her neck. She pulled back, but he held her ensnared in the steel of his arms. He drew her closer. Her eyes fluttered shut as his lips covered hers. She expected roughness, but the kiss was feather soft as his lips brushed over hers. Deepening the kiss, he coaxed her mouth open, his tongue exploring with a gentleness that surprised her. He tasted of unforeseen sweetness and of promised gratification. His fingers tangled in her hair, pressed against her back, forcing her breasts to arch into his muscular chest.

When was the last time she had felt a man's hands on her, the heft of his body against hers?

An eternity ago. But wait... She made a little sound of protest. Her hands reached up to push against him, but he held her fast. His lips left hers to travel across her cheek, nuzzling in the nook at the base of her ear. He drew her earlobe into his mouth, sucking. In spite of herself, she gasped, and this time it was from pleasure.

A little voice inside her whispered, *yes*.

With a sweep of his arm, he cleared the desk. The

bowl of apples fell with a clatter; fruit rolled in every direction. He pressed her backward, laid her across the desktop before she even knew what had happened. For a moment, lying there on the polished wood, she almost let go.

A pinprick of conscience punctured through the layers of desire. She struggled, pushing herself upright on her elbows. "Wait. You've got to let me go. I don't belong here."

"What about Nick?"

At the moment, Nick was the furthest thing from her mind. She had been converted into a mass of longing. Her skin was on fire, her breathing came in rapid bursts. Her desire had taken over, and the only thought she had now was Julian. She'd been ordained as a divine being, but this was the closest she had ever come to flying.

He leaned over her, capturing her mouth again. Withdrawing to look down at her, he whispered, "My angel."

It was like plunging into a bathtub full of ice. Instead of spurring her on as he'd undoubtedly intended, his words brought her thudding back to earth. Back to her duty. Her Assignee was out in the club this very moment, no doubt getting high with a bunch of prostitutes. And she…at this moment, she was no better. Pleasure had conquered her.

She lay panting on the desk. "You got what you wanted. Now give me Nick."

"We haven't even begun to explore what I want from you." His hands tightened on her hip, caressing through the fabric of her dress. "Your soul or his, love? Whose shall it be?"

"I don't know what you mean," she gasped.

He leaned over her, grazed a kiss next to her ear and whispered, "You know exactly what I mean."

An image floated into her mind's eye—an image of herself and Julian, bodies entwined on top of black silk sheets, their naked skin glistening with sweat. She squeezed her eyes shut and willed the picture out of her head. She could not sacrifice her body to this demon for the sake of a single human soul. It was forbidden.

"I don't want this."

"Sweetheart, what you want is irrelevant. I could take what *I* want right now." The tension in his body was barely controlled, his breathing ragged next to her ear. She had no doubt that he meant it.

"Please," she whispered.

He kissed her again, this time plundering her mouth with a force that made her arch up against him, pressing her breasts against his hard body and feeling the weight of him on top of her. She moaned, but whether it was in protest or in pleasure, she could not tell. He raised his head, his eyes flashing with lust.

She pushed against the hard plane of his chest once more. But he was impervious. He hovered over her for what seemed like an eternity, his gaze boring into her as though he might pin her there forever. The heat of him seeped into her, his strength barely contained in the rigid tension of his muscles.

When she heard her own voice, the desperation in it surprised her. "Please let me go."

He froze, as though the words had physically hit him. Then, something in him softened. He rose slowly, removed his hands from her body, curled them into fists. He stood away from the desk as she scrambled to her feet.

"If you intend to leave, *get out now.*"

His last three words were a snarl that sent a chill through her body. It was a warning. Why he should have warned her, she didn't quite understand. But she fled toward the door without looking back.

Julian watched her go, steeling himself not to give chase. A few grains of sand lingered on the polished wood of his desktop. She'd smelled like the beach. Like fresh ocean air. *Like happiness.* Something he hadn't known for a very long time. He swept the sand away with his fingertips.

In the pit of his stomach, something howled. Why had he let her go? Because she'd asked? She hadn't just asked, she'd begged. Like a woman fighting for her soul ought to beg. Like countless women before her had begged. Never once had he relented.

So why now? he asked himself.

She was unquestionably beautiful. But he knew scores of beautiful women, immortals among them. There was something very different about this woman. She was so vital and alive, still so new and so close to her humanity. For an instant, he longed for the fragile mortality that he had known for such an achingly short time. In the depths of her eyes, he saw everything he had missed—the brightness of a life throbbing with hope. In her presence, he felt a strange feeling he had not known for centuries. Something that was almost like peace.

He shook his head, brushing the feeling away with the last of the sand. Peace...happiness. He had moved beyond the need for such feeble emotions. He had a more important agenda now, and he needed to focus on it.

No. He had not let her go because of anything so weak, he told himself. He had let her go because now he had two victims instead of just one. He had no intention of releasing Nick. If he'd taken what he wanted, she'd have insisted that he free Nick. But if he waited, he could have both of them, on his own terms.

And because a quick kill was never as interesting as a long hunt. She was a challenge. Not like these mortals, who gave in to temptation so easily, so predictably. She had spirit, this one, and she had faith. That much was clear. Ultimately, though, she was no match for him. The inevitable outcome was that he would break her spirit and crush her faith, causing her to abandon her divine calling and fall victim to the latent desires he awakened within her. She would be relegated to hell for the rest of eternity. And this unfortunate little interlude would be a thing of the past for him.

He knew it would happen that way. Because that was what happened to every woman he chose to destroy. Because that was what had happened to him.

Inconceivable to think it, but once upon a time, he had been every bit as innocent as the little angel was now. Her scent triggered memories that lay long buried in the recesses of his mind. He tried to push them away, but they floated back into his consciousness anyway, scraps of memories…a sunlit summer afternoon spent wandering in a meadow with his mother, who toted his infant sister on her hip…his mother bending down to smile at him. "One day, Julian, all of this will be yours," she'd said.

He was born in England, in the idyllic countryside of Berkshire in 1752, the heir to a dukedom, at the pinnacle of a vast pyramid of wealth and privilege. Of his early childhood, he remembered very little, only snippets of those afternoon walks, the lavender scent his mother favored, the touch of her gloved hand on his hair. He had been well loved, and he had wanted for nothing.

One morning shortly after Julian's fifth birthday, his mother did not come to collect him from the nursery, as was her usual morning habit. Mother was ill, his nurse said, and not to be bothered. Julian, a sensitive child, heard the hush in the nurse's voice and knew that something was very wrong.

Some deeper instinct drove through the discipline instilled in him by his elders. He bolted from the nursery, down the long hallway that stretched into the wing of the house where his mother's suite was, and through the doors of her bedroom. He stood transfixed in the doorway, suddenly hesitant to approach the duchess as she lay on her bed amidst a jumble of covers. The cloying, sweet smell of the room was not the usual fresh scent he associated with her.

He took a few steps forward. "Mama?"

The duchess lifted her pale face, covered with the sheen of fever. "My little dove. Don't come near. Mama's very sick." In a rasping voice, she called to his nurse, who stood panting behind him. "Get him out of here."

As the nurse led him away, he glanced backward, saw his mother struggling to sit up. There was something infinitely sad in her smile as she watched him leave, and called out, "I love you, Julian."

He was sent to the outskirts of the estate, to the cottage where his spinster aunt lived. On the cold wooden floor of that spare cottage, Aunt Etheline made him get down on his knees and pray. There they stayed through the night, middle-aged woman and little boy both praying fervently for the salvation of their loved one. Their prayers were not answered. A few days later, the duchess succumbed to her illness, taking Julian's baby sister with her. Typhus, the "new fever," had changed Julian's world forever.

From then on, he lived with his aunt, who ruled his days by her strict religious code and sent him to sleep with bedtime stories of hell. The fiery pits into which sinners were thrown, demons who fed upon the entrails of the dead—these images became the source of recurring nightmares for the child. Julian, his aunt said, would be thrown into those very pits and burned for all eternity if he did not learn to behave like a good Christian. He thought of his mother often, wondered why God had chosen to take her. When he asked his aunt that question, he was answered with a hard slap and sent to bed without dinner.

After the death of Julian's mother, the duke became a living ghost. Julian often thought his father might as well have died, too. Julian visited the manor only on holidays, during which his father was always steeped in the scent of brandy, and with increasing frequency, in the garish perfume of whores.

God had abandoned him, Julian decided. For the better part of twelve years, his life continued to be a form of hell on earth. He had no peers or playmates, since he did not attend school, but was educated instead by private tutors who offered him little sympathy. He had never been a rebellious child, but the older he grew, the more outrageous his behavior became as he sought to vent his repressed emotions. He took to playing pranks on his tutors, destroying his schoolbooks, hiding from his aunt in the forest behind the cottage for hours on end. He disobeyed his riding master, galloping hard to the edges of the estate where he would linger and contemplate his escape. By the time he reached his fifteenth year, it was only a strange sense of duty to his family lineage, to the history of his heritage that kept him from leaving. Every act of disobedience earned him a week on bread and water, confined to his room. "Julian, you are mocking God," his aunt said, "and stepping closer to hell with every passing day."

He began to pray to the devil instead. It brought better results. A miracle of miracles occurred. A few months after his seventeenth birthday, his aunt died.

The timing of the event was fortuitous. He was sent to Oxford. It was the first time since childhood that Julian interacted with others his age. At university, his mind was blown open, and not only by what he learned in the classroom. He became aware of a world he had never experienced, never even knew existed outside the meager walls of the cottage. He was high on the sudden freedom that even his modest allowance afforded. His classmates were infinitely more schooled in the ways of the world than he. But at seventeen, he was a tall, broad-shouldered youth on the verge of manhood. And he was an earl who would inherit a duchy. Soon, he was accepted into the upper echelons of university life.

His Oxford days passed in a blissful haze of rowing on the Isis, of foxhunting and of horseback riding over the wide-open expanse of Port Meadow. There was the elaborate ritual of dressing for dinner every night in the Gothic, cathedral-esque atmosphere of Christ Church Hall. After almost every evening meal, Julian and his friends would retire to college common rooms to engage in heavy drinking, occasionally daring a foray into the taverns where students were not allowed. Classes were almost an afterthought, although he respected his tutors and inherited their enthusiasm for the latest philosophers of the Enlightenment: Rousseau, Voltaire, Kant.

After graduation, like so many other young men of his social class, Julian embarked on his Grand Tour, a whirlwind trip through Europe. Paris, the South of France, Barcelona, Madrid, Rome, Florence…he tore through the cultural, culinary and sensual delights of each place like a hurricane consuming everything in its path.

Then he arrived in Venice. *La Serenissima, the most serene republic,* a jewel poised on the edge of the Adriatic Sea. Venice was the antithesis to his suffocating childhood, a city of excess and courtesans. Venice was a universe away from his father, who was slowly but steadily rotting away in the ducal seat in Berkshire.

In the gambling salons, by some grace of the gods, he managed to parlay his allowance into a small fortune. He spent his mornings lounging in the coffeehouses. At night, he dined at the finest restaurants, made friends with Italian aristocrats, merchants, artists and intellectuals alike. Made love with his pick of the city's famous courtesans. Attended the opera, and found solace in the achingly beautiful arias of the sopranos. Riding on his charm and his good looks, he made love to them, too.

Oxford had been a pleasant diversion and a rich training ground. But it was in Venice that he finally took his place in the world. In Venice, he thrived, enjoying the full benefits of his station in life. He shed the shell of his past and emerged as a new man. For the first time in his life, he felt vibrant and whole. Potent. Alive.

And for the first time in his life, he began to notice the poorer citizens of *La Serenissima*. The beggars who squatted in the city's arched doorways, the vendors who hawked their wares in the open square of the Piazza San Marco. The servants who cleaned his living quarters and brought him his meals. His newfound confidence softened him, made him more charitable to all those around him. It became his habit to toss an extra coin into an outstretched hand, to speak a word or two of appreciation for a job well done. He even began to contemplate the tenants on his father's estate, how their lives might be improved, and what changes his power might effect when his father finally died. When *he* became the duke.

In short, he was becoming *good*.

Then, one day while he was strolling along a canal on a sultry afternoon, he met the woman who would be his undoing. In the sunshine of that bright afternoon, she blinked up at him with wide, pale green eyes. He stopped short on the narrow cobbled walkway, caught by her beauty and her seeming innocence. He hadn't foreseen how deadly she could be. Hadn't anticipated her betrayal.

It took her a decade to bait him into a hateful scheme that made him her pawn. But eventually, she achieved her goal. In her name, he fought a duel that cost him his human life. In that fight, he also took the life of another. That error cost him his soul. He lost everything.

At the time of his human death, he was thirty-two years old. A man in the prime of his life, on the verge of implementing the changes his father's tenants so badly needed. A man enraged. Not only by the betrayal at the hands of a woman. But enraged also by the betrayal at the hands of God.

Afterward, he wandered the realms of hell, tormented by the unrelenting heat and the perpetual regret. He became so miserable that he set about torturing other souls, without bidding from the demons. The Prince of Hell himself happened to pass by, and saw what Julian was doing. He was taken out of damnation and given a chance as a Gatekeeper, sent back to earth to do the devil's work.

He was spectacular at it. So spectacular that he rose through the ranking of demons like a flare fired into the night sky. The more souls he corrupted, the more powerful he became. He ascended to the position of Archdemon after a mere two hundred years, the blink of an eye in a demon's lifespan. He would not stop until he reached the top of the hierarchy. Until he answered to no one but the devil himself.

And after the disastrous way Julian's human life had

ended, he vowed that no woman would ever get the better of him again. Since then, none had.

This woman, this angel...she would be no different.

Chapter Two

Serena bolted. She fled out of Julian's office, back down the hallway and out into the crowded club. Pushing through the crush of bodies, she headed toward the VIP lounge where she'd last searched for Nick. This time, she had no difficulty finding him.

People were chanting his name, hundreds of voices shouting in unison: *"Nick...Nick...Nick...Nick..."*

His height and his extraordinary good looks made him difficult to miss in any setting. But here in Devil's Paradise, Nick was the epicenter of attention. Shirtless, with his tanned and muscular chest glistening under the nightclub lights, he danced on a table with a girl on each side of him. Surrounded by a tangle of snaking arms, a beer bottle dangled from his hand. Beneath him, the crowd basked in the glory of Nick's celebrity.

He threw back his head and howled, a long wolf cry that sent the crowd wild.

The guys howled back. The girls screamed and squealed. With his free hand, Nick wiped the traces of white powder from the bottom of his nose. Serena trembled, watching him. Deep in her gut, she knew that nothing and nobody could save Nick from himself tonight.

And if she stayed any longer, Julian would come for her. This time, he would not think twice. So she did the only thing she could. She ran.

As she pushed her way out of the club, a man stood in her way, exhaling whisky-steeped breath into her face. "Aw, baby, lookin' fine."

She veered hard left to avoid him. A cold wash of beer splashed down her arm and the side of her dress. Shivering with the shock of it, she pressed onward.

"Watch where you're going," someone else growled.

For once in her life, she didn't care about being rude. The only thing she wanted was to get out of this hell-hole. She shoved her way toward the exit of the crowded club. Toward freedom. She headed toward the doorway, a beacon of light in the midst of the darkness. Heaving open the door, she made to bolt past the bouncer. As she looked at him, a word flashed in her mind: *Gatekeeper*. Like Guardians, Gatekeeper demons roamed the earth in human form, blending in seamlessly with humans. Unlike angels, they were nothing but trouble.

He blocked her way, grinning. "Hey, darlin'. Where you goin' in such a hurry?"

She shoved past him and kept running.

Julian grabbed the champagne bottle and a pair of flute glasses, and headed back to the VIP lounge to check on Nick.

Hollywood's latest train wreck was still there, all right—making a massive spectacle of himself. So pathetic, really. Everyone, even Julian, who did not follow celebrity gossip, knew Nick's story. The son of a Brazilian financier and a famous American ballerina, Nick had been in the public eye since his birth twenty-six years ago. His parents' messy divorce had sent Nick bouncing between Sao Paulo and New York, cared for by a long string of nannies before finally being relegated to boarding school in Connecticut. His parents reasoned that they had given him everything a child could want.

Everything but their attention. And that was the thing Nick seemed to crave. Ironically, the higher Nick's star rose, the more his success alienated his parents. The more famous he became, the more they viewed him with distaste, eschewing the roles he picked as cheap and commercial. To numb the pain of their rejection, Nick had started on a string of benders that had turned the spotlight away from his acting career, and onto his now-legendary partying.

Now, Julian watched the bare-chested young man baying at the crowd.

Yes, Nick's star was teetering on the brink. If it fell, it would fall a long way down.

All the way to hell, Julian hoped.

However, right now, what Julian wanted was information. Specifically, he wanted the name of the little angel who had just departed Devil's Paradise. In three seconds flat, Julian put a halt to Nick's table-dancing show, located his shirt and sat him in a booth. Humans were so easy to manipulate, Julian thought. Especially humans who were coked to the gills. Nick's pupils were huge, dilated against the bloodshot whites of his eyes. His gaze flickered wildly, unable to focus on one point for longer than a few seconds.

Nick's female dance partners also settled into the

booth. Julian motioned for one of them to move. She did, but her heavy-lidded gaze told him she'd rather sit on *top* of him, not beside him.

"Julian Ascher," he announced. "I'm the owner of this place." He popped the cork off the champagne, eliciting a squeal from the girls.

The girl next to Julian leaned in to give him a view of her generous cleavage. She said, "I've seen your picture in magazines. You dated Brooke Bentley just before she cracked, right?"

Julian nodded, settling against the scarlet leather. He had all but forgotten about Brooke, a gorgeous young pop idol whose records had gone triple platinum after several hits. Poor, debauched Brooke was now living in a mental institution after their brief affair. Another resounding success on Julian's part. He turned to Nick and said, "A friend of yours came looking for you earlier tonight. A little blonde. Innocent as a newborn dove. Ring a bell?"

Nick shot out of his seat. "Serena St. Clair? Where is she?" His dark eyes zigzagged across the crowd, seeking her.

Serena. So that was her name, an ironic reminder of his beloved city. *La Serenissima.*

"She left," Julian said, masking his interest. "Didn't seem to be feeling too well. But she said to say hello."

Nick dropped back into his seat, like a disappointed little boy who had lost his favorite toy. "Did you talk to her?"

"Yes. She was sorry she had to go without seeing you." Julian smiled.

"That blows. I'm so in love with her," said Nick. The girl beside him pouted, but he simply ignored her.

Nick and Serena in love… Julian felt his jaw clenching beneath his tight smile. He wanted to kill Nick Ramirez now, to cut his body into a million pieces and send him straight to hell without any of the usual preliminaries. But he forced himself to speak civilly. "Tell me more," he said.

"What's to tell? You saw her, right? She's hot. Even hotter than Brooke Bentley. I'm telling you, dude, it was love at first sight."

"So she's in love with you?" Julian asked, in a tone he hoped conveyed boredom. The girls looked disappointed, so he poured some more champagne into their glasses to keep them quiet.

He sat back and frowned, assessing what lay beneath Nick's dark good looks. That slick Hollywood smile hid a nasty coke habit and a penchant for hookers, the pricier the better in both cases. As his Guardian, surely Serena must see that. Still, Julian could not resist picturing Nick and Serena hand in hand, gazing guilelessly at each other with wide eyes, the sheen of youth still fresh on their skin. The image of it made Julian want to retch.

"Not exactly in a romantic way…yet," Nick said. His shoulders slumped forward and he ran his fingers through his carefully spiked hair. "Serena's my yoga teacher. She acts like a nun or something."

Something inside of Julian rejoiced.

"Don't get me wrong," Nick continued. "Serena's not a prude. She's…special. She's not simply another beautiful girl. There's something different about her.

Something exquisite. She's the closest thing I've ever met to true unconditional love."

In Nick's famous brown eyes, Julian saw a sudden flicker of something, a flash of sobriety that broke through the drug high. Beneath his vacuous Hollywood exterior, Nick Ramirez understood Serena's true nature. It took Julian utterly by surprise.

"Forget about her for tonight. Everything you need is right here," Julian urged, running his hand down the arm of one of the girls. She was a pretty, young blonde, but still a poor substitute for Serena. "If there's anything else you desire, my staff will take care of you."

"Thanks, man. You're the best."

Julian left him in the VIP lounge with the girls and wandered back up to the observation booth. It was late, and brawls were starting to erupt on the dance floor. He watched the bouncers hang back as he'd instructed, waiting to break up the fights until after some serious damage had been done.

A fight of a very different sort was brewing between him and Serena. Angels, even fledgling Guardian angels, knew better than to cross his path. Most of them were either too smart or too scared to do so. Clearly, Serena St. Clair was neither. If she wanted Nick, she would have to pry him out of Julian's grip. How delectable it would be to break her when she tried.

Julian would win. Of that, he had no doubt. In the end, he always did.

Serena's lungs burned by the time she reached her well-weathered VW where she'd left it parked on the street. Unlocked the door with shaking fingers.

Collapsed into the driver's seat. Slammed down the lock and jammed the car into gear. The squeal of the tires sent a wave of pure relief through her as she peeled away from the curb and swung into traffic. But as she drove, her gaze flickered to the rearview mirror.

The demons were following her.

At first she sensed, rather than saw it. The car was a speck in the rearview mirror, just a little spot in the distance behind her. But then it increased speed, weaving through traffic with a dangerous momentum.

And then it was behind her, their car coming so close to her bumper that she could see them in the rearview mirror, laughing. It was the bouncer from the club, the one she'd just shoved past, and another demon. They drove behind her, inches from touching her. Taunting her. Threatening her. The blur of streetlamps and headlights whipped by as she merged onto the highway and pushed the car faster. *Fifty miles an hour...sixty...seventy...eighty...ninety.* The little car shook from the unaccustomed velocity.

From the passenger-side window, a winged goblin darted by, flying through the air like an oversize bat. It shot forward to hover in front of her windshield, blocking her view of the road. The cackle that came out of it sent a shudder through Serena. In those glassy little red eyes, she saw pure hatred. Without a doubt, it wanted to kill her. She floored the gas pedal and the car shot forward, smashing the creature against her windshield with a sick splat. A high-pitched squeal wheezed out of it, a sound like a pig being slaughtered. The reddish-black of its entrails smeared against the glass.

She flicked on the wipers and the carcass fell to the

side of the road. Streaks of blood blurred her vision but she kept driving, kept speeding down the highway with her foot pressed to the gas.

With the demons still on her tail, Serena gripped the wheel and waited for the flash of white heat, the sweep of death to overtake her. Fear, visceral and real, ripped through her.

It was not her entire life that flashed before her eyes, but a few moments of a single evening from less than a year ago. The image of the accident flashed into her mind. *The mangled metal, the sparks falling from drooping telephone wires. The roads slick with rain. No one else had stopped, so it was Serena who had pulled over at the side of the road and dashed out into the pelting rain. She'd pulled a woman and her young daughters out of their wrecked car without difficulty. The girls had been scratched and badly scared, shivering as Serena had hurried them to the safety of her backseat. Then she'd gone back to get the woman in the other car.*

She should have known as she worked at the door handle, her fingers scrambling against the cold wet metal. When she finally pried it open, the other woman looked at her with an expression that conveyed both gratitude and apology in the same instant. The car exploded, killing them both.

Serena knew that dying was nothing to fear. But God, she didn't want to go through it all over again. Death was a pain in the ass.

She braced herself, gripping the wheel and waiting for the demons to run her off the road. For the explosion she knew was coming. But it never came. Not this time.

She barreled down the road, checking the rearview and hoping the police didn't flag her down.

And as suddenly as the demons came, they were gone.

Serena exited the highway and drove until she found a residential side street. Pulled off the road and parked. The houses were quiet, most of the windows dark. Inside them, people slept, dreaming soundly in a world they thought was safe. In a world whose true nature they would probably never suspect. It was better that way, because if humans knew the extent of the invisible battle between angels and demons, most of them would probably go stark raving mad.

Her breathing slowed to normal. Her heartbeat stopped its frantic cadence.

But her chest ached as though it were going to implode. A single tear rolled down her cheek. She wiped it away with the back of her hand.

I will not cry...I will not cry.

Her throat swelled shut as she stared up at the riot of stars crowding the night sky above. A jumble of emotions swirled inside her. Hope for the young family she'd saved through her own death. Anxiety about Nick's safety. Despair at having failed him.

And something else. A tiny fragment of sorrow for herself. Maybe even some anger. Inside her, a little voice whispered how unfair it was that she'd been taken away from her own family when she was still so young herself. A family that had already been devastated by the death of her father, taken by a heart attack a decade before her own death. Half the family gone within a span of ten years, leaving her mother and brother behind to struggle with their grief. In the center of her chest, she felt a dull ache from missing them.

Sometimes life was downright cruel. And there were people—*demons*—in this world determined to make it even crueler. She shut her eyes and wished tonight had never happened. Wished she had never met Julian Ascher. Wished someone more capable had been assigned to guard Nick.

Wished she had never died.

But when she opened her eyes again, nothing had changed. Regret was a useless emotion. There was no point in lamenting things that could not be.

She started the car again and steered homeward.

Twenty minutes later, she pulled into her driveway in Santa Monica. She closed her eyes and tipped her head back against the headrest, listening to wind rushing through the palm trees overhead.

Lucky. She'd been incredibly lucky to get out of there tonight. Like he'd said, he could easily have taken what he wanted from her. Why he'd let her out, she didn't know. It puzzled her—he didn't seem to be the sort of man to give in. But whatever the reason, she was here now. Safe. She said a few quick words of thanks before heading inside, glad to know that her roommate was at home.

Meredith's curtain of red hair swung as she heard the door open, and her eyes flew wide when she saw Serena. "Thank God you're home! I could sense that you were in trouble, but I didn't know where you were," she said. Meredith's psychic skills, already developing during her human life, were still evolving now that she was an angel. "What happened?"

Serena collapsed into a kitchen chair and slumped forward onto the table, leaning her head on her arms. One of them was still sticky with beer, so she sat back upright. "Thank God we have each other. Nobody else would understand what I went through today."

There were dozens of angels in the city, but none who knew her as well as Meredith. As Guardians, they shared the top floor of this house. But as humans, Meredith and Serena had shared the last few moments of their mortal lives together. It was Meredith's car that the young mother had hit when she'd hydroplaned on that rain-slick road nearly a year ago. It was Meredith's door that Serena had scrambled to open, and Meredith's face that had been the last image of Serena's human life.

Now, her roommate handed her a mug of something from a stockpot bubbling on the stove. "Drink this."

"Do I have to?" Serena made a face at the murky brown liquid.

A nutritionist by calling, Meredith was a firm believer in the healing power of herbs, and she liked to boil them in large batches on the stove. "It's good for you."

Serena wrinkled her nose, but downed the liquid. It tasted even worse than it smelled—like old socks and dried mushrooms that had been boiled up in one pot— and it burned all the way down. "What is that?" she asked. "A healing potion?"

"It was supposed to be hot apple cider," Meredith said, clearly disappointed.

It might as well have been truth serum, because

Serena's story spilled out—her problems with Nick, the trip to Devil's Paradise, the car chase. And Julian. Dark, gorgeous, dangerous Julian. "I let him kiss me," she said miserably. "And I failed utterly at getting Nick out of that nightclub."

"You kissed a demon," Meredith repeated, her eyebrows creasing together into a little V in the middle of her forehead.

Heat crept into Serena's cheeks. "I thought…I thought he might release Nick."

"Didn't you remember Arielle's warning?"

"Warning?" Serena's eyes widened in alarm. She had no recollection of ever hearing their supervisor Arielle mention Julian before.

"She told me it was imperative to stay away from demons. I'm pretty sure she even mentioned Julian Ascher specifically. The name definitely rings a bell. I took some notes during my training sessions."

While Meredith searched her bedroom for her notes, Serena drank a glass of water and found herself hoping that her roommate was wrong. Why on earth would Arielle warn Meredith and not her? None of it made any sense.

Meredith came back with a notebook, and as she flipped through it, she muttered to herself. "Protection charms, angelic blessings, patron saints, medals…here it is. Demons. Julian Ascher, two-hundred-and-fifty-year-old Archdemon. Perhaps the most powerful demonic entity in Los Angeles County. Known associate of Corbin Ranulfson. Owner of a nightclub conglomerate that he uses as a front for other activities. Avoid at all costs. Here, I've underlined it twice," she said, holding the notebook out as proof.

Archdemon. Shit.

In Serena's gut, hysteria and Meredith's cider began to rise, but she swallowed them down. She might not have recognized Julian's name, but somewhere deep inside, she had known exactly how powerful he was. As an Archdemon, he bore the highest rank among demons, answering directly to the Prince of Darkness himself. Only a few dozen Archdemons existed around the globe, vying among themselves for the devil's highest favor. Of them, perhaps the most powerful was Corbin Ranulfson. Even the newest angel shook in terror at the mention of him. As his associate, Julian was a demon on the rise, a demon to be feared.

Serena groaned. "You've got to be kidding. I can't believe Arielle forgot to tell me this."

"Arielle never forgets anything."

The two women exchanged glances. A shiver stole down Serena's neck. *Oh, please, Lord, let there be some explanation for this.* "I'll ask Arielle at the Company meeting tomorrow," Serena said.

Meredith paused, considering her words before she finally spoke. "Sometimes it's difficult to understand Arielle's agenda. I'd be careful if I were you. In the meantime, don't worry about it. It was just a kiss, right?" Meredith smiled, a little too brightly.

Serena's stomach still threatened to regurgitate Meredith's brew, but she forced herself to return the smile and said, "You're right. It was just a kiss."

Just a kiss. She tried to remember that as she took a long, hot shower that did nothing to erase the sensation of his touch on her skin. Lying in bed afterward, that sensation still lingered. Trying to ignore it, she began to think about the real reason the encounter had frightened her so badly. What was this fear that had shaken her so badly tonight? Was it a fear of death?

No. Now that she had experienced death firsthand, she no longer feared death the same way that most humans did.

Her memory wandered back to another large gathering that had been held in her honor—her ordination ceremony, the divine equivalent of a graduation.

In the instant of her death, she had been borne into the angelic realm. Riding on that wave of light, she entered a vast amphitheater where hundreds of ethereal beings had gathered. They had come to witness the sacred calling of a small group of souls—Serena and Meredith's soul group. There among the angelic choirs, Serena's ears had filled with the chatter of melodious voices and the noise of iridescent wings shuffling. Wings that shone with colors she had never seen on earth, ruffling as loudly as the rush of a waterfall.

She was nearly overcome by the exquisiteness in the center of that radiating energy. At the same time, she knew intuitively that she was part of that energy, as much a part of it as the angels themselves.

Behind a massive, ornate lectern, stood the Archangel Gabriel. All eyes fixed on his flowing silver robes, the enormous spread of his wings trailing behind him. The angels stilled, waiting.

He spoke, the clear ring of his voice carrying over the crowd. "Death should not cause fear. Death is simply another event in the process of the soul's evolution, by no means its end." Most humans would be returned to earth in another mortal body, he explained, although most of them would never remember the process.

As Gabriel continued to speak, he explained that *all* souls were immortal. Every soul would live forever, although the vast majority of humans will never come to that realization within their current lifetimes.

And then he said to Serena and Meredith, "If you so choose, you will be sent back to earth in your human body, not as a reincarnated mortal, but as an angel in order to blend easily among those who are mortal. But once you decide to return in physical form, you will not be able to disincarnate without our assistance. In time, you may earn the right to transition between the angelic and the earthly realms. Your spiritual abilities will increase as you continue to evolve. One day, you will ascend from earth on your own energy and receive wings."

As Guardian angels, they would be impervious to injury and immune to aging and death, Gabriel said. The only threat to their existence was demonic energy.

Only a demon could kill an angel.

If a demon did manage to destroy the physical body of an angel, most likely she would be reprocessed. Sent back in her human body to continue her work where she had left off. *Recycling,* Gabriel called it, which caused the angels to thunder with laughter in the stands of the amphitheater. Serena hadn't found it that funny, but apparently they had a different sense of humor here in the divine realms.

For both Serena and Meredith, the choice was clear.

There were so many souls who needed guidance here on earth. In these challenging times, humans needed help.

And so Gabriel continued to lecture, outlining their duties and responsibilities. At the end of it, he explained, "Every soul has free will. Every soul has choices. In the material world as it currently exists, there are consequences to these choices."

What he meant was falling. If an angel fell, she risked going to hell. Just like any other soul. No being, including an angel, was immune from the consequences of free will. And plenty had fallen. Every last one of them, from the most exalted Seraph to the newest Guardian, was responsible for the consequences of her deeds. Gabriel delivered that last point slowly, his face stoic with the gravity of his message. Every angel in the amphitheater stilled, the stirring of wings silenced as he spoke. It was a warning, Serena knew, as she and Meredith stood trembling before the immense power of the divine.

Staring up at the shadows shifting across her bedroom ceiling now, Serena understood the reason she had felt so afraid tonight. Not because she feared death. No. She feared Julian because of the possibility of going to hell.

Just a kiss. She tried to comfort herself with that thought as she lay in bed, remembering the delicious heaviness of Julian's body weighing down on her and trying not to think about falling.

Chapter Three

*S*hame. Sunday morning, the memory of Julian's touch still hovered over the surface of her skin. Serena dealt with her shame in the way she always handled such emotions—she took it to the yoga mat. *Nick won't show up,* she thought as she drove to the studio. After last night, there was no way he'd make it to his private lesson scheduled this morning.

God only knows what that bastard Julian did to him.

But Nick was leaning in the studio's doorway, waiting for her with his rolled-up mat tucked under his arm. He was hiding behind silver aviator sunglasses and a baseball cap, with a scruff of beard stubble on his face. But he was here nonetheless.

When he took off the sunglasses, she saw the dark circles beneath his eyes. "You came to Devil's Paradise last night. I'm sorry I missed you," he said, his voice still hoarse.

In his raspy apology, she detected genuine regret. There was something else, something different in his soulful brown gaze. Perhaps a little more tenderness, almost as though he... She gave a little shake of her head, refusing to think about it.

"That's okay. I'm glad you made it this morning. It's good to see you," she said brightly.

She unlocked the door and led him into the studio, exhaling a sigh of relief as she passed beneath the vibrantly colored Indian scarves hanging from the ceiling. Inhaled the faint trace of incense that lingered in the air. Nick grinned, and it was almost enough to make her forget what had happened last night. It was his smile that set him apart from all the other hot young actors in Hollywood. His smile that made young girls scream hysterically when he walked down the street. Made grown women contemplate shameless acts.

She unrolled her mat on the hardwood floor. If she'd been human, she would have melted, too. But as his Guardian, what she felt was an overwhelming sense of platonic love, an emotion verging on the maternal. She wanted to protect Nick. He was here, back under her watch. Far from the grasping hands of Julian Ascher. *Safe.* She would do what she had to do to keep him that way.

They began to flow through the postures she'd taught him over the past few weeks. Nick's toned body seemed to soak up the movements easily, executing them with a natural grace. She alternated between demonstrating the poses and adjusting him, guiding him deeper into the postures.

"Good job. Your practice is really coming along," she said. "You're getting it, Nick."

He stopped and stood at the front of his mat, breathing deeply from the effort. In the sunlight filtering through the windows, she saw in his eyes the look she'd tried to ignore earlier. The look that was unmistakable now. The look that said, *I'm in love with you.* She'd seen it in the eyes of many different men, but never yet in the eyes of the right man.

An image of Julian flickered through her mind. She blinked, blocking it out and bringing her attention back to her Assignee.

Who was leaning in to kiss her.

Caught off guard, she pushed him away more abruptly than she intended. "Nick, don't!"

"Why not?" he said, pushing his hands through his tousled hair. "You're the only one who understands me. My parents don't give a shit about what I'm going through. I have no real friends. Everyone else just wants a piece of me. I thought you really cared."

She backed away, not sure how to respond for a moment. Nick's frustrated sigh tugged at her heartstrings. "I do care about you, Nick. As a friend."

He just wanted to be loved, she knew. In many ways, she could relate to the void he felt inside. Sensitive and artistic from an early age, Nick had been a misfit all his life. Ignored by his austere father and disliked by his high-strung diva of a mother, he was still struggling to find his own place in the world and to win their approval. His so-called friends treated him like a neverending fountain of free drugs and alcohol. The women he slept with were mostly professionals who demanded payment for their services.

Serena *did* understand him, though. She'd felt that same kind of void inside herself when her father had died. Like something had broken inside her that could never be repaired. Perhaps she had managed her hurt differently. Whatever the case, she knew she had been very lucky. For her, things could easily have gone very wrong.

The line between angels and demons was a fine one.

Yes, she understood Nick. But her job was to guard him and guide him; she could not return his desire. In time, he would deal with his feelings and they would evolve into a purely platonic relationship. At least, that was what she hoped.

Centering herself with a deep breath, she gave him an empathetic smile. "Come on. I'll help you with your handstands."

"Bet I can hold it longer than you," he said, grinning to cover his own embarrassment. "I've been doing handstands on grass since I was a kid. What's the difference between yoga and just showing off?" he teased.

"Yoga's not a contest," she said mildly, trying not to sound preachy.

"Afraid of a little healthy competition?"

They kicked up at the same time. Balancing in the center of the room, Serena concentrated on a spot on the floor. Felt the strength of her arms and of divine love supporting her. For one moment, everything in the world seemed right again. She felt the joy of pure play flowing through her body, felt it radiating out from her student, too. Finally, Nick gave a loud yelp and collapsed in a heap beside her, laughing while she remained balanced in the posture.

At the edge of her vision, something moved. From her upside-down position, she saw a familiar figure leaning in the doorway, watching.

"Hello, angel." His low, velvety voice swept over

her calm like a swell crashing on the beach, and she felt herself falling, falling…

Deva Yoga Studio was exactly the kind of place Julian hated. It was as though someone had taken Devil's Paradise and created its exact opposite. Here, they served tea at the front desk instead of tequila shots. The quiet unnerved him; he was used to the noise and chaos of nightclubs. The only thing that broke the silence was the sound of trickling water, surely designed to create a peaceful ambiance. It grated on Julian's nerves like Chinese water torture.

Serena, too, was the exact opposite of *him*. Maybe that was why he found her so incredibly attractive. There was something utterly compelling about the love/hate dynamic that he'd never been able to resist. He wandered down a quiet hallway, peering into empty rooms in search of her. In a large, sunny room at the end, he found her with Nick.

Balancing in a handstand on the hardwood floor, the line of her body was perfect. She was some sensualist god's idea of a celestial being. An homage to the human form, wrought by a divine hand and sent to torture him by deific forces. He prided himself on being a master of temptation, but somehow, with her, his finesse had abandoned him. No clever flattery came to mind, only animalistic instinct. He'd wanted her so badly last night that he'd botched a seduction that had practically been handed to him on a plate.

He didn't trust himself to do any better now, in the light of day. Well, he was going to have to try.

When he spoke two words of a greeting, she fell. He

watched her tumble as if in slow motion, landing catlike on her feet and glaring at him with those unforgettable eyes of hers.

"What are you doing here?" she demanded, rising to her feet instantaneously.

"I came to pick up Nick. I had no idea you were his yoga teacher," Julian lied smoothly. The lie was thinner than the yoga top that stretched over her luscious curves, but it gave him such satisfaction to see her eyes narrow with annoyance.

Beside her, Nick popped to his feet. "Good to see you."

"He's not finished yet," she said, unwilling to retract her claws from the clueless human.

He's mine, Julian thought as he smiled down at her. *You invaded my territory last night, and now it's payback time.*

Stubborn, she dug in deeper. "He needs to rest before he leaves. Nick, please take *sivasana* for fifteen minutes."

Sivasana. A bullshit name for lying on the floor, Julian almost said aloud. But he refrained. It wouldn't do to pick a fight in front of Nick. Not yet. Nick lay down complacently and the angel fussed around the room, covering him with a blanket in a gesture that was so very caring.

"*Namaste,*" she said, in a tone of voice one might use to say good-night to a small child.

"*Namaste,*" Nick murmured back.

How sweet. Julian wanted to vomit.

What disturbed him even more was that it looked like yoga was working for Nick. Here in the studio, the actor looked younger and happier than he had last night, the hard set of his drug-frenzied face smoothed away in his post-yoga sprawl. If he was this relaxed after a bender of a night—Julian had seen him finally crumple into a cab at around five o'clock in the morning—what would yoga do for him on a regular basis? Julian didn't like it one bit. Yoga went against everything he believed in. He'd always written it off as an exercise craze, targeted primarily to weak-minded women who fell for Eastern spirituality imported as a commodity and turned into a trendy sport.

But now more than ever, it seemed imperative he destroy Serena immediately.

He would find a chink in that virtuous armor of hers. He would work his way in and set about seducing her, taking her down with her own desire. In Julian's vast experience, a little corruption went a long way. She was so tightly wound, it wouldn't take much. All he would have to do was give her a little push. She would fall the rest of the way herself.

She sat down in a lotus position, watching over Nick as he lay on the floor. Julian waited. He would wait all day if he had to. Within minutes, the young actor was snoring loudly. He'd fallen asleep in a patch of sunlight slanting in through the large windows.

She got up, motioned for Julian to follow.

In the reception area, she flicked on an electric kettle. While she made tea, he pretended to peruse through the racks of books and yoga clothes displayed for sale. Out of the corner of his eye, he watched her pour the boiled water into a mug. It was a simple gesture, but she managed to perform even that task with supple grace.

"Chai?" she offered.

He grinned. "Got anything stronger?" In actual fact, as much as he plied others with alcohol, he rarely touched it himself. He was in the business of sending people to hell, not ending up there himself. Long ago, he'd realized that he needed a clear head to control the orchestrated mayhem that happened on a nightly basis at Devil's Paradise, as well as overseeing operations at his other clubs. But she didn't need to know that.

"Drink some," she said. "It'll be good for you."

"Thanks, but no. I've had enough goodness for one day." He felt an overwhelming need to knock that goody-goody halo of hers askew. He couldn't see it, but he knew it was there, radiating smugness into the core of him. Gesturing to a large statue of a six-armed goddess poised on a window ledge, he said, "Isn't that sacrilege? Won't your god strike you down for worshipping false idols?"

"I happen to be a multi-faith angel," she said, straightening defensively, those blue eyes of hers tracking him as he paced around the lounge. "All major religions share the same basic principles."

As she talked, he picked up a book with a photograph of a man with his leg behind his head, skimmed through the pictures inside. Ridiculous what people today fell for. Did they think they were going to reach enlightenment just by twisting their bodies into pretzel shapes? He set the book back on the shelf.

"That's a bit naive. There are vast differences between religions," he said, frowning.

"If we focused more on what people have in common

and less on our differences, the world would be a better place."

"Who wants it to be a better place?"

She lifted her chin, stared up at him with those magnificent blue eyes. "I do."

A sound broke from his throat, a laugh half-choked by bitterness. "What makes you think your side will win?" He stepped toward her. "Do you have any secret weapons we don't know about?" he mocked. And took another step. "You think you're any match for me?" He stood over her, looking down into the fiery blue blaze of her eyes.

"I know I am." She stared back, defiant. Obstinate. Beautiful.

"How do you know?" he challenged. "How can you be sure that your little Company of Amateurs is going to come out on top?"

Her answer died in a little gasp of protest as he snaked an arm around her waist. Pulled her to him. Kissed her. As she had the other night, she squirmed in his embrace. He held her, kept the pressure of his lips on hers. And then a miracle happened. She kissed him back, this time of her own accord, not out of coercion or force.

In the past two centuries, he'd lost count of the number of women he'd kissed. He'd kissed servant girls and crown princesses alike. Catholic nuns and courtesans. He'd kissed women at the top of the Eiffel Tower, in the secret enclaves of a Saudi sultan's harem, in London bordellos, in the open market in Marrakech and on the beaches of Saint-Tropez. Not one of those kisses was as memorable as this one.

There was a moment, when her lips first brushed against his, that he heard that same whoosh of unfurling wings he had heard when he'd touched her last night. This time, he knew it was no illusion. It pricked at his conscience for a moment—kissing an angel was surely some kind of sin, one more to add to the vast heap he'd accumulated. But then the kiss deepened and all notion of sin fled from his mind.

It seemed to him that the entire universe had contracted into this single, perfect moment. Past and future seemed to disappear in the sweetness of the kiss. There was only the present, the contact of their lips and the heat of her body calling to his.

He ached, wanting to pull her nearer. His cock pulsed, engorged and ready. He held himself back, knowing that to push too hard would be to lose her. With a gentleness that came from his deepest reserves of discipline, he ran his tongue along the seam of her lips. They parted, and he plunged his tongue into her mouth, exploring with a tenderness he never knew was possible.

It was the sweetest kiss of his life.

He didn't know how long they stood there, how long he reveled in the sensation of holding her to him, of feeling her woman's body melting against the hard planes of his maleness. It might have been two minutes; it felt like two hours. He had no idea what, after that disastrous interaction in the practice room, had made her relent. All he knew was that the kiss ended too abruptly when Nick's voice pierced his consciousness.

"Serena? Julian?" Nick's voice drifted into the lounge.

Julian released her. They leaped apart like two teen-agers caught necking behind the school bleachers.

"How long was I out?" Nick wandered out of the practice room, still blinking the sleep out of his eyes.

Serena had the dewy glow of a well-kissed woman, but her smile was as flat and wooden as the countertop she gripped for support. "Not long. Your body needed to recover. You'll start detoxing soon. As long as you take it easy on the hard stuff."

Nick grinned. "Thanks, Serena." He gazed at her with an infatuated devotion that made her smile soften into something genuine. It made Julian sick. Watching the two of them positively shining at each other, he wondered fleetingly whether *he* would ever be able to make her smile like that.

"Let's go, Nick," Julian said gruffly. "There's something I want to show you at the club."

"At eleven o'clock on a Sunday morning?" Nick asked, his gaze flickering to the angel.

It was Julian's turn to grin. Detox be damned. As far as he was concerned, a few shots of tequila and a couple of strippers could cure whatever ailed a man, no matter what time of day it was.

They stood poised in the classic triangular configuration Julian knew so well: demon on one side, angel on the other, unwitting human in the middle. All it took to tip the balance was for Julian to clap a proprietary hand on Nick's shoulder.

"Until we meet again," Julian said to Serena, slipping her a wink.

With that, he swept Nick out of the studio, leaving

her stunned and flushed, standing by the front desk of the yoga studio, gripping her mug of tea.

Serena arrived late for the Company's weekly meeting. She sprinted through the lobby of her unit's headquarters, which doubled as a legal-aid clinic during working hours. Banged on the locked doors of the boardroom, slinking in when Arielle opened them. The thirty other members of the unit, angels of every race and color, watched her as she crossed the room.

Do they know about Julian?

She collapsed into the empty chair beside Meredith. Like her roommate, many of the other angels also had psychic abilities. Some of the older ones were adept at reading minds, able to perceive minute details stored in people's memories. Serena glanced quickly at their faces, wondering who suspected what.

From the head of the boardroom table, Arielle smiled at Serena. "We were just going over the weekly status reports," she said, consulting her file. "I see you were assigned to Nick Ramirez's case three weeks ago. Why don't you share with us what you've accomplished so far, Serena?"

I kissed a demon. Twice.

Thirty pairs of jewel-bright eyes swiveled to Serena. Some of those brilliant stares held the recognition of her own thoughts, her own remorse reflected back at her. It was impossible to hide anything from the Company. Serena opened her mouth, but nothing came out. Arielle's question hung in the air.

The Company waited.

In the air-conditioned room, a rivulet of sweat

dripped down Serena's forehead. Finally she said, "I ran into Julian Ascher."

A collective gasp went around the room, and the angels began murmuring to each other. Arielle's face remained composed, but her lips twitched into an almost imperceptible frown. "Please carry on amongst yourselves," the supervisor said. "Serena, I'd like to see you in my office. Alone."

"Now?" Serena's voice came out in a tiny squeak.

Silence fell.

Never before had Arielle halted a Company meeting.

"Good luck," Meredith whispered, her forehead wrinkling in sympathy.

Alone with Arielle in her office, Serena talked without daring to look at the supervisor's face. The words seemed so sordid as they tumbled out of Serena's mouth. Heat flooded her face. Arielle would never understand. Her life was dedicated to the Company and the legal-aid clinic, and she ran both with a brisk efficiency that did not tolerate nonsense. Here in her modestly furnished office, Arielle's perfectly coiffed hair glowed halo-bright in the afternoon sun flooding in through the windows.

But when Serena finally glanced up, what she saw in the supervisor's eyes was compassion, not judgment.

"Don't be so hard on yourself, Serena," Arielle said, sitting straight upright with her hands folded neatly on top of Serena's closed file. "You did your best to perform your duty. Nick was supposed to be an easy assignment, suitable for a novice angel. The situation has become more complicated now that Julian Ascher has entered the picture."

"So what am I supposed to do?" Serena asked quietly.

"Continue to do your job. But keep in mind that you are not to sacrifice yourself again. I would have thought that with your one-year mark approaching, you would remember how tragically your human life ended."

Serena disagreed. By pulling that family out of the car, she'd saved three lives by giving up her own. To her, the simple math indicated that she'd done the right thing. However, one look at Arielle's face told her not to push that point.

"We've discussed this many times before," Arielle said. "Whatever happened during your human life, self-sacrifice is *not* part of your current job description. You would be of no use to the Company or your future Assignees if you martyr yourself for the soul of this one man."

"But—"

"Once is enough," Arielle said firmly. "Nick Ramirez has choices, and he's bringing this suffering on himself. You are doing your best to guide him in the right direction."

Serena dropped her gaze again, waiting until the lecture was finished.

"You're a Guardian now," the supervisor continued. "You have very clear instructions and a very clear goal. If you succeed at offering the correct guidance to your Assignees, you will continue to evolve through the ranks of angels. One day you will receive your wings. Regardless of the choices your Assignees make for themselves.

Do not give in to this demon, even if it means losing Nick's soul."

"What about kissing Julian? Aren't there...consequences?" Serena asked quietly.

Arielle shrugged. "There's no use fretting over it. You're a fledgling angel. Sometimes mistakes happen. You're not perfect. Yet." She smiled. "But be careful around Julian Ascher. He has the power to destroy you. He could have your soul in eternal damnation if something terrible happens."

"Like what?" Serena wondered aloud. She couldn't bring herself to say what was really on her mind: *Would sleeping with a demon automatically get you sent to hell?*

After a pause, Arielle said, "It would depend on the circumstances. But love heals all. If you keep love in your heart, you will always be safe." The supervisor scribbled some notes on Serena's file, then shuffled it closed and set it neatly to one side.

Serena sighed inwardly. "What circumstances?"

"I really wouldn't worry about that now," Arielle said, cutting off the question with a tranquil smile. "If you do find yourself in questionable circumstances, just avoid promising him anything. If you do, that promise must be honored. As you know, that is one of the most important rules governing the interactions between angels and demons. But otherwise, trust your intuition. You'll know what to do."

Something was not quite right here. Arielle usually made herself clear, but today she was being deliberately vague. In any case, Arielle shut Serena's file into a drawer. If Serena wanted answers, it didn't seem like she was going to get any today. Yet, there was one more thing she had to ask. Before she got up to leave, she said, "Why didn't you warn me about him?"

Arielle looked up, surprise glinting in her clear blue eyes. "What?"

"Why did you warn Meredith about Julian, but you didn't warn me?"

For a sliver of a second, a flicker of covert knowledge glittered in her gaze. She blinked, and it was gone. "Again, I wouldn't spend time worrying about that, Serena. You may go now."

Arielle smiled placidly and folded her hands on the desk, signaling that the conversation was unequivocally over. Serena knew better than to argue. But as she got up to leave, she wondered exactly what Arielle was hiding, and why.

Young angels were always so impressionable. The girl was remarkably like herself at that age, Arielle thought as she closed Serena's file. Now she picked up another file. It was Arielle's own file. There, under Arielle's name was written the name of her first Assignee.

Julian Ascher.

Two centuries ago, Arielle had been assigned to Julian when she'd been a fledgling Guardian herself. When he'd still been human. She'd been fighting for his soul ever since. Julian himself had never known, never suspected that he ever *had* a Guardian. He had refused to see the signs. Had thwarted all previous attempts to convert him. Now, the Company kept his activities under careful surveillance. And Julian had spent these past two hundred years wreaking havoc and amassing power.

Arielle's mandate was to stop him. This time, her secret weapon against Julian was Serena.

I knew this moment would come. Julian has taken the bait, Arielle thought. Yes, Serena had been assigned to guard Nick because it was inevitable that she would come into contact with Julian.

The Archdemon's major weakness was women—any fool could see that. And Serena seemed as though she had been tailor-made for him. Young, beautiful, so full of the vibrancy that Julian clearly craved. What more could a demon want? He was already hooked. And once Julian got his claws into a girl, he would not back down until...

Arielle leaned back in her desk chair and massaged her temples, willing herself not to think about the worst that could happen. Exposing a young angel to such dangerous forces was a risk, to be sure. But there was too much at stake. Julian's new nightclub, Devil's Ecstasy, would open in two weeks. When it did, it would draw thousands of people every night. Massive crowds would be exposed to temptation and corruption at Julian's whim. His influence was expanding at a terrifying rate.

He was becoming invincible.

Serena *must* succeed in her true mission. *To help Julian experience love.* She must not suspect the nature of that mission until it was accomplished. To make Julian fall in love, the object of his love must be genuine and true.

Love. Yes, love.

That was the only thing that could stop the damage Julian was unleashing. If it was possible to cause an angel to fall, it was possible to engineer a demon's redemption. A long time ago, a part of Julian had once been good. That goodness still existed in him. Serena would see that goodness, if she spent enough time with him. And she would make Julian see it himself. Of all the fledgling angels, Serena's heart was the most innocent. She'd never known romantic love in her human life, never been scarred by it.

Serena's innocence must remain untainted by the knowledge that she had been deliberately set up to lure Julian. He would smell that knowledge on her. Serena would be unable to hide it, since she was completely incapable of artifice or deceit. And if he sensed that she had an ulterior motive, he would never open up to her.

If Serena succeeded, it was worth the risk. Worth the enormous gamble of sending a fledgling angel on a dangerous mission she wasn't even aware of. To Arielle, there was nothing particularly surprising about that. Every day, humans and angels alike were sent on divine missions without knowing what they were doing. Or why.

Serena must succeed where I myself failed, the supervisor thought as she shut the file. She tucked it away in the cabinet and prayed for Serena's safety.

Arielle would be here to guide the young angel. And the Archangels would be watching over her from afar, even if they couldn't always be seen or heard.

But if Serena fell…there was nothing anyone could do to save her.

* * *

That night, Julian watched Serena sleep. As an Arch-demon, he was no longer bound by his physical body. He dematerialized at will now, moving between dimensions with the ease of a human crossing the street. Concentrating on the young angel's image in his mind's eye, he located her easily. Someone had cast a protection charm over her house, but the charm was weak and easily broken, rather like picking a cheap lock. After that, it was easy to gain entrance.

Serena's home was as pretty and inviting as she was. The large windows must have gotten a lot of sun in the daytime, because plants flourished everywhere. The furnishings were not expensive, but comfortable and homey—the kind of thing he supposed an interior designer might refer to as 'Shabby Chic.' Pastels and soft fabrics dominated. It was a style that was entirely too feminine for his tastes, and it made him vaguely uncomfortable.

As she lay in her frothy white bed—how cliché, for an angel, he thought—he perused her sleeping form. Drifting close, he paused, hovering over her in his dis-embodied spirit form. The covers were thrown back, revealing her pale limbs in the moonlight. She wore only a baby-doll T-shirt and a pair of boy-legged pant-ies. What a pity she didn't sleep nude.

He incarnated into his human body. It was the only way he could feel physical pleasure, and pleasure was his goal tonight. He was already hard and aching for her, frustrated by the abrupt end to their afternoon encoun-ter at the yoga studio. Edging closer, he stroked the soft skin of her cheek. She gave a little sigh of satisfaction. Awake, she'd never have let him touch her like this.

But now, as she slept, he took liberties that would have made her shriek with fury during waking hours. He got into bed with her, sliding under the covers with a carefully practiced stealth. Gently, he reached for her pert breasts, caressing one through the soft fabric of her T-shirt. The nipple hardened beneath his fingertips. She moaned, but rolled away from him. He brushed the nape of her neck and followed the touch with a gentle kiss. In her sleep, she fussed and swatted at the back of her neck.

She wasn't awake—if she were, she'd be screaming bloody murder. He withdrew a little and waited until her breathing resumed its slow, even pattern. Propped on one elbow, he studied her face, illuminated by the moonlight that spilled in through the sheer curtains. She might have terrible taste in interior decorating, but he'd rarely seen anyone lovelier, angel or otherwise. The crescents of her long eyelashes fell on flawless cheeks. He studied her perfect little nose, the moist curves of her perfect lips.

He slid a hand around her thigh, gliding along the silk of her skin, toward the bottom edge of her panties. In the next moment, she shoved his hand away and sat bolt upright in bed. "Julian, no!"

Just in time, he dematerialized. Awake, she peered straight at him in the darkness, a frown etching itself between her eyebrows as she clutched the blankets to her chest. She sat for long moments, staring at the air where he hovered, as though sensing, but not seeing him. Finally, she settled down again, closing her eyes and falling back into slumber. He slid away, disappointed.

Once again, he'd misread her. This afternoon he'd been sure that she was willing to surrender herself to him. And now, he was in danger of ruining his chances of having her.

But he would have her. He would simply have to be a bit smarter about things, he reminded himself again.

He would have to do things the hard way.

Chapter Four

At home that night, Julian swam laps in his outdoor pool to take the edge off. Having a human body was a pain in the ass sometimes, with its highs of physical pleasure and its lows of pain. He dove in, submerging his lust in the cool blue of the water, and tried not to think about Serena.

Instead, he thought about *choices*.

He cleaved his way through length after length, his thoughts racing. In his mind, he considered himself nothing more than a provider of choices when it came to the corruption of human beings. In the vast majority of cases, he found he could achieve his end goal without involving himself directly in criminal activities. No, there were plenty of middlemen willing to take care of that. He simply made sure he was around to make a full range of choices available. In Nick's case, for example, he'd simply provided the *choice* of partaking in illegal substances and illicit sex. In other cases, the choices Julian offered to other humans involved large sums of money.

His muscles began to ache, but he swam hard, his thoughts still churning.

Nobody has to choose damnation. Julian had never

forced a soul into hell. The power of suggestion went a long way, he'd found over the years. And where that failed, there was always good old blackmail. Almost everyone had made a choice or two in their past they'd rather keep hidden, a skeleton they'd prefer remained in the closet. He wondered if Serena had any skeletons in *her* closet. More than likely, he guessed that it was simply filled with pastel sundresses and yoga clothes. He was struck by a sudden desire to find out.

It was well after 1:00 a.m. when Julian stopped swimming and summoned his personal assistant. Harry, an African-American family man in his mid-thirties, had been happily managing an English pub in a quiet suburban neighborhood until his sudden and untimely death three months ago. He arrived, breathless, within minutes of Julian's call.

"I trust your children are all doing well," Julian said.

To provide for his four kids after he'd died, Harry had resorted to pickpocketing clubgoers at Devil's Paradise. When the Gatekeepers had caught him, Julian had found over four thousand dollars in cash on him and several handfuls of jewelry, including a silver bracelet filched off the wrist of the club's general manager. Julian had seen his potential, and hired him on the spot.

"Thriving, thank you," Harry said. "You've been very generous. I've been sending most of my salary to my wife. She thinks she's getting payments from a life-insurance policy."

"Excellent. I need you to do me a favor. There was a young woman who came in last night—an angel. Serena St. Clair is her name. Find out everything you can on her. I'd like to know what kind of *choices* might influence such a person, if you know what I mean."

"Consider it done, sir," he nodded, signaling that there was no further explanation necessary. He slipped back into the night as quietly as he had come, leaving Julian confident that the job was in good hands. Harry, of all people, knew the value of choices. He had become a demon because of a few unfortunate choices he'd made during his human life, choices that he regretted bitterly. And now he was willing to do all the wrong things for all the right reasons.

Oh, yes, it all came down to *choices,* a matter of finding which *choice* would determine the point at which a person cracked. Sooner or later, Julian would crack Little Miss Perfect. He just had to find out what that choice was.

Each day that week, the gifts Julian sent became more outrageous. On Monday, it was flowers and chocolate—three-dozen red sweetheart roses and the biggest box of Belgian truffles she had ever seen. Tuesday, a basket filled with French perfume. Wednesday, a tiny Yorkshire terrier puppy with a gigantic, floppy bow around its neck. A courier arrived with a jeweler's box on Thursday. Serena opened it to find a diamond bracelet glittering against the dark blue velvet. Friday, he sent her a ticket to Paris—on his private jet.

She sent each delivery back immediately, without so much as a phone call, a note or even a text message. It irked her that he thought she could be bought. That she would abandon her duty to Nick for a few expensive items, gifts that appeared to bear no personal thought behind them. They were the sort of offerings that a man might guess any red-blooded female desired.

But even more disturbing was her own reaction to the gifts—she wanted to keep them. Each and every one of them. What's more, she wondered about the man who had sent them. Who was he? And how far would he go to get what he wanted?

Oh, she was content with her life as a yoga teacher, and more than happy to perform her angelic duties with enthusiasm. But in the year since she'd been ordained, she'd lived frugally, without the comfort of family, or the little pleasures that men in her human life might have brought her when she dated them. In fact, in the past year, she'd shied away from male attention entirely, living almost like a nun.

How long had it been since anyone had sent her flowers or chocolate? She hated to admit it, but the gifts had brought a smile to her face when she'd opened the door. But none of them had affected her as much as the puppy. She'd snuggled him longingly, burying her face into his soft fur as he squirmed around to lick her. He had a tag on his collar that read *Milo*. It had almost broken her heart to send him back.

On Saturday morning, she woke up half expecting to see a new sports car parked in her driveway. But there was nothing.

As she drove to the yoga studio to teach Nick's private lesson, she told herself she ought to be relieved. But if she were totally honest, she had to admit that she also felt a tinge of disappointment. Apparently, Julian had an attention span of a fruit fly.

But it was probably—no, definitely—for the best.

Life would go back to normal now that he had forgotten about her. And that was what she wanted.

Wasn't it?

While Julian distracted Serena with the deluge of gifts, he planned. And a few days later, Harry came back to report. While Julian sat at his desk, Harry summarized what he'd found.

"Serena was born about six hours up the coast, in the town of Carmel. Mother and brother still live there. Father died of a heart attack at the age of forty-six, when the girl was thirteen. She went to college near home at UC Santa Cruz, traveled afterward, then taught yoga full-time. Died last year in a car accident on the Cabrillo Freeway. She was twenty-three years old." Harry paused, swallowing past what Julian guessed was a lump in his throat. "Joined the Company of Angels immediately upon termination of her human life. They relocated her to L.A., like they move almost all of their members, so she'd be around fewer of her friends and family who might recognize her."

Even if someone from her past did recognize her, Julian knew that if she created any glaring inconsistencies with human reality these days, the Archangels would correct her mistakes. They could lift angelic imprints off human memories as easily as wiping chalk from a blackboard.

Just as Julian himself could erase any trace of demonic activity.

"Vices?" Julian said. This was the part he'd been anticipating, always the most interesting part of someone's life.

"None. She was a quiet kid after her father died. Not much to report from her high school years. She partied like any normal college kid, but seems to have straightened out right after graduation. Otherwise, she had no apparent vices."

Impossible. "There has to be something. Maybe you didn't dig deep enough," Julian said, frowning.

Harry looked affronted. "I dug plenty deep. There just wasn't anything that interesting to find. She lived a good life."

Harry had more—pages of details on her class schedules, jobs she'd worked, her dedication to yoga, trips she'd taken, the kind of car she'd driven, who her friends had been. But nowhere in his report were the kinds of things Julian really wanted to know. A thousand other questions burned in his mind. *Who was the first boy she ever kissed? How many lovers had she taken? How many hearts had she broken? Had anyone ever broken hers? Had she ever known real love?*

Questions he could hardly ask Harry.

The report spoke of a life unlived, dedicated to service from a very young age. In Serena's human life, there had been precious little room for the passions, the desires, the joys and the screwups of being human.

"How pathetically short," Julian commented aloud. Her life had a sort of unlived quality that made Julian ache strangely for her. Harry, too, seemed to have been affected, deep in thought as he shuffled through the pages. There was nothing left to say, but Julian could see him standing there, trying to make sense of what he had found. *He's thinking of his own kids,* Julian thought as he watched the man.

"Thank you, Harry. That will be all for now."

After Harry shut the door, Julian was left in utter silence. He felt like someone had died, as though he ought to mourn her. She was a blank slate, this girl, the paper description of her life so bland as to make her seem expendable. But in person, from the very first time he had looked into her eyes, Julian had read so much more. He had seen her tenacious loyalty to Nick, the ferocious pride that gave her the courage to stand up to a demon—Julian himself—who was much more powerful than she was. And he had seen in those eyes a desire…a desire to know. To feel. To exist.

No, Serena was not a woman to be mourned. For even though her human life had ended, she was not gone, after all. She was still very much alive and kicking in the material realm.

And here in the material realm, he would delve into her unexplored desires. Would find a way to get inside of her and exploit whatever it was she most wanted to learn, to experience, to be. Would ply her with the things she had missed out on during her fleeting human life.

All he needed was a way in.

Perhaps she would be lured by material objects. He sent all the things that usually worked for him: flowers, chocolate, perfume, a baby animal, jewelry, a romantic escape.… But by the end of the week, all the gifts had been returned and Julian realized he would have to try another tactic. Family was always a good starting place, as Julian had proven so many times, most recently with Harry. At least the Company had kept Serena close to her family so she could watch over them from a safe distance. It was a fact Julian would certainly use to his advantage.

Maybe the brother...

On Friday afternoon, Julian wandered into Andrew St. Clair's photography gallery, a large, warehouselike space in the quiet seaside town of Carmel. The gallery's bare concrete walls were hung with pictures—portraits, mostly, some of them Julian recognized, and others he didn't. But famous or not, all of the subjects were lovingly photographed, shot with the careful eye of a true artist.

With the exception of one subject, perhaps a little *more* lovingly photographed than the rest. There was a substantial section of wall devoted to Serena, half a dozen photos of her at different ages and in various locales. Even as a baby, she'd been beautiful, the blue of her eyes intense in the photographs.

"Who's this?" he asked, keeping his tone bland.

Andrew shuffled up beside him, stuffed his hands in his pockets. Julian noted the family resemblance in his hair, a shade darker than Serena's, and his eyes, which matched hers exactly. "That's my sister, Serena."

"Is she a model? An actress?" he suggested casually.

"She did a little modeling when she was younger. She was scouted in high school, but she never had any real interest in it."

"Really? Why so?" Julian prompted.

Andrew shrugged. "Serena always had her head in the clouds. Used to wander on the beach for hours, just daydreaming. She studied philosophy at college and then she went to India for a year. Came back a changed woman, she said, and started teaching yoga."

"And now?" Julian said, prodding for the inevitable. He knew what had happened, but wanted to see the brother's reaction. He took great pleasure in the suffering of others.

Andrew smiled gently. "She died in a car accident last year."

"I'm sorry for your loss," Julian said, and was surprised by his own reaction. He meant what he'd said. He swallowed down the emotion that blocked his throat, not allowing it to surface. *How strange...*

"It's okay. Serena was a hero. She saved a woman and her two young daughters."

So she had a bent for self-sacrifice. Wasn't that interesting? He filed the information away for later. But surely the little angel had a vice or two, whether Harry or Andrew knew about that or not. There would be time enough to find out. He was in no particular hurry, except for the increasingly insistent needs of his body. And those, he could ease at any time. All he needed was a warm and willing female, and not necessarily Serena.

Andrew continued to gaze at the photos, lost in a moment of sadness. "I just wish she'd had more time. To live life. Serena was a beautiful girl, but she was so serious all the time. I'm not sure if she ever really knew how to have fun. I don't think she ever fell in love."

Interesting. But there was more there. Julian could feel Andrew's mind resisting, secreting away some bit of information that he deemed unfit to share. Julian wanted to know. He looked Andrew straight in the eyes and asked casually, "Why's that?"

"Maybe because she saw our father die when she was thirteen. He had a heart attack on the living-room floor, and Serena came home from school one day to find the paramedics trying to perform CPR on him. But they couldn't revive him. After that, she was never really the same. I think she might have blamed herself. I'm not sure why I'm telling you all of this," Andrew said, looking a bit startled.

Because your weak human mind is no match for mine, Julian thought.

Now, here was some information he could definitely use. Little Miss Perfect might not have any serious vices, but she definitely had vulnerabilities. A tendency toward self-sacrifice. Guilt about her lost father. Yes, he could work with that.

"What would you say about doing some publicity photographs for me, Andrew?" Julian said. "I'm having a party at my house in L.A. tomorrow, and a lot of important people will be there. I'd love to have you on board, if you're available."

He named a price.

Andrew's eyes widened. For the sum Julian named, he would be available. At that price, Julian guessed he might even have pitched in a pledge for his firstborn child.

As yet, Julian had no such party planned, but it would be organized at the touch of the speed-dial on his cell phone. He walked out the door and called his personal assistant.

Choices. Andrew had made the right choice. Perhaps now, his sister would be more amenable to choosing Julian as a potential companion.

* * *

When there was no word from Julian on Saturday morning, Serena began to breathe again. Now that she had a reprieve, it was time to rebuild. Time to concentrate on her students and the assigned souls she had been sent back to guide. On spreading the message of divine love.

Nick's yoga practice was progressing steadily. He'd had several lessons this week, and he was an enthusiastic learner with an innate grace. She'd forced herself to refrain from asking about the Archdemon. But some part of her, pathetically, hoped for the mention of Julian's name, of any snippet of news. She wondered if Nick knew about the gifts. If he did, he kept silent.

Nor did Nick try to kiss her again. Although it still disturbed her to see the smitten look in his eyes, at least he hadn't spoken of his romantic feelings for her since his last failed attempt.

Today, after his lesson, he handed her a plain white envelope. "Julian asked me to give you this," he said, proceeding to roll up his mat.

What now? Would the Archdemon resort to cold, hard cash? The deed to a condo? But when she opened the envelope with trembling fingers, all it contained was a folded note on heavy cream stationery. The handwriting was from another century, a sweep of elegant lines decorated with flourishes.

> *My dearest Serena,*
> *Please accept my sincerest apologies for intruding on your private lesson last Sunday afternoon. I am hosting an intimate gathering at*

*my home tonight, and I would be honored if you
would attend. You might be interested to note my
guest list will include someone with whom you
may be acquainted: photographer Andrew St.
Clair.*

   Yours, J.

There was more. Details of his address in Beverly
Hills. Mention of a dress code.

But she was too sick to read on. Her brother's name,
written in Julian's curling script, was embossed in her
mind's eye. *Andrew.*

He was two years older, but a hundred years wiser.
At the age of fifteen, Andrew had taken over as the man
of the house when their father had died. He'd been the
one who had stood next to her and held her as she cried
at their father's funeral, while they watched his coffin
descend into the ground. Her brother became her pro-
tector, her ally, her hero. But Andrew was only human,
and no match for a demon.

Bile rose up her throat and threatened to spill out.
The paper slipped from her fingers to the floor. The
room tilted dangerously, and for a moment, she thought
she might faint.

Nick was at her side in an instant, bracing her against
his muscled body, still damp from practice. "Are you
okay?"

"I'm fine. I'm just feeling a little under the weather
all of a sudden." She pressed her shaking fingers to her
temples, pushing away from him to stand on her own.

He picked up the note and glanced at it. "What's
going on between you and Julian?"

"Absolutely nothing." A rush of shame flooded through her. She never lied—not even little white lies like the one that had just popped out of her mouth. Since she'd met Julian, everything was changing.

"Don't feel obligated to go just because he's my friend."

"Of course not," she said lamely.

"And who is this Andrew St. Clair? You have the same last name. What is he…?" Nick's mind reached for the connection; divine intervention broke the link.

"It's purely a coincidence."

"Maybe you and I could go to the party together," he offered, his eyebrows raised in a question as he looked up from the note.

She paused for a long moment, not knowing what to say. But what option did she have? None. "Sure."

A smile lit like flame, spreading over Nick's face. "Fantastic. I'll pick you up at eight."

"Sounds like a plan." Good Lord, what was she getting herself into?

"It's a date."

Shit.

Nick left the studio happier than she'd ever seen him. Guilt screamed in her mind. She was leading Nick on. Worse, she was using him as a shield against Julian Ascher. While Arielle had never specifically spelled out why it might be wrong to use your Assignee as a buffer against demonic forces, Serena was absolutely sure it contravened the spirit of Company policy.

But the Archdemon had gotten personal. Her brother's life was at stake, and she would use everything she had to stop Julian. She would not let him win. She jammed the note in her pocket and headed out the door.

Later, Serena stood in her bedroom, staring at her open closet. Behind her, clothes were strewn around her usually neat room, which now looked like the aftermath of a Black Friday sale.

Evening attire, Julian's note said. Nothing in Serena's wardrobe, which consisted almost entirely of yoga gear and day dresses, remotely fit that description. But finding a dress for tonight was the least of her concerns. Trying on every piece of clothing she owned was merely a distraction from worrying.

About the fact that her brother's life hung in the balance.

Andrew.

She tossed another outfit behind her, feeling her chest constrict with sadness. In just over a decade, Andrew had lost both a father and a sister. It should have destroyed him. Left behind to mourn Serena's death along with their mother, he had somehow pulled himself together. Because Andrew believed firmly in that old saying: *whatever doesn't kill you makes you stronger.*

Andrew had been a good brother. He had loved her well. It tore at her heart to think that he was in terrible danger. And that he probably didn't even realize it.

"What on earth is going on?" Meredith stood in the doorway of Serena's room, eyes wide as she looked at the mess.

"I'm trying to find something to wear," Serena said, collapsing onto her bed, so tired she wished she could curl up and take a nap in the dark blue sundress she was wearing. In it, she felt about as sexy as a kindergarten teacher on a field trip to the zoo. "For a party tonight. At Julian's."

"Him again?"

"He's gotten his hooks into Andrew." The words came out of Serena's mouth as a forlorn little whisper, her voice thinner and more fragile than the wings of the crickets singing outside.

There was a long, terrible pause as Meredith absorbed the information. She swallowed and said, "So you have to go. If it were my brother, I'd do the same. But you're not thinking about going there by yourself, are you?"

"I'm going with Nick."

"The drug-addicted actor?" Meredith shook her head. "That's worse than going alone. I'm coming with you."

"It's far too risky," Serena said.

Her roommate gave her a sideways glance as she started to walk away, toward her own bedroom. Then Meredith glanced back and said, "Are you coming? We have to find you a dress."

When Meredith threw open her closet doors, she revealed a treasure trove of shiny, sparkly dresses. She grabbed an armful and spread them out on her bed. Serena stared, blinking at the array of colors, shocked that her roommate had been hiding all these clothes. Most of the time, Meredith wore plain white nutritionist's uniforms or jeans during her time off.

Her roommate noted Serena's expression, handing her a silk frock in emerald-green. "I'm still working on detachment from material possessions," Meredith said. "Arielle's perspective is that things will simply start to fall away as I'm ready to let them go. Until then, I can still appreciate a good cocktail dress." After a moment's pause, she said, "Speaking of Arielle, do you think we should consult her about this party?"

"Arielle was no help whatsoever," Serena answered, cinching herself into the dress and shifting uncomfortably. "Besides, what choice do I have? If Arielle tells me I have to abandon my brother to that…that hellhound, I can't very well follow her instructions, can I?"

"Sometimes Arielle tests people," Meredith said. "I've seen her do it before."

Serena paused. "It's possible. I just don't know why she would test *me*." She wiggled, trying to adjust the bodice. Both girls were slender, but Serena's natural curves refused to be constrained.

"Whatever you say." Meredith tilted her head as she assessed the dress. "That one doesn't fit you." She turned back to the open closet and continued to browse through her clothes. "Just be careful around that demon of yours."

Serena unzipped herself, blushing furiously. "He's not mine. Both times I ran into him, all that happened was a kiss."

Her roommate did not answer, but merely raised her eyebrows. She took the green dress and handed Serena a strapless white dress. Embellished with black embroidery and a black silk bow that tied at the waist, it fell just below the knee, an elegant length that emphasized the stretch of her long legs. "That's the one," Meredith said. "You look like a gift, with that bow on the front. Whatever you do, don't let him unwrap you."

Both girls stood looking at the dress in Meredith's full-length mirror. Serena felt a wave of desolation wash over her. *All my life, Andrew protected me from the worst,* she thought. *This time it's Andrew who needs protecting. How will I find a way?*

Meredith caught her gaze in the mirror and said, "You'll find a way. You will not let him down."

Chapter Five

What Julian had described as an "intimate gathering" on his invitation to her had ballooned into a gala evening for two hundred elite guests. A Gatsby of an evening, just the sort of sophisticated party that would jar Serena out of her element while appealing to her finer senses.

His Old Hollywood mansion made a glamorous backdrop for a summer party—the faint essence of scorned divas still clung to the hallways of the Mediterranean villa. An eight-foot-tall ice sculpture of a glistening winged creature dominated the foyer. Breezy chatter floated over the distant notes of the full orchestra tuning its instruments in the back garden, preparing for the dancing that would begin later. The cream of Los Angeles's elite had gathered. Among the politicians and actors, the models and business moguls, his staff circulated trays of champagne and hors d'oeuvres.

Julian sauntered through the house, wandering from room to room as the party gathered momentum. While he often remained apart from the crowd at Devil's Paradise, in his own home Julian was the consummate host. He shook hands and engaged in small talk. Encouraged people toward the lavish buffet set out in the dining room.

He kept an eye toward the entrance as he mingled. There was only *one* person he was intent on hosting. And when she arrived, theirs would be a truly intimate gathering.

But where the devil was she?

Harry skirted around the crowd, directing the staff and managing the smaller details. "Don't worry, sir," said Harry, catching the slight frown on Julian's face. "She'll come. Andrew's here."

Harry's right, Julian thought fleetingly.

Serena would not resist her brother's presence. Julian spotted the photographer snapping images of guests in front of the ice sculpture, and gave him a hearty handshake. He clapped him on the back and thanked the man for coming.

Andrew swallowed, unable to hide his awe. "Julian, your home is spectacular."

Revel House was Julian's pride and joy. He'd won the four-acre estate with its sprawling villa on a bet from a dying movie star in the 1950s. The bet had been rigged, of course. But that was something Andrew didn't need to know. "It's not a bad little shack," said the Archdemon.

"Thank you for the opportunity. I feel privileged to photograph your guests and your home," Andrew said, waving his camera in the direction of the ice sculpture. "Especially that work of art. The detailing on those wings looks so real."

As they stood admiring the statue, Andrew suddenly jumped backward, skittering behind Julian. "I could swear I...I just saw the damned thing wink," the photographer said.

"Of course not," Julian said, his voice calm. Of course, the sculpture *had* winked. The thing was a real demon he'd called up from the frozen Buddhist hell realms. It crouched still on its pedestal, pretending to be art. "Must have been a trick of the light."

For an instant, Andrew's brows knitted together. But he quickly recovered, face smoothing over. And if he thought anything was suspicious, he kept his mouth shut. They chatted amiably, and the more they talked, the more Julian found himself beginning to like the man. He stopped himself, reminding himself that Andrew's friendship was not what he wanted.

What he wanted was Serena. But in that regard, he was getting nowhere fast. He detached himself politely from the conversation, and then continued to circulate. Inside, he seethed.

What is it with men and multiples of women? Serena wondered as she and Meredith climbed into the back of Nick's limo. There was enough room inside for a soccer team. Yet he insisted the girls sit on either side of him.

As the limo sped along the Santa Monica Freeway, Meredith kept Nick occupied as they chatted easily, his eyes running over the redhead's vibrant green silk dress. Serena barely listened to their conversation, lost in anxiety about Andrew.

Under no circumstances would she let Julian sink his claws into her brother.

The limo idled in front of the gates to Julian's Beverly Hills home, waiting to enter his driveway. A chill ran through Serena as she gazed out the window.

"The Gates of Hell," Nick announced. "Copied from a Rodin sculpture, Julian told me. That's the famous *Thinker* figure up there, dead center at the top. Julian says he represents Dante, looking down on the characters from his epic poem, the *Inferno*. You can see the other characters sculpted on the edges of the gates. There are the legendary adulterers Francesca and Paolo. And there's Ugolino della Gherardesca, who cannibalized his children after they died of starvation," Nick narrated as he pointed.

As the gates swung open, Serena shuddered.

"You have a good memory," Meredith commented to Nick.

The actor shrugged, but his smile belied his pride. "That's my job. I'm an expert at reciting lines from a script."

His driver pulled up the long driveway, circling around an artificial lake. This was no house. It was a palace, a fantasy in white stucco. It could have been a luxury hotel on the Amalfi Coast in Italy, but it was Julian's private residence.

How did Julian accumulate all this wealth? Serena wondered. A thousand gruesome possibilities arose in her mind. She stopped herself from guessing. Better not to think about it.

"One man lives here alone?" Meredith asked, wide-eyed, peering out the limo's window.

Not a man, Serena brooded. *Evil incarnate.*

"One man and an army of servants," Nick said.

An army of hell beings, more precisely, she thought. Gatekeeper demons in doormen's uniforms opened the car door. She recoiled as one of them offered to take her hand, and she clung to Nick's arm. He mistook her terror for enthusiasm and smiled down at her, radiating warmth from his deep brown eyes.

Her heels clicked on the marble steps as they mounted the staircase. She shivered as they passed through the double doors that the Gatekeepers held open, and pulled her gauzy white silk wrap around her shoulders.

"There are so many celebrities here," Meredith breathed, as they paused at the entrance.

"Don't be fooled," Serena whispered back.

The crowd gathered in Julian's showcase of an entrance hall was worldlier than the drunken clubgoers who frolicked at Devil's Paradise. But the glittering dresses and expensively tailored summer suits did not deceive her. A dark energy simmered, barely contained below the genteel surface of the crowd.

Serena's gaze tracked upward. Towering above the crowd, a real *Nakara* demon smirked down at the party guests with a glint of mischief in its frozen eye. Overhead, a vaulted ceiling soared above the foyer, to the fresco of hell painted there. It depicted horned demons whipping the naked bodies of the damned, torturing them with hot irons, devouring their flesh with bared teeth. It seemed to Serena that, in spite of their cultured manners, the people gathered here could have fallen straight out of the painting above.

The night was still tender. Anything could happen.

But amidst the crush of guests, Julian was nowhere in sight.

Nick nabbed a couple of glasses of champagne from a passing tray, handing one to each of them. Then he grabbed one for himself. "Ladies," he said, raising the glass before he downed its contents in one gulp. "Here's to a great night to come."

"I don't drink," she started to explain, when one of the Gatekeepers approached them and made a little bow.

"Mr. Ascher requests the pleasure of your company in the back garden," said the Gatekeeper. "Please follow me."

He led them through a long arched hallway, through a set of high glass doors that opened onto a sweeping terrace. Serena felt as though she'd stepped into an old Audrey Hepburn movie. The terrace overlooked a vast garden that sprawled behind the house, strung with white fairy lights and twinkling with lit candles. At the bottom of a curving staircase, a swimming pool glowed a deep, eerie blue. On the lawn beside it, a full orchestra played while couples danced in slow circles on the grass and the white marble pool deck.

"Please enjoy your evening," said the Gatekeeper, bowing as he slipped away.

Surrounded by a cluster of beautiful women, Julian held court. In the fingers of one hand, a glass of champagne dangled. Something he said made the circle of women laugh, each obviously vying for his attention.

Next to him stood her brother, snapping photos with a camera that was strapped around his neck. Andrew turned. He lowered his wide-angle lens and gave her a long, odd look.

She froze as her brother stared.

Confusion swept across Andrew's face. Many people knew that angels walked among them. Only a few understood how closely. Most human minds were simply unable to hold the vibrations of divine beings. *"Think of that eerie feeling you used to get when you were alive,"* Arielle had explained soon after Serena's death. *"Like someone was watching over you? Or when you thought you recognized someone on the street, who seemed so familiar? That was not your imagination."*

Serena watched that feeling of near-recognition in Andrew's bright blue eyes now. Saw the shiver pass over his body as his mind churned, trying to place her. She had not seen her brother this close since her human death. A handful of times, she'd driven to Carmel to watch her mother and brother from afar, making sure to keep herself sufficiently hidden.

But now, she wanted to hug him. She wanted to cry.

Not just for herself, but for him.

Now here he stood, in the middle of this demon's domain. Because of *her*. In need of her protection. She had to get him out of Julian's grasp.

The Archdemon caught sight of her and raised his champagne glass to her in mock salute. As Julian's glittering gaze locked on hers, she felt the obsidian depths of his demon's soul pulling her toward him, threatening to draw her in.

At that moment, Serena wanted to kill him. Not just for putting her brother in jeopardy. But for luring Nick into increasing danger. For trying to seduce her. For all the evil he'd ever done to every soul who had crossed over his threshold.

The thought of murdering another person had never occurred to her before. But right now, she wanted to put her hands around his tanned, muscular neck and choke him senseless right in front of his crowd of privileged guests.

Oh, it would be so easy.

One act of recklessness to save hundreds of lives. Thousands. Possibly millions.

In the clear night sky directly overhead, a flash of lightning splintered across the velvet darkness. A sharp, loud crack pierced the sound of music and laughter.

A warning from above.

The orchestra ground to a halt and the entire crowd looked skyward. The only person not looking up was Andrew, who stood shivering as he stared, looking straight at Serena as though he was seeing a ghost. *In a way, he is,* she thought. Her brother shook his head, trying to jar himself out of his daze.

"How odd. Not a drop of moisture in the air," Nick said, scanning the sky. The orchestra launched seamlessly back into song and the guests resumed their chatter. The actor started down the stairs, toward Julian. "Let's say hello to our host."

The Archdemon bent down, whispering to Andrew. Who looked up at Serena again, this time without a trace of recognition. Smiling politely, her brother excused himself to go back into the house to photograph the ice sculpture.

Relief and disappointment both flooded her at once. Julian glanced at her, and the message in that gemstone gaze was clear: *If Archangels can erase angelic imprints, so can Archdemons.*

"So good of you ladies to grace us with your company," Julian said. Apparently amused by his own irony, he smiled slightly. "And, Nick, always a pleasure to see you, my friend. What a pity that you just missed meeting my new photographer. His name is Andrew. He's very talented. I'm thinking of taking him on board permanently."

"Really?" Nick said. "Sounds interesting."

"Andrew would love it. I can provide opportunities for him that he never imagined. He and I have been getting to know each other. We're practically best friends."

No. She would not let Julian have his way. Would not watch her brother's life go down the drain, no matter what Arielle had said. Her brother was in the prime of his humanity, and if Serena had anything to do with it, he would have every opportunity to live until he was a hundred. As she herself had not had.

"This photographer is very talented," Julian continued smoothly, placing his arm around the waist of a stunning brunette beside him. "And ambitious. He could be a great success with the right contacts."

The threat was subtle, but it hung in the summer air between them, charged like the lightning bolt that had electrified the sky moments before.

"Julian, I need to speak with you for a moment," Serena said. Beside her, Nick stiffened. But he wasn't in direct danger now. Her brother was. She turned to her Assignee and said, "I want to talk to Julian about the photographer. I need someone to take some photos of the yoga studio."

The brunette clinging to Julian's side pouted. He gave her a patronizing pat on the cheek and said, "I'll be back in a moment, darling."

In the same moment, Serena whispered covertly to Meredith, "Get my brother out of here."

Meredith nodded. Serena knew she had to count on her roommate now. She didn't dare look backward again as Julian led her into the house.

"You weren't supposed to come here with a date," he said quietly as he guided her through the winding hallways of his villa. The levity of his mood seemed to dissolve and he glanced down at her. "Nor were you supposed to bring your friend, Meredith. That's her name, isn't it?"

"You gave me no choice," said Serena.

He stopped short, turning to face her. "You always have a choice, Serena."

"Get your claws out of my brother," she said, refusing to back down beneath his intense gaze. "What you're doing is extortion."

"Such a negative view of the situation, my angel." He pressed her against the wall, leaned the weight of himself into her soft curves. "You need to loosen up. Your brother has been telling me all about you. He said you needed to have more fun."

Oh, how she hated Julian.

But she needed to keep him distracted. To give Meredith a chance to find Andrew and get him out of this godforsaken mess. She must stall for time. There was one way for certain that she knew how.

"I can show you how to have fun."

His voice was low and velvet, rolling through her body and vibrating deep inside her. She had the sensation that he was about to kiss her. Her eyelids drifted shut, and her lips parted slightly, ready to meet his descending mouth.

The sound of approaching laughter, of another couple

around the corner made him draw back. Julian drew a fingertip across Serena's lips. "Let's go. There's someone else I think you'd like to see."

Anger bubbled up in her. At her side, her hand curled into a fist. "Good God, who have you brought here besides Andrew?" she snapped.

He didn't answer, but tugged at her hand. He led her down a quiet hallway, toward his bedroom, she was sure. She stomped along behind him, struggling to keep up with his long strides. *Who on earth has he brought here, and why?*

At last, he opened a door that led not to his bedroom, but to his library. Leather-bound books lined tall mahogany shelves on every side of the room. Along one wall, a large sofa in chrome and leather seemed made for long afternoons of reading.

In a pen in the corner, she spotted the puppy he'd sent her, curled up in a little bed. His tiny head popped up when he heard the door open, and he scuttled over to the edge of the enclosure to greet her, tail wagging furiously.

"What's he doing here?" She crossed the room and scooped Milo out of his pen, laughing softly as he wriggled and licked her face. Her anger at Julian retreated momentarily. Perhaps he was not quite the monster she'd thought he was.

Julian shoved his hands in his pockets and leaned against one of the bookshelves, watching her. "I don't know why I kept him. I should have thrown him to the Nakara."

Horrified, she clutched the puppy closer.

"Maybe you'll rethink taking him home, after all,"

he said. "You wouldn't want him to get eaten, would you?"

"You wouldn't dare." She gave him her best glare, but it was hard to remain angry when she was holding this sweet puppy. Was it her imagination, or was there something like regret in the shadow that passed across Julian's face?

"My angel, I've done much worse," he said gently.

It was on the tip of her tongue to ask him what exactly it was that he'd done. But she stopped herself, realizing she didn't want to know. She cuddled the puppy closer, stroking Milo's soft fur. "Stop calling me that. I'm not your angel."

Milo struggled to get down. She set him on the floor; he wiggled off in search of something to satisfy his puppy's curiosity.

She investigated the books, browsing as Julian strolled so close behind her she could feel his breath on the back of her exposed neck. She concentrated on reading the titles, trying to pretend she couldn't feel the heat radiating from his powerful body. Machiavelli's *The Prince*, Aristotle's *Nicomachean Ethics*. A long shelf of Shakespearean plays. Sun Tzu's *The Art of War*.

"My, you're well-read," she said, swallowing down the growing realization that she was no match for Julian.

The books spoke of a man with a mind for strategy. A man who enjoyed delving into the ruminations of the world's greatest thinkers. Who had developed a sensitivity for the intricacies and vulnerabilities of human nature. A man who was infinitely more dangerous than she was equipped to handle.

His voice was soft behind her. "I've had a lot of time on my hands," he said.

On one wall hung a framed page of a manuscript, brown with age. She peered closer and read the lines of spindly handwriting.

In Xanadu did Kubla Khan
A stately pleasure dome decree...

"It reminds me of you. King of the pleasure dome," she said. Her gaze traveled down the lines, catching on the middle of the page.

A savage place! as holy and enchanted
As e'er beneath a waning moon was haunted
By woman wailing for her demon-lover!

She shivered, then turned to find him studying her intently while she perused the manuscript. "I know this poem," she blurted.

"Ah, yes, Kubla Khan. The Coleridge manuscript. It's an original, of course. He was one of my greatest accomplishments."

"What do you mean?"

His usual facade of detachment cracked slightly, and pride infused his voice. "Coleridge was an opium addict. He took a dose, then fell asleep. He always claimed that he had dreamed a few hundred lines of this poem. When he awoke, he started scribbling furiously, penning these first three stanzas. But he was interrupted by a knock at the door, and someone he called 'the man from Porlock' detained him for an hour. Afterward, he tried to re-create the masterpiece of his dreams, but of the three hundred lines, he could remember only fifty-four."

"So you're saying you were the man from Porlock?"

He smiled. "And the one who got him started on opium in the first place."

"But that must have been…" She trailed off.

"1797," he supplied. "The poem has some lovely lines, doesn't it?"

His gaze fell to her lips; she felt again that he might try to kiss her. She cut him off before he could, turning back to examine the manuscript. Behind her, he bent near. Her eyes scanned the words as he whispered them a hairbreadth away from her ear.

> *"…close your eyes with holy dread,*
> *For he on honey-dew hath fed*
> *And drunk the milk of Paradise."*

His lips brushed the tender skin beneath her ear. She trembled; her lips parted and her breath broke from her throat. She tilted her head back, giving him easier access to her neck as he feathered kisses along its most sensitive spots.

One of his hands rose up to skim the bottom of her rib cage, the other hand followed, venturing higher. Through the silk of her dress, he stroked her. Beneath his expert touch, pleasure washed over her.

Sensations set her body trembling. She was at risk of floating away on a cloud of bliss.

She wanted to reach back and kiss him with all the pent-up frustration of a week spent yearning for him, spent secretly fantasizing his touch on her body, the slide of his skin on hers. More than that, she wanted to kiss him with all the repressed energy of a year without intimacy with the opposite sex, a year of being stuck in a human body whose needs she denied at every waking moment.

But she did not. Could not. *Would not.*

As his heated mouth roamed the back of her neck, he steered her in slow steps across the room, until she felt her leg meet the edge of the sofa.

He turned her, held her to his chest, kissed the top of her head with a tenderness that was close to reverence. Without warning, she felt herself falling backward, her body suspended in his arms, until he deposited her on the sofa. She clung to him and he followed her down, easing his weight over her carefully as he caught one of her legs so that it rode the side of his hip.

It was the move of a master, choreographed so perfectly she had the sense that he must have performed it a thousand times before. He was as skilled as a gigolo and as smooth as Casanova. A warning signal popped up in the back of her mind, flagging her to the risk of the situation. She ignored it, lost in a swirl of sensual delight.

He looked down at her, easing back to stare at her with an expression of wonder that did not match his demon's nature. There was something human in him, too. Beneath that fiendish exterior still beat a man's heart. She saw it in his eyes, felt it in the gentleness of his touch, knew it from the tender brush of his lips.

Reading her body, his gaze pored over its curves and valleys, exploring her reactions and watching her face as he dragged his fingertips over the delicate skin of her throat, her collarbones. Her body came alive beneath his touch, and she reached out to slip her hands beneath his suit jacket. Through the fabric of his dress shirt, she ran her hands over his well-muscled torso, feeling the contours of his powerful body. Her hands roamed to caress the broadness of his back, sinewy like she imagined a bull's might be. He pressed against her, nestled in the junction between her thighs, the heat of him seeping through their clothes.

That little voice inside her whispered, *yes.*

He slowly pulled one end of the black silk bow encircling her waist, untying it. As though through a stranger's eyes, she watched the sash flutter to the floor beside them. Saw the wisp of fabric lying on the floor.

Fallen.

A jolt of panic ran through her. They must stop.

Surely Meredith has found Andrew by now and taken him to safety, Serena thought. *They must be gone.*

She caught his wrist, arresting the movement of his hand. "Julian, wait."

His hand stilled, but she felt the warm pressure of his fingers, his hand wrapped around the side of her waist, touching the place where the sash had been.

"Stay with me," he breathed, nuzzling the sensitive spot below her ear.

There was nothing in the world she would rather do, but the consequences were too dire. She thought about her duties as an angel, and pulled away, dislodging his hand. "I can't."

He sat up slowly, looked at her with an accusation in his eyes. "You can. But you won't."

She shook her head, and said firmly, "Julian, I won't let you ruin me."

"I'm ruining you? You're as hot and panting for it as I am, my angel," he said, a smirk playing around the corners of his mouth.

"Please, Julian."

His eyes levered shut. When he opened them again, the gentleness in him had faded, replaced by his usual disdainful facade. And she knew that this time, there would be no escape. Looking down at her, he said, "I should have expected that this would happen. I thought we could do things easily. But since you insist, it'll have to be the hard way. Come with me." He spoke in the same deep growl he'd used last Saturday night when he'd let her go.

This time, she sensed there would be no escape.

He grasped her wrist and yanked her to her feet, headed toward the door.

"Where are we going?" she said, pulling backward even though she knew it was futile.

His mouth set in a grim line. "To find your brother."

"Andrew's gone," she said defiantly. She drew herself up to her full height, but even in heels she still stood well below the bottom of his nose. "I sent him home with Meredith."

"I gave orders not to let them out," he said, tightening his grip on her wrist to a point just short of pain. His voice was as smooth and cold as ever, but fury burned in his eyes. "Shall we see whose instructions were more effective?"

Desire surged through Julian as he dragged her through the twisting hallways, back down to the garden. He could not remember the last time he had felt such a driving sense of immediacy, the rush of *emotion* burning through his veins. He'd spent centuries learning to control his emotions, because emotions always led to trouble.

Emotions clouded one's ability to choose wisely. Emotions led to mistakes, and mistakes landed you in hell. He, of all people, understood that. But tonight, this fledgling angel had pushed him to the brink. If she thought she could waltz into his home, kiss him and then *leave,* then she was the one who'd made the bigger mistake.

He would give her one last chance to make the right choice on her own.

In the back garden, Nick had taken charge of the microphone, belting out an old jazz standard with the orchestra. The fool was not half bad, Julian thought. Nick might have had a career as a rock star had he not found fame on the silver screen. As the song ended, the young man jumped off the stage to raucous applause, just as he spied Julian and Serena descending the staircase.

The angel peered at Nick beneath the twinkling lights as he approached, at the trace of white powder beneath his nostrils. "You've been using again," she said flatly.

"What else was there for me to do? My date ran off with another guy," he said. He wiped at his nose with the back of his hand, stared an accusation at Julian. He looked at Serena, gestured at the place where her missing sash ought to have been, and said flatly, "Part of your dress is gone."

Julian swept in front of her, blocking off their exchange.

"How would you like to come to Las Vegas with me?" he said to Nick on an impulse. "My new club is making its debut in one week, and I'd like you to be a part of the grand opening. I need to oversee the last-minute preparations, and I'd like you to be my guest at the Hotel Lussuria."

"What's in it for me?" Nick asked, eyes narrowing. His gaze darted behind Julian to the girl.

"I'll make it worth your while. You'll be handsomely compensated, of course. An executive suite, free gambling chips for the tables. All the booze you can drink," Julian said. Add to that the promise of more escorts than one man could handle and all the pure Colombian blow he could stuff up his nose, and Nick would be amenable to just about anything.

The actor jerked his chin toward Serena. "What about *her?*"

"She can come along, too," Julian said casually, turning slightly to watch her reaction.

She wore that adorable little scowl of hers. The heat of their kisses still stained her cheeks, and her blush intensified with her rising indignation. Angry, she was magnificent. "Not in a million years," she ground out. "Anyway, aren't you in the middle of filming right now, Nick?"

"I'm a star," he said, shooting her an irritated look. "If I want to take a week off, I can."

"This seems like a really bad decision. I don't think you should go anywhere with this man. I certainly won't," Serena said.

"It's your choice," Julian told her. "It's a pity Nick here will have to get along without his yoga lessons for the next week." Then he dropped the bomb. "Maybe Andrew would like to come with me, too. It might give us an opportunity to bond. And then there's Meredith…" He let his voice trail off for effect.

Serena gasped, her lovely blue eyes going enormously round. She was just as delectable when she was shocked as when she was angry. "You wouldn't."

"Why not? The more the merrier. Perhaps you might reconsider and join us, as well, my dear?" he said.

He summoned a pair of Gatekeepers, who brought the roommate and the brother from the corner of the garden, where they'd been detained on a thin excuse that had kept Andrew busy photographing shots of random guests. Julian caught the look of helplessness that passed between the two angels. His Gatekeepers had done their job and blocked Meredith's intended escape.

Julian strode up and gave the brother a hearty slap on the back. "Andrew, my good man. How have you been enjoying your evening?"

Andrew looked stone-cold sober, which was a disappointment. The Gatekeepers had instructions to ply him with alcohol and drugs, but Meredith must've succeeded in preventing that much. *Trust an angel to interfere with a perfectly good binge,* Julian thought.

"Fine, thanks, Julian," Andrew said. "I think I've got enough images for your publicity shots."

"Thanks so much for your help, Andrew. Your presence here has been very much appreciated. Listen, I have a proposition for you."

Julian felt a touch on his arm. Serena whispered, "Wait."

"What's that, my angel?" he said casually. He knew what was coming, but he tried to contain his smugness.

"I need to speak with you alone," she said, eyes downcast.

"Again, my dear? Andrew, Meredith, would you excuse us for a moment?" he asked, taking her by the hand and pulling her into a far corner. The roommate glared as Julian led Serena away. But the music from the orchestra and the mounting noise of the guests was enough to drown out their conversation from the redhead's prying ears.

Serena turned to him. "Let Andrew leave."

"Now, why would I do that? Andrew can make his own choices. It would be a once-in-a-lifetime opportunity for him to come to Vegas with me," Julian said.

"Let me substitute myself for Andrew. If you let him go, I'll come to Vegas with you."

Julian's heart soared, but he allowed no sign of it on his face.

"But I need to know I'll be safe with you," she demanded.

"I promise it. I swear it on my mother's grave," he said.

"For all I know, you might have knifed your own mother in the back. I want your promise in writing."

That hurt, more than she could know. The gentle touch of his mother's hand on his hair floated into his mind, the ghost of a memory so sweet it made him miss her, dead these long centuries. He shook the feeling away, forced himself to say lightly, "I loved my mother dearly, and of course I would never have harmed her."

She folded her arms across her chest. "Write it down or I'm not coming."

"Fine." He sighed. He took a pen from the inside of his suit pocket and scribbled on a napkin from one of the cocktail trays: *I, Julian Ascher, promise not to harm an angelic hair on the head of Miss Serena St. Clair during the week she has agreed to spend with me in Las Vegas.* He signed it with a flourish.

She scanned the napkin and blinked, hesitating for a moment. "I want you to promise to leave me, my family and my friends alone afterward."

"If you so desire, consider it done," he said, scribbling in the extra phrase to placate her. After seven days with him, Serena's prudish resolve would be broken, cast to the wayside. And he would have no further use for her family and friends, anyway.

"And separate rooms," she insisted.

He bent again to write, resisting the temptation to roll his eyes. If he wanted to take her, he would have her, separate bedrooms or not. Her fear of him bordered on the insulting. He'd never forced a woman. He'd never had to, and he wouldn't have to force *her,* either. She wanted him—he'd known that when he held her body against his and felt her submit. No, when Serena came to him, she would come willingly. More than willingly. He would make her crave his touch. Yes, he would have her writhing under him, calling out his name and crying for more. At the end of seven days, she would not want to leave him.

"Julian?" Her voice broke him out of his reverie. "Julian, did you hear a word I just said?" She held out the paper, glaring at him with that sweet little scowl.

"Yes, of course," he said absently. He hadn't heard her. He was too busy imagining her writhing bare-breasted beneath him.

"I want you to play fair," she said, scolding him like

an angry wife and snapping him back to reality. "No lying, no cheating, no trickery while we're together."

He grinned. "I may be a demon, Serena, but I'm an honorable one. My word is as good as gold." And as malleable as gold, too.

Oh, she was so naive. *An honorable demon.* Did such a being exist? Certainly, every demon had to observe the rules between angels and demons. Promises made between them must be honored, or there were dire consequences. Yes, he knew that. But even if there was such a creature as an honorable demon, he might not break the rules, but he would do his damnedest to bend them. And he had no plans to change his nature overnight. *No,* he thought, *that would be like asking a wolf not to hunt.* But since he knew she wouldn't appreciate that sentiment, he refrained from sharing it with her.

Instead, he headed back to where Andrew and Meredith stood. He clapped Andrew heavily on the shoulder, and said, "Here's what I wanted to propose. You've done such a wonderful job that I'm going to double your rate. Send me the proofs and I'll be in touch shortly. Can't wait to see those photos. I'm off to Las Vegas for a week with my lady friend."

Meredith's eyes went large and round. "But…but you can't!"

"It's okay, Meredith. We'll talk about it later," Serena said. She started toward the doorway, gesturing for her roommate and her brother to follow her.

Julian caught her arm. "Where do you think you're going? You and I are leaving now."

She stiffened, looking toward Andrew and Meredith. "I'm going home to pack."

"Don't worry about packing," he said. "Everything you need will be provided." He gestured to one of the staff, instructing the man to have a car brought around.

In the doorway, Meredith hesitated, waiting for Serena.

"Go," Julian said to them. "She's coming with me."

Serena stood by his side, the napkin with his scribbled promise dangling from her fingers. Her shoulders hunched forward and the corners of her mouth sagged as she nodded her assent. Meredith sent her a last worried look before ushering Andrew away. For a second, Serena looked so dejected that Julian felt a strange pang in his chest. It felt suspiciously like guilt. He ignored it, knowing it would eventually dissipate, as guilt always did.

She turned to him. "I need to make a couple of phone calls."

"That wasn't part of the deal."

She looked at him through narrowed eyes, with a particularly unangelic expression that he might even have described as murderous. "You get a phone call even when you're sent to prison."

The sensation in his chest intensified. He ignored it. "Forget it."

She clutched her cell phone, glaring at him. It was all so pathetic. But he refused to feel sympathy for her. She was the one who'd started it all by invading *his* territory last Saturday night, trying to mess around with *his* business. She was the one who'd embedded herself into his consciousness like an unscratched itch. She was the one who needed to learn to accept the consequences of her choices.

Julian reached over and took her cell phone, stuffed it in his pocket. A tear slipped out of the corner of her eye. She raised her hand to swipe at it, but he caught it before she did and blotted the tear with the pad of his thumb.

"Come now. It's only a week. Am I really that bad?" he coaxed.

She didn't speak, but he suspected he already knew her answer.

She was conspicuously silent as he led her back through the house, toward the front entrance. The party was just reaching its zenith, having mushroomed far beyond the original two hundred invited guests. People spilled out of every room, stumbling and laughing in the hallways. As Julian and Serena passed through the foyer, the Nakara caught sight of him. Apparently the creature had tired of remaining in its frozen position. As it saw him, it launched itself from its pedestal as though in protest for having been forced to endure hours of stillness. In a few flaps of its crystalline wings, it began soaring beneath the vaulted ceiling.

The foyer erupted into chaos. Guests began to stampede for the door, screaming and pushing each other down to get to the exit. Some ducked and tried to protect themselves from the Nakara's icy claws. As it flew, it let out a shriek that was like the sound of nails scraping down a chalkboard, but magnified through a loudspeaker. Julian shook his head at the flying monstrosity, directing it to return to its place. With a final shriek, it complied, winging back to the pedestal and settling grudgingly into place once again.

Julian bellowed over the noise of the panicking crowd, "No need for concern, ladies and gentlemen! It's merely a magic trick—an illusion for your entertainment!"

When they saw the beast had returned to its pedestal and resumed its petrified stance, the guests stopped. After a dazed pause, some began clapping. The applause escalated, and people clustered around the ice sculpture, speculating about how the trick had been done.

Serena said nothing. She glared at Julian through narrowed eyes, her lips pressed into a line.

"Your lips don't have their usual appeal when you flatten your mouth like that," he said, smirking down at her.

"Someone could have been seriously hurt," she said tersely.

"If there was any potential harm, it was from the humans themselves and not from the Nakara," he said. "Most of them would gladly have crushed each other to escape the danger."

Stepping through the crowd, he led her out the front entrance and ushered her into the passenger seat of his waiting Maserati. For all he cared at this moment, the damned ice demon could swallow the entire houseful of screaming humans. He wrapped his hands around the cool black leather of the steering wheel, and accelerated down the driveway.

He couldn't remember a moment in years that he'd felt this gratified. Let the staff deal with the aftermath of the party. He was taking Serena to Vegas.

Chapter Six

Serena awoke alone the next morning.

Thank heaven for small miracles, but at least there was that.

Only a thin crack of sunlight streamed in through a gap between the heavy velvet curtains. Otherwise, it was dark in the lavish bedroom where she lay, in a bed fit for royalty, on the softest sheets she'd ever felt. Overhead, filmy white fabric hung from a massive canopy.

Her mind scrambled for details of where she was, and how she'd gotten here.

And it all came flooding back. The party. The kiss in the library. The three-hour drive to Vegas at ninety miles an hour. The silence between them as Julian drove. Her fear as she'd clung to the door handle despite the smoothness with which Julian handled the break-neck speed. The towering hotel, its name emblazoned in ornate letters: *The Lussuria*. The grand lobby with its art-deco embellishments, its elegant color scheme of gold and muted blue.

Julian had settled her in this sumptuous hotel room and left her alone for the rest of the night. Relieved, she had bolted the door from the inside, removed her dress and promptly fallen asleep here on this haven of a bed. Into as deep a slumber as she could ever recall.

Now, lying here in this ethereally beautiful place, the horrifying realization of what she'd done began to sink in. *I've made a deal with a demon.*

A door swung open.

Not the front door she'd come in through last night, but a door she had thought was a closet. Clearly, it was *not* a closet.

And Julian had the key.

He stood in the doorway, clad in a white bathrobe, the color a stunning contrast again his tanned skin. "Good morning, sunshine," he said.

She flung the sheet over her half-nude body, but not quite fast enough.

His gaze slid over her, something dangerous stirring in those blue-green depths. "A very good morning, indeed," he mused.

While she scrambled to cover herself, he sat down on the edge of the bed, so close that she inhaled the scent of healthy male and a trace of cologne. He clasped his hands behind his head and reclined on the pillows. She struggled to move away from him, but it wasn't easy. The king-size sheet refused to cooperate as she yanked hard to free it from the foot of the mattress where it was carefully tucked.

"You might try the robe," he said. He gestured to the white terrycloth bathrobe that lay folded on a divan at the foot of the bed.

She slid awkwardly under the sheet to reach the robe and pull it on. Settled herself on the bottom corner of the bed, as far away from him as possible. "This was not part of our deal," she snapped. "We're supposed to have separate bedrooms."

He shrugged, toying with the belt of his own robe as he continued to watch her. "We do. But I never said I would stay out. Your room happens to adjoin my suite. I slept in my room last night, of course. I *am* an honorable demon."

She narrowed her eyes at him, wishing he wasn't quite so handsome. Or quite so close. Cinching the robe shut, she said, "You never mentioned an adjoining door."

"I'm still a demon, after all," he shrugged. "What did you expect?"

Lounging on the white sheets, he was magnificent. Six feet of tanned, athletic masculinity, displayed for her benefit. Without even looking, she could feel his half smile beckoning her. To reach out and touch him, to slip her hand beneath that soft robe. The belt was loosely tied, as easy to undo as the sash on her dress last night.... She turned her attention toward the windows instead, just for somewhere else to look. Swallowing, she said, "What time is it, anyway?"

"Just after two in the afternoon. Time for breakfast," he said. Then he picked up the phone and ordered room service, as nonchalantly as if it were the most normal thing in the world to be breakfasting in the middle of the day. As he spoke, his gaze raked over her. She wrapped the robe a little more tightly around herself.

When he'd hung up the phone, he told her, "You'll find other clothes hanging there for you in the closet near the bathroom. I took the liberty of having a personal shopper deliver a few items."

She didn't want to ask *when* he'd had time to do so. But he was, after all, an Archdemon. He could probably materialize gold from straw if he wanted to.

"Where's Nick?" she said, keeping her tone deliberately sullen. She might have agreed to spend a week with Julian, but she hadn't agreed to be pleasant.

"Stop worrying. Nick will fly in from L.A. with Harry later today. Your little friend will join us tonight for dinner, along with my business partner. Relax, angel. You and I are going to be spending a lot of time alone together this week."

Alone. With Julian. And all either of them had to do was reach out an arm across the expanse of rumpled bedclothes. Her heart began a rapid palpitation. She must put distance between them, she knew. She padded across the cool marble floor to the window. Throwing open the curtains, she blinked in the sunlight as her eyes adjusted to the brightness.

What lay outside was a spectacular view of the Las Vegas Strip. Even in the daylight, neon lights flashed, decorating the hotel and casinos lining the street as far as she could see. Next door, a miniature version of the Eiffel Tower stretched up into the cloudless blue sky. Across the street, fountains sprayed hundreds of feet in the air from the middle of a man-made lake. She sighed, dropping the curtains shut again. Julian's world was full of material extravagance and artificial beauty. But all the slick buildings, the mirrors, the gilt and glittering lights left her with a vaguely sticky feeling. All she wanted was to be back in her own home, and teaching classes at the yoga studio. Instead, she was here, in Sin City.

During her human life, she'd never been remotely interested in what this city had to offer. "What happens in Vegas stays in Vegas"—the popular motto of this adult playground—offended her sensibilities and went against everything she believed in. Gambling, drinking, strippers…everything this city stood for was in stark contrast to her life of moderation and constraint. And as an angel, coming here was completely out of the question. Unless Arielle had given her some assignment that brought her here, she would never have had a reason ever to set foot in this godforsaken place.

Why, oh, why had she promised to stay with him for a whole week? She'd fallen straight into Julian's trap. But with her brother as bait, there'd been no real choice. Andrew was a strong, ethical person, but clearly he'd been no match for Julian.

"The Lussuria," she said, testing the hotel's name on her tongue. "Pretty. What does it mean? Luxury?"

Behind her, he laughed, still lounging on the bed. "*Lussuoso* is the Italian word for luxury. *Lussuria* means lust."

She shivered, turning toward the bathroom. "I'm going to shower," she announced, hoping he did not hear the tremble in her voice.

He was gone from the room by the time she'd finished, presumably showering in his own bathroom. For the first time since they'd gotten in the car last night, she might have a few minutes alone. She needed to call Arielle. Julian had just used her room's telephone to call for room service, but now the phone was gone. He must have taken it with him. Peering behind the bedside table, she looked at the empty telephone jack and swore out loud.

She had to get out of here.

Yanking open the closet, she grabbed her dress, ignoring the other items that hung there. There was no sign of the strapless bra she'd worn last night, but she didn't have time to look for that now. She slipped into the dress, grabbed her shoes and ran for the front door.

Her heart pounded as she rode the elevator down, glancing at the illuminated floor numbers as she descended from the forty-fifth floor. She fished in her purse, gathering cash and a credit card in her shaking fingers as she began to formulate a plan. It would be easy enough to grab a taxi from the lobby, go to the airport, catch the next flight home. But what if Julian came after her? Would he try to stop her?

And suppose she did manage to escape. Would he unleash his wrath on Andrew or on Nick, as he'd threatened? Her Assignee would be arriving later today, and she knew that he would not be spared. She had seen for herself what went on at Devil's Paradise. Julian was capable of anything.

The elevator doors opened, and she stepped out into the luxurious lobby of the hotel. Tourists milled there, oblivious to the ominous air that chilled her to the core. A vast archway stretched into the casino, where on this bright Sunday morning the crowds were already massing amidst the ceaseless electronic beeping of the slot machines, the rattle of the roulette wheels. In the other direction, the entrance to Julian's club waited. A large silk banner above the closed doors announced the grand opening of Devil's Ecstasy next weekend.

She stood at the lobby's edge, surveying the scene. This was no innocent pleasure destination, designed for entertainment. It was a lair of evil, a sanctuary for demons. She could feel it in her bones, in the pit of her stomach. She wished to God she could walk out the front door and never look back.

But she knew that was impossible. She thought of Nick and Andrew, shivering as she speculated about what Julian might do to them if she left. No, she could not go. She knew what she had to do—she had no other choice.

Surprising Serena in bed was a moment Julian would savor for a long time to come. As he showered, his erection remained as his mind pored over the details of her body. She was deliciously built, with lithe, toned muscle giving way to soft curves that would fit his hands perfectly. It was as though she had been created to satisfy his every desire. He thought of her perky breasts tipped with rosy nipples. Looked forward to exploring every inch of her luminous skin, to arousing her erogenous zones and enjoying the height of her pleasure. And the height of his own pleasure, too.

He stepped out of the shower, dried himself with a thick bath towel and slid back into one of the hotel's robes. He sauntered through the living room and opened the door to her bedroom. The only thing there was silence.

"Serena?" he called. No answer. He checked her bathroom. She was not there, either. Then he saw that the closet was open, and her dress and shoes were gone.

Well, it was nothing that he hadn't expected, after all. She was a feisty little piece of work, and from the looks of things, not easily mastered. But she'd return. He would have bet on it.

He opened a newspaper and sat down to wait.

When Serena got back up to the suite, Julian lounged in an armchair with his feet propped on a footstool, his expression maddeningly relaxed. He smiled over the top of his newspaper as he saw her.

"So glad you decided to rejoin me, after all. You made a prudent choice," he said easily. "However, I don't feel I can trust you entirely. You attempted to break our agreement. If you do so again, I'm afraid I'll have no choice but to arrange for your brother to come out here to take some photographs."

Serena marched past him and into her bedroom without saying a word.

She slammed the door and lay on the bed, desolation washing over her. Julian had outmaneuvered her at every turn. If she'd been willing to stoop to his level, she wouldn't be in this mess right now. But that was impossible. Serena might not be able to talk to Arielle right now, but she was sure that at the very least, her supervisor would tell her to stick to her values. To play fair and have faith that the divine was on her side. That was becoming increasingly difficult, if not altogether impossible.

Oh, if she could just hear Arielle's voice, if only to assure her that there was someone out there who had some clue about how to undo the horrific situation she'd gotten herself into. About how to protect her brother without sacrificing herself.

It was the scent of fresh baking and bacon wafting from the living room that finally lured her out of the bedroom. She had to face Julian at some point, and she might as well pacify her growling stomach while she was at it.

A young woman in a hotel uniform was unloading plates from a room-service cart onto the polished mahogany table in front of Julian. "I wanted to bring up your breakfast personally, Mr. Ascher," she said. "We're so pleased to have you staying with us again. Mr. Ranulfson sends his regards and extends his invitation to dinner at our five-star restaurant, Firebrand. If you need anything, my name is Tiffany. I'm the chef's assistant."

"Thank you, Tiffany," he said.

The woman continued, "I hope you'll make use of all our amenities. If there's anything you wish for—" her voice dropped into a slight hush "—anything at all, please don't hesitate to let us know. I will be personally available to cater to your every need," she said.

Serena watched her, wondering if she was discreetly flirting with Julian. Well, who could blame her? Julian was a handsome man—a very handsome man—and obviously attractive enough to draw female attention. Even if he *was* pure evil.

Julian seemed oddly immune to Tiffany, despite the way she flipped her shiny brown hair and smiled at him almost adoringly. He indicated Serena, saying to the chef's assistant, "And the needs of my guest, Miss St. Clair."

Tiffany's smile thinned as she looked briefly at Serena. "Of course, sir."

As she walked out of the room, she threw one last glance at Julian, although he did not return it.

When the woman was gone, Serena collapsed into an overstuffed armchair, tucking her feet beneath her. "I thought only demons would work here. I didn't know there would be humans, too." Unable to help herself, she added, "She seemed eager to serve you."

He chuckled to himself, poring over the selections on the table. "We like to keep a mix of employees. Easier to blend with the human world that way." He heaped plates with eggs Benedict, buttermilk pancakes and fresh fruit, and handed one of them to her. "You're not jealous, are you?"

She straightened in her chair and balanced the plate on her lap. "Of what? You're perfectly free to associate with whomever you choose. Please don't let me cramp your style," she said, giving an egg yolk a vicious stab and watching it bleed yellow on her plate.

"You *are* jealous." His smile broke into a grin, and he forked a strawberry into his mouth. "Don't worry. She's got nothing on you."

They ate in silence. Having slept far beyond her usual breakfast time, Serena realized she was ravenous. She forced herself to eat slowly, although she wanted to devour the entire plate.

He gestured to a bottle of champagne that sat on the cart in a silver ice bucket. "Would you care for a little champagne? A mimosa, perhaps?"

"Why are you always trying to ply me with champagne? It's barely three in the afternoon," she grumbled.

"Come on and live a little. Have some fun."

"Fun?" The word escaped her as a high-pitched squeak. "Your idea of fun is perverse. Toying with people's lives and threatening to destroy them is not fun," she said somberly.

He set his empty plate aside. "And what's your idea of fun? Drinking chamomile tea on a Saturday night? Preventing other people from enjoying themselves? Your brother said he wasn't sure if you ever really knew how to have fun."

Tears welled in her eyes, but she blinked them away. She was not going to let him see her cry.

"You've gone too far," she said, choking back the sorrow that welled up in her, not only from Julian's taunting words, but also from the pain of missing Andrew. From hearing what her brother had thought of her. From realizing it was true. She stood, turning to head for her bedroom.

Behind her, Julian exhaled a long sigh. "Serena, wait. We have to call a truce. We cannot spend the next seven days bickering like schoolchildren. Let's be adult about this."

She folded her arms across her chest. "I am an adult," she said, wishing that she didn't sound like a petulant three-year-old as the words came out of her mouth.

"Then start acting like one. You agreed to come here, and you're not leaving. Accept the consequences of your choice. Look outside. All of Las Vegas is at our feet. Aren't you the least bit tempted to go outside and explore?"

"Choice!" she nearly exploded. "Coming here was hardly my choice. You coerced me. You threatened my brother and now you're insulting me to my face. You want *me* to take responsibility for my actions? Screw you. You have no idea how to be an honorable person, do you? If you even had the tiniest inkling of what that means, you'd let me go."

For a moment, she thought he might tell her to go to hell. Then he settled back in his chair and gave a long sigh. "I do know what it means to take responsibility for my actions. If you insist, I can at least be the one to take the high road and be the one to offer the olive branch." He paused for a long moment before he finally said, "I apologize."

It was perhaps the least sincere apology she'd ever heard, but there it was. She brightened a bit. "So will you let me go?"

"Of course not. Now, run along and change out of that dress from last night," he said. "There are plenty of new clothes hanging in your closet."

She went into the luxurious walk-in closet to look at the clothing the personal shopper had chosen. For several minutes, she stood wrapped in a bath towel, browsing through the items. The clothes were far more daring than her usual wardrobe, and far more sophisticated. There were low-cut dresses that were only slightly longer than certain T-shirts she owned. Most of the tops were either backless or transparent. None of the garments reached below the upper-thigh. But at least the clothes were beautiful. Whoever had selected this wardrobe had done so with good taste.

The undergarments were another story. She opened boxes to discover sets of lingerie in a gorgeous array of colorful silk and lace. But when she tried them on, she discovered that the bras were quarter-cups that stopped just beneath her nipples. The panties were either minuscule thongs or open at the crotch. She imagined he'd taken a perverse pleasure in instructing someone to buy these things for her.

It took her a while to coordinate an outfit that provided enough coverage in all the right places. In the end, she chose the longest of the dresses, which was cut from a paper-thin fabric that clung to her like water. And threw a silk pashmina wrap over it to cover the dress's plunging cleavage.

"Let me see," he said when she returned to the living room. Whisking away the pashmina, he gave her the once over and ended it with a nod of satisfaction. "You'll boil outside with that scarf. Otherwise, acceptable."

She resisted the temptation to cross her arms over her chest, and said, "Most of the things in that wardrobe look like they came out of the closet of a call girl."

"A very high-end call girl, if you must. Those clothes were expensive," he said mildly. "But if you insist, after we tour the Strip, we'll do some more shopping."

As they ambled down the palm-tree-lined boulevard, Serena marveled at the hotels, each with its unique theme. At the replica of Venice, gondoliers rowed their long black boats down the miniature canals. The office towers of New York and the Statue of Liberty loomed at another hotel. Yet another featured a live pirate battle waged between life-size ships. The sun shone; the day was deceptively bright. As they walked, Arielle's words came crashing back into her head. *He has the power to destroy you. He could have your soul in eternal damnation if something terrible happens.*

Something terrible…like sleeping with him? That much was still unclear to Serena.

She replayed Arielle's warning in her mind as Julian chatted easily about the hotels, about the fine weather, about his new nightclub and its upcoming grand opening. She said very little, since almost every response that came to her tongue was a sarcastic retort. But he did have a point, she realized—there was no point in keeping up this constant arguing. Gradually, as they progressed along the Strip, she found it very easy to be civil to him. Too easy.

"Tell me about yourself," he said, catching her hand and tucking it under his arm while they strolled among the crowds.

She struggled, trying without success to dislodge her fingers from his grip. "You've already managed to find out more than I could probably tell you in a day. Did you have someone investigate me?"

He smiled, reaching to smooth a wisp of her hair that tangled in the light breeze. Clearly, the answer was yes. "Aren't you curious about me?" he asked. He exaggerated a frown, but a little of that pretended hurt was genuine, she sensed.

"No," was the safest thing to say. The only thing she could say.

Of course she was curious about him. She wanted to

know everything—where he was born, what his childhood had been like, how he'd felt the first time he'd
fallen in love, how he'd died. All the minute details of
the circumstances that had produced this wildly handsome man who walked beside her, this remarkable physical body that housed such an embittered old soul.

As they walked, she started to formulate the answers
in her own mind. England, if she had to guess, judg-
ing from his comments about Coleridge and the hint
of an accent that crept into his voice at certain times.
He'd been a lonely child, she knew intuitively, from
the flashes of that tiny, abandoned boy she sometimes
caught when his guard was down. And the other thing
she knew with certainty, although she had no concrete
proof, was that his death had something to do with a
woman.

She stopped herself from musing any further. Whatever else there was, whatever else he meant to tell her…
it was most certainly better *not* to know.

Smiling, she tried to focus her attention instead on
the massive neon signs flashing overhead, even in the
bright sunshine. The wild stimulation of the Strip was
almost enough to distract her from wondering.

Passing their reflection in a large mirror in a hotel
lobby, he paused. "Look what a striking couple we
make," he said, drawing her close to him. She said nothing, but pulled away instantly, blushing furiously. But
she saw that he was right: his dark hair and tanned skin
made the perfect foil to her fairness. She was used to
attention from men, but she usually ignored it. As they
walked, she began to notice the admiring glances they

attracted from the tourists of both genders, and every size, shape and color roaming the Strip.

She reminded herself again, *He's not a normal man. I could lose my status as an angel, or worse.* She shivered. She'd slipped with him before, and it had been terrifyingly easy. What would happen if she *did* sleep with him? And what had Arielle said about it? She tried to remember her supervisor's words. *"It would depend on the circumstances,"* Arielle had said. Serena vowed to herself that it would never get that far. She must not let him kiss her again. She only had to last one week. Seven days and he would be out of her life for good.

If only she could talk to Arielle, get a moment away from him. She scanned constantly for pay phones as they walked, but every time she spotted one, Julian had his arm around her waist or a healthy grip on her hand.

They stopped at another hotel to see a garden habitat with baby dolphins. As they stood watching the young animals frolic in their watery enclosure, something maternal triggered in her. "How sweet," she said.

"Food for the Nakara." His tone was joking, but she wondered what he was capable of doing. When she turned to look at him, he hovered near, his gaze trained on her face, close enough that it seemed for an instant that he was going to kiss her. She froze, waiting for the descent of his lips to hers, the heady rush that would accompany the sweep of his tongue into her mouth. But he simply turned away with a wry smile. She followed, cursing her own disappointment.

They wandered onward, in and out of the casinos, through the infinite electronic arpeggios of beeping slot machines and the crowds of tourists. Senior citizens sat glued to stools, mindlessly plugging coins into games that seemed to absorb endless amounts of money. Groups clustered around roulette and blackjack tables, watching the ebb and flow of wins and losses.

He gestured toward the gaming tables. "Don't you want to gamble? We're in Las Vegas, after all."

"I don't bet," she said.

"I understand. You don't want to risk your own money. Take some of mine," he said. He pulled out his wallet, counted out several one hundred dollar bills, held them toward her.

She blinked, wondering if he really meant for her to take the money. Around them, the glittering lights, the mirrored walls, the garish pattern of the carpet and the noise were beginning to make her head throb. Outside lay a beautiful, sunny afternoon, but here in the casino, it might as well have been midnight. The artificial environment made her itch for natural sunlight. All she wanted to do was get out of this place. "No, really," she insisted, hoping he would relent so they could leave. "I don't believe in gambling."

His hand dropped slightly, and he frowned. "Not even a quarter?"

She shook her head.

"Come on. Where's your sense of fun?" he asked. The corners of his mouth twitched slightly. He was mocking her again.

Sighing, she took a quarter out of her purse, then plugged it in the nearest slot machine. After five seconds of electronic beeping and the digital spin of icons on the machine's screen, the quarter had disappeared forever.

"There. I lost. Is that supposed to be fun?" she said.

He covered his smile with his hand, trying not to laugh at her. "Perhaps you don't understand the element of chance if you've never won before. It's addicting, the thrill of not knowing where life is going to take you." He held up the cash he'd offered her. "Come, I'll show you."

With the money, he purchased four one-hundred-dollar chips. At a nearby roulette table, a croupier shouted out, "Ladies and gentlemen, place your bets!"

Julian placed all four chips on the black square with the number twenty-two.

"No more bets," the croupier shouted. Then he spun the wheel.

Serena watched the small white ball spin around the lacquered wooden wheel, the black and red numbers blurring as it spun. The wheel slowed, the ball teetering for a moment on the red number nine before settling into the pocket of the number twenty-two.

"Twenty-two wins!" called the croupier. He counted out fourteen thousand dollars' worth of chips and slid them to Julian. Around them, a small crowd gathered, attracted by the chips massing on the table. Julian bet the whole lot on black, grinning as the crowd clapped and cheered. Serena watched, wondering what would happen if he lost. Would he walk away disappointed, or stay and try to win again?

Of course, he won. He collected twenty-eight thousand dollars, cashing out the chips for stacks of hundreds. Pocketing a thick wad of bills, he instructed the cashier to deposit the rest in the hotel's security vault.

He grinned. "First rule of the game. Know when to walk away. Just like the song. Anything more would have been conspicuous."

"You cheated," she accused.

His grin flipped to a pretense of hurt, but his eyes still glimmered with amusement. "Of course not. You and I both have a certain amount of influence on the external world, and we're not afraid to use it."

"I don't use it for my own personal gain."

"Don't you? For every soul you save, you earn a certain number of brownie points. Surely, you're expecting to rise higher in the ranking of angels. Don't tell me there's no personal gain involved there."

"It's a very loose definition. I don't do what I do for money," she clarified.

"Maybe you should. Let's go spend it. I have a feeling that might appeal to you more," he said wryly.

He took her toward the shops. Serena tried not to notice the beautiful gowns that graced the windows of the upscale boutiques. Tried to remain neutral to the jewelry that glittered in the glass display cases, and the endless parade of gorgeous shoes and handbags for sale. She told herself that she needed to practice detachment. Material objects only led to the terrible kind of yearning she felt right now.

They passed a particularly stunning gown in a boutique window, a wispy dress in muted steel blue. He stopped, considering the delicate beading on the bodice suspended by thin ribbon straps. "That would look lovely on you."

She looked up at the dress and almost felt herself salivating. Yes, it would've looked lovely on her, she thought wistfully. But she didn't need it, and she didn't want to become indebted to him because of a silly piece of clothing.

"Let's go try it on," he coaxed. "You need something to wear to dinner tonight."

"I have the dress I wore last night. And there are other dresses in my closet," she said stubbornly.

"Not like *that* dress."

She knew he was right, but she remained firmly on the sidewalk as he walked toward the entrance of the boutique.

"If you won't try anything on, I'll simply have to send the personal shopper out again," he said. "You'll be deprived of the pleasure of choosing your own clothes, and you'll end up with things that make you uncomfortable."

"I'm not keeping the clothes you buy me."

"Suit yourself. Give them away to charity when you leave. But while you're with me, you'll do as I say," he said, taking her hand and finally pulling her into the shop.

The dress fit like it had been made for her. In the change room, she lowered the delicate layers of chiffon over her head, letting the airy fabric settle around her. It flowed around her as she walked out shyly to show Julian. He nodded appreciatively, coming to stand behind her in the three-way mirror. His hand settled on her hip in a gesture of possession; she made no attempt to move it. If he'd thought they were a striking couple before, there was no doubting it now.

"Wear this to dinner tonight," he said. "I want to show you off."

In the end, he bought her the dress and a dozen other outfits. He left directions for the clothes to be delivered to the hotel, and they left the shop.

"I plan to spoil you rotten, so you might as well enjoy it," he said as they walked back to their hotel.

"Thank you, but I don't need or want anything else," she protested. "Honestly, I'm happy leading a simple life."

"In relative poverty? There's nothing wrong with being wealthy. A person with more resources can do greater good in the world than someone without resources."

"Maybe," she said, "but not necessarily."

"Why would there be all this wealth on earth if humans weren't supposed to enjoy it? Those who are good are rewarded, sometimes with material prosperity. That's what you believe, isn't it? Otherwise, what's the point?"

"Don't tease me," she said. But it was hard to pretend she was angry.

"If *I'm* good, will you reward *me?*" he said, stopping in the middle of the sidewalk to pull her against him.

A shiver ran through her. He was about to kiss her right there, in front of all those tourists.

For a moment, she wished he wasn't a demon and that she wasn't an angel. She wished they were just like the rest of the crowd, normal people who came to Vegas for a bit of fun. People who could meet each other as human beings and not worry about the responsibility of lost souls or the consequences of falling from divine grace.

"But you're not," she said, more to herself than to him. She pulled away and continued to walk.

He strode beside her, the same little half smile tilting up one corner of his mouth. What he didn't seem to realize was that nothing could ever happen between them. She would never allow it.

Julian felt giddy, like a youth in the first blushes of love. As he readied himself for dinner, he stood before the gilt-edged mirror in his dressing room.

What a surprise today had been. In the shop, he'd felt genuine pleasure in choosing clothes to offset Serena's exquisite beauty. He also took pleasure in dressing well himself. He whistled a little as he admired the fine cut of the black, French-cuffed dress shirt he buttoned now. Appreciated the exceptional tailoring of his bespoke suit as he slipped on the jacket, made to measure on London's Savile Row.

He considered his reflection in the mirror, wondered what he looked like through her eyes. If they'd still been human, would she have found him attractive? Either way, human or not, he would never have had the chance to find out if he hadn't coerced her, threatened her brother's life. The thought of it depressed him somewhat. But no matter. She was here now, and for the next six days, she was his.

He wandered out into the living room to wait for her. Harry was there, arranging Julian's business correspondence neatly on a side table.

"How was your flight from L.A.?" Julian said jovially, sauntering over to the wet bar to peruse the selection. He poured himself a finger of single-malt Scotch, tossed in a few cubes of ice.

Harry frowned at him, blinking a little before he returned to the mail. "Uneventful, sir. I brought Nick Ramirez as you asked and checked him into a suite two floors down."

"Very good, Harry. Care for a drink?"

"No, thank you, sir." The assistant paused, obviously distressed by something as he looked more carefully at Julian. Then he said, "There's something different about you today, sir. You seem almost…"

"What is it, man? Spit it out."

Harry swallowed, paused, before he finally said, "Happy."

Julian could not remember the last time someone had said such a thing to him. Over the past two centuries, he had felt things in the vicinity of happiness. Pleasure, *certainly*. Gloating, *yes*. Superiority, *of course*. However, he had kept even those feelings under tight rein, within rigorously controlled limits. True happiness, *no. Never.* The suggestion came almost as an insult to him, and brought a frown to his own face.

"Never mind, sir," Harry said, clearly relieved to see his boss frown. "For a moment there, it did seem like there was something different about you. Like you were becoming less demonic."

Both men laughed at the ridiculousness of it. Julian took a swallow of whisky to cover his shock. With a wry smile, he told Harry, "When pigs fly."

The damage was done, though. Silence fell between

them, and then Harry left quickly, as though he didn't want to risk seeing any more happiness. As he shut the door, Julian knew that what his assistant had sensed was correct.

Serena was changing him.

"Play fair," she'd said last night. *"Don't lie, don't cheat."* He'd thought it impossible when she'd spoken those words last night. Strangely, this afternoon, he'd felt no desire to use his usual manipulative tactics. What a delight it had been watching her wide-eyed response to the delights of Las Vegas. Although she had tried to pretend they didn't, the gimcrack facades and the glittering lights had impressed her. Watching her experience the Strip was like seeing it himself for the first time.

Every moment he spent with her, he was a little more honest, a little less demonic. Even though she'd denied it, she was making him *good,* without even trying.

Since the first moment he'd laid eyes on her, everything had changed.

She had triggered something in him. Had reached the slivers of memory that had lain dormant in the deepest recesses of his mind. Had sent his thoughts reeling back to his human life, to a far-distant past that was at once satisfying and disturbing to remember.

It was terrifying. It was wholly unacceptable. It had to stop.

He must destroy her immediately. By doing so, he would destroy the last vestiges of his own humanity, would lay to rest the part of him that still yearned for the goodness of his human life. The part that still hoped. Still dreamed.

That was still vulnerable.

He would seduce her at last. He would do it slowly, taking care over the next few days to melt her reserve, to weaken her defenses. He would enjoy watching her struggle to maintain her cherished self-control. Then he would pounce, finishing the task with all the skill he'd honed in these two centuries of devilry and debauchery.

Serena entered the room, jarring him out of his thoughts.

Time seemed to stall, as it had the first moment he'd touched her a week ago in his club. Instantaneously, he forgot the worries that had surfaced during his brief discussion with Harry.

All he could see was her.

What surprised him was how casually she wore her beauty. He'd known so many beautiful women, but many of them had been vain and affected. They'd been worse by the time he was done with them, grasping and desperate after they'd ruined themselves through gluttony and greed.

But not Serena. He was struck by the realization that she wouldn't change, not even if he plied her with a king's ransom in gold and jewels. Now, as she stood before him in that beautiful dress, it was not the gown he noticed so much as the woman in it. She was ethereal, angelic. Magnificent. And yet, she held her graceful body with a sense of humility he had never witnessed in another being still incarnated in flesh and blood.

It humbled him. For an instant, he actually considered letting her go, sending her back to Los Angeles to tend to her lost souls and her task of spreading divine love.

But now, especially after what Harry had said, he knew he could not.

There was no way he would ever let her go. Not in a week.

Not ever.

"You look beautiful," he said, the gruffness of his own voice surprising him. He struggled to find words to express the pride he felt at having her by his side. Even if he had to trap her into staying there. He gave up attempting to search for a compliment that would not sound patronizing or irreverent. Knew that any further appreciation would just send her defenses up and make things even more awkward.

He took her hand, tucked it into the crook of his arm. As they walked to the door and mounted the elevator, he began to ramble. It was odd for him, as he was usually so firmly in command of language. But he found himself unable to stop. He talked the whole way down, describing the construction of his new nightclub in an overabundance of detail that made her gorgeous periwinkle eyes start to glaze over. He talked as they crossed the lobby of the hotel, through the casino, past the shouts of the winners and the cries of the losers, the calls of the blackjack dealers. He talked as they approached the hotel's premier restaurant, pausing only to speak to the maître d' so that the waitstaff could locate their host.

"Corbin Ranulfson's table, please," he said.

Serena looked up, her blue eyes enormous with shock. She recognized the name. *Of course.*

"Didn't I mention we would be dining with Corbin?

He's my business partner," Julian said, frowning down at her. On his arm, he felt her fingers tremble.

Corbin had a reputation for a brutality that had only been sharpened in the several centuries since his human life had ended. A descendant of Norman warriors, Corbin had a streak of pure cruelty that other demons feared and envied. He had no regard for mortal authority and answered to only one creature in all of existence: the devil himself. Julian had thought it wiser to cultivate him as an ally, rather than an enemy. So far, their business partnership had been problem-free, but Julian sometimes felt that dealing with the older Archdemon was like walking on a field of land mines waiting to explode.

Serena bit her lower lip as the waiter guided them through the sumptuous open space of the restaurant. They walked in silence through the dramatic room, past velvet draperies in deep blood-red and gold that hung from the ceiling. Past tables full of other diners, who turned to stare with envy and undisguised lust. Finally, they stopped at a large booth that overlooked the rest of the room.

In the booth sat the hotel owner, chatting with a dark-haired woman who had her back turned to them. As they approached, Julian wondered who Corbin's latest companion was, glancing at the glossy black curls cascading over the slender curve of the woman's exposed back. He thought idly that there was no way her beauty could match Serena's.

"Julian, m'boy," Corbin called, raising a hand in greeting. His companion turned.

She was every bit as gorgeous as she had been the

first day Julian had seen her, sauntering beside a canal in Venice, over two hundred years ago. And he was willing to bet she was every bit as evil.

"Chila," he said, blurting out the nickname he'd used when they'd been lovers.

"I don't answer to that anymore," she said, pursing her mouth just like she'd always done when she was displeased.

She'd lost almost all trace of her Italian accent, just as he'd lost his English one, many years ago. Like him, she'd become an American at heart. But her homeland was still there in her voice, if only in the slight musical inflection that was not quite native to these parts.

"Call me Lucy, if you must, but you know I prefer Luciana," she said, fluttering inky lashes over pale green eyes. "How long has it been, *amore mio?* Ten years? A dozen?"

He'd spent so long trying to forget the last time he'd seen her. But it was still branded into his memory, there along with all the other times she'd betrayed him over the centuries. His stomach jolted, threatening to toss its contents. He held it down and smiled urbanely, forced himself to bend and kiss her hand.

"Luciana, Corbin, allow me to introduce my dear friend, Serena St. Clair."

No longer focused on fearing Corbin, Serena's shocked gaze shifted to Luciana. Julian watched Serena's dazed smile as he made the introductions; she was less adept at hiding her shock than he was. But as they took their seats in the plush booth, she tilted her head, interrogating him without uttering a single word. With a mere look, he knew she wanted answers.

Chapter Seven

Serena had been brought to dinner with three powerful demons. But was she a guest, or was she the main course?

What flashed through her mind was the image of a serpent coiled on a tree branch, along with the sound of a slither and a hiss. She was aware of the very distinct possibility that this might well be her last meal, if she were indeed allowed to survive. She reminded herself of the rules when dealing with dangerous animals: *no sudden movements, and never let them sense your fear.*

She forced herself to switch her attention away from her own terror. Tried to distract herself by thinking about the brief interaction that had occurred between the demons.

Amore mio. My love. That's what Luciana had called Julian. She had the looks of an Italian supermodel, tall, slender and gorgeous as she rose to greet him. The raven-haired beauty gazed at him with an unveiled hunger as she perused his powerful physique. He leaned in to press a kiss against each of her alabaster cheeks. Jealousy simmered inside of Serena.

The demoness held out a hand to Serena. "*Buona*

sera, my dear. How pleased I am to meet you. Any friend of Julian's is a friend of mind," she said. Her hand was cool and delicate, and as soft as the famous silk from the shores of Lake Como. Those hands had once stroked Julian's muscled body, urging him to heights of pleasure as she, Serena, would never dare to do. Serena's jealousy almost bubbled over.

Apparently Luciana felt equally as jealous, because as Serena met the other woman's stare, she saw the cold calculation a rabbit might see in the eyes of a viper waiting to strike.

Shivering, Serena withdrew her hand and backed unconsciously into Julian, seeking the reassurance of his strength. Then she recoiled immediately, realizing that she might as well have been backing away from a viper and into the grip of a king cobra.

"My dear, you're lovely," Corbin said. Serena forced herself to hold her stance and the smile that was frozen on her face. If not for Julian, she would have bolted. By all appearances, Corbin Ranulfson, with his fair hair and amber-colored eyes, was a good-looking man in his mid-thirties. By now she knew that when it came to demons, a deceptive appearance was not just a possibility, but a general rule.

Corbin was famous. Or rather, he was *in*famous. His name was whispered in hushed tones by the angels, and every new Guardian, including Serena, had been specifically warned to avoid him. He was classically handsome, like Julian was. She might have taken a second look if she had seen him on the street. But he was infinitely more malevolent than Julian would ever be. And now, here she was, in the midst of his domain. With Julian as her only lifeline.

Serena tried to hide her dismay as Corbin bent low over her hand, mimicking Julian's continental manners. Vapors of alcohol wafted from him as he kissed her hand. As he rose, his gaze ran appreciatively over her curves. She could not control the shudder of fear that ran through her body.

He smiled a rattlesnake's smile. "Welcome to Firebrand. Won't you have an aperitif, m'dear? We've opened the evening with absinthe, as a tribute to Luciana's lovely eyes," Corbin said. He beamed at Luciana, whose chilling peridot gaze still rested, unwavering, on Serena.

She'd heard of absinthe before, vaguely remembered its rumored effects. Blindness, hallucinations, convulsions. If the demons insisted on maintaining this veneer of normality, she had no choice but to play along. She mustered a forced confidence and smiled. "No, thanks."

"What, not an absinthe drinker?" Corbin boomed. "How about a Cinzano, then? In honor of my dear lady's homeland."

"I don't drink," Serena said flatly.

"Come now," Julian said. "Surely you'll raise a glass on this one special occasion. You wouldn't want to disrespect our esteemed host's hospitality. Why don't you have the Cinzano—we both will," he said. "Unless you prefer champagne, my dear."

He spoke the words, but there was something rather hollow about his teasing. Something was simmering behind that debonair facade of his. It had slipped, only for a brief second, no more. But was it lust she'd seen flash in his eyes when he'd seen Luciana? For the first time since Serena had met him, his attention had wandered from her. She should be grateful. But it frightened her beyond words.

The other couple resumed their seats in the semicircular booth. Luciana sat on one end, with Corbin beside her. It seemed expected that Serena should take the place between him and Julian. She hesitated for a moment, until Julian nudged her forward, leaving her no option but to sit, sandwiched between the two men.

She forced herself to breathe deeply, to sit quietly without fidgeting. Julian's arm rested along the back of the booth, encircling her shoulders. His fingers skimmed her shoulder with a touch that was light, yet unmistakably proprietary. She was sure he could feel her trembling.

"Glad you could join us, old friend," Corbin said, leaning against her as he addressed Julian. "Construction's almost finished on the nightclub. The tradesmen are just putting the finishing touches on the painting and construction. Have you seen it yet?"

Julian shook his head no. Corbin looked at him quizzically. "What? You mean to say that you haven't had a chance to look at your coup de grâce?"

"I've had more important things to do," Julian said lightly.

"But your work has always come first," Corbin insisted. Then he eyed Serena and nodded knowingly. "Ah. I see."

"Perhaps they spent the afternoon indoors," Luciana said waspishly.

"I was showing Serena the Strip," Julian said, his tone still mild.

Luciana frowned, not bothering to hide her annoyance. "I bet you were watching *her* strip."

Serena's cheeks flushed with heat, but she ignored their banter, picking up the menu. She flipped through it, trying to think of a way to change the subject. "What do you recommend?"

"Spring lamb, skewered and charbroiled," Luciana said. "That would make a nice *antipasto* for you, Julian—an appetizer to whet your taste buds. You seem to have a taste for young and tender things these days. For the next course, perhaps the *capelli d'angelo*. Angel hair. How appropriate." She gave Serena a superior little smile. In the flicker of the candlelight, Luciana's smile seemed to contort into a demonic grin. For a moment, Serena thought she saw horns.

"Luciana, stop," Corbin chided. "You'll frighten the poor child."

But Luciana continued, unabated. "Pity there's no angel food cake on the menu. Julian will have to find another sweet for dessert," she taunted.

Serena had held her tongue long enough. She leaned forward and met Luciana's green gaze straight on. "It seems he's lost his taste for devil's food cake. All that darkness can become cloying after a while, don't you think?"

Luciana gasped. From the glare she shot across the table, it was clear that if Corbin had not been sitting between them, they would have had the beginnings of a catfight. Although Serena had never hit anyone in her life, she certainly wasn't going to hold back if Luciana attacked her.

Julian chuckled near Serena's ear. One of his hands still rested on her shoulder. Beneath the table, his other hand skimmed up her leg, skating beneath the hem of her dress and to brush the bare skin of her thigh. She tried to ignore the shiver of pleasure that tingled through her body.

Just then the drinks arrived, providing a momentary distraction. He leaned down to whisper in her ear, too low for the others to hear, "Better the devil you know."

While Julian whispered, Serena could have sworn she saw the demoness reach across the table, her pale hand hovering over his glass for an instant. But when she looked back, Luciana was fingering a pendant that hung around her neck.

The demoness raised her glass with an unexpectedly sweet smile, and said, "Cin, Cin!"

Serena had not intended to drink her Cinzano, but now she took a large swallow, letting the vermouth trickle down her throat. The liquor was delicate and sweet, an unexpected flavor among this gathering of demons. Then she noticed Corbin frowning, his gaze fixed on Julian's drink.

"Is that a crack?" the older demon asked, leaning across her. The nearness of him made her recoil as she followed his stare to the object of his disapproval. To her eye, Julian's glass was perfectly intact, without even a hairline fracture visible.

Nonetheless, Corbin called the waiter. The poor man sidled up to the table, his face as white as the pristine tablecloth. Corbin looked pointedly at Luciana as he handed the glass to the waiter.

"There's a crack in this glass," said the hotelier.

The waiter blinked, perplexed as he examined the glass. His face blanched even whiter. "I don't see one, but I'm sorry if there is a crack, sir."

"Leave it here," Luciana insisted. "Let Julian enjoy his Cinzano."

"Take it away," Corbin said. His tone remained neutral, but his mouth compressed into a bloodless line as he continued to look at Luciana.

The waiter cowered. "Yes, sir. Please accept my most sincere apologies, sir. I'll make sure it won't happen again. I'm aware that there are consequences of breakage."

"Go," Corbin ordered, cutting him off with a warning glance.

"Here, Julian, have my glass," Luciana offered.

Corbin reached forward and knocked it out of her hand. In that same toneless voice, he drawled, "Excuse my clumsiness, my dear."

A wordless exchange passed between the demon couple. Between them, an amber stain was spreading on the tablecloth. Serena could feel it crawling toward her. Just before the liquid reached her, Julian interceded, reaching over to toss a napkin on top of the stain.

"Let's forget about it," he said, echoing Corbin's mild tone. "I'll have a Scotch instead."

Then, as if the incident had never occurred, Corbin's demeanor shifted and he resumed the conversation.

Serena sat very still, trying not to look at any of them. What exactly had the waiter meant when he'd referred

to the consequences of breakage? She was hardly
stupid enough to ask aloud, but she could only guess
how Corbin treated his employees. Nor had she missed
the tension between the three demons, an uneasy truce
between them that seemed as though it might break at
any moment. If they caught her gaze now, they would
certainly see the fear in her eyes. She could feel Julian's
eyes boring into her, probing. "Everything all right?"
he asked.

Forcing herself to look at him, she smiled. "Perfect."
But everything was far from perfect. She prayed that
the evening would end quickly, and wondered how she
was going to survive a week of this peculiar kind of
hell.

Keep your friends close, and your enemies closer.
Julian perused his dinner companions as he sipped the
Scotch that arrived to replace his glass of Cinzano.
Julian knew, as the other two demons knew, that the
glass was not cracked.

Luciana had just tried to poison him.

From the corner of his eye, Julian had seen the subtle
flick of her fingertips as she slipped a few drops of some
undoubtedly lethal toxin into his glass.

Now, across the table, the she-demon simpered at
him with an unapologetic smile.

Was he surprised? Not really. Attempted murder at
the dinner table was practically *de rigueur* in his circles.
He hadn't thrived in the demon world for this long without learning to watch his own back.

Luciana was one enemy he knew inside and out,
quite literally. She was dangerous. Fiercely independent,

she'd managed to whore and trick her way to the status of Rogue demon, wandering among humans and leaving devastation in her path. On the outside, she was all alabaster skin and mist-green eyes. On the inside lurked a malevolent and unpredictable killer.

Julian could defend himself against her transparent rage. But the she-demon had clearly set her sights on Serena. Lord, if Luciana managed to get even a single strand of *real* angel hair between those teeth of hers, he would tear her limb from limb, and damn the consequences.

As for Corbin, Julian trusted him. *As far as he could throw him.* The waiter's face told a story of punishments and brutality. Of Corbin's ruthless methods of management.

He sensed Serena shift beneath his touch, shaken by the demons' behavior. The latent violence underlying their actions had clearly terrified her. She excused herself to use the ladies' room, and as she rose from the table he wished they were alone. So he could hold her and protect her. So he could tell her that he would never let them harm her.

But Luciana rose, as well. "I think I'll join you, my dear."

The angel's eyes widened with fear, but she went anyway. He had to hand it to Serena—she was a tough little cookie. He half rose from his seat, ready to follow them into the ladies' room to ensure that Luciana didn't harm Serena.

Corbin stopped him. "Luciana wouldn't dare hurt your little friend. Not here. This is my territory, and she's not supposed to act without my permission. If she steps out of line, I will fricassee her longer than the chef's special."

Julian settled back into his seat, but kept his gaze on the women as they receded. "Did she have your permission for that little stunt with the poison?"

"Old chap, I had no idea," he said blandly. Julian studied the other man's face, trying to decide if he was lying. But Corbin's icy gaze was as impenetrable as he said, "I would never have let her go through with it."

Perhaps, Julian thought, *but only because she didn't have your blessing.* Out loud he said, "Luciana's a handful, isn't she?"

"I vaguely recollected there was some harpy in your past, but I didn't realize it was Luciana," the older Archdemon said. "I only understood when you walked in tonight. Trust me, my good man, I'd never have taken up with her if I'd known. Golden rule, you know."

Julian doubted that Corbin heeded any human rules, much less the understanding between men that his friend's former lovers were off-limits. Yet, there was something oddly genuine in the other man's demeanor.

Corbin sipped his absinthe. "I don't usually take leftovers. But I wouldn't mind a go at your present delight. What heavenly creature have you captured? There's something quite exquisite about her."

Julian wanted to punch him. He wanted to cover Serena with a tablecloth and drag her from this den of demons, far from the prying eyes of those who might hurt her. Bringing her here had been a mistake. He had vastly underestimated the power of her beauty to draw Corbin's interest.

Corbin smiled, knowing Julian wouldn't dare to touch him. Only a fool would dare start a war with the second in command to the Prince of Hell. Besides, they were on Corbin's territory, surrounded by an army of his minions. "A Guardian, is she?" Corbin said idly. "How utterly delicious."

Julian's voice was a low growl. "Don't even think about it."

"I would never dare poach on your territory," Corbin said, smoothing over Julian's antagonistic tone with his suave manner. "Just admiring the view, old chap. What women never seem to realize when they go to the ladies' room together is that it leaves the men behind to talk."

Julian sent Corbin another warning glance. They sat in silence for a moment, sipping their drinks. If it came to an altercation, Julian wondered who would win. Corbin was powerful, but his power had been untested in recent years. Would Julian be able to take down the older Archdemon if it came to a fair fight?

If Corbin ever got his hands on her, Serena would suffer the worst kind of damnation imaginable. Corbin's sexual perversions ranged widely; he was capable of inflicting intense and extended pain. Once he was done with her, he would cast her mutilated body to his Gatekeepers. On the surface, he and Corbin might be allies, but Julian would fight to the death before he let her fall into the other Archdemon's clutches.

For Serena's sake, as well as his own, he vowed it would not come to that.

* * *

I'm way out of my league, Serena thought desperately. *I've got to call Arielle.*

The few minutes she had bought herself were precious, and she knew she had to make them count. Heading toward the ladies' room, she prayed that there was someone in there with a cell phone. Thankfully, a teen-aged girl was there, washing her hands.

But before Serena could even open her mouth to ask, Luciana walked in.

Serena went to the mirror, reapplied her lipstick and tried to ignore Luciana's obvious stare. At five foot six, Serena had never felt short, but Luciana loomed beside her, topping her by at least four inches. The demoness stood nearly six feet tall in heels—almost as tall as Julian. He and Serena made a striking couple. But paired with Luciana, the effect must have been breathtaking, with their eyes in complementing shades. They were two of a kind. Dark, sleek and powerful, like a pair of matched horses.

Or a couple of camouflaged bush vipers.

Luciana opened her purse and began touching up her makeup, as well. She looked down at Serena and said, "We ladies go through torture in order to make ourselves into creatures of beauty, no? Some have even used poison for its cosmetic effects. Do you know women once used belladonna, a very deadly type of flower, to make the pupils appear larger. To enhance the illusion of innocence. But I suppose you don't need any help in that department, do you? What a sweet dress you have on. So angelic. Did Julian pick it out for you? It's just his taste."

"As a matter of fact, he did," Serena said. She could not tell a lie, but it irked her to admit that Luciana was right, especially about Julian's preferences. She wondered how long they'd been lovers, how serious their relationship had been.

"He is fantastic in bed, wouldn't you say?" she said casually. "Knows exactly how to touch a woman. He makes you feel as though you're the most beautiful woman in the world. But of course, he is a master of seduction."

Serena remained silent, slipping her lipstick back into her purse and tucking an errant strand of hair behind her ear. She saw the flicker of Luciana's smile in the mirror.

"So you haven't found out yet?" Luciana laughed, a lilting, musical sound that grated on Serena's ears. "What a pity. I see he hasn't learned to stop toying with his prey before he goes for the kill. Such bad manners."

"I'm not prey," Serena ground out.

"You're no match for him, my dear. Julian eats girls like you for breakfast. Why, I've seen him devour half a dozen little angels in one sitting. I don't mean to scare you. Perhaps he'll finish the job quickly before he tires of you and casts you into eternal damnation once you've fallen."

Serena turned to face her. "Look, I don't know what's gone on between you two, but if you want Julian, you are more than welcome to have him. Be my guest. Trust me, I'm not your competition. Do us both a favor and take him."

Luciana glared at her, venom seething in the depths

of her demonic green eyes. Out of the demoness's open handbag, a foot-long snake slithered, its shiny green skin the same piercing shade as its owner's eyes. Luciana picked it up and kissed the top of its sleek head.

"Watch yourself," Luciana said languidly. "It would be a terrible shame if you had an accident during your stay here. You never know what creatures lurk in these desert locations."

The door swung open, and another unsuspecting human woman walked into the bathroom. The demoness tucked the snake discreetly back into her purse, as casually as if she were tucking away a compact.

It was on the tip of her tongue to retort, but Serena realized there was no sense in engaging in conflict with Luciana. She hated to admit it to herself, but when it came to Luciana, Julian was her ally. *Better the devil you know?* The jury was still out on that one, but between the two of them, she'd take Julian.

The roast vegetable soufflé Serena ordered was delectable, but she barely picked at it throughout the meal. Thinking of the poor waiter, her appetite abandoned her entirely. Luciana's warning and the presence of the demons around her didn't help. Julian chose neither the lamb or angel hair pasta that Luciana had suggested, but opted for seared sea scallops and pepper-crusted filet mignon. He proclaimed the food delicious. Luciana, for her part, spent the duration of the meal glowering over her lobster tail, shooting Serena threatening looks whenever the men's attention was diverted.

"The chef has outdone himself," Corbin declared, sitting back in satisfaction. "I'm always surprised at the incentive of everlasting damnation to put some drive into these mortals."

The three demons laughed. Serena wished they'd all go back where they came from: hell. She pushed the remains of her meal around her plate, thinking about how nice it would have been to curl up in the cozy armchair in her living room, beside the fireplace. She'd rather be anywhere but here.

A familiar voice made her head turn. "Serena, Julian! Here you are."

"Nick!" Serena almost leaped from her seat, she was so grateful to see him. "When did you get here?"

The young actor's face was shadowed with beard stubble, eyes bloodshot from a bad hangover. She wondered exactly how much he'd had to drink last night, what drugs he'd taken. She'd been so preoccupied, first with her brother's safety, and then with her own, that she'd had little time to keep track of Nick. He was still her Assignee, and she was determined to protect him as best she could. But he was sliding downhill at an alarming rate.

Even with his rumpled clothes and ashen skin, Nick was still a handsome young man in his prime. Luciana eyed him as though he were more succulent than the lobster she'd just eaten.

He grinned broadly and said, "Not too long ago." Then he saw Julian's arm slung casually around her shoulders and his smile faltered.

What a mess. Things were getting too complicated. She wanted to tell Nick there was nothing going on between them, that Julian had coerced her into being here. But she couldn't. Especially not in front of the Axis of

Evil gathered here at the table. Satan's three helpers would eat both her and Nick alive.

"Looks like it's double-date night," Nick said, flustered as he eyed them together. "I don't want to be a third wheel…"

The demoness batted her eyelashes like an old-fashioned actress as she held out her hand for Nick to kiss. "*Tesoro,* you're hardly a fifth wheel," she said, her accent pronounced as she mangled the idiom. "You're more like…dessert."

Nick laughed, lapping up her outrageous flirtation. He bowed gallantly. "It's you who is utterly delicious, madam," he said, making a show of admiring Luciana's figure.

"Come and sit next to me." The demoness slid in closer to Corbin, pushing him closer to Serena, who was forced to lean even closer into Julian. Luciana patted the smooth leather next to her, signaling for Nick to sit.

"Aren't you adorable? I'm going to make you my pet, my dear," Luciana cooed.

Nick grinned. "But I'm not properly trained. Do you mind the kind of pet that bites?"

The demoness giggled. "I absolutely prefer it. You don't mind, Corbin, my darling, do you?"

Corbin's pale gaze revealed nothing. Nick slid a glance in Serena's direction to make sure she'd caught their innuendo. She wanted to leap over the table and warn him. But of course, she couldn't. It would break protocol to reveal the existence of divine entities. Besides, his human mind would never believe her. But Nick was her responsibility. It was her job to keep him safe. She had to find some way of keeping him out of Luciana's clutches.

But by the time dessert was served, it was clear that Nick was dazzled by the demons' charisma and their glamour. Luciana flirted shamelessly with him, feeding him chocolate-dipped strawberries as if they were lovers. Serena watched them from across the table and stirred at her crème brûlée, but found that she had no more appetite for the delicious dessert than she'd had for her dinner.

Between the two women, Corbin had gone quite still. Serena wondered what was going on in his mind. It seemed to her that watching his lover flirt with Nick ought to drive any red-blooded man wild with anger, but it was impossible to tell what Corbin thought. From his earlier behavior, she fully expected him to burst into a fit of rage. Yet, he sat observing the scene as though there was nothing amiss. Serena watched as Luciana flirted simultaneously with both men, touching each of them frequently. But the demoness also threw Julian surreptitious glances. Serena wondered, was the she-demon trying to make Julian jealous?

Corbin drained his drink and set the empty glass on the table. "Why don't we swing by Devil's Ecstasy and have a peek inside."

"Right now? It will be completely empty," Luciana said, stroking his cheek with the back of her fingers. Her pale gaze widened in mock innocence. "Whatever will we do there?"

On her other side, Nick said, "I'd love to see it bare, without any people."

"That's not the only thing he'd like to see bare," Serena muttered under her breath.

Julian raised a questioning eyebrow at Serena and whispered, "Jealous?"

She shook her head, feeling the fabric of Julian's suit jacket slide against her bare arm where they touched. Yes, perhaps she was a little jealous. Although not of Nick, but of Julian.

"You must be tired, Nick," she said, hoping the actor would take the hint and save himself. "You flew all the way from L.A. today. Don't you want to rest?"

Nick shook his head. "No, *Mom*. The flight only took an hour. I'm good to go."

"Well, *I'm* feeling a bit sleepy," Serena said, trying not to feel slighted by his little joke. "I might turn in early."

"I wouldn't hear of it," Julian glowered.

The nightclub was a short walk across the lobby from the restaurant. As the group moved, she hung back, pulling Nick aside. "Be very, very careful. These people are dangerous," she whispered.

He shrugged and said, "They seem pretty cool to me. Serena, you need to cut loose a little. Have some fun!"

Fun. For the second time that day, Andrew's words echoed in her mind. She knew how to have fun. She just liked to do it safely.

Nick had no idea that his life was in jeopardy. All he could see was the shiny surface of the demons' wealth and beauty. She wanted to shout it to the rooftop pool that the three people walking in front of them were demons. Wanted everyone in this sinfully luxurious hotel lobby to turn and stare at them, to drag the demons away and destroy them. But that was impossible. *"Supernatural occurrences must never be disclosed to humans, except under exceptional circumstances,"* Arielle had told her at the beginning of her training. *"It can be done, but you must always seek my permission first."* Which Serena didn't have. Furthermore, demons swarmed the hotel, by far the majority here. Overpowering them on their own turf would require a massing of angelic forces that was beyond her capabilities at this moment.

She whispered to Nick, "There are things you don't know about these people. As your friend, I just want you to make the right decisions."

Julian glanced over his shoulder, breaking off his conversation with Corbin. "What are you two talking about back there?"

She clung to Nick's arm, glaring a warning at the Archdemon. Julian merely smiled.

They walked into the club, and a feeling of déjà vu swept over her. In design, the club was similar to Devil's Paradise. But the new club was more garish and more opulent. Crimson draperies swept from the ceiling. A grand staircase rose up from the main floor to the unknown pleasures of the second floor. Through a massive set of glass doors at the far end of the club, an outdoor pool was visible, its still waters gleaming in the moonlight.

Julian climbed the short staircase to the DJ booth, and a moment later, an old, slow song played over the sound system. She recognized it immediately as Chuck Berry's "Earth Angel."

Nick took Serena's hand and led her to the dance floor. He was pulling her into his arms when Julian stopped him.

"Not this time, son. It's my club, and I'll christen the dance floor," Julian said. To Serena, he said, "We didn't get to dance at my party."

Luciana stood at the edge of the dance floor, scowling. "There's so much saccharine in here, it's making me sick. I need some air," the demoness announced loudly. She dragged Corbin by the sleeve out the glass doors toward the pool. Nick trailed after them.

Serena pulled away from Julian to follow Nick. The young man was her responsibility, and if something happened to him, she would never forgive herself. But Julian resisted, holding her against him.

"Let them go," he insisted. "They wouldn't dare do anything here. It's my territory."

She sent another worried glance in the direction the three of them had gone. "You'd better be right," she said. Then, as Julian's arms pulled her closer, she protested, "You're holding me too tightly."

He eased his hold, releasing her slightly. They danced slowly, circling to the music. It was strange, knowing that the latent power in the arms that held her might turn on her at any second. And yet, he held her with such care, such infinite gentleness. She inhaled the scent of him. He wore an expensive cologne mingled with the subtle undertones of maleness that arose from his body. He was intoxicating, and if she wasn't careful, he would seduce her before she even realized it.

"'Earth Angel.' What a cliché," she said, breaking the silence. She didn't bother to mention that she and

Meredith danced around their living room to this song on a regular basis.

"Where's your sense of humor? I bought this record in 1954. *Hey, Senorita* was the B-side. Marilyn Monroe married Joe DiMaggio that year. The French were defeated in Vietnam and the country was partitioned into North and South," he said, nostalgia seeping into his voice.

"Very impressive. Anything else?"

He paused, looking up toward the massive vaulted ceiling. "The world lost Frida Khalo and Henri Matisse. Oh, and one more thing. The words *under God* were added to the Pledge of Allegiance."

"How do you remember these things?"

"Details become important. They're the easiest way to mark time. When you're immortal, time becomes your best friend and your greatest enemy. You'll learn that," he said, his mouth setting into a thin line.

"Why?"

"Because you have all the time in the world to do the things you've always wanted to do, learn what you've always wanted to know. Then one day you'll come to a point where there's nothing left to learn. Nothing left to know. Oh, you'll never master everything. That's not what I'm saying. But there comes a point where none of it means anything anymore. Details are the only thing that distinguish today from yesterday, or the last month, the last year or the last decade."

"I'm still struggling to keep things together," she said. "But I can't imagine a time when life is meaningless."

"You're new. One day you'll understand."

No, she wouldn't. Life would always have meaning

for her—her life, and the lives of those she loved. As she looked up at his face, she realized that he was miserable. And so alone. But there was probably no point explaining that to him. He would never understand. Could a demon understand love?

The sound of splashing caught her ear. Then, Luciana's high-pitched shriek pierced the melody of the music.

"Nick's in trouble," she said. Julian resisted, but she broke from his embrace and started toward the pool area. This was all her fault. She'd allowed her attention to wander, and she'd left Nick alone with those monsters. He was just a defenseless human, incapable of defending himself. She should have known better.

She heard Julian sigh, but he followed her as she broke into a run.

"Did you plan this?" she shot over her shoulder. "Did you deliberately distract me so your friends could get their evil claws into him?"

"Of course I didn't. I may be in league with the devil, but I am not in league with *her*," he said.

"I never should have trusted you," she snapped.

Nick was in trouble, all right, but not the kind she'd anticipated.

The three of them were waist-deep in the pool. Luciana's dress was molded to her body like the water they stood in, and every bit as transparent. Pressed between the two men, Luciana stood with Nick in front of her, his face lost in the valley between her breasts. Corbin stood behind her, and her head was tilted back as she kissed him, open-mouthed and moaning.

Serena gasped.

The three of them turned at the sound and stood motionless as they gazed at her, an erotic tableau that was strangely beautiful in the moonlight.

Luciana's gaze swept past Serena, to Julian. "Come join us, *amore mio*. The water's warm," she said with a suggestive smile.

"You can even bring your little angel if that's what floats your boat, old chap," Corbin said, his gaze sending a shiver of fear up Serena's body.

"Nick, you're making a huge mistake. Come out of there right now," Serena said.

He stood rooted to the spot, his eyes daring her. He clearly wasn't going anywhere.

She moved forward, ready to leap into the pool after him. At the edge, Julian caught her, holding her back. She tried to shake him off, but couldn't. To the demons in the water, she called, "You harm Nick, and you'll have to answer to me."

Luciana tossed back her glossy black hair and laughed.

Chapter Eight

Julian stepped forward. "You harm him, and you'll have to answer to *me*."

His voice reverberated over the water. Everyone froze.

Moonlight reflected off the surface of the pool, spangled light splaying on their wet skin. Corbin nodded only once, but solemnly and with respect. Luciana fell silent. A glint of that pale light shimmered ominously in her eyes. Julian would gladly have separated her head from her body if he didn't think there would be consequences, not only with Corbin, but with higher authorities.

And Nick. Julian didn't care what happened to Nick. The little bastard could go to hell in a handbasket for all he cared—it certainly looked like Luciana was perfectly happy to take him. But Serena had consistently put herself in grave danger trying to protect her Assignee. Julian knew his only chance of getting her out of here was to guarantee Nick's safety.

"Is that a yes?" Julian demanded. "I need to hear it. From both of you."

"Yes," Luciana said, her mouth tightening from the force of holding in her resentment.

For a moment, Corbin merely grinned. That grin was a mask. He might be ruthless with his underlings, treating them like disposable objects if they made the slightest mistakes. But with another Archdemon, it was not so simple. He was bound by his understanding with Julian, an uneasy alliance that stretched thin between them now, a wire drawn to the breaking point.

But then Corbin relented. "It's all just an innocent game, old chap. We wouldn't harm a hair on his head. Unless he asked us to."

An Archdemon's word was enough. Satisfied, Julian exchanged a nod of acknowledgment with him.

Nick remained where he stood, still clutching the demoness's body. Oblivious to the currents that swirled around him. "Why would they harm me? I'm a big boy. I can fend for myself," he said, a hand tightening on Luciana's breast. "Serena, just because you don't know how to have fun, it doesn't mean you have to spoil it for the rest of us."

In his grasp, Julian felt Serena flinch. But she gritted out, "Nick, you have no idea what you're getting yourself into. If you have any sense at all, you'll get out of that pool."

Julian had to haul the angel away resisting. He pulled her back through the club, back into the hotel lobby. When they were safely inside the elevator, he finally released her. They didn't speak a word on the way back up to their suite. She stood with her lips pursed and her arms folded.

"Aren't you going to thank me?" he said, trying to coax her out of petulance.

"*Thank* you?" she said, terrifyingly quiet. "Why on earth should I thank you?"

It was true. He had brought both her and Nick into this mess. He had invited them to dinner with Corbin, and inadvertently exposed them to Luciana. It was entirely his fault. Normally, he would have relished the experience. Tonight, he felt like he had lost something precious.

"He'll be all right. I promise you," Julian said. It was the first real promise he'd made in an eternity that was largely unmotivated by evil. He still wanted desperately to bed her, and he supposed that played a large part in his actions tonight. But more than that, he'd extended his protection to Nick so that she wouldn't have to worry. Still, she didn't seem to understand that.

"They're going to destroy Nick. It's only a matter of time."

Julian leaned against the elevator paneling, sidling closer to her. "Relax. They were just playing down there in the pool."

"Were they?"

"Nick was probably pulling threesomes long before tonight. The first time I saw him, he was snorting coke off a hooker's ass. Like he said, he's a big boy. He can take care of himself," Julian said. But as he spoke, the words sounded hollow even to him.

"The problem is that he can't. *I'm* supposed to take care of him." She crossed her arms and leaned against the far side of the elevator, her mouth set in a firm line.

Her stubbornness irked him. It was an obstinacy born of the same need for control that caused people to believe she was incapable of having fun. Yet, what annoyed him the most was that, in this instance at least, she was right.

The elevator bell pinged and the doors slid open. Her silence grew from an annoyance to a sting; he felt its bite intensify as he escorted her down the hall and into their hotel suite. When he finally closed the door behind him, she turned to glare, her stance set for a fight.

"Damn it all to hell," he said, turning to go. "I'll go get Nick. You stay here."

"I'm coming with you."

"No, it's far too dangerous," he growled. Then he turned and headed back downstairs.

The three of them were still in the pool, their wet clothes shed and scattered on the deck. Luciana's bare breasts shone in the moonlight, Nick suckling at them. Julian was of half a mind to warn the young man right then and there that Luciana was a murdering she-demon from the depths of the underworld, hell-bent on destroying Serena and anyone associated with her to boot. But he refrained. After all, it would be a case of the pot calling the kettle black. Considering that the pot himself was very, very black.

When Luciana heard the scrape of his shoe on the poolside tile, she turned. "Julian. You've come to join us, after all, *caro mio.*"

"No, Luciana, I've come to break up the fun." He waded into the pool and grabbed Nick by the scruff of the neck.

"Spoilsport!" she pouted.

Corbin paused, his hands still filled with her breasts. "What's gotten into you, my man? Is it the male to female imbalance you're upset about? We could easily recruit a few of the ladies from the casino."

"My club, my rules," Julian said. "You two can do whatever you damned well please. Go fornicate in the fountains of the Bellagio, for all I care. But Nick is here by my invitation, he's getting paid on my dime, and he will abide by my terms. And I don't think it's unreasonable for me to ask him not to participate in a threesome in my brand-new pool."

"Serena put you up to this," Nick said through gritted teeth. He hunted through the sodden clothes for his underwear.

"We'll go to Corbin's suite, then," Luciana said loftily, wading out of the pool after them. "Feel free to join us."

Julian tried not to stare, and said, "Not if you were the last woman on earth."

He heard her outraged gasp behind him, but he dragged Nick, still shirtless, by the ear behind him. They walked through the lobby, leaving a trail of water behind them. Julian's trousers were soaked through. He wondered if his Savile Row tailors had contemplated the effects of chlorine when constructing the garment.

Around them, people turned to gawk. Two women stood beside them as they waited for the elevator. "Isn't that Nick Ramirez?" the first asked.

"It can't be! He looks terrible," the second whispered back. They lingered, trying to hear every bit of conversation they could before the elevators slid shut again.

As the elevator doors opened, there stood the attractive chef's assistant who'd delivered breakfast this afternoon.

"I've seen every one of your movies, Nick," Tiffany said shyly. "I loved you in *Ascent to Heaven*. You were so believable as a depraved monk."

Nick gave her a sloppy grin.

"Is there anything you require before you turn in?" she asked.

"What he needs is a babysitter," Julian muttered.

Tiffany's gaze played fleetingly over Nick. Julian could tell by looking at her that she wasn't exactly the type of girl to fall in bed with just anyone. But with a coy little smile she said, "For the right guest, anything can be arranged."

At any time in the past, Julian would happily have accepted her subtle offer and let the two of them have at it. But Serena definitely wouldn't approve. So before Nick could answer, Julian said, "Thanks, but Nick will be fine on his own tonight. Won't you, my friend?"

Leaving the disappointed girl in the elevator, Julian hauled Nick to his room. Sat him on the bed. Standing over the actor, he said in a deep and rumbling voice, "Do not leave this room tonight. Do you understand me?"

Nick trembled, looking up at him blankly, his defenseless mind saturated by Julian's order. "Yes, sir."

Humans. So pathetic.

"You're feeling very tired now," Julian instructed him. "So tired you want to close your eyes and go to sleep."

Nick yawned, his eyes shuttering closed as he succumbed to Julian's suggestion, body contracting into a fetal curl. Just before he passed out cold, he muttered, "Sometimes I think she's an angel."

Julian left him there to dream of feathered wings and halos, and took off to find Serena.

In their hotel suite, Serena scrambled to find a phone. Now she had another chance to call Arielle, and she must succeed this time. The situation had become far too critical. She needed her supervisor's advice, *now*. She scanned the living room, but Julian had apparently removed the phone here, too. Damn him! *His bedroom. Maybe he's left a phone in there.*

She hesitated at the door. Invasion of privacy was not her favorite modus operandi, and the feeling of crossing into a demon's territory—into his most private and personal space—sent a chill over her. Shaking, she opened the door. The room was a mirror image of hers, only with Julian's personal effects neatly arranged. She sat down on the bed and dialed Arielle's number. As the phone rang, she prayed, *Pick up, please pick up.*

Arielle's voice on the other end of the line was the most comforting thing she'd heard in days.

"It's me, Serena! Arielle, thank heavens you're there," she nearly shouted, before she reminded herself to keep her voice to a whisper.

"Don't panic. Meredith told me exactly what happened at the party." Arielle sounded strangely calm. But it was her job to remain calm when her supervisees got into scrapes. "She found someone to cover your yoga classes."

Yoga classes? Serena was shacked up with a demon,

and the first thing Arielle commented on was covering her yoga classes? *I'm not sick with the flu. I'm in grave danger of eternal damnation.* "Aren't you worried that I'm staying in a suite with Julian Ascher?"

"It's not the ideal situation, I know. However, what happened couldn't be helped. But it's *you,* Serena. I know you'll do the right thing. And in any case, you'll be out of there by the end of the week."

"Arielle, this place is crawling with demons! Corbin Ranulfson owns the hotel where we're staying, and there's a female demon here called Luciana who seems extremely dangerous. Nick is in terrible danger of falling under their influence. What do I do? I wish I could just leave right now."

"You gave your word, Serena. It's too much of a risk to break a promise made to a demon. There would be consequences."

"Consequences?" Serena stopped breathing. "Could I die? Only a demon can kill an angel, right? That's what Gabriel told us at our ordination ceremony."

"The soul never dies, even if the body ceases to exist. You know that, Serena."

So technically speaking, the answer is yes, she thought. *I might be recycled again, like the Archangels explained before. But my body could still die again.*

There was a long sigh on the other end of the phone. "Serena, these things happen in the course of our duties, darling. You're doing the best you can. I know it's difficult, but it is imperative that you stay with Julian."

These things happen? Serena pulled the receiver away from her ear and stared at it. Something was definitely very odd. Arielle's cryptic answers were downright frightening.

"What's going on, Arielle?"

"I can't tell you exactly what to do," the supervisor said. "But there is one piece of advice I can give you. Find the inherent goodness that still exists in Julian and make him see it in himself. He must come to the realization on his own, but you have to help him."

Serena heard the front door open. Heard Julian calling her name.

"He's coming. I have to go," she whispered into the phone. "I'll try to call again tomorrow."

"Remember, you must keep love in your heart," Arielle said before she hung up.

Serena listened to the Archdemon's footsteps striking across the marble floor.

Love, she thought wildly as the sound approached the bedroom. Arielle had gone completely insane. What place did love have in a situation like this? *Goodness? In Julian?* That was pushing things a bit far. *Why does Arielle think she knows what's inside Julian, anyway?*

The door opened.

"Who are you talking to?" He came to stand at the foot of the bed, looming over her. Water from his soaking-wet dress pants dripped onto the marble floor.

"It was just…my roommate. I wanted to make sure the cat was fed." She opened her eyes wide, trying to feign innocence.

He stripped off his suit jacket and threw it over a nearby chair. "You're a terrible liar. You don't even have a cat. If you had one, do you think I would have sent you a puppy? What's the punishment for lying, angel?"

She ignored his question. What concerned her more was the thought of poor Milo, cared for by demon servants in Julian's big, empty house. Instinctively, she moved away from him, sidling toward the head of the bed. "What did you do?" she said, eyeing his wet trousers.

He kicked off his shoes, and bent to peel off his damp socks. "What do you think I did? I jumped into the pool and fished Nick out."

"Where is he?"

"In his room. Tiffany offered to babysit him. She seemed pretty keen, but I knew you would disapprove. Don't worry, Nick's not going anywhere."

Relief flooded through her. Nick was safe, at least for the moment.

But was *she* safe?

Julian dropped his pants, left them in a wet heap on the floor. Next, he unbuttoned his shirt and tossed it on top of the pile. He was magnificent, pure muscle, his body as chiseled and symmetrical as a statue of a young Roman god. He stood in his soaked boxer shorts. They clung, and through the wet fabric, she saw that he was already hard.

He wanted her. That much was very clear. What was also clear, although far more disturbing, was the fact that she wanted him, too. All she could do was stare as he rid himself of the last vestige of clothing. Her mouth went dry. She blinked, her eyes fixated on that glorious male hardness that jutted from his body.

"I'll bet you were calling for help," he said. "Rest assured, angel, no one can help you now."

He bent to reach for her. She expected his touch to be cold and damp, but his fingers were warm as they stroked the line of her jaw.

"I just did you a big favor. Perhaps you could think of some way to thank me."

She slid away a few inches, shying from his touch. "Don't you ever do anything that isn't for evil purposes?"

He smirked. "What, out of the goodness of my heart?" He rubbed his thumb over the sensitive swell of her lower lip. "Serena, my sweet girl, will you ever learn? I'm a demon. This is what I do."

"Find the inherent goodness that still exists in Julian," Arielle had said. At times, Serena had forgotten that Julian was a demon. Had sometimes looked at him as though he were a normal man. But never had she considered that actual *goodness* might be lurking somewhere in him. Despite his own denial of that goodness. Still…maybe the possibility wasn't as insane as she'd originally thought.

Right now, however, most likely he had *not* saved Nick out of the goodness of his heart. His ulterior motive seemed pretty clear.

"I don't owe you anything," she said hesitantly, still confused about Arielle's advice.

"You're right," he said in that low, velvet voice of his. "You don't. But you're not doing this because you owe me. You're doing it because you want me."

She closed her eyes, felt her hair cascading around her as she shook her head. "I don't."

"You're trembling. It's not cold," he said.

"It's been a difficult night," she cried. "Maybe it's the alcohol." Her gaze wandered toward the open door, and she wondered how she could maneuver herself off the bed.

He tracked her gaze to the exit, raised an inquiring eyebrow. "Where would you go?"

Where, indeed? Back to L.A., even though Arielle had practically ordered her to stay here and honor her promise? Back to Carmel, where her brother was safely at home? He would not be safe for long if she did leave. There was nowhere to go, not when those she loved most would be put in danger by her actions.

"What do you want from me?"

"All I want is for you to lie back and take the pleasure I'm going to give you."

Slowly, he laid her on the bed. He drew his fingertips down the curve of her chin and the smooth length of her neck. He traced her collarbone, spanning its width, before his touch traveled lower, to the slope of her breasts.

His blue-green gaze was intense as he looked down at her. "You were beautiful tonight," he said. "All through dinner, I wanted to touch you like this."

His fingertips trailed down, skimming over the surface of her dress where it covered her breasts. He watched her, drinking in her every reaction, from the moist slip of her tongue over her parted lips, to the rise and fall of her breasts with her rapid breaths.

"I wanted to kiss you like this," he said.

He claimed her mouth with a groan that seemed to rise up from deep inside him, from a night's worth of repressed desire. A night he'd spent watching her, wanting her. And she knew it. Secretly, although she was loathe to admit it to herself, she liked it. Now, with his lips and tongue, he teased, sending a white-hot flash searing from her lips down to her core. While he kissed her, his fingers found the zipper at the side of her bodice, unfastening it in one expert flick of his wrist.

She caught at the side of her dress, holding the parted fabric closed. "What are you doing?"

"You're full of silly questions tonight, aren't you," he said. He caught the lobe of her ear in his mouth, gently suckling. His breath was warm and heavy. "What does it look like I'm doing?" he whispered. "I believe in equality, and it seems patently unfair that one of us is still fully dressed."

He kissed her again, muting the weak sound of protest that died as a mewl in her throat. While his tongue made a stealthy invasion of her mouth, he pushed the frivolous straps of her dress from her shoulders. Then he broke the kiss, his breathing in shallow pants as he eased the silk down. Beneath the dress, she wore a strapless corset from the collection in the closet. She'd had no time to replace the lingerie he'd chosen for her. The corset had been the most tasteful item among the selection, black lace over delicate pink tulle. His inhale was sharp when he saw it, and on his exhale, he whispered, "Exquisite."

He removed her dress and turned to toss it aside as though discarding a handkerchief. She lay in the corset and its matching G-string, a garment that was no more than a triangular scrap of black-and-pink lace. A garter belt held up back seam stockings, and she still wore her high-heeled sandals. He stripped each item from her one by one. The shoes he tossed in the direction of his own. His fingers were steady and sure as he unclipped her garters and drew each stocking down. He didn't falter for a second as he unfastened the row of hooks on the corset's front. He was so familiar with the workings of women's underclothing that it shocked her. Then she realized that she should hardly be surprised. She was in the hands of a master.

He drew the corset open, reverently baring her breasts. For a moment, he stared, feasting on the sight of her naked flesh, her nipples already beginning to harden beneath his gaze. He took one of her breasts in his hand, squeezing gently and flicking the sensitive bud with his thumb. She arched upward, and he increased the pressure, softly pinching the nipple between his forefinger and thumb until it was erect.

As he touched her, she reached out to explore his body, the surface of his tanned skin, the light patch of hair on the hard contours of his chest. She traced the lines that separated his chiseled abdominal muscles, the sinewy bulk of his arms. Even for a demon, he was beautiful, his body honed to a work of art.

His head dipped, and a groan escaped him as he closed his mouth over her breast, laved the tip with his tongue. He teased, sucked. He moved to the other breast, took its peak between his teeth, carefully stretching, elongating it, until she cried out from the intense mix of pleasure and pain.

Her panties were the last to go, his fingers hooking into the thin elastic string at her hip, pulling them down over her hips to discard them in a second. Then she was naked, under him on the bed as he leaned over her, touched his lips to hers. He smoothed a hand down her stomach, caressing her all the way down to the blond curls between her legs that covered her most secret place. She closed her legs, trapping his hand there. He stilled, looking down at her, the question unspoken but clear in his eyes: *Will you let me?*

If they stopped now, nothing would change. She would still have her status as an angel. She sat up, put her hand on his wrist. He stopped, but did not withdraw his hand.

"I think we should stop," she said in a gasp.

"Spread your legs for me," he said, low and smooth.

"I can't. It will be the end of me." She watched his face, knowing that if he pressed her, she would probably succumb.

But he said with infinite patience, "Serena, I've kissed you, touched you before. Do you think just because I touch you here that something will change?"

"You make it sound like it's nothing," she said, still holding on to his wrist. She dared a glance into the sea of his gaze, saw the storm gathering there. "You know where this is going."

"Do you really think that you could be damned just because I put my hands on your body? What kind of divine justice would allow that?"

She hesitated. He had a point. Arielle had been so deliberately vague that Serena wasn't sure what the consequences of sleeping with Julian might be. She tried to remember again what Arielle had said. *Keep love in your heart.* She had no idea what that meant. Did it mean that if she was in love with Julian, then anything was permissible? It was safe to say that she was *not* in love with him, so where did that leave her? Whatever Arielle had really meant, in the intensity of this moment, it was impossible to figure it out. She had to stop. She needed time to think.

Julian sighed, closed his eyes for a second. She watched him swallow, fighting with himself. They both knew that he could flip her on her back in a second and take what he wanted, without so much as exerting an ounce of force. Her defenses were down; she was vulnerable to his charm. She hoped he wouldn't use it.

"If that's what has you worried, I promise you that we will not have intercourse," he said finally. "I don't want to take anything that you're not ready to give."

"How can I trust you?"

"Trust me? Temptation is my weapon of choice. Coercion, if necessary. But never force. You and I both know that there are rules in the game between angels and demons. Rules that must not be broken. I would be punished severely if I broke my promise. It's yourself you're not sure you can trust."

"But you're the demon," she protested, not wanting to listen.

"I may be, but I have a human body and human desires. And so do you. Serena, I hunger for you. Let me pleasure you. I swear, I won't go any further than you want me to."

He was right. She did have human desires. She'd been made sexless by her divine role, despite being embodied in flesh and blood.

"Forget I'm a demon. Forget you're an angel. Let's be

together as man and woman. There are no rules against that."

For a moment, she relented, let go of her grip on his wrist and relaxed her thighs. His hand moved forward in the subtlest of gestures, the tip of his index finger stroking the opening of her most sacred place. The contact of his touch was so intimate and so pleasurable. And so utterly wrong.

She pushed against him then, levering her legs over the side of the bed. She bolted for the door, not stopping to pick up her discarded clothes. She dared to look back at him, fearing that he might come after her. Some tiny, hidden part of her hoped that he might.

But he made no move from where he reclined on an elbow, watching her with an urbane smile. "Run along, then, angel. It's only a matter of time before you succumb. And when you do, it will be all the sweeter for having waited."

She ran back to her own room, slammed the door, locked it behind her. There was no real way of keeping him out, she knew. If he wanted to enter her room, he would find a way. But if only there were some way to lock herself *in*.

He was right. It wasn't him she couldn't trust. It was herself. She now realized that he wasn't her greatest tormentor. It was her own desire. He was waging a constant siege on her virtue. But that siege was only effective because she found him so difficult to resist. Without that, she was in no danger whatsoever.

Andrew...Nick...myself. There's too much at stake, she realized. *I must resist.*

She stopped pacing and leaned her forehead against

the windowpane, looking out at the flashing lights of the Strip. The illuminated fountains across the street shot plumes of water into the air; crowds of people gathered in front to watch. She remembered what it was like to be one of them, normal and human. And completely oblivious to the workings of the preternatural world.

Above the city, the sky was a starless black velvet, even though there hadn't been a cloud in sight for days. The glare of the city lights obliterated the celestial light from above. She wondered how people here in Vegas made their wishes. Then she realized that here, they wished on the beeping lights of slot machines, on the flicker of neon signs and nightclub disco balls.

Maybe it wasn't luck she needed. Perhaps she needed to appeal to a higher power for help. She closed her eyes. *I pray that I'm doing the right thing. I'm not sure what I'm supposed to do or how far I'm supposed to go.*

When no answer came, she opened her eyes and gazed up at the night sky again. Then she realized it. *The stars are still up there,* she thought, *it's just that you can't see them.* She wished she could hide, just like the stars above Vegas. Wondered if she would appear invisible to Julian if another woman suddenly appeared, blinding him with a brighter light than her own.

Who could she find to distract him? Women seemed to flock to him, as Tiffany had been drawn to him this morning. A hundred other women had slid covert glances over his tall, athletic body as they'd strolled along on the Strip in the afternoon. But the women of Vegas did not deserve the likes of Julian set loose on them. Serena wouldn't wish a demon on any human being. Not even Tiffany.

The only remaining possibility was Luciana. Something latent and dangerous existed between them, something that might ignite again with a little help. But they were both more powerful than she was. Together, they could destroy her before she had a chance to escape.

Her mind spun, churning through possibilities and options. But in the end, she could not imagine a viable way out. The only realistic solution lay within herself, with her own self-control. She must resist this desire within herself that was threatening to destroy her.

One day finished, and six more to go.

If she survived this week intact, she would consider it a miracle.

Please, help me find some way to bear this.

She closed her eyes, and let her wish rise up to a star she could not see.

Julian was losing his grip on his demon's nature.

Once again, he watched her go. He heard her door shut, and the sound of the lock clicking echoed in the marble-floored suite. It was the sound of finality, and in this moment it felt as though she was barred from him forever.

Drawing a shaky hand through his hair, he collapsed back on the bed, breathing in shallow pants until the intense feeling of loss passed. How he had managed to remain so casual at the end was a mystery to him, when he'd wanted to dive between her spread legs and taste her, to tease her for an hour or so until she finally came. He'd wanted to take her by the hips, to drive into her until the words *demon* and *angel* had disappeared from her vocabulary and she was reduced to a quivering mass of boneless contentment.

Screw waiting. He'd flung those words out carelessly, because there was nothing else he could say. He stared at the ceiling, still fully erect and frustrated on more than just a physical level. He wanted her, no, he *needed* her in more than just body. He needed her in *soul*. That is, if he even had a soul anymore.

Briefly it crossed his mind that he had a key to her door, and that he was fully capable of using it. In the past, he would have done so without remorse. He would have gained access to her room, and easily overcome her faltering willpower.

But now? What was stopping him?

Absolutely nothing. Rising from the bed, he opened the door and paced out into the living room. Went to stand by her door, listened for noise from within. Heard only silence. His hand, holding the plastic card key, hovered over the doorknob for a very long moment.

A single swipe of the key would open the lock. One small push of the door would open it.

The only thing that prevented him from going in was a promise.

He marched back into his own bedroom, bolted his own door shut, turned off the lights and cursed the thoughts that rushed into his mind.

Somewhere along the line, although he didn't know where or when, this had stopped being a game of seeing whether he could seduce an angel. She was no longer just another passing conquest, or a challenge to alleviate his boredom.

He was dangerously close to falling in love.

Who ever heard of a demon in love?

Lust, he could handle. Lust could be easily slaked by any number of women who would be more than willing to satisfy his needs. No, lust was not the problem. By far the more disturbing emotion was a vague feeling throbbing in the center of his chest, infecting him like a virus integrating itself into his body. Perhaps it *was* too early to call it love, but if left unchecked, Julian was certain that this emotion would develop in that direction. Love was a sentiment for weak-minded fools. He'd been a fool for love during his human life, with Luciana, and it had not ended well. Certainly, he'd succeeded without love for the past two centuries. In fact, he'd dedicated himself to destroying love wherever he found it.

The most obvious solution was simply to release the girl—let her go home untouched and innocent, with her faith in the goodness of the world intact. But at the idea of it, every muscle in his body clenched, and his mind screamed against it.

No. He would keep her for the week she had pledged to him. But if he resolved not to seduce her, he would spend the next six days battling his desires, with the likelihood that the frustration he'd felt last night would mount to a fever pitch. And where was the fun in that? He was not particularly fond of masochism; he did not wish to submit himself to that particular kind of torture.

He must pour all of his energy into accomplishing her seduction. To destroy the innocence about her that was driving him to such distraction. Once rid of that innocence, her appeal would be gone and he would no longer be at risk of falling prey to the affliction of love. Mastering her sexually would mean recovering his power not only as a man, but as a demon.

Because he needed to get back to business. Tonight, Luciana had tried to poison him. He had put himself at considerable risk in order to save Nick. Exposing his potential weaknesses to the other demons was not acceptable. He needed all of his energy, with no distractions and no vulnerabilities.

Yes, bedding Serena would be worth the risk.

But he realized now that she had a high level of immunity to physical pleasure. His little angel had a will of iron. Tonight, he had worked her supple body into a passion that he was sure matched his own. Her self-discipline was admirable, but her defenses were not impossible to overcome. However, he would have to approach her seduction from a different angle.

Coercion had only gotten him so far. If he continued to threaten her, she would eventually surrender her body, but he wanted more. Appealing to her body had gotten him past certain barriers, but he sensed that if he wished to go further, he would have to appeal to her mind. He would have to dig deep into his most powerful tactics.

He would have to convince her that she was saving him. That was the only answer, the only possible way she would allow herself to be seduced. All angels believed in the healing power of love. If she thought that making love to him might lead to some kind of redemption, she would surrender herself to him.

It was a process that would break her. Once he was finished with her, she would be fallen, like him, relegated to the demonic world. If he tired of her, he would simply abandon her. But as they said, misery loved company. If there were still some inkling of interest after he'd stripped her of her angelic shine, she might make a fine companion in eternal damnation.

Three floors up, Luciana and Corbin lay in his magnificent bed. Luciana stretched luxuriantly, arching her back to show off her lush breasts, slick with sweat from their lovemaking. *"Così bene, caro,"* she said with a little sigh of pleasure. She was so convincing he almost believed it.

"You should have told me, darling," Corbin said in a conversational tone, tracing a fingertip idly between those luscious orbs. "It would have been useful to know that you and Julian had been lovers."

She looked up at him with a doe-eyed innocence that she might have counterfeited from Julian's little angel. "You're not jealous, are you, *amore mio?* That was ages ago. Julian completely slipped my mind. He's nothing to me. Especially not now that I have you." She reached up to kiss him, her tongue snaking its way into his mouth.

"Apparently you think he's disposable," he said when they finished the kiss. "But you should have asked for my permission before you tried to poison him."

Tonight, for the first time in the many months since he'd met Luciana, he saw her clearly. She was a whore and a liar, willing to do almost anything to get what she wanted. She was trying to use him. That much was obvious. He should have known the moment she'd appeared three months ago, just after the press release had announced the plans for Julian's nightclub. His mind worked back, searching for other signs he'd missed, blinded by the pleasures of the flesh she offered, and by her exorbitant praise. That oh-so-pleasurable flesh writhed beneath his fingers now, the cadence of her honeyed Italian whispers dripping into his ear.

She would have to learn that Corbin Ranulfson was no fool. But first, he would destroy Julian.

What a shame. Once, it had seemed that Julian might be a true ally, someone with whom he could collaborate. A man whose tastes and opinions were not unlike Corbin's own. But lately, Julian had been getting too big for his britches. Oh, there was no end to the ambitious young demons who aspired to challenge Corbin's leadership. But Julian was different. Julian made him nervous. Julian was strong. In Corbin's many centuries of demonry, he had rarely seen another demon so powerful.

It was time to cut Julian down to size.

"I'm going to help you destroy Julian," the Archdemon said. "He's a fool for trying to protect Nick, but we can use that against him."

"What about that little bitch who ruined our fun tonight?" Luciana pouted. "*Tesoro,* I want you to get rid of her."

"Don't worry, darling. I'll take care of her."

Oh, yes, he would take care of her, although perhaps not quite in the way that Luciana meant. So young, so vulnerable, the little blond angel Julian had picked up as a pet. What fun it would be. And perhaps he would keep Serena afterward…after he'd tired of Luciana and thrown her to the Gatekeepers.

Nobody crossed Corbin and got away with it.

He was rising again, aroused by the thought of the two women at his mercy, begging for their lives. He reached for Luciana, kissed her deeply, imagined he was kissing Serena. The night was still young, and there were infinite possibilities to explore.

Chapter Nine

Dawn. The rising sun stole over the city and blossomed, for a brief instant more glorious than the bright lights of the city. Julian stood at his bedroom window, glowering into the brilliance of daybreak. Sleep had proven elusive last night. Serena had left him aching and tormented by the feeling of her supple body arching beneath him.

The night had been torturous, but he had survived it.

Several times during the night, he'd stood at her door on the verge of unlocking it. But each time, he concluded that it would only serve to break the tenuous thread of trust hanging between them. And with Serena, he was finally beginning to realize that trust was the real key.

He opened his bedroom door and went into the living room, surprised to see her there, practicing yoga on the bare marble floor. Leaning against the doorway, he watched her drop backward from a standing position, her supple body arching as she reached back to land on her hands. Her skin gleamed with the dew of perspiration in the morning sunlight. He wondered how long she had been out here. Wondered if she, too, had been unable to sleep.

She caught him watching and straightened out of the pose immediately, pulling herself up to standing. A pretty blush washed over her cheeks. "I wouldn't have come out here if I'd known you were up," she insisted, her cheeks staining a deeper shade of scarlet. She patted her face delicately with a towel. "But since you're here, we should talk about last night."

"Haven't you heard the saying? Whatever happens in Vegas stays in Vegas," he said, mustering a nonchalance he didn't feel.

"Somehow I don't think that rule applies to angels," she grumbled.

"I swear, it will never happen again if you don't want it to," he said. *Oh, but you will want it to,* he thought. He had reawakened her body to pleasure last night. She might protest that she was immune to his advances, but her body told a different story.

There was more truth in the way she'd trembled in his hands last night than the words that came out of her mouth this morning. The memory of her curves undulating beneath his palms made his cock twitch.

It was imperative that they get out of the suite immediately. If they stayed here, he would be sorely tempted to drag her into his bedroom and bury himself in her. With a little coaxing, she might be willing. But his instincts told him to wait. With enough patience, she would come begging for it.

"Get ready in fifteen minutes," he said, aware of the gruffness in his voice. He made an attempt to gentle it.

"I have some work to do at the club, and you're coming along."

She blinked up at him with wide-eyed innocence. "I'd rather stay here. I'd like to check on Nick when he wakes up."

"Nick is probably still sleeping off his hangover from last night. He won't be awake for hours. You'll spend the day with me," he said, leaving her standing in the living room with no opportunity to argue.

With a handful of days to go before the opening of Devil's Ecstasy, the club was buzzing with painters, designers and delivery people. Julian settled Serena in a corner booth, resentfully reading a magazine. Then he took a walk around, watching as the workers hung curtains from the ceiling, put the final touches of paint on the trim, stocked the bars. Upstairs, a team of trainers from his other clubs instructed the new staff, teaching the bartenders how to juggle bottles, the shooter girls how to flirt outrageously, the bouncers how to control the opening-night frenzy.

Every time Julian asked whether anyone needed instruction, the answer was always the same: "No, Mr. Ascher, everything is under control."

In short, everything was running smoothly. So smoothly, in fact, that there was nothing for him to do.

In the past, opening a new club had been a real challenge. He'd enjoyed diving into his work, always ready to learn something new. But this time, there were no surprises, nothing new to learn. He'd done this dozens of times before in other cities across the country. Vegas was just another place on Julian's long list of clubs.

He looked at Serena, sitting cross-legged in the booth, flipping idly through her magazine. Even with her hair in a makeshift bun, she drew interested glances from the male workers bustling around her. Serena was oblivious to their attention.

From across the room, Julian watched as one of the carpenters finally got up the nerve to approach her. She looked up, surprised, her face beaming with a platonic smile. Julian didn't need to hear their conversation to know what was going on. The guy was hitting on her.

Julian crossed the room in long strides. "We're leaving," he said to Serena. He shot the carpenter a territorial look that all beta males understood. There was a moment of hesitation while the mortal deliberated whether he should stand his ground. Serena was worth fighting for, but the man took another look at Julian and scuttled off without a word.

"I thought you needed to be here to supervise," she said, clearly unimpressed by his rudeness. He didn't care. He just wanted to get her out of here, away from the prying eyes of others.

"Harry can supervise," he said. His personal assistant could certainly be trusted to oversee the minutiae of the club.

The only thing Julian wanted right now was to be alone with Serena.

The only thing Serena wanted right now was to get away from Julian.

"I'd rather stay at the hotel," she said as they walked

through the hotel lobby toward the main entrance. "I can go back up to the suite if you have somewhere to go. I won't try to escape, I promise. Get one of your Gatekeeper demons to guard my door if you don't trust me."

He leaned down, captured her chin lightly in his hand. "You have a choice," he said, his voice low and silken. "Either we spend the afternoon as I had planned, or we can spend it tucked away in your bedroom. Which would you prefer?"

His face was poised inches from hers; she could feel his breath on her face, the caress of his strong fingers along her jawline. The thought of spending an afternoon in bed with Julian was so delicious her mouth started to water. But it would be wrong. So utterly wrong, she reminded herself.

"I'm not leaving Nick," she said, standing her ground.

"By all means, let's go check on him together," Julian said with a little smile. "I can guarantee you he's not awake yet."

He was right. When they knocked on Nick's door, there was no answer. She didn't ask why Julian had a key to her Assignee's room, but when they opened the door, Nick was tucked safely in bed, snoring loudly.

"See? There's no use in you hanging around here while he sleeps," Julian whispered with obvious satisfaction. "I'll make sure my employees look after him."

They stopped by the kitchen to pick up a picnic basket containing a lunch the hotel staff had packed. From there, Julian led her up to the roof. On the circular helipad, a helicopter waited, black-and-silver metal sparkling in the morning sun.

She hesitated, wondering where the pilot was and where they were going. He saw her face and grinned. "Don't worry, angel. We're just going for a little joy-ride. Today, I'm going to show you that demons can fly, too."

Him. He was going to pilot this thing. She hung back, eyeing the helicopter with skepticism. He loaded the picnic basket into the back. He settled her into the jump seat, next to the pilot's seat, buckling her in and putting a headset over her ears. He flicked on the flight controls, starting the engine and the rotation of the blades. The vibration of the helicopter sent a shiver down her back. He launched them from the pad with a sudden lift that left her body weightless for a moment. The shadow of the helicopter receded on the pavement beneath them. As they rose, she forgot that she had ever been afraid.

They flew high above Las Vegas, soaring over the Strip in the noonday sun. From above, she watched in wonder as the man-made volcano blew. The sun glinted off the gigantic hotels lining Las Vegas Boulevard: the pyramid of the Luxor, the enormous artificial lagoon of the Bellagio, the Eiffel Tower of Paris. Behind them, gigantic azure swimming pools were crowded with people lounging in the heat of this perfect July day.

Julian veered east, away from the Strip, as they flew over neat rows of suburban houses. Then they were out of the city, leaving it behind them, a man-made mirage shimmering in the desert. He narrated through the headset as he flew over hills of scrub-covered earth, pointing out the dark brown-and-black volcanic rock that lay in the folds of the valleys. Heading over the famous Hoover Dam, Serena marveled at the blue-green surface of Lake

Mead, separated into two different levels by a miracle of engineering. Time seemed to collapse as she peered down at the wonders far below.

He flew as easily as he drove, holding the control stick steady between his knees with a light but expert touch. He was a man in command of his surroundings, manipulating the controls with the same deftness he'd used on her body last night. He concentrated on his task, calm but alert. A slight smile played on his lips as she considered his profile. His athletic body was relaxed— he obviously enjoyed flying.

Flight seemed to be, for Julian, an innocent pleasure, unconnected to any evil goals or motivations. She furrowed her brow, trying to reconcile this side of him with the demon who had threatened her loved ones. Even in bed last night, there had been a part of him that had seemed gentle, free of any demonic impulses. He had touched her with a tenderness that had almost seemed human.

But they were not human. He was not, and neither was she. She must never forget that.

She snapped her gaze back to the landscape below. They had been flying for about an hour when they flew over a mountainous rise, and on the other side of it, the land dropped away into the dramatic basin of the Grand Canyon. The layered rock walls rose in tiers around them. His voice came through the headset. "The canyon was formed by erosion, by water, ice and wind forcing the land apart over thousands of years. I've always thought she has a soul of her own."

Julian guided the helicopter around the rim of the canyon, flying for another half hour as he pointed out the unusual land formations—pinnacles, mesas, buttes. "There are several peaks that are called temples here," he noted. He pointed them out as the helicopter flew past—Shiva Temple, Buddha Temple, Zoroaster Temple, Brahma Temple. She gazed wide-eyed at the craggy rock formations that jutted skyward. How apt that they had been given spiritual names. The canyon was a place of profound tranquility, a place to meditate on the mystical. It was an odd place for a demon, though.

He landed on a plateau, a tabletop of bare rock thirty feet across, the sides of which sloped downward at a steep vertical drop. He switched off the helicopter and let the blades stop their rotation, turned to her as he removed his headset.

"This is the reason I brought you here," he said, pointing to the gorge below them. "Bright Angel Canyon. There's a Dirty Devil River in Utah that was named by the same explorers in the mid-1800s. They said they wanted to honor the good spirits as well as the bad," he said with a grin. "There's a lookout point at the Bright Angel trailhead, but it's often packed with tourists. We have a better view of the canyon from here."

There wasn't another soul in view. The trip had taken over two hours, but this canyon might have been a universe away from Vegas. They sat without speaking for a few moments, simply staring at the grandeur of nature around them. Her gaze traveled along the stratified gray rock, layered with red, and below, to the greenish-gray waters of the Colorado River. For the first time in two days, she felt at peace.

Hopping out of the helicopter, he laid out blankets on the ground, began unloading the picnic basket. She followed, drinking in the clean canyon air. Wandering over to the edge of the plateau, she looked down, suddenly vertiginous at the drop where the cliff dove straight into the canyon below. She shivered, although it was far from cold.

There was a shuffling of gravel beneath her, and then his strong hand closed around her upper arm. A few rocks came loose from the edge and tumbled two hundred feet to the bottom of the gorge below. As he stood behind her, she felt safe. Instinctively, she knew he would never hurt her, that he would keep her safe from harm.

"Come away from the edge," he said, his voice low in her ear.

He tugged her backward, toward the picnic blanket. He began to unpack the items the hotel staff had packed: an assortment of cheese and crackers, delicate roast vegetable sandwiches, a large bottle of cold lemonade. He poured her a plastic cupful of the beverage and she sipped its sweetness, wrapped her hands around it, cooling them.

He had brought her here, to this place of penetrating beauty. Unable to find words adequate to express her awe and delight, she said the least she could say. "Thank you."

"It gives me pleasure to see you happy," he said quietly.

He paced around the edge of the plateau, peering down and covertly watching Serena finish her lunch. She made a pretty picture sitting in the center of the rock formation, surrounded by the rising strata around them, with her sun-gold hair whipping in the wind and her cheeks flushed pink from the summer heat.

He had meant what he'd said—it gave him immeasurable pleasure to see her so enchanted with her surroundings. But it was terrifying to hear those words coming out of his mouth—more terrifying than if he were hanging from the plateau's edge, about to plunge into the canyon's abyss. The safest way to deal with those uncomfortable emotions was to cut them off before they could blossom any further, to stifle the tenderness that was beginning to bloom in his heart. He needed to change the subject. So he began to talk.

"The Grand Canyon was one of the places I came when I first arrived in this country," he said, coming to stand at a point on the lip of the plateau. "I came from England on a steamship, long before I developed the power to dematerialize. It was the middle of the nineteenth century. London was in the middle of a cholera epidemic, packed to the gills with disease and poverty."

How odd. It was not the subject he had expected to arise. He had wanted something trivial, something light. Normally he didn't disclose his personal history to women, but for some reason, he felt compelled to tell her. Here, in the midst of these craggy undulations, the landscape pulled at the emotions brewing within him. He wanted those enormous blue eyes of hers to shine with understanding, instead of the wary suspicion that he usually read in them. Instead of stifling his feelings for her, those emotions were intensifying. But he found it impossible to stop.

"England under Victoria was repressive, full of

societal rules and sexual hang-ups. Of course, behind that prim and proper superficiality, the criminal underworld was as seedy as could be. But England reminded me too much of my lost family. Even my father had been dead for over half a century, and I needed a fresh start. America was wild back then. I thought New York City would be a good place for me to make a new life. But that city, too, already had established its ranks of demons. I wanted uncharted territory. So I came west with the Forty-Niners—the gold prospectors who were headed to Northern California in 1849. I saw a few men strike it rich, and a lot of men leave empty-handed. It wasn't until twenty years later that the Powell Expedition began to explore the Grand Canyon."

But it had still been unmapped land when he'd first set eyes on these cavernous depths. He told her of gingerly riding on horseback down the zigzag trail the Hopi Indians had carved in the slanting incline. He had come here looking for something—not gold, but *meaning*. Perhaps it seemed logical that this was where the opening to hell should have been, if such a place had been accessible on earth. After half a century of demonry, by the time he arrived at the Grand Canyon, he was sick of watching men fall, sick of being the one to tempt them into debauchery. He had stood at the bottom of the gorge in the rain, waiting for the devil to reclaim him. Waiting for a flash flood to sweep him back to hell, or a lightning bolt to strike. But none came.

"After the gold rush was over, I took the considerable profits I had made and headed south, to Los Angeles. In the early days, it was known as the roughest town in the country. There were territorial wars between the Mexican-born and the Anglos. Lynch mobs ran all over town, and the murder rate was ten to twenty times higher than it was in New York City at the time. It was heaven on earth for a demon trying to make a name for himself. I opened a saloon, bided my time, and the rest, as they say, is history."

Serena blinked, the blue of her eyes brighter than the clear summer sky. They were so clear, he could see her thoughts passing through like clouds, her mind absorbing his words. They sat in silence awhile, digesting the meal and his story.

After a while, she spread her arms out to indicate the vastness of the canyon. "But it's so beautiful. I don't know how you can doubt the power of goodness when all this beauty exists."

"Good and evil are equally balanced. Besides, you should know by now that what is beautiful isn't necessarily good," he said. "Despite what mankind may think, Keats was wrong when he wrote, 'Beauty is truth, truth beauty.' You can't deny that I'm beautiful, but I'm fundamentally evil."

"You're wrong. The balance of good and evil is a fallacy. You're not evil," she said firmly. "You're just… mistaken." She turned her face toward Bright Angel Canyon, a worried little frown on her brow.

"This canyon is a place of beauty, but it is also a place of death. Nearly six hundred souls have found their final resting place here. Murder, suicide, plane crashes, hypothermia, dehydration, drowning, rock slides, falls. Every sort of ending imaginable has occurred here. And you don't think the devil makes his presence known?"

She said quietly, "I think the devil is just another

mistaken soul. He was a fallen angel. What's to say he can't go back? That *you* can't go back?"

He laughed. "I'm sure he would think the same of you. You could fall," he said. Her gaze darted to the plateau's edge, and to the steep drop below. He opened his mouth to say that she could fall very easily, but stopped himself. He wanted to lull her into a false sense of security, not put her defenses up.

"Why did you choose darkness?" she protested. "What happened to you, Julian?"

Her blue eyes searched his face for an answer, but she didn't want to know, not really. If he told her, she would feel sorry for him, and he didn't want that. He didn't need her pity. So he changed the subject yet again, rattling on about the details of that early trip, his returns to the canyon, his many explorations on foot and on horseback.

Reaching into the picnic basket, he took out the red velvet cake the staff had packed for dessert, handed her a piece. Continued to speak as she ate. A tiny movement along the edge of the plateau caught his eye. The writhe of a familiar reptile, a thin whip of bright green, intense against the dusty canyon rock. A snake whose color hailed from the forests of sub-Saharan Africa, not native to the canyons of Arizona. A snake that had been brought here, not one that belonged here.

He opened his mouth to call her name. But he was too late.

It was the noise that caught Serena's attention, the whisper of skin sliding on earth. When she looked down, she saw the green snake coiled there, its pop of color bright and deadly. Exactly like the one she'd seen slither from Luciana's handbag last night.

How strange. For a moment, she wondered if the snake was real. Then it moved. In a quick slither of blurring colors, its shiny black head rose. Dartlike, it shot out and sank its fangs into her ankle. The pain was not intense, but startling.

Only a demon can kill an angel, she remembered.

Was Julian conspiring with Luciana, after all? Fleetingly, it struck Serena that she might be just one more prize in his quest for power, yet another victim whose destruction would increase Julian's ranking in hell.

Her body began to numb.

Perhaps Julian *was* pure evil, after all.

Chapter Ten

Julian watched her fall. Heard the rustling of wings, not unfolding this time, but sinking to earth. Her body swayed, still graceful even in her fall. She crumpled, breaking the fall with arms already weak, and lay on the ground, breathing in shallow gasps. Around her, her golden hair fanned like a halo in the dirt. Her forehead contracted, and her gaze tracked him, full of alarm and hurt. Full of accusation.

He stood, rooted to the ground, mind scrambling to process the slick bands of color as the snake slid from her hand. For a sliver of time, his body froze from the shock of it. With her, he felt some part of himself falling, some part of him that was ripped away as he reached out, realizing that he was too late to catch her.

He *must* save her, or a part of him would die with her on this desert rock.

Serena whispered his name. And he shook himself out of his paralysis.

He picked up the snake in one hand, heedless of the danger, and hurled it into the empty space of the gorge. It arced out, hanging suspended in the open air for a moment before it began to fall, disappearing into the depths of the canyon below.

"I can't die," she murmured, her chest rising and falling as her lungs labored in their fight for air. "Not again. Not so soon."

Oh, but Julian knew very well that she *could* die. Not in a spiritual sense—the soul could never die. But her physical body was very much susceptible to destruction. Yes, she would probably come back to earth. *Somewhere. Sometime.* But who knew where or when? There were certainly no guarantees. Especially not after what had happened between them....

He had seen this particular trick before, although not used to destroy angels, but other demons. In fact, he had assisted in carrying it out. The snakes Luciana carried with her were just babies, but charged with demonic energy, even a newborn green mamba's venom accelerated death, able to destroy a body that was otherwise immortal. What would normally take hours would happen in a matter of minutes. There was only one way to stop it.

Antivenom. The only known treatment for a green mamba bite. To be more specific, a particular kind of antivenom that someone he knew carried at all times. She carried it because she was so fond of this particular modus operandi that she would never risk being without it herself, just in case one of her precious little pets decided to bite her. That person, of course, was Luciana.

He cursed himself. He had brought this on Serena. He was the one who had taken her to Vegas, had exposed her to Luciana. If the angel died now, he would never be able to forgive himself. He would kill Luciana. Rip her head clean off her body, and he didn't care whether he was damned for all eternity because of it.

He dematerialized, reappearing just outside the doorway to Corbin's penthouse suite. Julian banged on the door until a Gatekeeper opened it. He barged in without the usual formalities, searching for that familiar flash of raven hair. "Where's Luciana?"

The Gatekeeper, recognizing the Archdemon's power, cowered and pointed down a hallway. In the spectacular living room, the two demons were lounging on sleek leather sofas. *And so was Nick.* There was no time to ask what the young human was doing there. Julian simply ordered him, "Go back down to your suite and bolt yourself in. Don't ask questions. Just do it."

Nick complied. The second he left the room, Julian went straight for Luciana, dangerously close to letting his rage explode. "What did you do to her?"

Luciana widened her spring-colored eyes, play-acting the innocent as she reclined on a pile of cushions. "I don't know what you're talking about. *Sei pazzo!*" *You're crazy.* It was something she'd said to him often when they were lovers. It had annoyed him then; now it made him want to strangle her.

He towered over her, hoping his physical presence would intimidate her so that he wouldn't have to resort to force. "Drop it, Luciana. You're not fooling anyone. Give me the antivenom."

Corbin stood and leaned against the wall, watching their interaction. "Julian. To what do we owe the pleasure of your company?"

"Ask her," Julian said. When the demoness remained silent, he said, "Serena was bitten by a poisonous snake that someone packed in our lunch."

"Your new girlfriend should watch what she eats. Or

what eats her," Luciana said, a tiny smile playing around her evil little mouth. What he'd ever seen in that woman was beyond him. She might be beautiful, but she was one hell of a manipulative bitch.

Julian sprang forward, grabbed her by the collar. "Give me the damned antivenom. Or I will make sure you rot in hell for all eternity to pay for what you've done."

Her eyes widened then, this time in genuine fear. Corbin didn't make a move, merely stood by, observing. She choked out her assent and Julian released her. While she disappeared into the bedroom, he stood with his arms crossed, conscious that every second he stood here was a second of life that was draining out of Serena's body.

Finally, Luciana came out with a small vial and a syringe. "Take it and go," she pouted.

Antivenom in hand, he turned to leave. "If you ever so much as touch a single strand of hair on her head, I will exterminate you," he said quietly.

Then he leaped back into the void. Time was his greatest enemy now.

Bright Angel Canyon. So still, so peaceful. A beautiful place to experience death. Again. Here in this remote part of the earth, her physical body would decompose naturally, returning to the soil as the bodies of other creatures did. As her previous body had. It was simply another part of the cycle of nature, as inevitable as the rising and setting of the sun, the changing of the seasons, the turning of the tides. *Dust to dust…*

The soul never dies, even if the physical body ceases

to exist. This time, she was ready to return to the Archangels, safe in the knowledge that they waited for her above.

She began to let go, drifting up toward the light.

Serena felt herself spiraling upward, sailing into the clear afternoon sky. A sense of peace washed over her. In the distance, it began to rain. Just over the peak of the Buddha Temple, the sunlight refracted in a thousand different colors, each more vibrant and more beautiful than the next.

Julian had disappeared. He had left her to die, alone in the midst of the deserted canyon. It was a fact that would have devastated her if she'd still been incarnated. But now, hovering above her body, she was no longer bound to its sensations and emotions, and she viewed the situation without judgment. Death was simply part of reality.

She floated, watching her physical form sprawled on the ground beneath the blanket Julian had spread over her. The breath had gone out of her, and she lay still, as though sleeping, one hand curled beside her head. A pair of crows circled overhead, sensing the proximity of death.

And then Julian reappeared.

She watched as he drew liquid into a syringe from a small glass vial. He injected the liquid into her arm, then began administering CPR. As he pumped her chest with a strong, even rhythm, he spoke gentle words of encouragement. "Stay with me…don't leave me now, angel." The clouds moved closer, and rain began to pelt down, first in fat drops, then in a steady downpour as he worked. The deluge slicked his hair, soaked his clothes. Around him, the dusty red soil turned into mud.

Removed from her physical body, she did not feel the rain. She drifted, still at peace. From above, she heard a rustling of outspread wings. The Archangel Gabriel appeared, radiating pure white light. An overwhelming sense of harmony infused her. She wanted nothing more than to merge with the universal energy toward which Gabriel would guide her.

"He's trying to save me, isn't he?" she mused.

The Archangel smiled, his incandescent form untouched by the pelting rain. "Yes. Your physical body is dying again. But you will not leave at this time. You must return to the material realm. You have a divine mission to carry out."

"Of course. Nick, my Assignee. Won't Arielle just find another angel to replace me if I don't come back?" She wondered briefly whether her supervisor would even register her loss.

"Your mission goes far beyond that, little one. It's not your time yet."

"What do you mean?" she called after him.

But Gabriel didn't answer. She looked up at the storm-darkened sky as he surged upward on a single beat of his vast wings. And Serena spiraled back down to earth, landing in her body with a thud.

It was so very cold, so very wet here on the ground. She shivered, her limbs trembling from it. She opened her eyes. Julian was bent over her, hands poised over her chest, ready to compress again. There was concern in his eyes, emotion so real that, for a moment, it made him seem human. How odd for a demon.

"I thought you were trying to kill me," she said. Her voice came out as a croak; it hurt to talk. Her teeth chattered.

"Don't try to speak. Just rest," he said. He laid a hand on her forehead, and closed his own eyes for a moment. He whispered something that she couldn't hear, but that she thought sounded like an expression of gratitude.

He scooped her into his arms, carried her to the helicopter. Laying her carefully on the backseat, he spread a dry blanket over her, placed the headset on her. His mouth set into a thin, white line. "I'm sorry this happened. It was entirely my fault," he said. "I should have known Luciana would pull something like this. But you must know that I would never hurt you." She shut her eyes, trying not to throw up, and felt his lips graze her hairline before he shut the door.

The vibrations of the helicopter jarred her body, making her nausea worse. Two hours seemed to stretch into an eternity. There was no question of death now, only the intense pain burning in her lungs and stomach. Gradually, though, her shivering stopped. The pain came in ebbs and flows, leaving her wondering when it would stop, how much more she could take.

Still, she thought about how full her existence had been. She'd left her human body at a very young age, and she was still young. It saddened her that there were still so many things she would never experience in physical form, like true love—the kind Andrew had always said she'd missed out on. Yet, it was not herself that she worried about the most. Rather, she worried for her Assignee, her brother and her roommate. If she died again, there was no telling what might happen to them in her absence. She thought of Nick, so vulnerable in the midst of all these demons.

Would Julian still carry out his threats if she were gone? She did not believe he would. Over the past few days, she was beginning to recognize a certain quality about him that she might have described as 'goodness,' had he not been a demon. A certain quality that had led him to save her life, when he could just as easily have left her to die on that plateau. The image of his steady hands manipulating the helicopter controls was the last thing she registered before she slipped out of consciousness.

When she next opened her eyes, Julian was placing her between the clean sheets of her bed at the hotel. She was warm, dry and stationary. She gave thanks and vowed never to take those simple things for granted again. She nestled her cheek against the softness of the pillows and allowed her eyes to drift nearly closed.

"Will she die?" An unfamiliar voice spoke in a hushed tone; she turned her head to see a nice-looking black man standing there, his dark eyes shining with concern. *Demon,* her mind spoke warily. Yet, this one seemed different. Of all the demons she'd encountered, none except for Julian had retained the kind of compassion for other beings she sensed in this man.

Perhaps that's why he's here. Because Julian trusts him, she thought.

"No, Harry," Julian said. "I've seen this before. She's out of danger now. But stay with her. Call me if she shows any signs of distress."

"As you request, sir."

Julian turned back to the bed, smoothed her hair with

a gentle hand. "I'll be back shortly. There's something I need to take care of."

She turned her head, hating the neediness in her that wanted him to stay. Her mouth was as dry as though it were filled with the red dust of the canyon. Just as well. If she tried to speak, she would not have liked what came out. *Please. Don't leave. Stay with me.* Words that were better left unspoken.

Julian lifted a glass of water to her lips, held it while she drank. Then he went out the door. She struggled to sit up, but nausea crashed over her like a riptide, rocking her with a dizziness that she never thought possible on dry land, and laying her out flat again. She closed her eyes for a moment, then tried again. This time she was more successful. The wave of sickness was gentler this time, nauseating but bearable.

Harry rushed forward with an empty wastepaper basket, ready for the worst. "Miss, try to save your strength."

She sat up, struggling to keep down the contents of her roiling stomach. She had to find the strength to get out of this bed.

If the demons tried to kill me, God only knows what they could have done to Nick.

She imagined the worst. An image of Nick floated up, his tortured body bloodied and torn to shreds. Gabriel's words rang in her mind: *You have a divine mission to carry out.* A mission that went far beyond taking care of Nick. She had an awful feeling that mission had something to do with Julian.

But even in her weakened condition, she needed to know that Nick was safe. He was still her Assignee, and he could be in grave danger. Still, the only way to get out of here, it seemed, was to get Harry to help her. How she was supposed to do that, she had no idea. So she did the only thing she could do, and just started talking.

"You seem like a nice guy," she said. "How long have you been working for Julian?"

Harry paused. Swallowed. "Three months."

"You seem too nice to be…" She closed her dry mouth, wondering how she could remove her foot from it.

"A demon?" He laughed. "Is that supposed to be a compliment? There are certain benefits to working for Julian," he said. Some bittersweet memory crossed his handsome face, and she wondered what it was.

"You can leave me. I'll be fine. We angels have incredible powers of recovery, just like you demons," she said. In theory, she knew that to be true. Right now, every second she lay in this bed felt like an eternity.

He smiled awkwardly, obviously uncomfortable with his role as her caretaker but committed to carrying on nonetheless. "No, miss. Mr. Ascher assigned me to watch over you, and that's what I plan to do."

He settled into a chair in the corner, sitting down to wait as if he expected to be there for a long time. Inside her, the urgency built. She could think of no other tactic than to simply blurt out the truth.

"I need to go, Harry. I need to check on someone."

"Nick. I know all about it," he said. His voice sounded almost as tired as she felt.

"He's my responsibility. Don't you remember what it's like to be human? And scared? Underneath all his bad behavior, Nick is both of those things. I need to find him. To see if he's okay." Without knowing why, she added, "He's just a kid."

The last word seemed to soften something in Harry. His expression shifted. "You're just a kid yourself. How can *you* look after him?"

He was so close to the truth that she wanted to cry. But she would not. She swallowed past the lump in her throat and said, "That's just the way it is, Harry. Sometimes we don't question these things."

"I can't help you," he said softly. "I'm sorry."

"Of course you can't," she said, closing her eyes as another wave of exhaustion hit her. "You're a demon."

There was a long silence, broken only by the creak of Harry's chair beneath his shifting weight. In that small sound, she could hear his increasing discomfort.

With her eyes still closed, she spoke, barely a whisper. But a whisper she hoped would be enough. "Perhaps I was sleeping. Perhaps you went into the living room, and the door was left open. Perhaps I snuck out of the suite so quietly you were unable to hear me. Perhaps that's what you would tell Julian if he found out."

Another long pause. Another creak as Harry shifted again. Finally, in a tone as quiet as hers, he whispered, "Perhaps."

Her eyes fluttered open and she saw him looking at her, regarding her from his corner chair. He felt sorry for her. And she felt so sorry for him. Because in that instant she knew what utter hell it must be for someone like him, someone who had a heart, to do what he did. She had no idea of Harry's circumstances, but she imagined they must be dire if they had brought him to this.

She licked her dry lips and closed her eyes again, gathering strength. "Thank you, Harry. I won't forget this."

His chair creaked as he stood. "This conversation did not take place. If you tell Julian that I helped you, I will deny it. All I know is that I was sitting in the living room, and I had no idea how you got out," he said.

She wanted to leap from the bed, to hug him, to kiss him on the cheek, but he had gone from the room by the time she opened her eyes. Serena stood up, taking in a deep breath when dizziness threatened to overset her. Serena got her balance and, discarding the night-gown she wore, she pulled on jeans and a T-shirt. She crept out of the bedroom, mouthing a silent *thank you* to Harry, who was engrossed in a book in the corner of the living room, pretending not to see her. From there, she slipped out the front door and into the hallway.

Serena had already thought of the worst that could happen. She might run into Julian, who would bark and growl. But he had saved her life today, and she was beginning to doubt that he was really capable of hurt-ing her. She might run into Luciana. But she needed to make sure Nick was safe.

What she had not anticipated was the weakened con-dition of her own body. Beneath her, her legs wobbled. She collapsed onto the floor, bracing herself with her hands. Taking a few deep breaths, she willed herself up again. Pushing herself to standing from the floor, she stumbled into the elevator and leaned against the wall, panting as she watched the illuminated numbers creep downward.

The journey two floors down might as well have been a trek across the Sahara. Every step was excruciating. She tried to walk upright, not wishing to draw attention to herself. But passersby looked at her with worried expressions. A bellboy stopped her, concern etched on his face. "Ma'am, are you all right? Do you need assistance?"

"Thanks, I'm fine," she murmured. She could not risk asking for help—every employee in this hotel reported back to Corbin.

Finally, she made it to Nick's room. She raised her hand to knock. Laid her head against the door frame as she waited for him to open the door.

Luciana was still in Corbin's suite when Julian found her, lounging across the hotelier's lap. He wanted to destroy her, to send her back to the depths of hell for the pain and fear she'd caused Serena.

"It was just a harmless prank," the demoness purred, stretching to caress Corbin's cheek. Her raven tresses gleamed in the dim lamplight. "It was just a little game."

Julian glared, wondering how he'd ever deluded himself into thinking he had once loved this wretched creature. What an idiot he'd been in his human life. "You don't play with what belongs to me."

"I gave you the antivenom, didn't I?" she said, pouting. "Stop overreacting. It was just a snake. If I had wanted to, I could have…" She paused, exchanging a covert little smile with Corbin.

"What?" Julian demanded.

"Nothing," she said. "That little *zoccola* is tougher than she looks."

Slut was what she had just called Serena. It was the last straw. Julian said to Corbin, "If you don't ask her to leave, I'll consider it a declaration of war between us."

Luciana sent him a glare so icy it would have frozen hell over. She started to rise, no doubt about to launch into one of her histrionic screaming fits, when Corbin held up a placating hand. "Calm down, old friend. Who's to say Luciana was responsible for this?" the older Archdemon said.

Julian stared him straight in the eye. "That picnic basket originated from your kitchen. No one else would have dared tamper with anything on your turf without your permission."

"Let's just let bygones be bygones," Corbin drawled.

"I can't keep Serena here safely," Julian said. "You and I have been working on the opening of this night-club for over a year. It's scheduled to open in five days. Luciana is using you. If you let this harlot come between us, our business partnership will be severely compromised. You've got to choose. Luciana or the business. You're a smart man, Corbin. Make the right choice."

Julian made his way out of the suite, shaking with rage. He swallowed, trying to lubricate the dryness in his mouth. He had just delivered an ultimatum to the most powerful demon in the country. Tomorrow, he might be toiling in the pits of the underworld, back where he'd been when he'd first lost his human life.

What the hell. It had been worth it. *Serena* was worth it.

As he waited for the elevator, the door to the suite opened. Corbin came out, his face as inscrutable as ever. "Luciana will be gone in the morning," he said in a neutral tone. He turned to go back inside, but before he did, he paused, turned back to Julian and said, "Don't ask me for any more favors."

Julian slumped against the side of the elevator, relieved. Luciana would be furious, but Corbin had come through. For the first time in hours, Julian allowed himself to breathe. But his relief was short-lived. When he went back down to his own suite, Harry was slumped in an armchair, snoring noisily, and the angel was nowhere to be found.

Chapter Eleven

Down in his suite, Nick was pissed off. He sat hunched in front of the TV, arms crossed and feet propped up on the coffee table. The walls of the room were like a cage, penning him in.

"Who does Julian think he is?" Nick muttered to himself, flipping through the channels.

Stole my girl. Treats me like a child.

Not like Corbin and Luciana. Now, *they* understood him. Not only that, but they understood how to *live*.

An hour ago, they had offered him an entrée into their world. A way to bring his wildest dreams to life. The dreams he had never spoken aloud to anyone.

"We can make your life magical," Corbin had said to him, as they lunched in the penthouse suite. With its huge windows overlooking the Strip, it seemed to Nick as though the whole world lay stretched at his feet.

Nick was no stranger to privilege. He had grown up surrounded by wealth and beauty. But most of his youth had been controlled according to the strict rules of his uptight parents. Who barely ever had a moment to pay attention to him. And when they did, it was only to disapprove.

Corbin was different from anyone Nick had ever met. Because Corbin *listened*.

"Tell me what you want," he'd said.

"Respect," Nick had told him. That was what Nick wanted most. For his culture snob of a mother to watch one of his movies without wrinkling her nose in subtle distaste. For his ultra-conservative old father to watch one of his movies, *period*.

The only time he'd ever gotten respect from his parents was once during prep school, the first time he'd ever been onstage. He'd played Romeo, only because the girl he'd had a crush on had been cast as Juliet. His parents hadn't actually made the time to come see the play. But at least they'd each nodded with approval when he'd told them about it during his separate visits to them at Christmas break. That play had begun Nick's acting career, although he had never done Shakespeare again. Afterward, the crush had died quietly. The girl had gone on to a minor career in commercials, and after graduation Nick had gone to Hollywood. But nothing he had accomplished since—neither his fame nor the money he made from his own talent—had ever been enough to earn his parents' respect.

Corbin had understood. He had taken Nick seriously. "You're a man of substance, Nick. You deserve a role that will put you in the running for an Oscar. I can arrange that."

Nick didn't doubt it for a second. Corbin was *connected*. That much was obvious.

"Just stick with us," the hotel owner had said coolly, sipping his cocktail. "You'll see how easy life can be."

Then Nick had remembered his yoga teacher's re-action last night, when she'd seen them all in the pool. "Serena won't like it."

"What are you, some kind of six-year-old?" Luciana had said, trailing her fingers down his arm. "You don't have to listen to her."

Nick had paused after that. He didn't have to listen to her but, for some reason, he still wanted to. He still wanted *her.*

"She ran off somewhere with Julian this morning," Corbin had said coolly. "Left you behind. You're never going to have a chance with her, unless you find some way to get rid of Julian. But don't worry. We can help you fix that, too."

Before the discussion had gone any further, Julian had burst in and ruined everything.

Julian promised me this trip would be fun. But every time I start to have fun, Julian gets in the way, Nick thought furiously. *Now I'm stuck in this stupid hotel suite, and he's with Serena. I'm gonna go nuts if I have to stay in here any longer.*

He went to open the door, desperately wanting to leave. To go back upstairs and continue his conversation with Corbin. But when he reached for the doorknob, his head started to pound. Worse than if he'd been struck by a massive hangover, worse than his most painful migraine. *Don't leave,* Julian had said. That thought bounced around the inside of Nick's head, making him back away from the door and collapse back on the sofa.

He picked up the remote again, flipping through the channels and becoming more and more frustrated.

Until he saw his own face flash across the screen, smeared with fake blood and sweat in a gladiator flick he'd done a few years ago. He'd never thought much about it previously. For some reason, it made his blood boil now. He hated the sight of that stupid movie, hated his whole stupid career.

With all of his strength and pent-up rage, he drew back his arm and hurled the remote at the TV. Cracking the plasma screen with a burst of breaking plastic. The image of his face splayed into a billion tiny bars of flashing light.

He wanted *more*. He wanted what Corbin had. And he wanted Serena.

He would do anything to get what he wanted.

Serena heard the crash inside Nick's room, and raised her fist to knock on his door. Just before she made contact, a powerful hand closed over her wrist. Without question, she knew whose fingers stopped her. As she turned to look up at Julian, she saw the worry in his eyes. Emotions shifted across his face, worry merging into another expression, something altogether more dangerous. Something more like anger.

"What the hell do you think you're doing down here?" Julian growled.

She opened her mouth to shoot back an answer, but the door opened a crack, and Nick stood there frowning. He froze as he saw them, Julian still clasping her wrist. Clearly irritated, her Assignee said, "What's going on?"

Relief flooded through her at the sight of him. "I

wanted to make sure you were okay. I just heard a loud noise coming from your room."

"As you can see, he's fine," said Julian. She wanted to look into Nick's room to see what had been broken, but the demon started to pull her away.

Nick's brows snapped into a vee as he poked his head out a bit farther, peered closer at her. "What happened to you, Serena? You look like hell. Is he…?"

"I'm fine. Just feeling a bit under the weather," she said. Nick did not need to know what had gone on in the canyon today, nor would he ever be able to understand it.

"Why don't you shut the door and take a nap?" Julian said, leaving Nick no choice but to comply.

Nick's frown deepened, but he shut the door nonetheless.

"You should have trusted me," Julian whispered, close to her ear. "I told you he would be fine." He slipped an arm beneath her shoulders, ready to hoist her into his arms.

She pushed away from him, trying to walk on her own. "I can walk by myself."

Beneath her, her legs buckled traitorously.

"You are the most stubborn woman I've ever met," said the demon. "And the most foolish. What were you going to do if Nick wasn't here? If the others really had taken him somewhere?"

"Go down to the lobby and call Arielle," she admitted lamely.

His breath made a hissing sound. "You're too damned honest for your own good. You should learn how to lie. It makes life a lot easier."

Ignoring her protests, he swept her into his arms, carrying her the rest of the way back to their suite. Where Harry was sitting on the ornate sofa, head in his hands. He jumped up when he saw them, springing to his feet with anxiety spread all over his face.

"Harry, you may leave," Julian said quietly.

"I'm so sorry, sir," Harry said. "I never meant for her to escape. It was entirely my fault."

Serena chimed in, "It's not his fault, Julian. It was my fault."

Julian waved a dismissive hand in Harry's direction. "Just go."

Harry's eyes went wide, but he said nothing. Serena wanted to say a few words to comfort him. She hoped he was not in trouble because of her. But she could almost see the storm clouds gathering over Julian's head. She knew it was best to remain silent as Harry slipped out the door.

Julian went to the minibar and poured himself a drink. Then he turned and went out onto the balcony. It was clear that he wanted to be alone, but she followed anyway.

A muscle twitched in his cheek as he gazed out over the view, not looking at her. "Luciana's gone. She won't hurt you again," he said.

"What happened between you two?" she asked softly.

It was the question he'd been asking himself for the past two hundred years. He exhaled a long sigh and said, "Luciana is the reason I became a demon."

"Oh." It was barely a whisper, a mere puff of air with

a little bit of voice that was carried away on the breeze. "You don't have to tell me."

"I want to make you understand," he said. More than that, he wanted to make *himself* understand. He pulled her inside to sit on the sofa as he started his story. "Once upon a time, there was a spoiled young English lord…"

"You're *Lord* Julian?" she interrupted.

He half smiled. "That part of me died more than two hundred years ago. It means nothing now. But, yes. At one time, I was the Earl of Leyburn."

It all came pouring out. His human life history spun before him as he talked, weaving in and out of the present as the hours slipped by like fluid. Outside, the sun melted toward the horizon, the mountains a shadow in the background outside before darkness claimed the city.

The tale of his early years and the death of his mother brought tears to Serena's eyes, despite his best efforts to recount it in a neutral tone. He had known the story would: the loss of a parent at such young an age struck the chord of her father's death. He continued, pushing through the pain of his adolescence, his hard-won neutrality lightening to fond remembrance as he talked about his Oxford days. He was almost grinning by the time he spoke of his Grand Tour of Europe, and finally, the joys of exploring Venice. From there, he steeled himself for what must come next.

"It was in Venice that I first saw Luciana. She was a silk merchant's daughter, barely seventeen the first time I saw her, sauntering along the Grand Canal on a fine summer's day."

He paused to order room service, editing the story in his head as he perused the menu. There were things Serena didn't need to know about. Things that would hurt her. Like the memory of Luciana's dewy beauty. With her dark hair and pale emerald eyes, Luciana was the most gorgeous creature he'd seen on earth, until he'd met Serena. The day they'd met, Venice had been as hot as Hades. Luciana had looked as cool as a fresh breeze off the Adriatic. He had stopped her on the pretense of having lost his way. Luciana had kindly pointed him in the right direction. She had laughed at his poor attempts to speak Italian and had shyly spoken a few tentative words of English.

From that day onward, Julian had conspired to meet her every day in the same spot, near the Rialto Bridge. They would stroll along the canals, conversing brokenly in two languages and laughing at each other's linguistic mistakes. He began to bring her small gifts: flowers at first, trinkets from the market, pieces from the Murano glassblowers, lengths of Burano lace. It wasn't long until their innocent walks progressed past flirtation, straight through the doorway of Julian's rented rooms.

But Serena didn't need to know any of that, so he picked up the story where it seemed relevant. "Luciana was hell-bent on defying her parents' wishes and marrying an English lord. When I came swaggering along at the age of twenty-two, full of naive arrogance, Luciana must have seen me as a walking target.

"I fell immediately for her charms, and I planned to marry her, even though my father would have disowned me if I had arrived home with an Italian bride in tow. He was a moldering old man, and I knew his attitudes were wrong. I was ready to risk my inheritance for her. But somewhere deep inside me, I suspected that her love was neither as deep nor as constant as she pretended it to be. I waited for her to prove me wrong. Impatience got the better of her. She pressed me, and I resisted. All it would have taken was a modicum of loyalty on her part, a few weeks more of playing the devoted young ingenue. But that was too much for Luciana. In a fit of anger, she refused to see me. Less than a month later, I heard that she was to marry Thomas Harcourt, another unwitting English sap, who was also on his Grand Tour. Harcourt was a baron; it was then that I realized I was just an expendable sucker. To her, I was simply a title and a pocketbook. Luciana had never cared for me, and she replaced me as easily as she had found me.

"I was shattered. Even though I had been hesitant, I had fully expected that we would marry. After the shock of her desertion wore off, I went back to England. My father's health was in decline, and I realized it would be in my best interests to return home. I set about accomplishing some of the plans I had begun to make while I was in Venice: improving the lots of the tenants' lives, providing for the education of the children. I lived the life of a country nobleman, shouldering the responsibilities of a benevolent lord.

"I didn't speak to Luciana again for almost ten years. Her name was bandied about in society. I glimpsed her a few times across crowded ballrooms, and once at a museum exhibit. It was rumored among the upper classes that she was a social climber, a ruthless gossip, and that she was cuckolding her husband with his own valet.

"But then one day, she came to me in my town house in London. Years had passed, but she still looked like an exotic flower plucked from an Italian garden, clothed in the finery of an English baroness. But she carried no delicate floral scent. She reeked of desperation. She was gravely discontent with her lot in life. She told me that her husband was beating her. She blamed me for her unhappy marriage. She came to me for comfort."

That moment was branded into his mind—Luciana, dressed in an elaborate embroidered gown of pale lilac silk, on her knees, begging for his company. A soft cashmere shawl trailed across her shoulders. She had let it slip to the floor beside her, an invitation that suggested the rest of her clothes might follow. He'd been lonely, still unmarried at thirty-two. And he had relented. Taken her to his bed. Stripped the fashionable garments from her and mounted her, without regard for her husband or for his own safety.

He glossed over those details to spare Serena, and continued, "It was then that she asked me to help her end it. She wasn't talking about divorce. She wanted me to kill Harcourt. Her husband was ruthless, she claimed. One day she came to me with a broken arm, sobbing because she was convinced he would soon end her life. The only thing that would stop him was death. Of course, by that time, I was a fervent man bent on goodness and justice."

Serena's voice broke through the silence. "And so you killed him?"

Julian nodded, the memory of it shaming him. He had never thought himself capable of killing a man. But he'd believed himself justified in salvaging Luciana from a life-threatening situation. He could still feel Harcourt's blood on his hands, warm and sticky and smelling of rust. Felt the nausea rising out of his gut as he spoke of it, even two centuries later. Only one thing tempered the feeling of self-loathing the memory evoked. And that was the memory of his own lifeblood draining out of him, pooling with Harcourt's as their lives faded away.

"It was inevitable. We dueled over Luciana. Pistols were his weapon of choice. It was a frigid December day when he called me out. We were both excellent marksmen. We both hit our targets. Trailing blood, he crawled across the snow, over the tracks of our paces. And swore to me that he had never harmed a hair on Luciana's head. She'd faked the proof of it—she'd sustained the injury to her arm when she'd fallen off a horse.

"Luciana had simply tired of having him as her husband, Harcourt said, and she wanted an excuse to get rid of him. It was that simple for her. She didn't think twice about using me. Both of us died. Luciana lived another year, the time it took for Harcourt to claw his way out of hell and finish her off himself.

"She caused me to fall. I have never forgiven her for that. Even though, over the years, I have sometimes faltered and succumbed to her charms. There are times when I've even believed she could love."

And times when she had behaved like a monster.

But he had been equally as monstrous. He had ruined countless women, caused so many to fall. Willfully seeking out beauty, he had derived a great deal of pleasure in destroying it. It was an act of vengeance, not just against Luciana, but against God. The God who had allowed his mother to die. The God who had finally delivered him from the hell of his aunt's upbringing, only to strip him down to misery again when his human life ended.

"Whether Luciana had killed anyone before that, I doubt," he said. "But afterward…"

Afterward, he had witnessed her performing countless other acts of torture and murder. Luciana had a complex about aging, although she'd been only twenty-eight when she'd died, and the signs of age had not yet begun to erode her beauty. Once, he'd caught her bathing in a bathtub full of blood taken from virgins. It was an old European beauty trick, she'd claimed. He found out later that she'd heard tales of the seventeenth-century Countess Elizabeth Bathory, a woman who had committed many such heinous murders. Luciana's crimes would have had Serena groveling on her knees for his protection if she knew about them. But Serena was blissfully ignorant, and Julian saw no reason to frighten her.

"Back in England, the life I left behind crumbled into dust. Despite his poor health, my father survived me by thirty years. When the old duke finally died, his estates and all of his possessions ceded to a distant female cousin. There was no male heir, so the title became extinct. From afar, I watched our family legacy dissipate into nothingness."

Serena looked at him with compassion in her eyes. "The legacy you should have continued."

The legacy he didn't deserve. Instead, he began to rebuild.

"As a new demon, there were rules to learn. I had

no property on earth, since everything I had owned reverted back to the estate when my human life ended. I needed to make a living, and I needed to blend in. So I started to work in a village pub, as a barkeep. I was a fast learner, and for the first time in my existence, I understood the value of hard work. The villagers were also easy to manipulate, and provided an amusing distraction from my misery." *Especially the village girls,* he remembered. If he'd been popular with the ladies before his life had ended, as a demon, women had flocked to him.

"From barkeep, I progressed to owning my own tavern. Over the years, I worked and saved, bought another. And another. Little by little, I arrived here in the twenty-first century, the owner of a chain of nightclubs, with a substantial amount of material wealth. Despite my relatively young age for an Archdemon, there were only a handful of others more successful than me. It was my goal to become the most powerful among them. By allying with Corbin, I believe I've surpassed all of them, except for him."

"And now?"

"Now all I want is you. And that's why I need you to save me."

"Save you." She blinked, not knowing what to say. Was he being honest, or was this just part of his game? Why had he revealed himself to her tonight?

"You believe in the healing power of love, don't you?" For a moment, she thought he was joking. But she looked at his face and saw that he was serious.

Is Arielle right? Is there some part of Julian that is still good? she thought wildly.

She shifted, inching away from him on the sofa, where they had been sitting for hours as he spoke. Of course there was no love between them. Perhaps she felt a certain amount of love for him, in the vague, fuzzy sense in which she loved all living beings. Even demons. But love, in the most intimate sense of the word? The romantic sense? Last night, she'd been sure that she *didn't* love him. Did she?

Oh, Lord.

Her hand shook. The remnants of their dinner lay on the cart, now cold. Her stomach growled, she wandered over to the cart, removed the cover from the vegetarian entrée she'd ordered. It was not appealing, so she dropped the plate. Tried to pretend that everything was normal. That nothing had changed between them.

Everything had changed.

Dropping back onto the sofa, she heard the little voice inside her whispering again. She wanted him, she realized. Wanted him to seduce her so she could protest, as she normally did. But he didn't. He was looking at her, she realized, waiting for her to say something. Not knowing what to say, she covered her confusion with a smile.

He wasn't fooled. "Love never fails," he said.

Instantly, her smile dropped away. "How dare you use those words," she said. "Don't talk to me of love when you have dragged me here and kept me against my will."

"You could walk out at any time. There's the door," he said.

"So you'd let Nick go, and leave my friends and family alone?" she challenged, meeting his gaze even though her cheeks burned.

Something flickered in those jeweled depths, but whether it was humor or admiration, she didn't know. "I'm not willing to go that far. I will promise you one thing. I won't take advantage of you tonight. You're a snakebite victim. You haven't much strength. It's been an emotional day."

She sighed, laid her head back into the soft cushions of the sofa and closed her eyes. "Every day with you is an emotional day."

"Poor, tired little angel."

She heard him move. Opened her eyes. He leaned over her so carefully she might have been made of delicate crystal. Brushed a kiss across her lips. Followed it with another, equally as soft.

She felt safe with him. Her defenses were so weak right now that she would have succumbed without an argument. But he didn't even try. Instead, he helped her off the sofa, and gave her a little push in the direction of her bedroom.

"Serena, I am a changed man, I swear to you. We have five days left together. I will prove to you how much I've changed."

For a moment they stood, separated in distance by only a few steps. This time, when she looked in his eyes, what she read there was clear. Desire, yes. But also respect. And a touch of wonder. Her heart raced. She turned, walked calmly into her bedroom and shut the door, as though she hadn't just been witness to something so remarkable, so miraculous that it was unthinkable. Could it be—dare she believe it—could a demon really fall in love?

Chapter Twelve

The next morning, they sat on the sweeping terrace of their suite, breakfasting beneath the cool shade of potted palms. Lounging in his white bathrobe, Julian leaned back in his chair and regarded her as he casually sipped his coffee.

"Nick is going to spend the evenings with Harry while we're here in Vegas," he announced. "My assistant may not be able to handle even a neophyte angel, but he can babysit a human being."

"Nick is *my* responsibility," Serena shot back. "It's my duty to spend time with him, especially at night when he's most vulnerable."

Over the rim of his cup, Julian's blue-green eyes flickered. "Call it outsourcing. Nick will be safer with Harry than he would be with you, Serena. Unlike you, we demons have no qualms with using mind control on humans. It's not my preferred method of operation, but it gets the job done. Would you rather be chasing Nick around Vegas at night, just like you were doing in L.A.?"

"That's my job," she said stubbornly.

"Remember, you came here with *me*. We have a deal."

On that point, Julian was immobile. He would not listen to another word of argument, blocking off all conversation with one of his urbane smiles. But beneath that smile, a deeper emotion lurked, and she knew better than to stir it up. Julian could crush Nick if he wanted to. And if he were given the slightest reason to do it, he might.

The next few days passed in a blur, as Julian lured her deeper into his world of exquisite debauchery. He took her to dine at top-rated restaurants, where he plied her with the most expensive wines. From box seats at a concert, they listened to a famous diva lull a packed auditorium with a love ballad. He brought her to see a magician walk through sheet metal and escape from a locked tank of water. At the Cirque du Soleil, she loved the colorful costumes and the gymnastic feats that seemed to hover on the edge of the mortal realm. Throughout all of it, each time Serena stole a glance at Julian, he was watching her more closely than he watched the performances.

She told herself that his interest was as much an illusion as the magician's tricks, or the exotic acrobat-animals dangling in contorted shapes from the ceiling. Reminded herself that at the end of the week, she would go home to Los Angeles and resume her everyday life. *Without Julian*.

Sitting in darkened theatres with the weight of his hand on her thigh, or his fingers tracing circles on her palm, she knew that somehow, sometime in these past few days, she had fallen in love with him. She knew it in her gut, as surely as she knew she had never felt this way before. Despite his dark exterior, there was a human side to him. Why else would he have left her untouched these past few days?

Nights were the hardest part. The first night, she'd lain awake for hours, waiting for Julian to come to her. When he didn't, her imagination ran wild. She imagined him sleeping, imagined herself getting out of bed, going to him, pressing her body against his. Over and over, she steeled herself against it, knowing that to do so would be her ruin. Unable to focus her mind, her thoughts were repeatedly drawn back to the darkness of Julian's bedroom and the pleasures that lay within it.

Her cherished self-control was slipping. She was a fool for trusting him, and even more of a fool for wanting him. And she knew that. But strangely, rather than praying for their time together to end, she had begun to dread leaving.

In this city of illusions, Serena was losing track of herself.

And Julian was winning.

Her self-control was not the only thing slipping. So was her influence on Nick. Nights were becoming Julian's domain. But in the broad light of day, Serena decided to recover the parts of herself that she felt slipping away. She must get back to yoga, she realized, to guide both herself and her Assignee back to normality.

"Every morning at ten o'clock," she suggested to Nick, "let's meet on the terrace of my suite and do yoga together."

Eager to spend time with her, he happily agreed. They rolled out their yoga mats on the smooth marble.

As the desert heat warmed their bodies, she hoped her teaching would be enough to dissuade Nick from falling into the mounting distractions of Vegas. Feared it wouldn't be enough.

Nick was jealous.

One morning after their yoga session, he and Serena soaked in the blazing rays of the sun beside the private pool reserved for the hotel's most elite guests. She could feel Nick's gaze even behind the mirrored lenses of his sunglasses, roaming over the stretch of flesh bared by her bikini. But she was comfortable with her own body, and she decided to simply ignore him, willing platonic thoughts into her Assignee's head. However, the tension proved too much for him.

"Are you sleeping with him?" Nick demanded flat out.

She shifted in her deck chair, resisting the urge to wrap a towel around herself as he stared at her curves. "No."

"Has he tried?"

"None of your business," she answered curtly.

"It *is* my business," Nick insisted, leaning toward her with that earnestness that took her by surprise. He slid the sunglasses to the top of his head and gave her a long, searching look. "You met him through me, in a way. There's more going on here than meets the eye. I think Julian might be…"

Does he know? she wondered.

"…Mafia," Nick finished in a conspiratorial whisper.

She resisted the urge to laugh. Oh, if it were only that simple. She supposed Julian *was* mafia—just not the human kind. Serena let out a long sigh. "Don't worry, Nick. Julian and I are not together."

Still not entirely convinced, Nick relaxed a fraction nonetheless. "Good. You need to be careful around him. He's very dangerous."

Nick was right. Julian *was* dangerous. He said he had changed—he vowed it on a daily basis. But he had voiced no plans to stop the opening of his nightclub, nor to halt the damage caused by the dozens of other clubs he owned. Next week, he would begin corrupting thousands more souls on a nightly basis. If anything, Julian was only going to get worse.

Her Assignee settled back in his chair, content for the moment to lounge and allow the passersby to discreetly ogle his perfectly etched abs. She sighed, thinking about the divine mission the Archangel Gabriel had mentioned. Gabriel's words seemed to indicate a responsibility that extended beyond lounging poolside with her Assignee. If she had been sent here to stop Julian's corruption, she had no idea how she, a newly minted angel, was going to accomplish that. She had no weapons with which to fight him, and he was slowly wearing away at her defenses. She no longer trusted herself.

When she looked over at Nick again, he was gazing at her with something like adoration. In a soft voice, he said, "He can never love you the way you deserve, you know."

Love. Nick was right about that, too. In fact, he was proving himself to be much less vacant than he'd originally seemed.

"I'm not looking for love right now," she said. *Or ever.* Serena closed her eyes and felt the sun's rays soak into her face. Long ago, she had reconciled herself to the fact that she was never going to experience romantic love. It was simply not in the cards for her. And especially not with Julian.

On Thursday night, Julian and Serena joined Corbin for dinner.

When Corbin had extended the invitation, Julian knew he could not refuse. They were not friends, but nor were they enemies. To preserve the business relationship, Julian knew it was vital to keep his partner placated. Especially since Corbin had gotten rid of Luciana. Yet, Corbin was dangerous, and Julian knew he could pose a threat to Serena.

Having drinks in the restaurant lounge, though, the three of them made an awkward trio. Without Luciana or Nick, there was nothing to divert the tensions that ran between them. Without Nick, there was no lightness to the conversation. And without Luciana, there was nothing to distract the hotelier's gaze from Serena. The older Archdemon's eyes missed nothing. Corbin watched Serena walk across the room after he'd sent her to request a song from the jazz ensemble playing there.

"There's a sparkle in your eye I've never seen before, my boy. Come up to my suite tonight," Corbin insisted, his gaze still fixed on the girl. "I'm having company later. Bring your little angel or not, but if you do, be prepared to share her."

At that moment, Julian realized the impact of what he'd done. He'd jeopardized something he loved. Corbin's interest had fixed on her, and he was ruthless in satiating his desires. Serena returned to the table and sat, oblivious to the danger she was in. The danger Julian had put her in. He would send her home first thing tomorrow morning. There was no way he was going to keep her any longer.

If Corbin decided he wanted her, he would take her. There would be nothing playful or joyous in it. He would simply maul her physically and spiritually, leaving the empty husk of her violated body. Corbin had done this to countless mortal women. There was nothing stopping him from doing it to Serena.

Tomorrow morning, Julian would locate Luciana—wherever she had gone after Corbin had kicked her out—and impress upon her the necessity of leaving Serena alone. And then he would release the angel. Tonight, he would find a woman and release the terrible urge that was building inside of him.

Sex with a stranger would be good for him. He was a mess. He had endured five days of this peculiar and painful type of torture, and it could not go on. He would get rid of Serena, flush her out of his system.

Having made his decision, he felt somewhat better. Serena was not for him. She was a pretty thing he could admire for the few remaining hours he would spend with her, and then she would become a memory, a bright reminder of true beauty in two and a half centuries of falseness and facades.

After dinner, Julian and Serena returned to the suite. He poured himself a glass of whisky and paced around the living room like an animal pacing the limits of its cage.

"You seem restless tonight," she said, a touch of

anxiousness clouding her sky-bright eyes as she watched him. "We could go out somewhere. Find a club if you'd like, or go play the tables."

She had never before offered to spend time with him. At every opportunity, she had fought him. Now, suddenly, after he'd made his decision, she looked at him with that sort of pleading in her eyes that he had seen in the eyes of countless women before her. But she was utterly unlike any woman he'd ever known. She was everything he had ever wanted, but could not have.

"I'm not in the mood," he said, looking her straight in the eye, unwavering in his dishonesty. He had lied like this so many times before that it came naturally, the words rolling easily off his tongue. Yet, lying had never before sparked in him this feeling of being slightly hot and uncomfortable. He shook it off and said, "Corbin is hosting a networking event. Strictly business, you understand."

There was nothing he wanted more than to pull her into his arms and make love to her. He needed to get out of here. His desires were building up fast, and if he stayed here alone with her any longer, he was going to crack. He smiled his urbane smile.

She said nothing, but sank onto the sofa, draped there like some Grecian goddess in another sumptuous gown, this one of dove-gray silk. There was something in her eyes—something smoldering there. A wanting. She was calling to him. She traced her hand along the neckline of the dress. "We could stay in for the evening. Together." Her voice was full of meaning.

"I imagine it would bore you," he said. He turned

away, unable to bear looking at her. He made a quick call on his cell phone, arranged for a Gatekeeper to sit outside the suite while he was gone. "I'm putting a guard on the door. I won't be long," he said. He swept out the door and didn't look back.

Corbin's suite was a playboy's fantasy. Gorgeous women and trays of champagne circulated. Corbin always had an eye for premium goods. Most of the girls were half naked or in even more advanced states of undress. In the corners of the room, exotic dancers performed on platforms, slithering up and down stripper poles doing acrobatic tricks worthy of a Romanian gymnastics team. With a little more luck, they might have been aiming for the Olympics. Instead, they were here, dancing topless, at this hub of debauchery.

After five days with Serena, he was hot and ready to go. The party was just beginning to pick up—he could feel it pulsing with raw energy, ready to take a turn to the truly wild. It was almost enough to make him forget about the angel he'd left alone downstairs. *Almost.*

From out of the crowd, Corbin appeared, a blonde on each arm like a young Hugh Hefner. The only thing he was missing was a smoking jacket. He gave Julian a hearty slap on the back. "Glad you could make it."

As if he'd had any doubt. Julian smiled coolly. "Wouldn't have missed it for the world."

"What can I get you? A drink? A girl?" Corbin grabbed a glass of champagne from a passing tray, offered it to him. Julian shook his head, made a beeline to the bar. Tonight, he needed something harder—something that would knock out his senses and the scent of

Serena, erase the feel of his fingers tangling through the silk of that miraculous golden hair. Something that would make him forget.

For a demon with two and a half centuries of experience, Julian was almost as bad a liar as Serena.

She slumped on the sofa, staring at the door that he had just shut, her heart racing. He had never been this transparent, never allowed his pent-up emotions to simmer so close to the surface. Something was wrong. When he walked out the door, he had torn her heart out. He wasn't going to a business meeting. That was for sure. Julian had not left her side for five days, and the idea that he would have left her now, for the reason he'd stated, when they had so little time left together, seemed highly unlikely.

Something had shifted in him. And something had shifted in her, as well. It was impossible to deny. The handful of days they had spent together felt like an eternity. Something deep inside of her, something beyond all rationality, had taken root. A tendril of something wondrous had grown. That tendril reached out to him now.

She had seen the goodness that still existed within Julian, exactly as Arielle had told her. *Make him see it in himself.* But how could Serena do that when he was dead set on betraying the goodness within himself? And dead set on betraying *her*.

Serena had seen the look of longing he tried to hide behind his veneer of sophistication. And she could smell the betrayal coming off him. He had physical desires, physical needs, and he intended to slake them. She knew it as surely as she knew her own name.

Then again, there was nothing to betray. They had made no promises to each other. There was no love between them. Was there?

She didn't know. But the little voice inside of her said, *Go. Stop him.*

She opened the door. Julian was not taking chances. It was the first time he'd left her in days, but he'd left a Gatekeeper outside the door. The demon sat on a chair in the hallway, stoically staring into space. Beside him, a goblin sat on the floor, cackling to itself as it pored through the contents of a woman's purse, undoubtedly stolen from some unwitting tourist downstairs.

The Gatekeeper smiled amiably. "Hello, miss."

She gave him her prettiest smile back, hoping that would soften him.

The demon's name was Simon. He seemed to be a nice enough fellow, well mannered and polite, probably because he feared recrimination from Julian. But he showed no signs of letting her leave. "Mr. Ascher warned me about you. Said you'd try to talk me into letting you go. Unfortunately, I just can't do that, miss," Simon said, folding his arms across his bulky chest.

The goblin, hideous little watchdog on the floor beside its master, gave her an evil grin.

How, just how am I going to get out of here?

"I'm really sorry to have to do this to you, Simon. You seem like a nice guy," she said, hoping the trick up her sleeve would work. It was the last option she had left. But it was worth a try. It had not worked with Julian the night she'd met him at Devil's Paradise, but

Julian was infinitely stronger than the Gatekeeper he'd left to guard her. The question was, was the Gatekeeper stronger than *her?*

"Do what, miss?" Simon asked, frowning.

She concentrated hard, willing a bright light into his head. The harder she focused, the brighter the light became.

Simon raised a massive hand to squeeze his temples. "Shit, that hurts."

She concentrated harder. The light gained intensity, a blinding orb of energy that pulsed through his brain. He clutched his head, the agony dropping him from his seat to roll on the floor.

Serena ran.

The goblin scrambled after her, squealing in rage like a stuck pig. She gave it a vicious kick and sent it sprawling into a wall. Bolting down the hallway, she jammed on the elevator button.

Come on, come on.

Down the hall, she could see Simon lumbering to his feet, clutching his head in pain. Just in time, the elevator bell pinged and the doors slid open. Inside, she hit the button for the penthouse, and at the same time jammed her finger on the button to slide the doors closed.

Catching her breath as the elevator made its ascent to the top of the hotel, she smoothed her hair, willing her heartbeat to slow.

Yet another Gatekeeper guarded the penthouse suite, this one bigger and meaner-looking than Simon. Outside in the hallway, music, laughter and cocktail chatter drifted from the party. The Gatekeeper loomed over her, running his eyes over her outfit with the kind of leer that made her want to cross her arms over her chest.

She gave him a big, sunny smile. "I was invited to Mr. Ranulfson's networking event tonight, but I'm afraid I lost my invitation."

The Gatekeeper smirked. "Girls don't need no invitation tonight. But this ain't no networking event."

"I was speaking euphemistically," Serena said, covering quickly. *I knew it.*

"Huh?" he snorted. Clearly, he'd been hired for his size and not his brain capacity.

"I meant a *networking event,* if you catch my drift," she said, with a lewd wink. "I'm in *business,* you know. A *working girl,*" she said, hoping he'd catch the hint.

He eyed her gray silk dress. "You're not like the rest of Josie's girls," he said frowning. "You look, you know…classy."

"Thanks, I think," she muttered as he finally opened the door.

She walked inside, feeling a shudder rack through her body. Corbin's suite was enormous. The Gatekeeper ushered her through the circular vestibule down a long hallway, which opened into a high-ceilinged space. Enormous windows showcased a spectacular view of the Vegas Strip at night. Perforated brass lanterns were strung across the room, light twinkling through cutout stars that hung over the clustered guests. It was not a huge party, but it seemed to be an exclusive one, at least from the male perspective. There were far more women here than men. And the women were all clearly professionals, hired for the occasion. It was certainly no networking event.

She glanced around, looking for a sign of Julian. When she found none, she pushed deeper into the party.

Fingertips traced down the exposed skin at the back of her neck. She knew before she turned—it was not Julian. She whirled to find Corbin standing behind her. He bent low and swept a kiss over the back of her hand. He played the part of the charming and successful entrepreneur, rather than the lecherous demon host of a party where all the female guests had been bought and paid for. Yet, the latter part of him ebbed, barely hidden beneath the surface of the facade he wore for her benefit.

"So glad you could join us, my dear. I wasn't expecting you, but I'm pleased you came," Corbin said. He handed her a glass of champagne.

She forced a thin smile, took a sip of champagne to cover her dismay. Julian might be beholden to this man, but when she looked at the older Archdemon, she felt nothing but fear. She saw what he was—pure evil— and no amount of grooming or ambiance could cover that up. Unfortunately, at this moment, she stood at the epicenter of his power, at the mercy of his legion of minions.

So she maintained her smile and said, "Have you seen Julian?"

"He said he wasn't going to bring you," he said slowly, running a finger up her bare arm. "Does this mean it's open season?"

Being touched by Corbin was like being brushed by a rat that had been wallowing in a landfill. She steeled herself not to move. It would not do to start a fight. "I'm not prey," she told him.

"Too bad. I thought wings were on the menu tonight." He traced his fingers along her back, following the curve of her shoulder blade. "They're my favorite. Wouldn't you like to give me a taste?"

His hand swept down to cup her buttock, and she jumped, shocked at his touch. She tried to back away, but Corbin's hands were too quick, reaching for her before she could escape. Where was Julian when she needed him?

Please, God, don't let Corbin hurt me, she prayed.

In another of the many rooms in Corbin's penthouse, Julian reclined on a bed, watching an exotic dancer grinding around a pole directly in front of him. How thoughtful that Corbin should have accommodated his guests' needs so thoroughly that such an amenity was a built-in feature.

It was a room designed for sex—not just the pole, but the mirrored ceiling, the muted lighting, the garishly ornate bed with its covers of burnished copper silk. The girl who danced for him had introduced herself as Lexus, at which point he'd almost laughed out loud and asked why nobody ever chose Toyota or Volvo as stripper names. She was clad only in a silver-colored bra, a matching G-string and a pair of platform heels. Lexus arched and turned, showing off her tight, curvaceous body in a way that Serena would never do for him. He should just reach out right now and take her, this girl who was so intent on pleasing him, as Serena was not.

The dancer bore some resemblance to Serena—they had the same long fall of blond hair, the same wide-eyed youth—which was why he had selected her. But Lexus might as well have been born of a different species from Serena, they were so fundamentally incomparable. For all her grinding and gyrating, her big breasts and her firm ass, nothing about the stripper turned him on.

He took a swig from the bottle of gin he'd finagled from the bartender and tried to concentrate on getting it up.

The girl released from the pole, reached behind her back and unclasped her bra. Her impressive breasts sprang forward, dark nipples puckered, already erect. He should be panting for her by now, but he felt nothing. She moved onto the bed, crawling toward him on all fours. He inhaled her perfume. It was not a cheap scent, but it was still somehow sticky and cloying.

She straddled him, pushing her tits toward his face. He reached out, fondled one, rolled the nipple between his fingertips. Closed his eyes, tried to pretend she was Serena. But her breasts were implants, firmer and denser to the touch than Serena's natural curves. She moaned, "Yeah, baby," but that was also fake.

On any given night before he'd met Serena, he would have found this stripper sexy, but instead he'd had enough. "Sorry, sweetheart. Not tonight." Pushing Lexus off him, he ignored her disappointed sigh. He extracted his wallet from his back pocket, took out a few hundred dollars and tucked the bills in the side of her G-string.

She stroked his thigh, inching her hand up toward

his groin. "You sure, sugar? You don't have to pay me. I'd do it free of charge. I'll let you drive."

Wincing at the pun on her name, he tossed her an extra couple of hundred. "It's not you, gorgeous. My mind's somewhere else."

He picked up the bottle of gin and headed into the hallway. For an instant, he paused, wanting to go back down to the suite he shared with Serena. But he was not sure what would happen if he did. He couldn't trust himself to be near her. He was raging with need—a need that no other woman could fill.

Then he caught a scent on the air, subtle but distinct. A hint of something too fresh, too innocent to be in this debauched place. He moved toward the main room, seeking it like a wolf following the scent of its next meal, wanting a taste of prey to satisfy his burning hunger.

Serena was there, pressed against the edge of a table, cringing away from Corbin's seeking hands. Julian charged forward.

Corbin backed away instantly, a hound releasing a captured rabbit from its jaws, caught poaching on another's land. "Ah, there you are, old chap."

Her face relaxed when she saw Julian, and she leaned toward him, eyes eager and pleading. *Don't. I'm no better than Corbin,* he thought. She was too innocent. She did not deserve to be mauled by demons, himself included. But he wasn't sure whether he could stop himself. He held out a hand. Wide-eyed, she took it.

Neither of them spoke as he led her away from Corbin. He wanted her alone, now. He dragged her into the bedroom he'd just vacated, slammed the door and locked it behind him.

Only when he heard the click of the lock did he realize what a mistake he had made in bringing her here. There was nowhere to look but the bed. That was the last thought that shot through his mind before it went blank with desire.

The bottle of gin he held clattered to the floor.

"Thank you for rescuing me," she said. Her voice washed over him, fluid tones of a siren's call. He saw the subtle glimmer in her eye and knew what she offered.

This was hardly a rescue, and she knew it. *He* was the one who had lured her here to begin with, against her will. To Vegas. To this hotel. To this room.

"You don't belong here," he ground out. His own voice was rougher than asphalt, rasping in his parched throat. "Go home."

Ignoring his warning completely, she sauntered toward him, crossing the floor in a few long strides. Took a spin around the stripper's pole. Grasped it with one hand and spiraled like a seasoned dancer. He tried to avert his gaze. But he couldn't tear his eyes away.

She wound her body around the pole. The smile hovering on her lips was more playful than seductive. But her movements showcased the litheness of her body. He blinked hard, trying to clear the illusion from his sight. When he opened his eyes, she was still there. Beckoning. Teasing. In the lean stretch of her body, he saw the formula of ideal proportions at work. He watched the camber of her hips, subtle counterpoint to the curves of her breasts as she experimented with the pole, arching and turning. Not as smoothly as Lexus, but a thousand times more seductive.

He itched for her to continue, to shed the confines of her dress and let him prostrate himself before the splendor of her nudity. Instead, he muttered what he *should* say. What he *ought* to say. "Stop it, this isn't you. Don't do this for my benefit. Where did you even learn to dance like that, anyway?"

Her tiny smile flickered, taunting him. "There are pole-dancing classes on college campuses. Even soccer moms do Cardio Striptease at the gym these days. It's perfectly innocent."

It was not innocent. *She* was not innocent. Not tonight.

His cock twitched in his pants, hardening as he watched her. The dim lighting turned her pearl-gray minidress to liquid silver that poured over her flushed skin as she danced. His brain grasped for some semblance of sanity. When had she managed to invert their roles? His mind scrambled to pinpoint that moment. But all rational thought escaped him now.

He must regain control. He was the master of temptation, not its servant. The seducer, not the seduced. Hunter, not hunted.

He must let her go. He must *force* her to go, immediately. Push her away so that she would be far from the stain of his touch. Clearing his throat, he moistened his dry lips and spoke. "Didn't you hear me? You're free to go. Back to L.A., back to your little yoga studio, where you're safe."

Instead, she released the pole and moved toward the opulent bed. The click of her heels on the marble floor echoed over the muted sounds of the party outside. She brushed past where he stood. Trailed her fingers across his chest—nothing more—then sank to sit on the bed's edge. So close he inhaled the scent of her: fragrance of amber, cinnamon and female arousal.

Then she leaned back on her elbows, with the ease of a she-lion stretching in a patch of sunlight. Displayed herself for his benefit, her blond hair spilling against the bronze bedclothes. Dangled a shoe off the toe of one foot. Tilted her head to one side so that a feathery lock of hair fell across her high cheekbone. Slowly, ever so slowly, she reached up to flip it away. In the same instant, she raised her eyelids, licked her lips and gave him the sultriest come-hither look he had ever had the supreme pleasure of witnessing.

He raised his voice to a roar, trying to scare her. "Who do you think I am? Do you want me to make you fall?"

"I won't fall." She didn't even blink. She looked up at him through inky lashes, fully aware of her own sensuality and shockingly adept at using it. "There's no passage in the Christian Bible that specifically forbids sex between unmarried people. It's not in the Torah, either. Nor does Buddhism forbid premarital sex, as long as it's consensual and doesn't harm others. I know what's in my heart," she said. "I want to share my body with you."

She was enough to test the patience of a saint. Last time he'd checked, his application for canonization had been denied. He didn't stand a chance. His hands burned to touch her; he curled them into fists to stop himself from reaching out. "Don't even suggest it. Serena, I'm a demon. Any intimate contact with me would be unclean. Immoral."

"Then come to me not as a demon, but as a man," she said, her voice dropping to a whisper. "Whatever you've done, you will be forgiven."

Would he? Staring into the vivid clarity of her eyes, he actually wanted redemption. Longed for it as he had never done before, not in all the centuries of his existence.

He heard her high heels drop to the floor, first one then the other. She posed on the bed with her breasts accentuated, the molten silk of her minidress sliding over her. The dress stopped midthigh. She shifted so it rode higher.

What she wore beneath it was pure sacrilege—a scrap of black lace trimmed with scarlet that caught his gaze and brought him to the edge of delirium.

His hands fisted so tight the muscles of his forearms strained. "You're too naive to realize what will happen to you. You exist in a world of rainbows and butterfly wings. Look around you. Do you know where you are? You're in a demon's lair. Unless you want to stay here forever, *get out*."

That little smile flickered. "I know what I'm doing."

He came to stand by the side of the bed, uncurled his fingers and looked down at her. "You don't. I'm going to destroy you."

"I don't think that's possible, but I'll take my chances."

She was determined to undo him. He was already undone. He tried, one last time. Tried to steel himself to drag her from the bed, out the door. But it was futile. His resistance had been worn away by stages, the way a river erodes rock. Every minute he spent without touching her seemed like a year. Now, after what felt like eons, his defenses had been worn to their foundation. She offered an enticement he couldn't resist.

He leaned down and kissed her, licked open her lips. She tasted of champagne, intense and provocative. Addicting. Her lips parted as a sigh of pleasure broke from her throat. He drank it in.

Free-falling into that heady space, he dove deeper, hands mapping out the places he was coming to memorize, roaming over the contours of her breasts, the flat terrain of her toned belly. His lips set about unlocking the secret places he was still learning to navigate: the spot beneath her ear, the curve of her jawline, the tender divot between her collarbones. His fingers tangled in the brightness of her hair, curled in the sterling of her dress.

Raising his head, he paused, waiting. The room was loud with the sound of their mingled breathing, shallow gasps of craving that echoed off the walls and reverberated in the crevices his unfulfilled infatuation had carved inside him. Their union would mean the certain destruction of them both. He half expected the floor to open and swallow them, right then and there.

When it didn't, he kissed her again. Dared both God and the devil to take them.

He had made his choice.

Chapter Thirteen

In the moment before he kissed her, Serena lay on that burnished silk bed, watching him deliberate over his choice. He stood utterly still for an instant that seemed to stretch into an eternity. His jaw was so tight she could see the muscles of it flexing. A small vein emerged in the middle of his forehead, a valve about to blow.

She should leave now. Take his offer and walk out the door, as she'd wished so many times in the past five days. Shut all memory of him into an iron box in the very back of her mind and never open the lid. She closed her eyes for a moment, staring into the blue-black darkness behind her closed eyelids.

I won't fall…I know what I'm doing. What brought her to speak such brave words a moment ago, she had no idea. But the little voice inside her that she had ignored so long—the one that regretted leaving her human life behind so early, that yearned to experience love—that tiny whisper would no longer remain silent.

She thought of Arielle's words, also: *Keep love in your heart.* Sex was a physical manifestation of love. If she kept love in her heart, surely she would always be safe. She had understood that as she'd lain dying in that canyon, and as he'd rescued her from that beautiful death.

When she'd first come to Vegas, she'd prayed to be released, to go home. Now, faced with a choice, she prayed he would want her to stay. Because even though she had seen the goodness in him, she still needed to make him see it in himself.

Then he reached down and slid his hand beneath her neck, bent to kiss her. Strong yet gentle, dangerous yet infinitely tender, his lips descended on hers, claiming, capturing, drugging her into a haze of desire. His mouth ventured across her cheek to envelop her earlobe, his breath echoing in her ear. She opened her eyes. In the mirrored ceiling, she saw them reflected, her bright hair splayed against the copper-hued silk, and on top of her, the broadness of his back as he leaned over her.

That voice inside her, which had now risen to a roar, shouted, *Yes!*

"Not here," he said, his voice low and gruff. "Come."

He led her out of the suite, past Corbin's party guests, into the elevator. At the door of their own suite, Julian slid his card in the lock. At that moment, he turned to look back at her and asked, "Are you sure you want to do this?"

"If you keep asking, I might change my mind," she answered.

He bent low, swept a kiss across the back of her hand. "But then you'd miss all the fun." He went to the stereo and selected something low and sultry. He dimmed the lights. Then he kissed her. As his lips brushed over hers, she sank against him, all urge to resist gone out of her. Tonight, all she wanted was to love him.

He took her hand and led her into the bedroom. When he moved to turn on the light, she stopped him. "Leave it," she said. He shrugged. Light spilled in from the hallway, illuminating the room without the brightness of lights overhead.

With infinite care, he bent down and kissed the place she'd been bitten, where the puncture wounds of the snakebite had healed over. "Perfect," he said. "You are perfect in every way."

"So are you," she said. "You just don't realize it."

He shook his head, sorrowfully. Painfully. "I'm the antithesis of perfect, Serena. I'm everything that is evil."

"Every being is divine. Even demons. I think you've just made a mistake."

"Then how do I get to the other side?"

"Love," she said. Then she kissed him, fearlessly. She had no fear of him—love had washed it away.

His hands moved over her, sliding over her curves. This was no slow exploration of her body. This time, he was ravenous for her. She knew that nothing short of a lightning bolt sent from the heavens would stop him. She answered his passion, kissing him back with equal fervor. She ran her fingers through his hair, reveled in its softness. His scent enveloped her: the sensuous notes of his expensive cologne mingling with the scent of pure man.

They stripped out of their clothes, fingers fumbling, made suddenly clumsy with wanting and speed. Panting, he lowered her onto the bed and levered himself over her, laying his weight carefully along her, one knee pressing into the space between her thighs. He kissed a trail leading down the side of her neck, across her chest to the tops of her breasts, lower, to her stomach, and lower still.

He stripped off her panties, pausing as his gaze roamed over the freshly waxed curves of her pubic mound. "Beautiful," he murmured, a little smile playing around the corners of his lips.

"I've spent so much time at the spa in the past few days, and I..." She blushed, too embarrassed to admit that she had known it would come to this.

"Hush, darling. No need to explain. It was a thoughtful gesture, and you deserve to be thanked." He reached a hand forward to touch her, gently sliding his fingertips over her pubic mound to explore the bare folds of her. He caressed her closed slit, feeling the satin softness of the skin. Then he nudged her to open wider, so that the lips parted, exposing her wetness and the delicate peak of her clit. His gaze lit, fixed between her legs as though he had discovered a rare jewel. Featherlight, he brushed his fingers up the insides of her lips, deliberately avoiding her clit. "You are the most beautiful thing I've ever seen."

He continued to explore, teasing her until she tilted her hips upward, wanting more. He slipped a finger into the moist core of her, slowly testing the grip of her body. He inserted another finger, stretching her, and muttered, "God, you're so tight."

Then he dipped his head between her parted legs. His tongue swept over her in long strokes, delving repeatedly into her opening, plunging as far as it could reach until it retreated to travel upward, along the sides of her lips. He paused, his hot breath fanning her skin. Finally, he kissed the sensitive bud of her clit. It was no more than a whisper of contact at first, a mere brush of his lips over her wanting flesh. Then he laved his tongue over it, hot velvet drawing over her. And again. He lapped slowly, urging her hips to rock with his rhythm. His tongue moved lower, to drive again into the opening to her body. Retraced its path upward to flick her clit with the tip of his tongue. She arched upward, lost in the pleasure of it.

He filled his hands with her ass, kneading her buttocks, and growled a low, guttural sound of appreciation. Then he dove in, licking and sucking and driving her so wild that she grasped the sheets in handfuls to keep from bucking off the bed. He reached up and circled the nipple of one breast with his fingertips, pinching it until she almost came.

"I want you inside me," she gasped. "I want to feel you moving in me."

He sat up, wiping his mouth with the back of his hand. Instead of his twitching erection, he slid his middle finger into her, circled her clit with his thumb. She closed around it, instinctively clutching for more. "I want you to beg me for it. You've been such a tease all week. I want to hear you say it."

She shifted on the bed, pinioned there by a single finger.

"See how it feels to be teased?" His smile was sin incarnate. He waited for her to beg, but she would not relent.

She narrowed her eyes, "You're a bastard."

He kissed her, long and deep, driving his finger farther into her. Waiting, he withdrew his finger, traced her own moistness across her nipple. "Say it. Say the magic words."

She gazed into the brightness of his blue-green eyes. "Fuck you."

He laughed. "No, those are not the magic words." He took his thick cock in his hand, rubbed its head in her slit until his erection was slick with her desire. Close to her ear, his breath was hot on her neck. "Say it," he whispered. "Say it or I won't do it." He teased her clit with his cock, playing there until she panted and whimpered.

She reached down, closing her hand over his, running her thumb over the crown of his glorious penis. "I can wait. We'll see who does the begging."

She rolled so that she was on top of him, slid down the length of his body, tracing the same path that his mouth had taken on hers. From his muscled chest, she kissed down the chiseled plane of his stomach, traced her fingers through his curling pubic hair before she stopped to admire his impressive manhood. She took a moment to study it, for the first time examining the veins that traced the smooth skin of the shaft, the ridge that ran beneath it. He watched her, his gaze intense with anticipation.

Then she ran her tongue along the ridge, licking up the length of him up to the head of his cock, where a clear drop had emerged. Tasted the saltiness of it. She took him into her mouth, swirling her tongue around the head of his cock, then flicking it over the ridge as he pressed his hips upward.

He moved to kneel, and she shifted to her knees, as well, arching her back and supporting herself with one hand while she wrapped the other around his male hardness. He gathered her hair in his hands, gently cradling her head as she sucked his cock, taking in as much of him as she could. He might have driven for the back of her throat, but she kept her hand around him, controlling exactly how far he could thrust, savoring the feel of him in her mouth. She drew her other hand down the hard muscles of his thighs, reached beneath to caress his balls. She sucked until she sensed that he was close to orgasm, then she took him out of her mouth, kissing and licking more gently to bring him back from the brink.

Pushing him down, she climbed on top, legs straddling him. Instead of pulling him inside her, she hesitated. She lowered herself so that her pussy was poised above his twitching cock, and rubbed herself against his hard shaft so that he groaned. "Who's going to do the begging now?" she whispered.

She looked down into the blue-green depths of his eyes, saw them glittering with humor. Then he rolled, switching their position so that he was on top, nestled between her widespread thighs. "It seems that neither of us is in the mood to beg tonight," he said, lowering his head to brush a conciliatory kiss across her lips.

He guided himself to her opening, then he slowly inserted himself into her, pausing an inch inside of her as she gasped at the size of him. She blinked, trying to breathe deeply as she shifted to accommodate him. He waited, bending to kiss her hairline. "Are you all right?" She nodded, and his cock pressed farther, stretching her with every inch, pushing deeper into the core of her until she thought she would faint from the ecstasy of it. "That's it, sweetheart," he said. "Take all of me."

With one hand, he grasped her hip, his fingers digging into soft flesh. She ran her fingernails gently up his back, clung to his shoulders as he pumped into her. The pleasure built, rising to a pitch so exquisite she wished she could keep him inside of her forever. He reached down and slid his hand between them, stimulating her clit in slow circles with his fingers as he thrust.

The moment of her climax came with a flash of lucid truth: he was neither demon nor human, but pure energy, light that shone so brightly it merged with the light that was her light. She knew, beyond a doubt, that he was not merely himself, she was not merely herself; they were both part of the universal energy that encompassed the existence of all living beings.

Entering her was the sweetest thing he'd ever felt. In two centuries of existence, he'd experienced nothing like it. It was like coming home. He felt his body dissolving, not like he felt when he was dematerializing, but as though he were merging with a shower of ethereal gold. The light wrapped around him, melted into him.

He rode the waves of her orgasm, grinding his hips into her so that the tip of his engorged cock, so deep inside her, seemed to touch the very heart of her. He came with her, pouring his pleasure, his elation, his joy into her body, like a deluge of rain pouring from the heavens onto a parched plain.

For a moment, they lay still together, joined at that sacred place. His cock pulsed inside her as the last drop throbbed out of him. He rested on top of her, wanting to stay inside her body forever.

Time seemed to stretch, to elongate, measured out by a new scale where every inhalation was momentous, and every exhalation, a precious event. He wanted to stay here, like this, forever. Not moving, not speaking. Just being. He felt her breathing with him, synchronized as though the flesh and bone and blood of their bodies could bridge the divide between heaven and hell.

Finally, he pulled himself out of her and rolled to one side, covered in sweat and gasping for breath as if he'd just run a marathon. He glanced over. She lay with one knee bent upward, an arm flung over her head and the other hand resting on the stretch of her stomach. He could see her ribs where her skin drew over them, wanted to count them from the bottom upward, until they merged into her magnificent breasts. He could not believe she had just allowed him to take her. Not simply allowed him. Had coaxed and cajoled him to be with her. He felt privileged and proud like he never had before.

Before, sex had been about pleasure, and about other, darker things: temptation, humiliation, exploitation. In two hundred years of debauching women, it had never occurred to him that sex could be like this. He had always ridiculed the idea that intercourse could be about spiritual union. Possibly because he had never experienced it himself. But *this*. This was an elevation of consciousness, and the moment had been eternal. He had felt himself merging with her, and more than their bodies had united. It was as though their souls had fused, and not simply during the moment of copulation.

They were linked, he and she. He wasn't sure if he could ever go back.

And it scared the shit out of him.

Well, it hardly mattered anyway. Frankly, he was surprised she hadn't already disappeared, sucked into an abyss that opened up in the floor, or struck by a lightning bolt cast down by her puritanical god. In the morning, certainly, she would be gone, sent to hell by divine wrath.

And he would go on doing what he'd always done. Corrupting humans. But now, he would live in a special hell of his own: a world without Serena. It was a punishment only Satan himself could have dreamed up. Julian would probably even get a promotion. The thought of it made him want to fight, to kick and scream, to punch a hole in the wall. But he knew his rage was useless.

If things had been different, if they'd been human, he would have claimed her for his own. Taken her in his arms and never let her go. But they were not human. He was a demon, and she, for one last glorious night, was an angel. And since they were to have only one night together, there was no time to waste.

His cock twitched, not quite recovered from their first round of lovemaking, but already rising to attention again. He reached out and closed his hand over her luscious breast.

In Corbin's bedroom, Luciana lounged in an armchair next to the bed, her raven tresses curling over her pale, naked breasts. Outside, the party raged on, the music seeping through the walls, accompanied by shrieks of laughter and the occasional orgasm. Corbin reclined on a pile of pillows among the rumpled bed-clothes, running his hands idly along the lush curves of the showgirl he had just had sex with. Luciana watched, although she was somewhat bored after all of the girls he'd had tonight.

"How much longer must I hide in here? It's no fun, spending all day alone," she said, toying with a silk stocking she'd tossed onto the floor earlier.

Corbin lifted his head, fixed his tawny gaze on her. "Aren't you having fun, darling? You know that if you leave this suite, Julian will be able to track you. As long as you're here, you are under my protection. You'll just have to keep yourself occupied for a few more days until we've caught Julian in our trap. Be patient. Didn't you enjoy the aesthetician I sent up from the spa today? You have a refreshed glow about you."

Luciana thought about the facial she'd had this after-noon. The little aesthetician had been so talented, truly gifted at her trade. Afterward, with a single flick of her practiced wrist, Luciana had snapped the girl's neck. She had the Gatekeepers drain the body and dispose of the corpse while Corbin was away, and then gave herself a lovely facial with the girl's blood. She eyed the show-girl who was now stroking Corbin's enormous member, ready for another round. Corbin flicked his tongue over the girl's nipple; she giggled and threw her head back, her honey-blond hair spilling down her back and onto the bed beneath her.

"I detest being cooped up," Luciana pouted, barely entertained as Corbin frolicked with the showgirl. "But I can't wait until we get our hands on Julian's little puritan of an angel," she said. Corbin's eyes flared, his mouth still lapping at the showgirl's breasts. He maneuvered his face between the girl's legs, and bent to taste her, staring into Luciana's eyes as he did so.

He would tire of this human quickly enough. And after that, the showgirl might share the fate of this afternoon's aesthetician. Corbin probably already had plans for her. Sometimes he liked to dismember human women after he'd had his way with them, just for the fun of listening to them scream. Once, she'd seen him cannibalize the body of a human woman who was still alive, the blood running down his chin as he savored the taste of her living flesh. The thought of it made Luciana shiver, even in the heat of Corbin's too-warm bedroom. Watching him pound his cock into the showgirl's willing body, it pleased her to know that the human girl would be dead within the hour. The pretty mortal's flesh would be torn apart, her limbs severed by the force of the Archdemon's bare hands.

And as for Serena… Luciana smiled, wondering what it would be like to bathe in an angel's blood.

Chapter Fourteen

Hell is surprisingly comfortable, Serena thought as she drifted out of the dark space of sleep. She was warm, although not burning hot, and she had the sensation that someone was trailing fingertips across her back. Hell was not just comfortable. It was downright pleasurable.

She opened her eyes. She wasn't in hell. She was lying with her head resting on Julian's chest, in his bed. Except for the rumpled sheets, the bed was bare; all the other bedclothes had been thrown off during the night. Julian opened his eyes, so clear she might have been peering beneath the blue-green surface of a glacier-fed lake, shot through with streaks of gold sunlight. His fingertips rounded over the globe of her buttock.

"Good morning, angel."

Good afternoon, more like it. Day streamed in through the half-open drapes, and outside, the sun was already high and the sky, blazing blue. She stretched her sore body, muscles still tender from the rigors of last night's marathon of pleasure.

Last night.

She shot upright, not bothering to hide her nakedness. He had seen it all anyway, had kissed and caressed every curve of her body, had worshipped every inch of her bare skin last night. Still, that brilliant gaze roamed over her, as hungry as though he'd never laid eyes on her before.

"I'm still here," she said. She had not been sucked into a vortex and carried off to hell. But why not? Wasn't that what happened to fallen angels? Whatever she'd said to him and to herself last night about keeping love in her heart, there was still a little niggling doubt in the back of her mind that was not sure about what might happen. In any case, she was pretty sure that angels who fell weren't just left to their own business the morning after committing a carnal sin.

Julian reached for her again; she swatted his hand away. "I need to figure out what's going on." She thought, *I need to call Arielle. So I can find out whether there were any consequences after last night. Whether it's safe to remain here for another two days.*

"Stop worrying." His mouth curled into a sexy little smile. "What could be more important than this?" he said, dipping his head to catch her nipple in his mouth.

Involuntarily, she stretched back at the pleasure of it. Ignoring her own desire, she tried to push him away, tried to push away the sensations that were building in her. He was ready for her, his heavy member erect. She twisted, seeking the clothes she'd discarded on the floor last night. But he pulled her to him, running his hands up her back and continuing to trail kisses along her breasts. His faint beard stubble rasped against her soft skin.

"I have you until midnight tomorrow. Then you are free to leave. Not a moment earlier," he whispered.

Panic started to rise in her. Mixed with desire, it was a potent cocktail as he rolled on top of her, spreading her thighs. In a single, powerful stroke, he entered her. He pushed deeper, claiming her, plunging into her with an intensity that swept away all her worries of falling.

She arched up to meet him and they soared.

I'm no good for you, sweetheart, Julian thought as they lay sated after their lovemaking.

Her head rested sweetly on his chest, his fingers sifted idly through the silk of her hair. The half-drawn curtains muted the bright afternoon; her hair brought the sun into the room and washed him in strands of light. He thought of the gold rush that had brought him to this part of the country. It had taken him a century and a half to find the real treasure.

She gave a little sigh, running her fingers through the light curls on his chest.

It was abundantly clear to him that he must let her go. He had staked his claim, but now he was going to have to abandon the treasure. Or his selfishness would ruin her. His plan to destroy her had crumbled to dust. Now, there was no way he could relegate her to eternal damnation, not even if it meant that she would remain by his side forever. Better never to see her again and know she was safe.

Tomorrow night at midnight. They had agreed on it. Ordinarily, he would not have let a contract scribbled on a cocktail napkin dictate his pleasure. He would have found a way around it. Because he, Julian Ascher, was adept at such things.

This time would be different. This time, he would let her go, not only because his honor demanded it, but because it was the best thing for her. In her absence, he would survive. He, Julian Ascher, master of temptation, connoisseur of pleasure, would simply go back to his old ways. Find himself another woman, maybe two, to divert his attention. Or so he told himself.

In the meantime, a few dozen hours remained. He stirred again, considering the thousands of ways he could pleasure her, wondering how many of them he could squeeze into those remaining hours. He bent to kiss her. Tried to ignore the certain knowledge brewing within him that he was kidding himself that his life would ever be the same without her.

After they made love, they lounged in bed for another hour, feeding each other ripe strawberries from the room-service cart. Serena was still worried about her status as an angel—Julian could see it in her eyes. But to him, she appeared to be resigned to spending one last day with him. So they lingered, savoring the sweetness of the berries and of each other's bodies.

A knock at the front door interrupted them. Julian threw on a bathrobe and went to answer it.

In the hallway, Corbin stood waiting. He cast a knowing glance over Julian's attire, and said, "You sly dog. Still in bed at two in the afternoon, eh?"

Julian grinned hard, wishing Corbin would just go away. He tightened the sash of the robe. "What do you want, Corbin?"

The hotelier walked into the suite, peering around, probably for signs of Serena. "You left early last night. Too bad. It was memorable. I haven't had so much prime tail in one night since the Summer of Love back in sixty-seven." He grinned, all dazzling white teeth.

Julian smiled along with him. But unlike Corbin, he didn't need an orgy to satisfy his sexual cravings. All he needed was Serena.

"Just dropped by to let you know I'm hosting a high-stakes poker game tonight. It would be good if you could join us," he said, looking pointedly at Julian. It was not an invitation. It was an order. "The buy-in is a million dollars."

Julian cleared his throat. The money wasn't an issue. Money could be made in the blink of an eye. But when Corbin gambled, he didn't just play for money.

He played for souls.

Tonight, Julian had planned on one last secluded evening alone with Serena. Tomorrow night, they would be surrounded by crowds when the club opened. And then he would let her go.

Corbin knew that. He was already betting on it, even before the poker game started. He wanted Serena, had finally succeeded on getting his hands on her last night, if only briefly, at his party. But Corbin wanted more of her. Julian could see it in the other Archdemon's eyes.

Take the angel and leave. Go somewhere and don't look back, Julian thought to himself for an instant. Then he realized how impossible that would be. Running away was not something in an Archdemon's arsenal of tricks. He would lose everything he had worked these past two centuries to achieve. Would open himself up to vulnerability. *No.* Julian would not run. Not because of an asshole like Corbin.

"I'm not the keenest poker player," Julian told him. Which was the furthest thing from the truth. Poker was a staple in the backrooms of Devil's Paradise and his other clubs. He was an expert at it. And it never hurt to start bluffing early.

"Don't worry about that. I'll see you tonight." Corbin smiled. "And bring Serena. She can watch from the gallery."

"Of course," Julian said, concealing his dismay.

He shut the door and returned to bed, knowing with dead certainty that behind that cold gaze of Corbin's, something truly horrific was brewing.

Weak means strong, strong means weak. That was the secret to most poker "tells"—the clues hidden in a player's body language that would tell whether he or she was bluffing. A player who leaned back in a chair with slumped shoulders was probably holding a royal flush. A player with a puffed-up chest, who sat a little straighter than usual, most likely had a pair of deuces. There were other clues: the subtle fidget with the edge of the cards, the nervous flicker of the eyes, the minuscule twitch of a smile.

But not here. Not at Corbin's table, where an elite group gathered on Friday night, closed off from the prying eyes of the crowds in the main casino outside. Each of the six players around the table—all men, all high-ranking demons—were masters of deception, well schooled in the art of bluffing. They bantered easily among each other, cracking jokes and telling stories. But every fidget, every flicker, every twitch was carefully orchestrated to create the illusion of the casual, the human. With these players, there were no tells.

In front of each player, stacks of cash held together with paper bands stood beside piles of the ivory poker chips Corbin used for all his high-stakes games. Serena sat in a chair nearby, legs elegantly crossed. Julian smiled to himself. In a little black dress, with her blond hair swept back off her face, there was an air of sophistication about her that Julian had never seen before. Yet, she still looked angelic. Behind that virtuous facade, nobody would ever have guessed that they'd spent the afternoon fucking.

Beside her, Nick slouched with his arms crossed and a sour look on his face. Whether that was because of his thwarted crush on Serena, or because he had not been invited to the table, Julian did not know or care. The human would have been decimated at poker with the current set of players within ten minutes flat, in any case. Poor fool.

Corbin's voice broke through Julian's solitude. "You look like the cat that got the cream, my boy."

Julian could not resist a smirk. "Maybe I did."

The dealer shuffled, throwing the cards with an efficient flick of the wrist. Across the table, Corbin ruminated behind dark glasses, as though he needed to hide his already inscrutable expression. Yet, emotions did not need to appear on a man's face to be self-evident. Julian could feel his envy. Just like Nick, Corbin wanted Serena, and he wanted her badly. Julian could see it in the twitch of Corbin's body, the tension in his posture. No dark glasses could hide that.

The storm was brewing, and soon it would break.

Corbin stood and spoke. "All right, boys. Welcome to the table. It's no-limits five-card stud. As you know, it's a one-million-dollar buy-in."

The play began. The hands went quickly, each player responding much faster than a human would. These men did not waste time. After a mere fifteen minutes, two of the demons were eliminated, their cash and chips absorbed into the hands of the other players. Soon after that, the other two players folded, until only Julian and Corbin were left.

"Poker's not exactly your game, eh?" Corbin said, taking off his glasses for a moment to rub his eyes. "You misled me this afternoon, my friend."

Julian shrugged, considering his hand. He and Corbin were roughly even. He wished they could stop so he could leave. He looked at his watch. It was almost midnight. Tomorrow at this time, he would say goodbye to Serena. *One more day with her. That's all I have left.* Ironically, time, which he'd had in abundance over the course of his existence, was the most valuable thing in the world right now.

Corbin was toying with him, cutting short that time.

"Raise you twenty thousand." Corbin pitched another few bricks of cash into the middle of the table, where the pot was massing.

"I call. And raise you three hundred grand," Julian said, upping the ante. He pitched in the money, knowing that when the cash game came to a head with Corbin, the real betting would begin.

Beside Serena, her Assignee's discontent was brewing as the game continued. Maybe it was obvious from the way Julian looked at her that something had changed.

"Who cares about poker?" Nick muttered as he glowered at Julian. "Let's get out of here."

"Not right now," Serena said, watching the play at the table intently.

Poker normally bored her silly. But the vast sums of money tossed on the table made her breathless and nervous on Julian's behalf. While all of the other players wore dark glasses, Julian played with nothing to shield his expression. Amidst the clink of the poker chips and the shuffling of the cards, his posture was relaxed, but she sensed his intense concentration on the game.

Corbin slipped off his glasses for a moment, and looked straight at her. Something dark and wicked flashed in his pale gaze. Danger. Lust. Barely contained and ready to explode. She wondered when it would happen, and hoped that she was far away when it did. She shuddered, unable to control the fear that rippled through her. He slipped the glasses on again and returned his attention to the game.

She could no longer bear to watch. Leaning over to Nick, she whispered, "I changed my mind. Let's take a walk."

Two burly Gatekeepers trailed after them, no doubt following Julian's instructions to track their every move.

They stepped into the main area of the casino. Unlike

the exclusive atmosphere of the high-stakes room, gamblers from every walk of life teemed around the tables and at the slot machines, come to test their luck on this night as the weekend began.

"I'm worried about you," Serena said, trying not to sound too matronly. "Everyone's waiting for you in L.A. so they can continue filming your movie. Why don't you do the right thing and go back to work?"

But Nick completely ignored her concern. Instead, he said flatly, "You slept with him."

"Don't be angry with me, Nick," she said, knowing there was no point in trying to deny it. "I told you that you and I could never be more than just friends."

He shook his head in disbelief. "I warned you about him. Serena, that man is pure evil. You made a huge mistake. You could have been with someone who really loved you." He turned to leave, but not before he paused and said, "You could have been with me."

"Where are you going?" she called after him.

He didn't answer, but left her standing there in the middle of the crowds, with the noise of the slot machines beeping all around her. One of the Gatekeepers trailed after him, no doubt going to alert Harry to babysit him once again.

Nick might hate her, but she had done her job nonetheless. She had kept him safe.

She checked her watch—it was just past midnight. Tomorrow at this time, she would walk out the front door and leave this debacle behind her. Somehow, she would convince Nick to go with her. She would go back to Los Angeles and resume her life.

She would forget Julian.

I have the strength to do all of that, she knew. *All except maybe the last part.*

Serena can go to hell, Nick thought as he went up to Corbin's suite, where Luciana was sipping a drink that matched her eyes and staring blankly out the massive windows. Her boredom vanished in an instant when she saw him.

"You were right about Serena," he told the dark-haired beauty, collapsing on a chaise longue. He felt like his heart had been torn out. "She chose Julian."

Luciana came to sit on his lap, smoothed her fingers over his hair. Kissed him so sweetly that he *almost* forgot about Serena. Trailing a finger down the front of his shirt, she popped open the button of his jeans and whispered against his lips, "Forget about her, *mio caro.* Tonight, you're here with me."

Down in the VIP lounge, Lady Luck was smiling on Julian.

In his hand, the flat faces of four kings stared out blandly. It was an excellent poker hand. *Should be enough for me to win,* he thought. But it was impossible to anticipate what the other Archdemon held. At this point, the cash meant nothing to him. A little less than six million dollars sat on the table, but all Julian wanted was Serena.

He pushed his remaining pile of cash and chips into the middle of the table. "All in."

"What a pity the game has to end so quickly," Corbin said, pretending to be dismayed. "Let's at least make it interesting."

"Call it or fold," Julian said, irritated by the other man's delaying tactics.

"You're anxious to leave, I see. Perhaps we need to bet something more meaningful than money to make tonight memorable. Something truly precious. I'll bet the deed to the hotel." As casually as though he were scribbling a grocery list, he wrote a note on a marker, tossed it into the pile. He sat back and folded his arms, waiting for Julian to react.

That piece of paper called to Julian. It beckoned him. If Julian won the hotel, Devil's Ecstasy would be entirely his, free from Corbin's demands, unencumbered by the older demon's influences. The quickest way out of his obligations to the hotelier was to *become* the hotelier. Julian would have a shot at living a clean life, without crime, without evil.

Maybe one day…after centuries of atonement…*a life with Serena*.

"What are you willing to risk?" Corbin asked, the tone of temptation infusing his voice. "What do you have to bet that rivals the Lussuria?"

Julian swallowed, knowing full well what he was after. But he was unwilling to give Corbin that satisfaction. Not without a fight. So he said, "Devil's Ecstasy."

Corbin sat back in his chair, crossed his arms. "But your club is in my hotel, so I practically own it already. What's more, it hardly matches the value of my hotel. You've got to wager something proportionate. That's how poker works, old friend. We each bet something of equal value."

Unfazed by Corbin's condescending snarl, Julian

told him, "I own clubs across the country. Take your pick."

The other demon shook his head, sending a pointed glance at the empty chair where Serena had been sitting earlier. "Spare me the list of your other possessions. There's nothing I don't have except for one thing," Corbin said. He leaned across the table and said, "The girl."

Julian glanced quickly over his shoulder to make sure she hadn't returned to the room. Mercifully, there was no sign of her. "Never. I don't own her."

Corbin's lips twisted into a smile. He didn't bother to hide it. Maybe he couldn't. "You own one more night with her."

"This entire hotel against one night with Serena." Julian smiled. "That's ridiculous."

They both knew it was not. Hotels could be built. Within a matter of months, given the right amount of money. If Julian won this one, Corbin would simply build another hotel down the Strip. And he could have it fully constructed by the winter, if he wanted to.

What Corbin really offered wasn't simply a chance at winning this property. If Julian won, his relationship with Corbin would be severed forever. If he lost, it wasn't just his relationship with Serena that would be destroyed. It was Serena herself.

"No." Julian stood to leave.

Corbin shrugged, leaning his arms against the poker table. "What a pity. I'm giving you the chance to save her. Considering that I'm going to take her anyway once you're done with her." He spread his hands on the green baize of the gaming table, smoothing them over the fabric covering as though he were stroking the skin of a woman's body.

Julian's mouth went dry. The thought of Corbin's hands on Serena's skin sent blood pounding through his temples. He could feel the pressure in his veins and arteries increasing, pressing to the limit. "You wouldn't."

"Why not? She's fair game."

"You and I are business partners," Julian ground out. "She's under my protection."

Corbin merely shrugged and smiled. "All's fair in love and war, my friend. Play me for her. At least then she'll have a fighting chance at survival."

Survival? What in hell's name did he intend to do to her? Julian's hands tightened into fists. He was ready to explode over the table and beat Corbin to a pulp. Behind him, he heard the Gatekeepers stir.

"I'm simply giving you a choice. Just as you pride yourself in giving others their choices," Corbin said.

But when it came down to it, there was no choice at all, Julian realized.

"All right." Julian sat, trying to contain his rage. He cursed Corbin. He cursed himself. He should have let the angel go long ago, when he had the chance, and damn the consequences. Should not have brought her into this, left prey to the many dangers her beauty attracted, himself among those dangers.

He scribbled her name on a piece of paper and tossed it onto the pile. As it slipped from his fingers, he could feel his heart tumbling with it, landing to rest atop the pile of cash and poker chips.

"One more condition," Corbin announced. "We bet

on a single new hand. Sudden death. Winner takes all."

"Fine. I want a new dealer. And a new pack of cards," Julian insisted.

"You, Gatekeeper," Corbin said, snapping his fingers in Simon's direction. "Come here and deal."

"A neutral dealer. Someone who doesn't work for you," Julian said.

"Every dealer in this house works for me," Corbin said in a low rumble. "Every croupier, bouncer and cocktail waitress. Every hotel clerk, porter and busboy. This is my domain. You will not find a soul on this property who is not partial to me. Harry's your man," he said, jerking his chin in the direction of Julian's manager. "And the girl is already half in love with you."

There was no way to argue with Corbin, so Simon took a seat at the table. They were cheating, and Julian knew it. Lame fury seized his entrails and wrenched. Was he going to sit here and let Corbin cheat him out of the only thing that mattered to him?

"You're losing your poker face, my boy." Corbin laughed. He toyed with a stack of chips, the clinking sound grating on Julian's nerves as the ivory discs dropped against each other.

Julian said nothing. He began to sweat, wondering if Corbin could see the tiny beads of moisture forming on Julian's upper lip, his forehead.

"Deal a single hand," Corbin told Simon. "Best hand wins."

He picked up his cards. So it had come to this. Julian sat for a moment, staring at the pair of jacks and the pair of fives in his hand. Lady Luck had deserted him.

Corbin laid his own hand on the table. "Royal flush."

Impossible. The odds of drawing a royal flush on a single hand of poker were astronomical. Julian stared at the cards fanned neatly on the table: ten, jack, queen, king, ace of diamonds. The face cards smirked, their subtle smiles taunting. Julian's hand could not beat Corbin's royal flush. Nothing could.

Julian did not bother to show his cards, but instead placed them facedown on the table. He would not walk away. Even if Corbin threw him into the deepest pit in hell, he would fight to his last breath. He would protect Serena with every ounce of strength he had.

"You're cheating," he said flatly.

At the other end of the table, Corbin rose. "How dare you," he snarled. "I won her fair and square. I'm going to enjoy her, not only because she's fresh, nubile angel flesh, but also because I won her from *you.*"

Raising his chin, Julian stared straight into those dark glasses. "You're cheating, and you know it."

"You lost. Too bad, my friend." Corbin picked up a poker chip from the table, flipped it so that it landed in front of Julian. "Take this. Consolation for a game well played. Walk away now, if you know what's good for you."

"There's too much at stake. I'm calling your bluff, Corbin."

"Your nightclub is on my property. I could ruin you. Not only here on earth, but in the bowels of the underworld. If you want to spend the rest of eternity living out your darkest nightmares, keep it up."

Julian folded his arms across his chest.

On all sides, the Gatekeepers loomed, waiting for Julian to make a move. If he showed the slightest hint of aggression toward Corbin, they would jump him. But he would not walk away. There must be some way he could protect Serena. Or perish trying.

His brain churned as he sat and stared at Corbin, the malice seeping from behind the other demon's dark glasses. Corbin would destroy Serena, and they both knew it.

Julian did something he hadn't done in centuries. He began to pray, and not to the devil this time. Not for the hotel—he could care less about Corbin's palace of sin. Nor did he pray for himself—he was a lost cause and he knew it.

He prayed for Serena. He prayed like he'd prayed for his dying mother and his baby sister, those centuries ago, as he had knelt on the wooden floor of his aunt's Spartan cottage. Right then and there, he made a bargain with God. *Lord, if you help me keep Serena safe, I swear, I will let her go.*

Corbin reached for the piece of paper from the center of the table with Serena's name on it.

It was then that Simon cleared his throat and spoke. "Julian's right. Corbin's cheating. He marked the cards."

Corbin towered over the Gatekeeper, his face contorting into a mask of fury. "How dare you accuse *me*. You will be severely punished for this."

"We fixed the decks before dealing," Simon blurted, backing away. "He didn't get that royal flush by chance. He used ink that can only been seen with those glasses."

Julian studied Simon's face carefully. Was he telling the truth? Or was this part of some elaborate plot Corbin had schemed up?

Between the two demons, which one to believe? Simon or Corbin?

His gut said Simon. Standing over his minion, the old Archdemon's face flushed deep red. To cross him meant risking everything, Julian realized. But that risk was his only choice.

"I believe you, Simon," Julian concluded finally, his voice calm but firm.

Corbin let out a short bark of laughter. "It's his word against mine. Both of you boys are out of your league."

"There's a simple way of proving this. Give me the glasses, Corbin," Julian said.

"Go fuck yourself, you insubordinate jackass. This is mutiny," the older man spat.

The other Gatekeepers tensed nearby, ready to intervene. "Whose command do you obey?" Corbin barked at them. "Take him!"

But they didn't move. Like Simon, it appeared that the others had also endured enough torture at Corbin's hands. Julian drew himself to his full height. "No need for this to get ugly. Just give me the glasses and we'll settle this like gentlemen."

The older demon launched himself across the table at Julian, sending chips and money flying into the air. Julian hated to fight, but he knew how to defend himself. Corbin came at him. Julian deflected him easily to one side. Corbin whirled, managing to sucker punch Julian in the gut, winding him momentarily. There was no holding back now. Julian threw one punch to Corbin's windpipe. The older demon was laid out on the floor, struggling to breathe.

Julian picked up the glasses. If he was wrong about this, Corbin would never forgive him. Not only would Julian lose the investment and effort he'd put into Devil's Ecstasy, but he would be discredited and disgraced before the entire hierarchy of demons. He would lose the respect of the Gatekeepers. He would never be able to function as an Archdemon again.

And Serena would be lost, destined for certain destruction at Corbin's hands.

His hand shook as he put the glasses on. He fished some cards out of the clutter on the table. At first, it didn't seem like they were marked. Perhaps he had made a mistake. His heart began to race, his palms sweated. He turned the cards over, searching for a sign.

Then, as he examined the cards more closely, he saw that Simon was right. In the corner of the face cards, there was a tiny mark on the bottom left of each card. Marks that could only be seen with these glasses. He whipped the glasses off, handed them to the nearest Gatekeeper to verify.

"I knew you were cheating," Julian said, exhaling finally. He looked down at Corbin, squirming on the floor.

"You don't realize what you've just done," Corbin snarled. "You've started a war. Over that whore of an angel."

"I should kill you."

"You can't. We still answer to the same master. I am

still his second in command. Kill me, and you'll spend the rest of your days in the deepest reaches of hell."

Julian sighed. "I don't want to fight with you, Corbin. I don't even want the hotel. But leave Serena alone. I want to hear it from your lips. Say it. Promise me you won't harm a hair on her head."

"Take the hotel. It's yours. You've won it fair and square, haven't you?" Corbin snarled. "But that whore of yours had better watch her back."

Julian increased the pressure of his foot on Corbin's neck. "You dare threaten her? I really *should* kill you." On the floor, Corbin started to choke. Julian refused to let up. Let the demon die if he wasn't willing to promise Serena's safety.

Corbin flailed, waving his arms. Julian released his foot ever so slightly. "Fine," the old demon choked. "I won't…harm her."

Julian released the pressure slightly. "How do I know your word is worth a damn?"

Corbin grasped his neck, coughing and spluttering. "Trust me. We've been working together for quite some time, old chap. I swear it on my honor as a demon. I will not hurt Serena."

Why would Corbin honor his word, given what had occurred tonight? But Julian had little choice. If he didn't find some way to let Corbin go, he would have to find some way to either keep him in captivity, or kill him. There would be hell to pay for that, quite literally.

"You have no honor. I want your promise in writing. A blood contract," Julian said.

The older demon winced, but nodded his assent.

Julian let him up. Watched as Corbin requested a clean sheet of paper, a pen, scribbled out a sentence and handed it to Julian for approval.

I, Corbin Ranulfson, hereby swear never to harm Serena St. Clair.

Julian nodded, then watched as Corbin signed his name. Taking a pocketknife from one of the Gatekeepers, the beaten demon slit his index finger and smeared scarlet on the page over his name.

He had executed the most extreme bond a demon could give, a contract sealed in blood. The blood contract carried dire consequences for any demon who dared to break it. It ought to be insurance enough. In addition, Julian would keep a close watch over Corbin. And assign a detail of Gatekeepers to guard Serena. Never let Corbin get close to her again.

Corbin brushed off his clothes, straightened his suit jacket. With the same remote smile he always wore, he said, "See you around."

Julian's poker hand lay facedown on the table where he'd left it. Corbin flipped it over and laughed. He strode toward the doors, passing Serena on the way out. He laughed and told her, "Julian lost you on a pair of jacks."

Then he was gone.

Julian stood, amazed. He had worked for years to partner with Corbin. Now he owned the Lussuria. Strangely, he didn't care about any of it, the material trappings, his newly gained power. All that mattered was that Serena was safe.

"Thank you," Julian said to the Gatekeepers, as they were about to walk out of the room.

"I didn't do it entirely for your sake. I did for myself, and all the other Gatekeepers who worked for him. He treated us like shit," Simon said. His gaze slid toward Serena. "And I did it for her. Even though she gave me the worst headache of my life, she didn't deserve to wind up with Corbin."

What wouldn't a man do for her? It was no wonder that Simon had risked his life to protect her. Corbin had lost his hotel because of her. Julian had made a fool of himself over her, staking everything that he had, everything he was.

He had one more day with her, and that was all. He had not forgotten the bargain he'd made with God, who had failed him on every occasion but this one. Julian had sworn he would let her go, and he would honor that promise.

"A pair of jacks," Serena said, her voice flat. "I don't even play cards, and I know those odds are not good. What did he mean when he said you lost me?"

Julian pulled her into an embrace so tight it cut off her breath entirely for a moment before he eased back, looking straight into her eyes with such openness that she forgot all her anger. "Don't ask. Please don't ask. I've been through hell tonight. Serena, I would never willingly risk your safety. I hope you know that by now. Come. We're going to enjoy our last twenty-four hours together. I want to dance with you again before I let you go."

She hated him. She loved him. He was unbearable. He was addictive.

Then she realized that none of it mattered. She only

had one more night with this man, and after that, she would return to her usual life, without distractions. Without passion. Without Julian.

As they crossed the lobby, the Gatekeepers bowed to Julian as he passed by.

"Is there something you're not telling me?" Serena asked.

"I won the hotel from Corbin while you were gone. He won't be bothering us anymore," he said, in the banal tone he used to cover deeper emotions. "News seems to spread through the staff like wildfire."

The king is dead. Long live the king. Those were the words that floated into her consciousness. By the time she tried to figure out where they had come from, they had already passed, drifting back out of her mind as they entered the doors of Devil's Ecstasy.

Chapter Fifteen

Devil's Ecstasy was cavernous, deserted. Less than a week had passed, but it seemed like a lifetime ago that they'd last danced together in the eerie emptiness of this luxurious space. Serena waited in the dark, illuminated only by the glittery light reflecting from a disco ball hanging high above the dance floor. Julian disappeared into the DJ booth, and within moments an old recording of Elvis played over the sound system.

"Come and take a turn around the dance floor," Julian said, holding out his hand toward her. They drifted into the empty space, and the music washed over them. She knew the song well. "Can't Help Falling in Love." Elvis sang of fools rushing in. *If fools rush in where angels fear to tread, where do demons fear to tread?* she wondered. Then it hit her.

Love. Love is the place where demons fear to tread.

Sadness welled up inside her, for the life she wished she could have with Julian. A life she knew could never be. A week had passed like a blink of an eye. Tomorrow night, they would part. One day without him would stretch into two, three, a week, a month, a year. Decades would pass. Time would rush onward. She would always remember the time she'd spent with him, but the details would grow hazy. Those first, heady kisses in his office at Devil's Paradise and in the library of his Beverly Hills mansion. Exploring the Vegas Strip with him. The feverish nights they'd spent, beginning to know each other's bodies. The chaste kiss on the forehead he'd given her after their day at the Grand Canyon. And finally, their elated union last night, the ecstasy of it sweeping her into a different realm.

These things would recede into the past, fading to distant memories. She knew this with absolute certainty, as she knew that human life must end, and people came and went from the earth like the ebb and flow of the ocean's tides.

She rested her head against his shoulder as they circled slowly. At last, she knew love. Finally, and without question or reservation. It was so beautiful she wanted to weep, both for the fact that she'd finally found it, and for the fact of its impossibility.

"Don't cry," he said, brushing away the tear that slipped down her cheek with the pad of his thumb.

"I'm not. There's something in my eye."

"Bullshit. I thought you angels were made of stronger stuff."

The tears fell, dripping onto his shirt to leave watermark stains. She tried to turn her head, but there was no way to hide from him.

"Let's get some air," he said.

He led her upstairs, to the terrace overlooking the Strip. Out there in the City of Dreams, the lights glittered beneath the black velvet sky. People partied. They gambled. Won fortunes. Lost their savings. Celebrated.

Cried. Got married. Had flings. Drank themselves into oblivion and forgot why they'd come here. Serena wished she could forget, but Julian was etched into her memory forever. Nothing would erase him.

She shivered a little in the cool night air. He came to stand behind her and pulled his suit jacket around her. Kissed the top of her head and murmured, "Remember this night. Look back on this time we had together, this time we stole from both God and the devil. I may be sent straight to the inner circle of hell for saying this, but you made me believe in love."

"I can't believe you would be condemned for believing in love," she said. "If angels can fall, can't demons be redeemed?" Desperation churned in the pit of her stomach. She swallowed to keep it down.

Behind her, he sighed, and it seemed as though she could hear years of weariness exhaled on that one long breath. "Sweetheart, I don't think so. I would have to save a continent of starving children in order to atone for the damage I've caused."

"But there must be some way." Even as she spoke the words, her mind could not contemplate a solution. She leaned back against him, searching for something to say. "Maybe you could start by praying," she said finally. It was a naive suggestion, but the only one she had.

He let out the tiniest snort of breath, and when he spoke, she heard the ironic amusement in his voice. "To whom do you suggest I pray?"

"To whatever higher power you believe in. If you're not comfortable with that, then appeal to the goodness within yourself."

"I've always gotten much better results appealing to the other side," he said, the irony spreading to curl the corners of his lips.

She peered up into his face, searching for a sign there, some glint of hope that he might be willing to fight. "Somewhere in you, there's faith in the power of the divine. You just said you believe in love."

"It's not the same thing."

"Isn't it?"

They stood in silence for a long time, wrapped in each other's arms, looking out over the night skyscape of this city of legends, this city that had sheltered their extraordinary love affair, if only for a week.

They made love slowly, tenderly in Julian's bed.

"We don't have to do this if you don't want to," he said, trembling as he laid her back onto the sheets. After tonight's events, he was grateful that she was here, safe in his arms.

She kissed him then, more passionately, more ardently than he had ever hoped she would. "I want to."

He had succeeded in achieving his goal: he had made her crave his touch. But in the process, he had lost himself to her, utterly and irrevocably. He had never experienced such openness with a woman, nor had he guessed himself capable of such gentleness. When they made love, it was not the wild, acrobatic sex he usually engaged in. Staring into her eyes as she climaxed, he realized that he had meant it when he'd told her that she'd made him believe in love. Because he had fallen in love with her.

He had opened up in ways he had never thought

possible. He made love to her, trying to memorize every curve of her body so that the memory of it would last him a lifetime. Longer than a lifetime—an eternity. He would spend an eternity without her. Afterward, as they lay entwined in the dark, he contemplated his new definition of hell: existing without Serena. Satan himself could not have thought up a crueler punishment.

Serena and Julian lay entwined, still awake as the night began to relent. He watched shadows flicker across the ceiling, wishing he could freeze these past few moments with her. *The warmth of her body against his. The twinned sound of their breathing. The satin softness of her skin as he held her.*

All week, he had fooled himself into thinking that he could keep her. At this moment, he was the most dangerous thing to her. It was a miracle she hadn't already fallen, but if she stayed with him, her fate would be sealed. He would destroy her. She would become another version of Luciana, a bitter demoness who seeped evil from every pore. Or worse, he would break her. Serena would become a dried-out shell of the woman she was now, a frightened little scrap of a creature whose existence had been ruined.

He had always known that. How many lives had he ruined in exactly the same way? Now, faced with the decision, he knew he had to let Serena go. Not just because he had made a promise to God. But because it was the right thing to do. The right thing for *her*.

The clock showed that it was almost four in the morning. Nearly twenty hours remained until their agreement expired. *Midnight on Saturday night.* But he knew that if he was going to give her up, he must do it *now,* before his resolve was burned away by the broad light of day. Before he saw her face radiant in the sun's glow. Before he changed his mind and decided to ruin her forever.

He rolled slightly, pushing her away from him and sitting up to turn on the bedside lamp. Avoided looking at her face to see the hurt there. Whatever he did, hurting her was inevitable. He would simply have to do it as swiftly and as cleanly as possible.

"I've made a decision," he said. "I'm releasing you from our agreement. You're free to leave."

She pulled the sheet up to cover her nakedness while he pulled on a pair of pants. She cleared her throat a little and said, "We have almost another whole day left. Don't you want to spend it together?"

He forced himself to turn, to look her in the eye with a steady gaze that was as impenetrable as his poker face. "That's not a good idea," he said with feigned casualness. "I've had my fill of what I wanted from you."

She gave a soft little laugh, threw an arm above her head with a little sigh. "I don't believe that for a second. Not after how you just…"

…reveled in the splendor of your body? Felt your soul vibrate beneath me, on top of me, within me? He cleared his throat and made himself say, "Do you think I haven't pleasured countless numbers of others in exactly the same way? Serena, I think you should go."

She sat up, her glorious hair tumbling in disarray around her, falling to cover her naked breasts. "Are you kicking me out?" There was disbelief in her voice. Shock. A hint of rage.

"Our week together has been fun," he said, keeping

his tone cool. "But I'm afraid I'm not interested in pursuing any further contact with you."

"You're in love with me," she said. He had never heard it as an accusation before, and it stung. "You were always criticizing me because I was afraid to have fun. You're afraid to fall in love." From the bed, her eyes challenged him.

"Don't lecture me about fear, Serena. Until you've experienced the deepest reaches of hell, felt the fires of damnation burning the flesh from your bones, you have no right to judge me." It was almost unbearable to look at her. Tears were beginning to form in her large blue eyes, pooling along their rims and threatening to spill over. He wanted so badly to look away, but he held his ground.

"You're afraid love will destroy you," she whispered. "Do you know what I think? I think you're acting out of fear. You've been corrupting people for so long, you don't know what would happen if you stopped. If you don't corrupt other people, you won't be an Archdemon anymore. You'd just be another one of the damned. You're afraid you'll lose your power."

Let her believe that. He thought of a demon he'd known years ago, who had stopped one day. Just stopped. Refused to do his job, wouldn't tempt another human. The Prince of Hell himself had ordered the demon to resume his responsibilities. That demon was now burning in the deepest reaches of hell, stripped of his demon status, flayed alive by Satan's minions for the rest of eternity. Despite that, Julian would have suffered the fires of hell for her. But let her think he was releasing her for his own sake. She'd go with less of a struggle.

"Demons are only angels who've made a mistake. They think they need to be punished, but all they really need to do is forgive themselves. Divine love heals all wounds," she said.

"Are you excusing my sins, Serena? Are you willing to forgive me for letting you go?"

She dropped her gaze. "I'm not the right person to ask if you want atonement. You know who you need to ask."

Fury burned through him. That would happen when hell froze over. He walked to the bed and ripped the sheet away from her, exposing her nakedness. "Go."

She scrambled off the bed, tears tumbling down her cheeks.

"What did you think would happen? That we'd end up living happily ever after? Life is not a fairy tale, Serena. I'm not Prince Charming."

He made himself continue. Because if he didn't, she would make it her mission in life to reform him. And that, he knew, was utterly impossible. She would ruin herself in the process. "This was just a game," he said. "A diversion. I saw you. I wanted you. I had never been with an angel before, so I took you."

"I don't believe you," she shot out.

"What makes you think this conquest is any different from anything else I've done before?" She glared at him. *Let her hate me. Let it be easier for her this way.* He said the one thing she would not refuse. Could not refuse. Not when she was bound by duty. "Take Nick and get the hell out of here."

He stared out the window at the neon lights of the Strip below, not daring to look at her. Tried to focus on the world outside because he couldn't bear to see the hurt and sorrow etched on her face, emotions he didn't need to see because he could *feel* them in the place where his heart might have been, if he'd had one. Instead, the center of his chest felt as though a thousand shards of glass were exploding there.

"I'll send your clothes after you," he muttered.

"I don't want the clothes."

Of course she didn't. She wanted *him*. Better that she didn't take anything that reminded her of him. He would destroy it all, leave behind nothing to mark their time together. "Suit yourself," he said. He turned and walked out of the room.

In the living room, he poured himself a drink, downing two fingers of scotch like it was water. He poured himself another, and tried to ignore her crying, the muffled, breathless gasps that ripped at the core of him. He snatched up the bottle of scotch and went out onto the balcony.

Choices. For once, he had made the choice to put someone else before himself. It was better that she left, went back to Los Angeles. Back to her safe little life, far away from him. It was the oldest adage in the world: *if you love something, let it go.*

In a matter of minutes, she had dressed and gathered some things from her bedroom. She swept through the living room and out the front door, leaving him standing in the night air, staring out at the dark sky over Vegas.

She was gone. In her place, there was only emptiness.

* * *

Tears were still pouring down Serena's face as she banged on Nick's door. For the longest time, there was no answer. Was he even in there? Julian's Gatekeeper thugs were supposedly keeping him safe. But maybe Julian had failed her in that, too.

She was about to give up when Nick opened the door, just a tiny crack until he saw it was her. His hair was rumpled, and he squinted in the hallway light. He took one look at her face and said, "What's wrong?"

She heard the faint rustling of sheets coming from a bedroom that was out of view. Just inside the door, a woman's high-heeled shoes lay on the floor, apparently kicked off in haste. Perhaps Tiffany had managed her way into Nick's bed, after all.

Whoever it was, Serena didn't want to know. But there was one thing she did know: whoever was in Nick's bedroom had not managed to dim the infatuation shining in his eyes as he looked at Serena now. And she would use that infatuation, say whatever she had to say in order to get Nick out of here.

She wiped at her tears with the back of her hand. "I'm going back to L.A. If you care about me at all, you'll come with me now. Please."

Baiting him with his feelings for her was unfair. But she could think of no better strategy to lure him away from these demons. She must succeed this time. She had come here for this purpose, to protect him. She would not get another chance.

"Wouldn't it be better to wait until morning?" he said, blinking again. His gaze slid to the interior of the hotel suite, toward the bedroom.

"It's dangerous. I need you to come with me, Nick," she pleaded. "I'll explain on the way."

Along with the concern, desire flickered in his eyes. Every other time she'd seen that desire, she'd ignored it, discouraged it. This time, she looked back, letting her gaze lock with his.

"Give me five minutes and I'll meet you in the lobby," he said.

Crossing the lobby, Serena paused, watching the hotel guests pass through. Even at this hour of the morning, it was still busy with people stumbling in from last night. Julian's new nightclub hadn't even opened its doors yet. He was now the owner of one of the most successful hotels in Vegas. She imagined him strolling through the lobby, king of his domain. Or standing above it all, watching the casino from a vantage point beside the pit boss. No wonder he had sent her away. Julian had bigger things to keep him occupied.

She sank into one of the lobby's leather sofas, suddenly exhausted from everything that had happened that night: the poker game, their dance in the empty club, the last act of lovemaking with Julian. The day had drained her. In fact, the whole week had drained her. Yet, her gaze still tracked toward the elevator, hoping against hope that the polished metal doors would slide open, and Julian would emerge. Tell her that he loved her. That they would never be apart. She prayed for him to change his mind. To come after her.

From across the lobby, she heard a man call, "Serena! Wait!"

Had her prayer been answered? Harry scuttled

through the crowds, waving wildly. Her heart leaped. Surely Julian had sent him. He had sent Harry to bring her back. They would be together. Everything would be fine.

"Thank God you haven't left the hotel yet. Julian sent me to find you," Harry said, a little out of breath. "He wanted me to give you back your cell phone." He handed it to her.

She stared at the little object in her palm, tried for a faltering little smile. "Thanks."

Harry put a hand on her shoulder, steadied her. "He told me to arrange a car for you, to take you to the airport. Or if you prefer, to drive you back to L.A."

What she really wanted was to go back upstairs, back to Julian. To fall into his arms, to cry until she'd run out of tears. But Julian had made it clear that he didn't want her.

From behind her, Nick said, "I'll take her home. My driver will pull the car around front."

In the back of his limo, Nick held her hand. Not asking for an explanation, with that small gesture he comforted her. Not as a lover but as a friend. As the car swung onto Las Vegas Boulevard, the road ahead of them was all but deserted at this hour of the morning. She kept her tears inside this time, numb from the shock of leaving.

In that moment, she realized that Nick had finally come to understand platonic friendship. Ironic, the Assignee offering support to his Guardian. But as her hand settled in the warmth of his, she realized that she had inadvertently fostered something in her Assignee that she could not have done by simply sheltering or continuing to babysit him.

Nick had learned compassion.

Julian sat at the hotel bar, plugging twenty dollar bills into the electronic poker game built into the bar top. He was on a losing streak—none of the money came back. A half-empty highball of gin and tonic sat beside him, the latest of eight in a row since Serena had left. He downed it in one chug.

At long last, he was the master of his domain. Corbin was gone. He had no one to answer to. Devil's Ecstasy would open its doors to the public. It would be outrageously successful. He should be happy. Instead, he was sitting here, drinking himself into a stupor.

"Sir?" Harry's voice drifted behind him. "Are you all right, sir?"

Julian turned and looked at him through squinting eyes. "Fine, Harry," he said, although he felt far from fine.

"She's gone, sir. Nick took her home."

Harry sounded sorry for him. The last thing Julian needed was someone's pity. But he had it. Harry stood awkwardly, wringing his hands as though he might hug his boss at any moment. Julian scowled and said in a gruff tone, "Put a bodyguard on her, Harry. I don't trust Corbin."

"It's done, sir," Harry said gently. "I've already arranged for a team of men to watch her and a detail to follow Corbin, as well. I suspected you would want a follow-up."

"Tell them to be discreet. I don't want her knowing they're there." Julian's shoulders slumped. If he couldn't be with her himself, at least he could still offer his protection.

"Don't worry, sir. Corbin promised not to hurt her. He signed a contract. In blood," Harry said, grimacing.

Julian wanted to howl. Corbin was forever making bargains, but he always found some way to manipulate himself out of them. He was a master of twisting the rules. Although he ought to have been bound by them, somehow he never was. Julian could only hope that the blood contract would restrain him. He had no other option. Keeping Serena might protect her from Corbin, but it would not protect her from himself.

Instead of howling, Julian snorted a laugh. *"Never bet the devil your head.* Haven't you ever heard of that old saying, Harry?"

Harry's forehead furrowed and he shook his head.

"It's from an Edgar Allan Poe story about a man named Toby Dammit, whose favorite saying is, 'I'll bet the devil my head.' The devil challenges Dammit to jump over a certain obstacle. When Dammit goes to jump, his head is severed off by a sharp metal bar over the obstacle. Moral of the story: you can't trust a deal with the devil."

Harry climbed onto the stool beside him. "But Mr. Ranulfson isn't…"

"The Prince of Evil? Not quite. But close enough." Julian gave Harry a hearty clap on the back. "Sit down, Harry. You have a lot to learn if you're going to survive in this business."

He ordered another round of gin and tonics. Outside, dawn was about to break. But here in the casino, the night was far from over.

* * *

In the penthouse suite of the hotel across the street, Corbin pulled back the curtains and stood looking at his beloved hotel. Luciana joined him at the window, her hair still tangled and her lips slightly bruised after just leaving Nick's bed.

"You should not have gone to the human's room," he frowned, turning to her. "Julian could easily have found you."

"Julian is too busy to care tonight, and you know it," she shrugged. "He has *that girl*."

"The hotel staff are on his side now. But no matter. It's merely a temporary setback. We'll regain the ground we lost with Julian and Serena. And we will make them pay."

"And Nick?" she said, hopeful.

"Are you becoming attached to him, my dear? Your new lover will come in handy soon. He's easily led, and he'll do as we say. For now, it's best that he's gone along with Serena. Until we can figure out a way to use him."

Luciana nodded. The time for vengeance was near.

Chapter Sixteen

Nick stroked his fingers through the silk of Serena's hair as she slept, stretched out in the back of his limo as they drove back to L.A. Even in slumber, her face showed signs of stress, her forehead pinching into a little furrow as she dreamt. She *still* outshone every girl he knew, even the ones who got paid to be beautiful. Why she didn't seek out fame or attention for her beauty, he had no idea. But it made her all the more extraordinary.

Julian is a fool for letting her go, Nick thought. *Once Serena and I are finally together, I'll never let her go.*

His driver pulled up at the address she'd given, a weathered two-story house in Santa Monica. Respectable, but not luxurious. Nick would change that. He would make sure she never had to work a day in her life again. And she would change his life, too. He would finally have the love he had always craved. They would both be happy at last.

And he would make sure she never, ever came into contact with Julian Ascher again.

Gently, Nick shook her awake. She blinked, disoriented, still looking fragile and sad. He wondered what exactly had gone on between her and Julian, but knew better than to ask. She would tell him herself in time. When she was ready.

"Thank you for bringing me home," she said, delicately rubbing her eyes as she sat up. Then she smiled, leaned over to kiss him on the cheek.

He grasped her arm, gently but insistently. He knew he should probably wait, but he just couldn't stop himself. There was something he needed to say, and he needed to say it now. Because Julian was finally out of the picture, and Nick had already been waiting for so long. "Serena, wait. I need to tell you something. I'm in love with you."

She swallowed as she looked at him, her exhaustion apparent in the dark circles beneath her eyes. "Oh, Nick. I'm so sorry. I don't feel that way toward you."

"I know the timing must seem odd," he blurted, trying to find some way to make her understand. "But I hope you'll at least consider the possibility of things changing between us."

"It's not a matter of timing," she told him. "I'm afraid I'll never be able to return your feelings."

"Why not?" he said, leaning forward from the black leather seat, trying to stop himself from appearing too concerned. He tried to mimic Julian's coolness. But real life was not like playing a role. There were real emotions involved. Real hurt.

"Apart from the fact that we're both just hours away from being with other people? There are reasons that I can't explain. But it all stems from the fact that I'm your—" Something hovered on the tip of her tongue, suspended there by a thin invisible thread. "I'm your friend, Nick. And I can never be more than that to you."

"You could be if you gave me a chance," he said, starting to lose his cool. "You fell in love with Julian, didn't you?"

"Of course not," she said.

He watched her face, the pained compression of her pretty mouth and realized exactly how mistaken he had been. She still wanted Julian, and she would for a long time to come. Her words were so hollow, her grief so deep that she was absolutely incapable of hiding it. Her inability to act was no longer so refreshing.

She looked back at him, a hurt look in her eyes. She said, "I'm sorry. See you at the studio tomorrow?"

He turned to stare out the car window, brooding. *What would Julian say?* He had no idea. He'd never been particularly good at improvising. Now, without a script, he was lost for words.

"Nick, I know you're upset." She sighed, the weariness evident in her voice. He knew she was searching for words, too. But there was nothing left to say. What she finally came up with was weak. "This, too, shall pass."

But it wouldn't. Serena wasn't the kind of girl you forgot easily—Nick knew that in the pit of his gut. He watched helplessly as she climbed out of the car. And he realized that she was the kind of girl you would remember on your deathbed, as the one who got away.

"Thank God you're back!" Meredith said when Serena dragged herself through the front door of their apartment. "You look like you've been through hell."

"In a way, I have been," Serena said wryly. She wanted to collapse the moment she stepped through the door, to crumple into a little heap on the kitchen floor. Instead, she settled for one of the kitchen chairs.

She thought of Nick, looking so dejected in the limo. He needed more from her, she knew, needed reassurance and guidance. But she had nothing left to give. She was utterly and completely tapped out. She had run dry.

Meredith gave her a look of absolute compassion. Serena didn't say a word about what had happened, but her roommate seemed to understand completely. "You're back now. Whatever happened, forget about it. Leave it behind. Get some rest. Tomorrow you'll be back to focusing on your work, and you'll move on."

Serena wanted to explain, searching for the words to make it all sound reasonable. When she did speak, her words sounded weary. "There's goodness in Julian. He's just afraid of it. If you knew him like I do, you would understand."

"I know him as well as I'll ever want to know him," Meredith said. "I've seen what goes on at his house. You're better off without Julian. In time, you'll forget him."

But Serena knew that she wouldn't. Julian had been emblazoned on her memory forever. The memory of his touch, of the feeling of his lips on hers, might fade. As much as she wished she could forget him, she knew she never would.

Alone in her bedroom, she crashed on her bed, too tired to sleep. Beside her, the bed felt huge and empty. She smoothed her hand over the soft surface of the duvet

cover, over the space where Julian's body ought to have
lain. And wished there were some way to bridge the
gap between heaven and hell. But they were on opposite sides of a natural divide. Good and evil. Angel and
demon. There was no way around the impossibility of
loving him.

Julian awoke late Saturday morning with a massive
headache to the sound of jackhammers pounding on concrete. Then he realized that the drilling was only inside
his own head. He hauled himself out of bed, his stomach struggling to keep down the contents of last night's
meal. Which had consisted solely of gin and tonic.

"What is the cure for a hangover?" he muttered to
himself. He thought briefly about his old standby, Hair
of the Dog cocktail. Gin, hot sauce and a slice of chili
pepper. Disgusting, but it always seemed to do the trick.
To get the ingredients, he'd have to go downstairs and
find a bar, or pick up the phone and call room service…
To hell with it. Might as well fight fire with fire. He
grabbed a full bottle of gin and headed for the roof.

The gin eased the hangover, replacing it with a buzz
that numbed the ache of missing Serena. From the roof,
Julian launched the helicopter and took off toward the
desert. He flew like a madman, bearing toward his goal
at a speed only a man hell-bent on suicide would attempt. He wanted to crash the helicopter. He wanted
leave his body to rot out in the desert. Unfortunately,
killing himself was not an option. His body would
simply regenerate, returning him to the same situation
he was trying to escape. Or else he would be returned
to the underworld, to the ceaseless burn of those fiery

pits. For a demon, there was no easy exit strategy. There was only this unending hell of existence.

But Julian was no coward, and suicide was the coward's way out. He was, however, tired. Exhausted by living. Exhausted by the centuries of endless corruption, of unrelenting vice. Any pleasure he'd taken in it had gone forever when Serena had walked out the door.

He flew for hours, taking the same route he'd flown with her the day she'd almost died. Landed on the same plateau where they'd spread their picnic. Feet from where he'd parked the chopper, where she'd lain in the dirt and fought to stay alive, had grasped the edge of life as it had slipped away and had pulled herself back. She was a fighter, that one. A fighter until the end. She would not be one to wallow. He tried to picture her now, back in Los Angeles, sitting in her apartment or teaching at her yoga studio.

He sat in the helicopter, staring at the layered rock formations, down into the wide mouth of Bright Angel Canyon. What had once seemed beautiful now seemed merely vacant without her. He'd been right about Keats. Beauty did not always amount to truth. Beauty could be evil, and it could also be empty.

His bright angel had left him. He had forced her to go. She was better off without him.

When his buzz started to wear off, he grabbed the bottle of gin from where he'd tossed it on the passenger seat, took a swig and let it burn down his throat.

Would Serena think of him? If she did, what would she remember? The worst, probably. That he'd coerced her into the trip in the first place. That he'd exposed her to Luciana and that nearly lethal snakebite. That he'd bet her on a card game and almost lost her. That he'd made love to her, then abandoned her like a one-night stand he'd picked up in a bar somewhere.

She would not remember that he had fallen in love with her. That she meant more to him than any other person or thing he'd ever encountered in his two centuries of existence.

Because she would never know.

At the same time that Julian was drowning his self-pity in gin, Nick was numbing out the pain of living by taking copious amounts of prescription painkillers. He didn't remember calling Corbin and Luciana. But on Saturday afternoon, they showed up on the doorstep of his bungalow in L.A. He peered at them through his drug-induced fog.

"We made the trip from Vegas just for you, my friend," Corbin said, as the couple walked in and made themselves comfortable in his living room. "We knew you would need the support."

"Finally, some real friends," Nick said, collapsing onto the sofa beside Luciana. "Nobody takes me seriously, not even Serena. I want what you have. I have wealth and fame. But I don't have any real power. Nobody respects me."

"Hush now, *amore,*" Luciana said, stroking her long fingers through his hair. "We respect you."

"We can make everything easy," Corbin offered. "It's going to require one small sacrifice. But afterward, you can have whatever you want."

"Like what kind of sacrifice?" Nick asked.

Luciana laughed. "*Caro,* have you ever thought about what a pain life is?"

"Of course," Nick said irritably, wondering what she was getting at. "But so what?"

"You don't have to feel so much pain. If you're no longer alive…" said Corbin.

Nick almost laughed out loud. "What, kill myself? You're kidding, right?"

Neither of them even cracked a smile.

"Don't worry, death is not as difficult as it might seem," the hotelier said. "Once you get over the pain of living, you'll be much stronger in your afterlife."

Of course they were joking. For all of the pain life had caused him, Nick had never once contemplated suicide. But looking into Corbin's eyes, a new idea began to form inside his head. *Yes. Of course. I might as well end it now.* Nothing had ever been so clear to Nick. So he said, "You're right. I'll be much stronger in my afterlife. The only question is, how do I get there?"

"We'll be here with you," Corbin told him. "But you have to decide how you want to go."

"Well, there's one easy way that comes to mind." Nick opened a drawer in his coffee table. Inside was his smorgasbord of drugs, a collection of baggies and bottles that he kept on hand for parties and other little emergencies. *Cocaine, Ecstasy, Percocet, heroin, Vicodin.* All his favorites were there. And then some.

"Let me help you," Corbin said, perusing the stash. He took out a small handful of pills here, a few grams of powder there. "Yes, this should do the trick."

Later that afternoon, when Serena awoke after a long nap, the shock of leaving Julian had begun to dissipate. But now the real pain set in. Pain so intense she thought she might die from it. Wished that she would lift right out of her physical body and ascend back to the heavens, back to disembodied bliss. Wished she could burst through the thin membrane of life that bound her to the material realm.

She had finally experienced love, and it hurt more than anything she had ever known before. Yet, life without Julian would go on. Somewhere deep inside of her, Serena knew that. Whether she would ever get over loving him…now, that was another story.

Yet, as painful as it was, she knew she could not simply stay at home and mourn forever.

She did what she had always done in times of pressure and pain. What she had done when her father had died. She went to the yoga studio and rolled out her mat on the studio floor.

In only a matter of days, her body felt like it had aged a decade.

She moved slowly, allowing her muscles the chance to readjust to the familiar movements. It hurt, this confrontation with the unavoidable reality that she was yoked in this physical body. As she flowed through the postures, her mind returned again and again to Julian. *To Julian's touch. To Julian's kisses.* To the day he had come into the studio. The room hadn't changed, and neither had her yoga practice. Yet, nothing would ever be the same. He had become a part of her. She closed her eyes and pushed on, trying to lose herself in the waves of her breath, counting each inhalation and exhalation and letting that steady rhythm carry her through the practice.

Afterward, she lay on her back in corpse pose,

looking up at the bright patterned scarves on the ceiling. Before, this place had always felt like home. Coming to the mat, she had always felt whole and complete. Now, she felt like something was missing. She tried to discipline herself not to think of him. She didn't *need* him, she told herself. He was not essential to her life, like oxygen, or water, or food.

Somehow, she would go on without him.

Her phone beeped. Ordinarily, she turned it off the moment she entered the studio, but today she hadn't, not only because she was waiting to hear from Nick. But also in the pathetic hope that Julian would call. Her fingers shook as she picked it up, clicked on the message that she'd just received. Julian had not called.

It was a one-word text from Nick.

Goodbye.

The word sent a chill over her. What did that mean? *Goodbye?*

Oh, no.

She slammed out of the yoga studio, fingers shaking as she locked the door behind her, heart thundering in her chest as she jumped into her car. She had taught Nick's first yoga lesson at his West Hollywood home before moving his sessions into the studio. As she drove there, foot heavy on the gas pedal, every minute seemed to stretch into an eternity. Time expanded, and it seemed as though she had slipped into a surreal nightmare as she sped toward the inevitable.

Outside Nick's bungalow, an ambulance was parked, its lights still flashing. She got out of her car and approached the open front door. Inside, a team of paramedics pumped the chest of the body lying on the living-room floor.

Just like her father.

And just like her father, Nick was dead by the time she arrived, his body cold and lifeless.

"May I see him?" she asked, moving toward him. She stood over him, tears slipping down her cheeks. Laid a hand on his forehead. At rest, Nick looked so peaceful, finally. Angelic, almost.

"Are you his girlfriend, miss?" someone asked.

"No," she whispered. "He didn't have a girlfriend."

Nick had lived and died, just as Serena had herself, never knowing true love.

Nick's death was ruled an accidental overdose, the result of a lethal combination of illegal drugs and prescription painkillers. The text Serena had gotten moments before his death told her otherwise. Nick had participated in his own death. Serena sat in Arielle's office, trying to make sense of what had happened.

"Where did he go?" Serena whispered. She felt like a complete failure, so full of shame that she had lost Nick.

"Nowhere we've been able to track," Arielle said. She paused before admitting, "However, we strongly suspect that he may have become a demon."

Serena gazed out the window at the beach across the street. Nick should have been out there on this hot summer's day. Lying on the sand beneath his aviator sunglasses and a baseball cap. Not lying on a cold mortuary slab beneath a sheet of plastic. She bit her lip to stop herself from crying. "Nick killed himself because of me."

Arielle's sharp, intense look made her bright blue eyes almost frightening. "You must *never* speak like that again. Nick's death was not your fault. We all lose Assignees. It's an unfortunate reality of being a Guardian. Every soul makes its own decisions. We do not blame ourselves." She paused, something warring in her perfect, beautiful face. At last, she said, "I couldn't tell you before this, but I lost my first Assignee, as well."

"You?"

"Yes. And I've spent an inordinate amount of energy lately trying to get him back," said Arielle.

Julian.

In Serena's head, the pieces started falling into place, a rush of information that made her review every interaction with the Archdemon since they'd met. In a split second, all the assumptions she'd made about him, and about Arielle, had been shattered. "But how can an angel be assigned to a demon?"

"I was assigned to Julian when he was still human. I've been fighting for his soul for the past two hundred years," Arielle said. "I've tried everything. Direct interventions, scores of other women. Nothing has worked. Until you."

Emotions bubbled inside of Serena: anger, frustration, sadness. They swirled inside her, an internal cyclone that threatened to sweep her away. Yet, she remained, anchored here by her supervisor's calming presence.

"But I didn't work, either. Julian wasn't saved." She paused to digest the information.

"You got closer to him than anyone ever has."

"Is that why you left me alone with him? To try to convert him to our side?"

Arielle smiled gently. "You were never truly alone. The Company had angels with you all along, watching over you."

"Even when I…" Serena blushed. Did Arielle know *everything* that had happened?

"Slept with Julian? Well, no. Not then. We understand the need for privacy, you know."

Barely. The fact that the Company knew she had slept with Julian was humiliating enough.

Arielle gave a long, bemused sigh. "Dear, there's nothing wrong with sex as long as it stems from love. You knew that already. What you did was natural. You didn't hurt anyone, and you didn't hurt yourself. In fact, we had hoped it would happen. For the sake of the assignment."

"I still don't understand. How could you have let me go through all that anxiety…for nothing? Why did you let me think I had no support?"

Arielle smiled gently. "It wasn't for nothing. Everything happens for a reason. There were things we needed to keep from you, for your own good. For instance, you needed to learn to stand on your own two feet. Every Guardian must learn to walk alone. And you did. Perhaps more importantly, if you had known about Julian, he never would have fallen in love with you."

"So what do I do now?" Serena asked. "Nick is gone. I failed my mission."

"*Failure* is a harsh word. No experience is ever wasted," Arielle said gently. "For now, take some time off from your work with the Company. Go back to teaching yoga for a while. In time, you'll see the lessons you learned from this mission."

The supervisor's words were little comfort. Serena closed her eyes, swallowing down the grief that threatened to wash over her. She wished that none of it had ever happened. Whatever Arielle said, it did not change the fact that Nick had killed himself on Serena's watch.

He had been *her* Assignee. *Her* responsibility. She had failed him. She had failed the Company. She had failed herself.

As the afternoon began to fade into evening, the weather turned gray and drizzly, unusual for midsummer. While his family grieved his loss privately, all of Los Angeles seemed to be mourning Nick Ramirez along with them. At his home, paparazzi swarmed and a massive pile of flowers began to accumulate on his doorstep. T-shirts with Nick's face emblazoned across them cropped up in the city and began to spread across the country.

Thousands of his fans turned up for an impromptu memorial that someone had organized in the back of an old warehouse. It quickly turned into a rave, where people danced late into the night because everybody who attended agreed, "This is what Nick would have wanted." News cameras hovered in helicopters overhead to capture the crowds for posterity.

Alive, he was just another disaster of a young actor, his frequent missteps merely more fodder for the gossip magazines.

Dead, Nick had become an icon.

* * *

Devil's Ecstasy was on the verge of its opening night. And Julian didn't give a damn.

Downstairs, people thronged in the lobby of the Lussuria, a crowd stacked with celebrities waiting for Julian to open the doors and officially start the party. The debauchery. The excessive drinking. The exotic drugs and the wild, unimaginable sex. He should have been down there, celebrating his greatest accomplishment to date.

Instead, Julian didn't care.

Not because he was still stuck wallowing in self-pity. *No.* Because arriving back from his helicopter joyride in the desert, Harry promptly told him the bad news.

"Nick Ramirez is dead," his personal assistant said in a hushed voice. "And Corbin and Luciana have been spotted in Los Angeles."

Julian immediately saw what a fool he'd been. Rather than wasting time flying around in the desert and feeling sorry for himself, he ought to have been planning. Amassing his forces against his enemies, anticipating their revenge. Instead, he had been temporarily blinded by loss. By grief. *By love.*

"We need to find Corbin and Luciana, and we must act quickly before they do any more damage. I should have taken care of them properly last night, or even today, but I…" For an instant, he was without words, flushed with shame, silenced by worry. *I've got to make sure Serena is safe.*

"You had your hands full, sir," Harry said quietly. "Don't worry. We'll find them."

For once, Julian was grateful for his assistant's

compassion, the very trait he had been trying to cultivate out of Harry.

"Thank you, Harry," he said. "Get the Gatekeepers to track down Corbin and Luciana. I'm going to find Serena."

By the time Nick realized that Corbin had tricked him, it was far too late.

The process of dying had hurt like hell. Nick's physical body had been racked with pain from vomiting copiously. He'd fallen to the floor, convulsing from seizures, his heart pounding as though it were about to explode, when mercifully his brain had finally shut down. Then his soul had taken a gory trip to hell, where he'd seen things he'd never imagined possible. Things that were burned into his mind, things he would never forget. Now, at least he was back here on earth. A strange fear had set in, though, and an overwhelming sense of guilt at having thrown away something tremendously precious. At having wasted his human life.

Corbin laughed scornfully as he asked Nick, "Did you really think it was all going to become magically easy? You're an idiot."

"You said I would become like you," Nick whined, "but I'm not. What am I now?"

"Nothing. Less than nothing. You're at the bottom of the totem pole, lower than even the Gatekeeper demons. You've got to prove yourself if you want to become a real demon."

It was all so fucking depressing.

"Here's your first assignment if you want to become

one of us," Corbin said. "You're going to help me get Serena."

"Why do you need my help?" Nick whined.

Corbin stared at him for a long time. He used the same neutral tone as always, but now it scared the shit out of Nick. Because now Nick knew what lay behind that pretense of neutrality. Now he knew what Corbin really was.

"Stop asking questions, Nick," the Archdemon said. "Just do as I say."

Serena sat at the back of the yoga room, watching the rows of spandex-clad bodies lying on their colored mats, as they rested in *sivasana*. Corpse pose. A mimicking of death. A pose for the living to learn to let go. What could Serena teach these students about real death? Even though she'd been through it herself, she still struggled with it. Struggled with letting go. Nick's death permeated her thoughts. And despite Arielle's advice, Serena found it impossible to ignore the crushing disappointment of her own failure.

Her phone beeped, the noise loud enough to startle a few of her students out of their repose, heads turning toward the disturbance. She apologized and checked her phone. It was another text from Nick.

I'm with Andrew. Meet us at Devil's Paradise.

Even the dead had trouble letting go.

Julian was just one step behind Serena, so close he could feel her vibration lingering in the places she'd been. The first place he'd tried was her home, but he found Meredith there instead. The redhead had opened the door a crack, looking out at him with the watch-fulness of a pit bull on guard against an approaching thief.

"Is she here?" he'd asked, impatience getting the better of him.

"Why would I tell you if she was?" the roommate said, crossing her arms and staring him down.

"Because I'm in love with her." Had he said that out loud before? He didn't think so. He wished he had picked a better time to announce his feelings, wished he could have told Serena herself instead of her angry friend.

"Well, it's a cold day in hell," Meredith smirked. "But if you hurry, you just might catch her. She's down at the studio, teaching a candlelight yoga class."

Angels. So goddamned self-righteous. For the first time he could remember, Julian didn't care. But when he dematerialized, arriving at the yoga studio a moment later, Serena wasn't there, either. He stood in the reception area, where he'd once kissed her. He'd already been half in love with her then. Her students filed past him on their way out the door. And he wondered where on earth she had gone.

"Don't go into Devil's Paradise by yourself, Serena," Arielle ordered into the phone as Serena sped toward the nightclub. "The Company is coming to help you."

The nightclub was ominously quiet for a Saturday night. There was no trace of the crowds that usually swarmed the club, no lineup of fashionably dressed club-goers waiting outside. It was as if she were walking into a ghost town. Not a single Gatekeeper was around to guard the place. *Where is everyone?* she wondered.

Standing outside, she shivered in the warm night air. Then she heard the faint cry of her brother's voice, coming from somewhere inside the darkened club.

"Serena! Come quickly! I need you!"

The little voice inside Serena whispered, *Don't go in. Wait for Arielle and the others.* But Andrew was in there. Fear raced through her, spurring her on. She had to go in, and she had to do it *now.*

The heavy front doors of Devil's Paradise creaked as she hauled them open. Inside, the dark, empty space felt eerie without the glittering lights and the well-dressed crowds. In Vegas, she'd felt safe with Julian, alone with him on his territory. Now, a frisson of doubt swept over her.

The door clanged shut behind her, cutting off the outside world and shrouding her in complete darkness. "Andrew? Nick? I'm here," she called out.

While her eyes adjusted to the dimness, she stood for a moment, listening for movement. She took a few tentative steps, trying to recall the interior layout. "Where are you?"

As if in answer, the building creaked a tired groan of complaint, then settled back into silence.

There was a large foyer, she remembered, before the main dance floor. She stopped, peering into the darkness. She could make out the high ceilings, two stories overhead, and the pillars rising up to support them. Somewhere at the back of the club, a door slammed. She jumped, skittering like a spooked animal.

A shadow darted; she heard the shuffle of quick footsteps around her.

"Andrew? Nick?" she called again. Silence. She started to retreat toward the front doors.

The sensation of a hand brushing her arm stopped her cold.

"I knew you would come."

When she saw Nick, she knew immediately. He was no longer human. He had become a demon. Physically, he had not changed at all, even though she knew that his body was now virtually indestructible, just as hers was. From one glance into his eyes, the change was apparent.

His eyes had been soulful when he'd been human, their warm brown depths had held a range of emotions that changed from one moment to the next. Now, they had the cast of a demon's eyes, a fixed stare of pure hatred that Julian and the older demons kept masked with their practiced expressions of boredom.

Evil emanated from him, an energy surrounding him that was invisible yet wholly tangible. The kind of energy that older demons knew how to hide, as well. With Nick, that malevolence was so fresh, so new it was almost electric, and it chilled her to the bone.

"Where's Andrew?" she managed to squeak.

Nick laughed. "I have no idea. Probably at home."

"But I just heard him call for help," she said.

"I'm a very talented actor. My impersonations are second to none. But then, you wouldn't know that, would you? Because you never cared to ask," Nick said, his stare holding steady as he moved closer.

"How did you know Andrew was my brother? And

how did you get in here?" she said, anger rising within her. She had only ever tried to help Nick, had only ever wished the best for him. Now, he had tricked her.

"I know a lot more than I did before," he said carelessly. "Now I have help."

In the darkness, she heard another movement, the touch of feet so light on the floor it was barely perceptible. The air beside her shifted, and suddenly he was there, beside her. *Corbin.* Her body froze as he circled around her. Overhead, a woman's laugh echoed. The dim light flickered, and Luciana descended a metal staircase, coming toward Serena at a frightening speed. As the demoness drew nearer, Serena saw the knife glinting in her hand.

"Nick?" Serena asked. "What have you done?"

"I've finally realized how to get what I want." There was bitterness in his voice, unshielded by any artifice now. "You care more for that asshole of an Archdemon than you do for me. You may be in love with Julian, but I can still have you. I know what you are now, angel."

"I'm sorry, Nick. I never meant to hurt you. But whatever the demons told you, I wouldn't believe them. They're full of lies."

"And you're not? You lied, too, even though you were supposed to guard me. Oh, I think you made a genuine effort at the beginning. Then you started sleeping with Julian. I had to find guidance elsewhere."

In that instant, Serena glanced downward, her gaze catching on Luciana's black satin shoes. The ones she'd seen kicked off inside the door in Nick's hotel room the night they had left Vegas. *Nick and Luciana.* Her mind struggled to process it.

"So Luciana was in your room when I came to get you?" she asked.

"She told me to go with you," Nick said. "Said you needed my support. Luciana's not the jealous type."

Serena didn't believe that for a second, but she bit her tongue. Instead, she asked, "How long have you been… with them?"

"Not long at all," said Nick. "This is a new beginning for me. And it will be for you, too, Serena." The three demons laughed, the sound roaring in her ears and sending her pulse rocketing into panic mode.

"We'll show you the error of your ways, m'dear. No more of this angelic nonsense. You'll have much more fun with us," Corbin said.

"We can all be together," said Nick. "The way it was meant to be. Don't worry. We know how to share."

Corbin interjected then, pushing the younger man aside so hard that Nick fell to the floor. "You're wrong about sharing, my young friend. You haven't earned that privilege yet," the Archdemon said blandly. He reached out to run his hand down the front of Serena's body, squeezing her breast and slipping his hand between her legs. She slapped him hard across the face, the *crack* of it resounding in the empty space. For a long, terrible moment, he held his hand to his cheek.

"Feisty little thing, aren't you? Not scared of death, I see. What more will it take to teach you to fear me?" Corbin asked her.

Oh, God, please keep me safe.

Luciana danced around them, gleeful. "We're going to throw you to the Gatekeepers after we're finished with you," she crooned. "By then, you'll be a shred of a woman. And when the Gatekeepers have had their fill, I'm going to drain you. Virgins' blood is the best beauty secret. You're far from a virgin, but your blood might do just as well."

Corbin said in a disapproving voice, "We'll do no such thing. We'll keep her as a pet, chained to the bedroom wall."

Serena shuddered. She didn't know which was worse. At least if they killed her, she would probably start the recycling process again. The pain of it would be hideous, but at least there would be an end to it. But if Corbin kept her…there could be nothing closer to hell on earth than being a demon's slave.

"Please," she said. "Don't hurt me."

"Oh, I won't hurt you, dear," Corbin said. "I promised Julian I wouldn't harm a hair on your head. You'll love it when we fuck. But I can't vouch for what Luciana might do."

The demoness held up her knife. The silver blade gleamed, picking up a shard of light in the darkness of the nightclub. She ran it along Serena's cheek. Blood seeped out. Luciana drew her finger along the cut, stinging. Serena felt the vomit rising in her throat, threatening to spill out.

She closed her eyes and prayed.

God in heaven, protect me.… Please, God. Send help.

There was one last obvious place for Julian to look, and a phone call from Harry confirmed it.

"They took her," his assistant said, breathless on the other end of the line.

"Who?" Julian demanded.

"Corbin, Luciana and Nick. They killed the Gate-keepers you sent to watch her. One of them managed to get us a message before he died."

"Where is she?" Julian asked. His gut began to churn. What a fool he'd been. He'd broken the cardinal rule of the demon world. Never underestimate your opponent. Worse, he'd underestimated his own attachment to the girl. Even Corbin saw what Julian couldn't. That she was the only thing in the world that would bait Julian into a trap.

Love had blinded him. By fearing to ruin her himself, he'd pushed her away, into a danger worse than he ever could have inflicted. His mind began to run through all the possibilities. He shut his eyes and shook his head, willing the gory images out of his head.

Harry said, "We're not quite sure yet. But somebody phoned in a bomb scare to Devil's Paradise. Cleared the place out. It's empty. I'm sending over a team of Gate-keepers as we speak."

"I'm going now," Julian said.

He closed his eyes and concentrated on Los Angeles, on his West Hollywood nightclub. He arrived in front of the carved wooden doors of Devil's Paradise. And as he had last night, when he thought he had lost Serena to Corbin, he prayed. Prayed for guidance. Prayed for assistance. Most of all, he prayed for Serena's safety. Not knowing whether his prayers would be answered, he did it anyway.

He hauled the doors open and entered. In the darkness, he navigated from memory, visualizing the space he knew so well, his steps echoing in the massive room.

Light flooded the dance floor, illuminating two figures there. Corbin and Serena. He'd tied her to a post, and her once-bright hair was dulled, matted with blood. Good God, what had Corbin done to her? Julian would kill him. But first he would torture him, frighten him as much as Corbin had frightened Serena. He would sever Corbin's genitals from his groin, and make him bleed like he'd made Serena bleed.

A third figure huddled on the floor, cowering in terror. *Nick.*

"Ah, Julian," said Corbin. "The knight in shining armor, come to rescue the damsel in distress."

Serena looked up then, shock in her wide blue eyes. Corbin had stuffed a gag in her mouth, but she screamed anyway, a muffled sound of frustration that stoked Julian's rage to a white heat.

"Let her go, Corbin," Julian growled. "You win. Take me instead. Take the hotel. You can have whatever you want."

"Thanks to our young friend Nick, I already have what I want. I want her," Corbin said easily.

"Let her go. She's innocent," Julian told him.

"All the better. It's not as much fun killing guilty people all the time. I enjoy a little tragic injustice once in a while. Don't you?" A trace of satisfaction glittered in Corbin's cold blue gaze. "In any case, why should I let her go when I can have both of you?"

The older demon moved toward Serena. At the side of her throat, he held the blade of a knife. As Julian walked closer, he saw that her face, her neck, her arms were covered with thin cuts.

"Don't worry, I promised I wouldn't hurt her. This is

all Luciana's handiwork," Corbin said. "So don't come any closer. I wouldn't want to break my promise."

"Coward," Julian ground out. "Why don't you fight me, like a real man? Instead of torturing an innocent girl." He squared his stance, ready to take on an attack.

Serena shook her head, and screamed again. Julian could see the message in her eyes: *Get out. Save yourself. Leave me here.* As if he would ever do that.

Corbin held the knife at her throat, and Julian could see the blood that dulled the sheen of the blade. "Shall I cut the jugular or the carotid? It would be so easy to slice right through either. And wouldn't that be a pity, if she bled out here? Rather ironic. Devil's Paradise, the final resting place of an angel. It'll make your club even more popular," he said.

Julian's blood raged. "You can't kill her. You know the rules."

"Perhaps you're right. But we can certainly cause a great deal of pain."

We?

Out of the corner of his eye, Julian saw the flash of black hair beside him. *Luciana.* She came toward him with all of her pent-up vengeance, two centuries of rage that had grown into an uncontrollable force all its own. He dodged and she swept past, overshooting him in her fury. As she spun to face him again, he grabbed her sideways, wrestling a knife out of her hand. It clattered to the ground, and he kicked it away.

He wrapped his hands around her neck. "Let go of Serena. Or I'll send Luciana straight back to hell."

Corbin just stared at him with that inscrutable gaze. "Go ahead. You'll be doing us both a favor."

"*Arrogh'e merda,* Corbin, you piece of shit," Luciana shrieked. "How dare you?"

"Didn't anyone ever tell you, sweetheart? Never bet the devil your head. He'll screw you every time," Julian said, thrusting her away from him. "Come on, Corbin. Fight me. Show me what kind of a man you are. Just the two of us. I'm the one you want. I'm the one who took your hotel. I'm the one who made a fool out of you. Crushed your reputation. Usurped your power."

What happened next seemed to occur in slow motion. Corbin dove at Julian, just as he'd done in the high-stakes room at the hotel. Julian feinted, knocking the knife out of his hand. But this time Corbin's weight caught him square in the chest and sent the two men crashing to the floor. Pain seared through Julian's back as they landed, Corbin's body crushing him as they fell.

Beneath them, the floor of the material world gave way and they continued to fall, spiraling down into emptiness. Down into hell.

They were gone. Julian and Corbin had disappeared, leaving Luciana gawking in their wake. The demoness turned, fixing her serpentine gaze on Serena, still bound to the post. Their heads turned in tandem. On the ground between them lay a discarded knife, still wet with Serena's blood.

Luciana smiled as she bent to pick it up. "Now, where were we?"

In that instant, half a dozen burly Gatekeepers lunged

through the door, scattering as they entered the club, their eyes adjusting to the darkness. They paused, glancing at the two women with some confusion.

God in heaven, help me…

"Take her!" Luciana ordered, pointing at Serena.

But the Gatekeepers did not move. They took their instructions from Julian, and in Julian's absence, they hesitated. Then one of the Gatekeepers advanced, not toward Serena, but toward Luciana.

"*Maledizione!* You're demons, aren't you? She's an angel! Idiots, why won't you listen to one of your own kind!" Luciana screamed. She held the point of her knife at Serena's neck, its tip pricking against her skin. "Stop right there or she dies."

Serena felt her pulse beating against the metal edge of the knife. A strange calm came over her, knowing that even if she died, she would be safe. Luciana yanked loose the rope that bound her to the post, freeing her and shoving her forward.

The doors to Devil's Paradise swung open on a gust of cool wind.

In the doorway, Arielle stood, her blond hair blowing around her, bright as a halo. Behind her, half a dozen members of the Company stood, their presence radiating strength. The supervisor stared down Luciana and said, "Harm Serena and you will never know a moment's peace again. The Company will hunt you down. We will find you. And you will understand the consequences of killing an angel."

The two women stood, glaring at each other. Time seemed elastic, and in the moment that they stood transfixed, Serena sensed the power struggle between them, a showdown of unspoken threats in the space between their locked gazes.

"Let her go," Arielle ordered.

The demoness's breath hissed through her throat, the steam of her fury escaping through a pressure valve. She still had the potential to blow. Finally, with a vicious thrust, Luciana hurled her captive into the heavy doors of Devil's Paradise. Serena's head connected with the wooden door frame. Pain splintered through her skull. She felt Arielle's arms catch her as she fell, cushioning her descent.

"Luciana's getting away!" someone shouted.

It was the last thing Serena heard before she passed out.

Chapter Seventeen

Serena wandered in a haze among the red mists of hell, through a labyrinth of rooms. At each turn, she saw clusters of demons torturing the damned, gnawing at the entrails of mutilated human bodies, digging out their eyeballs with great, curving claws that trailed strands of bloody nerves. In her dream, the demons hissed, pale green snake eyes glowing.

She ran, twisting and turning through the snaking corridors, until she came to the center of the maze, where she found Julian, tied to a rotting wooden bed frame. He turned his head, imploring her with blue-green eyes bright with fever. Beneath her, her feet were rooted, unable to move. From behind, a demon caught her, claws slicing into her shoulder, and...

She awoke in her own bed at home, surrounded by the familiar froth of her white duvet. Her head ached like she'd been hit with a two-by-four. But she was still alive. Her wounds would heal. At least on the outside. Bile surged in her stomach and threatened to rise up her throat. She swallowed hard and willed it down.

Arielle perched on the edge of her bed, leaning over her with concern. Serena croaked, "What happened? How long was I out?"

She remembered Corbin and Julian dematerializing from the floor of the empty nightclub. The imprint of their struggle lingering in the empty air they had just vacated. Then, like a ripple in a pond, all trace of them had vanished and the space had gone still again.

"A few hours. Things went a little differently from how we had planned," Arielle said. "None of us anticipated that Nick would disappear, but he did and he's lost to us at the present time. Perhaps at some point in the future we'll be in a position to reach him. But more importantly, we achieved our primary goal. Julian is no longer a demon. He no longer has the power to corrupt humans. Your work is done."

Nick is lost to us. That was Arielle's way of saying that Nick was in hell. As for Julian…Serena knew where he had gone, too. Her dream had not been a dream. Corbin had taken Julian to the underworld.

Arielle confirmed it, but then added, "It's not your responsibility to save him. Julian believes he needs to be punished. And as long as he believes that, no one can save him."

There was silence between them as Serena's mind flipped back to the nightmare images that had ripped through her sleep. *The damned, tormented by demons. Julian, chained to a bed.*

She flipped back the covers. Her whole body ached; her injuries were still not fully healed, but she would not let that stop her. She would not sit in bed while Julian burned in the underworld. There was no time to waste. "Then I'm not finished. We need to get Julian out of there," she announced. "I'm going to hell."

"You're willing to take the chance that you may end

up sacrificing yourself for all eternity?" Arielle asked. "Think about what that means, Serena. The rest of your existence in hell. Your mission is not to sacrifice yourself. Remember, you've already done that once before. The risk is far too great. It's time to let Julian go."

"I love him. I have to try," Serena said, regretting that her actions had impacted her supervisor in ways that Serena herself had never considered. Still, she could not give up on Julian. "I don't believe that God would allow me to get stuck in hell. I'm not afraid. Besides, Julian risked himself for me."

Arielle pursed her lips, silent as Serena rooted in her dresser for a pair of jeans and a simple blouse. Finally, the older angel said, "I wish I could go with you, but I can't. Corbin specializes in taking people into their own personal version of hell, modeled on their darkest fears and traumas. Only someone Julian trusts enough to let into his subconscious will be allowed to enter his version of hell."

Serena turned to face her, clothes in hand. "How do I know he'll let me in?"

"You don't. Not until you get there. But you won't go alone. The Archangels have the power to enter any part of hell. You'll have to ask Gabriel if he will guide you."

"How do I do that?"

"Call and he will come." Arielle rose from the bed, came to squeeze Serena's hand. Around them, white light flared for an instant, its brilliance gathering to surround Serena with a luminous aura. "Use the light to protect yourself when you're in hell. Remember to keep love in your heart. And one more thing—always remember that you're a fully enlightened being."

Julian burned. The fires of fever consumed him, his mind wandering through a delirious nightmare of images. He slipped in and out of consciousness, unable to distinguish exactly where he was, only that he was strapped to a surface, lying flat with his belly and chest exposed. He writhed, he twisted, but he could not escape the pain that seared through his body.

Corbin loomed over him, the flesh of his face melting away to skeleton, the eyeballs uncovered and bulging. Corbin's bare skull, teeth bared in a permanent grin, white against the exposed jawbone. "You remember Brooke, don't you, Julian? You ruined her life. She's been down here, waiting for you."

Brooke Bentley's vibrant beauty had already been ravaged during her years on earth, but hell had transformed her into a creature Julian no longer recognized. A being no longer human, a grotesque parody of the woman she'd been in life. The skin he'd once caressed was now torn and hanging from her in ribbons of gore. Desiccated weeds tangled in her matted auburn hair, and a putrid stench arose as she moved toward Julian. At the ends of her fingers were no longer fingernails, but the claws of a bird of prey, a Frankensteinian version of a harpy's hand.

"This is for what you did to me. For all of the women you destroyed," she shrieked, plunging one of those talons toward the pit of his belly.

"No!" Agony roiled in the pit of Julian's gut; his

insides buckled as though she had impaled his abdomen with a glowing hot iron. But when he looked down, his shirtless body was unmarked. Was it an illusion, this torture? Whatever it was, in this nightmare of a hell realm, the pain was very real.

Brooke laughed then, her cackle spiraling up into a ringing echo, infernally loud in the cavernous space around him, even as he clenched his eyes shut against her.

Nothing could save him. He was damned, and he would remain here, trapped in this endless suffering. Because he deserved it, he knew. He may have prayed for Serena when he needed the support of the divine. But for himself, Julian knew he was beyond prayer. Beyond hope. Beyond redemption.

Regret. Since the end of his human life, centuries ago, the word had signified nothing. When the shot of his pistol had pierced the heart of Luciana's husband, he had known regret. But upon his human death, immersed in the blaze of hell, that regret had burned away, licked into flames the same way paper dissolves in fire. His regret had melted into the ember emotions of bitterness and malice.

He thought of Serena. Through experiencing her love, he had recovered the meaning of regret. He deserved to be punished. For all of the countless lives he had ruined, for all the people who had suffered exactly like this. His actions had resulted in the torture of thousands, and for that, he deserved to be punished. Most of all, he deserved to be punished because he'd placed Serena's life at risk. He had toyed with divinity, and he had come very close to corrupting it.

As Brooke plunged her needle-sharp claw into his stomach once again, Julian's single consolation was that at least Serena was safe.

The sky in Julian's hell was a deep gray, the clouds pregnant and threatening to burst at any moment. They rolled overhead at a terrifying speed, giving Serena a feeling of vertigo as she walked behind Gabriel. To quiet her stomach, she focused on his white wings, brilliant against the drab landscape.

In the distance, the outline of a ruined English manor house dominated a hilltop. Gabriel said in a hushed voice, "That's Julian's ancestral home. It's here, in his version of hell, because this is the scene of his deepest fears."

"Where is he?" Serena asked, shivering. It was supposed to be hot in hell, not cold, wasn't it?

The Archangel motioned for her to follow him. Entering a forest of withered trees, they walked until they reached a dilapidated cottage. The thatched roof was crumbling, covered in patches of mold, and the garden rambled, overgrown with weeds, roses decomposing in mottled shades of dried blood. Without knocking, Gabriel pushed open the door and entered.

Inside, a thick layer of dust covered the dark wood floors. The few sparse pieces of furniture were broken and decaying. As Serena took a step forward, the floorboard beneath her foot creaked and then gave way. Gingerly, she pulled her foot out of the hole and continued behind Gabriel.

From another room, they heard a man curse, and another groan.

Gabriel held a finger to his lips, signaling for silence. As quietly as she could, Serena followed him. He pushed open the door.

Julian was chained to a child's bed, its wooden frame rotting, exactly as it had been in her nightmare. He was shivering, sweat running down his face.

Serena knelt, smoothed a hand over his forehead. "What's wrong with him?"

"Typhus," Gabriel said. "Before mankind invented antibiotics, it was an illness spread by body lice."

"So it's treatable?" she asked.

Gabriel nodded. "With modern medicine, it is completely curable."

Julian opened his eyes, the crack of a fevered gaze showing through his encrusted lids. "You shouldn't have come here. I can no longer protect you—I've been stripped of my powers. Please go. Before he gets back."

A chill ran up the back of her neck, and she sensed the approach of something ominous, the way a cat might sense a coming storm. Her back was turned toward the door, and she whirled to protect it from the approach of evil. As she did, she saw that Corbin stood in the doorway. Not a Corbin she had ever seen before, but she recognized immediately that it was the essence of the demon uncovered, stripped down to the bone. Remnants of flesh, veins, arteries clung to his skeletal limbs and head, but he moved like no living thing she'd ever seen. Serena drew herself up, standing tall even though her entire body trembled. "Speak of the devil."

Corbin slammed the door shut behind him, closing the space of the small room. The walls seemed to constrict, the four of them cloistered in the enclosure, steeping in the rot of illness. "Why, this is an unexpected visitation. Angels in hell. And not yet fallen, I see," Corbin roared. "You've pushed your luck a bit too far, I'm afraid. Now that you've come, you're here to stay."

"We've come for Julian," Serena announced, knees buckling under her as she spoke. If she failed here, there would be three souls lost, not just one. She had known it, trusted that Gabriel, her guide, would protect them from the heinous forces that dwelled here.

And Gabriel towered beside her, glorious even in this pestilent squalor. Hell did not diminish the glow of his luminous down wings, nor could it dull the gentle beauty of his face. He stood silently, but Serena drew courage from his presence.

Corbin sneered as he regarded them. "Julian's not going anywhere. He's going to rot down here in hell for the rest of time. And you'll rot with him."

She took a deep breath and said, "You have no power over me, Corbin. You may have been able to best me once, but I don't fear you anymore."

That bony grin answered her. In a blur of shadow, the demon whipped forward and grasped her arm. "I'm going to give you a taste of what your life is going to be like from now on. We're going on a little tour of your own personal hell."

She felt her body dissolving, wavering in the small cottage bedroom, transported out of it. Dematerializing. *Remember that you are a fully enlightened being,* Arielle had said. Serena stared hard into Corbin's eyes and concentrated on that thought: *You are a fully enlightened being.*

He fought against her, his willpower outstripping hers. Around them, a different scene started to materialize: that of a rainy, cold day one year ago. She stood on the side of the road, soaked to the skin. Fifteen feet away, two cars had collided, their windows fogged, obscuring the occupants. But Serena knew who was in those cars. In one, a mother and her two preschoolers. In the other, Meredith. The scent of gasoline hung in the air, omen of the explosion that fate had ordained.

But when she tried to run to save the trapped family, she was unable to move. Corbin stood beside her, gripping her arm. "Welcome to hell," he said.

"I'm not afraid," she shouted, against the breathlessness of cold that rushed into her mouth as she opened it. "Even if I can't save them, that family will be with the angels. Even if they pass to the other side, they are safe."

Around them, the rain began to beat down harder, setting a chill in her bones. Thunder boomed like an amplified timpani, and Corbin laughed to its accompaniment. "Not here. Not in hell. You and your loved ones will stay here in *my* domain. You. Julian. Your father. You will dwell in the principalities of the lost forever."

"How dare you speak of my father. You have no power over any of us. We have done nothing to deserve being caught here with *you*." She looked Corbin in the eyes again, unafraid. "I've already been through hell with you, and I'm not doing it again." Again and again, she thought, *You are a fully enlightened being. You are a fully enlightened being.*

He grabbed her and spun around beneath the downpour. "Do you think it's that easy? That you can just wish hell away? It doesn't work that way. You're playing by my rules now."

"I'm not playing at anything, Corbin," she said, her voice rising. "The time for games is over."

She willed harder. *You are a fully enlightened being. You are a fully enlightened being.*

The scene shifted yet again. This time, as it materialized, Serena stood at the front door of her childhood home in Carmel. She looked down at herself, saw her old favorite pink hooded sweatshirt on her adolescent body.

Oh, God, no. She knew what lay inside the house. She did not want to go in. But something compelled her to reach forward and push open the door. Time slowed to a crawl. A team of paramedics knelt on the floor, performing chest compressions on a man whose blue eyes, the same eyes she had inherited, stared blankly at the ceiling.

One of the paramedics turned to look up at her. His amber gaze burned into hers. The rest of the figures froze, their movements suspended in midair. Corbin stood and walked toward her. "He made a deal with me," said the demon, latching on to her arm with a grip that was terrifyingly strong. "You'd never guess what kinds of things he traded away."

"That's not true!" Serena shouted. "My father was a good man. You have no hold over him, and no hold over me!"

"You're close to becoming a demon yourself, girl," he snarled.

"You couldn't be further from the truth." She stared right back into his eyes, concentrating on the phrase Arielle had said to her. *You are a fully enlightened being. You are a fully enlightened being.*

She thought of all things good. Of waves crashing on Carmel Beach. Of the mother and the little girls she'd saved, safe and happy together. Of Meredith's crazy potions and late-night advice. Of lying in Julian's arms, the synchronized rise and fall of breathing, their bodies twining in divine union. She imagined light pouring from her heart, into the dark abyss of this hell to which Corbin had brought her, willing happiness to every being that existed inside of it and out. The scene around them flickered, shimmering like a background image projected onto a life-size screen.

Words tumbled from her lips, the most powerful invocation she knew: *Lumen de lumine. Deum de deo. Deum verum de deo vero.* She chanted the words again, in Latin and English both: *Lumen de lumine. Deum de deo. Deum verum de deo vero. Light of light. God of God. True God of true God.*

It was then that she truly realized that Corbin had no power over her. His demonic abilities extended exactly as far as her willingness to believe that he could harm her. She had always known that nothing was as powerful as the divine light—that the balance between good and evil was the biggest misunderstanding plaguing mankind. But she had never understood that more fully than now.

"Hell can't hold me. I don't believe in it," she said, shaking off the demon's hold for the last time.

Summoning white light to herself, she concentrated hard, willing the energy into a compact ball that she directed straight toward the demon. That radiance flashed in the space between them, elongating and wavering for an instant before she streamed it right into the center of his forehead. He stumbled away, clutching his head and uttering a high-pitched shriek that threatened to pierce her eardrums. His bony body seemed to shrivel before her eyes, wilting into a heap of decomposing remains.

Over the horrible noise of his screaming, Serena shouted, "You stay here and rot, Corbin. I'm going back for Julian."

She gathered the bright shield of light around her once again, protecting herself. Held in her heart the knowledge that nothing and no one could harm her. That she truly was a fully enlightened being. Then she set the scene in her mind, willing herself back into the sickroom of Julian's nightmare.

Gabriel blinked, smiling. "You've come into your power, little Guardian. And you've learned to dematerialize."

So she had. She had no idea what had become of Corbin. Wherever he had gone, he wasn't here. She knew, beyond all sign of a doubt, that if she ever met him again, she would prevail. She was strong enough now that she could overcome him through the sheer power of her faith, the strength of her hope, her belief in love.

But there was no time to waste. They must get Julian out of this place immediately, she knew. She knelt by

Julian's bed, untying the bonds that held his wrists to the decaying wood. She spoke quietly as she worked at the knots. "Hell only exists because you believe it exists. It's an illusion. Julian, you have the ability to walk out of here. The demons have no authority over you. All you have to do is believe."

He looked up at her with such suffering in his eyes that she almost stopped right then, weighed down by the pain of it. "Believe in what?" he asked.

She forced herself to hold the thought in her mind, *You are a fully enlightened being. You are a fully enlightened being.* "Believe in love, my dearest."

He shut his eyes, turned his head away. "But I need to atone for the things I've done. For the lives I've ruined. I deserve to suffer."

"What's done is in the past. Your suffering isn't going to help anyone, not even those people whose lives you ruined. The only thing you can do is let go of the past, and go forward with a pure heart. You've learned your lesson. Repair what you've done, if possible, and start helping others instead of hurting them."

"I deserve to suffer for what I did to you."

"You did nothing to me. I learned the true nature of love. And I'm not giving up on you. The only one holding you here is yourself."

"I'm beyond redemption," he said. His voice was so mournful that for an instant, she wavered, wondering if he really was lost.

Behind her, she felt the radiance of Gabriel's energy, emanating into her and through her, the force of him so powerful it illuminated this place that seemed forsaken by God. She looked deep into Julian's eyes, sapphire shot with emerald, beautiful even in his suffering. And she said, "Nobody is beyond redemption. Divine love is universal and unconditional. I love you, Julian. All you have to do is believe."

I love you. Since his mother had died, countless women had said that to him. Most of them in the throes of sex. He had heard it thousands of times, but never once had it rung true before. It did now, coming from the lips of this little angel who had braved hell to rescue him.

How could she be right? It was not possible to end suffering just by believing it could end. Was it? And if so, what exactly was he supposed to believe? Believe that he was worthy of being released? That some good might come out of his existence if he tried to help others? The thought was ridiculous. Impossible.

There was a rustling of wings. *Archangel.* Julian had never seen him before, but through his feverish stupor, he knew what he saw. In the dank room, the magnificent angel shone. It seemed as though Serena, too, had grown brighter. She was no longer a frightened little fledgling. She had learned to fly.

Chapter Eighteen

Back to earth. Back to the safety of Serena's comfortable apartment. Back to something Julian had not experienced in centuries.

Peace.

"What am I, if not a demon?" Julian asked Gabriel, once they had finally returned.

The Archangel smiled, benevolence shining from his face, brighter even than the sunlight streaming into Serena's living room. "Perhaps you never realized it, but your true nature is angelic. That's what demons are. Fallen angels. Redemption is within the reach of every last one of you."

"But I don't know how to be…good," Julian protested, glumly thinking about the weight of his past, its temptations, its transgressions. Its sins.

"You have Serena to guide you. And you've already been protecting *her*. From now on, that will be your task. You are each other's Guardians. You must also know that your mother is always keeping vigil for you," the Archangel said. "Your father, too, will one day find his way back to enlightenment and remember his soul's true nature. You will all be reunited. I promise you that."

Julian realized that, even when he'd been in the depths of damnation, some small part of that *had* always known that his mother had always been watching over him. He'd never truly been alone.

"What about *my* father?" Serena asked, her forehead creasing into a worry as deep as Julian had ever seen it. "I saw him in hell. Corbin said…he told me my father had made a pact with him."

"All will be revealed in time, child," the Archangel answered.

"I will help you find the truth," Julian vowed. "There must be some way to uncover what really happened to your father. Corbin isn't to be trusted. He's full of lies."

"I know."

"And you've got to help me, too."

"With what?"

"I'm going to live the life I wanted to live two hundred years ago. I'm going to use my power for good instead of evil. The profits from the clubs will be used to help the poor. I'm going to bring joy into people's lives, instead of misery."

In the end, even Julian himself was stunned at how quickly that happened, and how easily it was to accomplish. He appointed Harry to redesign the clubs, and in the weeks that followed, Angel's Ecstasy was a bigger success than Julian ever imagined. The new Vegas club was an instant hit, even though its doors had remained closed for a week before reopening under the new name.

On the night of its second debut, Julian and Serena stood on the upper level, looking down over the dance floor, the masses of sinewy limbs below moving with joyous abandon. "This is how it should be," he shouted over the surging beat of the music. "No crime, no drugs, no prostitution."

Next to him, she grooved to the rhythm, her blond hair shining under the disco lights. "But pure fun. Even angels are entitled to a bit of that," she called back, winding her arms around his neck and pulling him into the beat.

He had no idea what the future would hold. He had no idea whether he could live up to the expectations she had of him, or that he had set for himself. He had no idea whether he would be able to resist life's temptations for the rest of his days. The only thing he knew was that he wanted to be with her forever.

Taking her hand, he descended the stairs to merge onto the dance floor. Together, they found the pulse of the music, their bodies moving in sync as they danced late into the night among the crowd of exuberant souls.

Exactly one year had passed since Serena's human death, and on that day, she brought Julian back to her hometown. Back to Carmel. Results of her subsequent attempts to dematerialize had proven unpredictable, so they opted to take the Maserati. This time, she drove.

They cruised along the Cabrillo Freeway, curving their way up the winding coastline with its dramatic crash of waves. "One year ago today, I was driving home on this very road. I stopped to help at the scene of an accident and I died."

As she drove, she reminded herself of the differences.

That day last year had not been a day like today, clear and sunny. Toward evening, the colors of the sunset had not blended into amber and pink, as they did right now. But as they veered along the highway, emotions warred within her. Sorrow. Fear. Doubt.

The sun disappeared into the ocean, vanishing out of view by the time she finally worked through the lump in her throat. "I saw a part of your human life that was very personal. I brought you here because I wanted to show you a part of my human life, too," she said, reminding herself of the reason they'd come. "I want you to know me as intimately as I know you, Julian."

As they neared the crash site, worry washed over her thoughts and panic threatened to capsize her. She wanted to turn the car around. To drive back to L.A. She had not counted on the feelings that flooded through her as she traveled this stretch of road again.

Mercifully, they arrived.

Without the rain and the crush of metal, it was simply a spot on the road, unremarkable but for the small wooden plaque that bore her name and Meredith's, along with a few bouquets of flowers to mark the occasion of their passing.

Yet, this was not what Serena had brought him here to see. She took Julian's hand and guided him into the forest, lighting their way with a flashlight. She knew where they were headed, the ground beneath her as familiar as her own backyard. They walked in silence, all the familiar scents and sounds from childhood coming back to her. The fresh, pungent smell of the pines and cypress trees around them. The rhythm of any waves growing louder as they hiked toward the ocean.

Overhead, stars cluttered the night sky, their shine un-hindered by the competing glow of city lights.

She lifted a finger to her lips. Led him clambering up a large rock, pulled him to peer over its edge. She whispered, "Look."

They stood on a cliff, looking down at a crowd that had gathered on the craggy shoreline of Point Lobos. Where a hundred points of light illuminated the shore-line, sending light back to the stars above.

She had brought him home to witness her one-year memorial. She had brought him to help her say goodbye. She had brought him with her, willed here by the silent wishes of her family and friends. By their hopes and their tears, beneath the glitter of stars and the flicker of candles. The group gathered was small in comparison to the thousands Nick's death had drawn. But during her life, they had loved her well. She pitied Nick, wherever he was, closed her eyes and said a silent prayer for his soul. One day, she would find him.

Just as one day she would find her father.

Tonight, she was here. Watching over the people who had come to pay tribute to her human life. Her mother stood at the front of the crowd. In the warm breeze, Serena stood absolutely still, quiet as possible to hear the faint resonance of Muriel's words rising up to reach Serena.

"It's been a year of firsts for us," she said. "Our first Thanksgiving without her, our first Christmas. Her twenty-fourth birthday, the Fourth of July. Life has been a little emptier without her. A little quieter. But I still feel her with us, watching over us. Sweetheart, we love you."

Andrew came to stand by their mother, putting his arm around her to comfort her. A few people wiped away tears. Serena wanted to cry, too.

I love you, too. And I'm so much closer than you'll ever know.

Muriel turned to look up at Serena. Her mother could sense her standing there on the cliff—Serena was sure of it. She sent love down to all of them. It still made her intensely sad to know that she would never be able to comfort her family and friends physically, to put her arms around them. But in her absence, they would comfort each other. And she would never be too far away to watch over them.

Her human life may have ended. But she understood now that her time on earth was just beginning.

She had the Company now. And she had Julian by her side.

In these past few weeks with him, despite the trials they'd undergone together, or perhaps because of them, she finally understood the true nature of romantic love. With him, she felt whole, as though whatever had broken in her during her human life had finally healed. Whatever was missing, she'd finally found. The little voice inside her was finally at peace, no longer whispering of bitterness or resentment.

Behind them, a noise sounded, the faintest brush of movement, too quiet to be human. They both turned at the same time, to see Arielle making her way up the rock toward them. Serena's heart felt as though it had cracked open and a warm glow spread over her. In that instant, all of time seemed to collapse into one single moment, and all beings seemed connected by a single unifying force: love.

* * *

Nearby, under the dense cover of foliage, a pair of green eyes as verdant as the cedar trees glinted in the night. Luciana hid, watching, and fingered the vial of poison that still dangled from her neck. She tilted her face upward in the cool night air, gazing up at the stars through the canopy of forest overhead. And gave thanks. Sent gratitude to the dark forces that had helped her to escape, once again.

Her run-in with the Company had been a setback, and it had drained her energy, to be sure. But she was free. And just as Serena had come home, so Luciana would return home, to a city on the shore of another ocean.

Home to Venice.

To recuperate. To recover. And to plan her revenge.

* * * * *

Acknowledgments

Thank you to my very own set of earthly guardians:

Valerie Gray, executive editor at MIRA Books. Thank you for your wholehearted support of this series, and your unwavering commitment to great storytelling. In the past year, your lessons in craftsmanship and your creative guidance have made me a better writer. You have taken me beyond what I could have achieved on my own. House calls much appreciated.

Kimberly Whalen, agent extraordinaire at Trident Media Group. Thank you for taking care of the business side of writing, for your expert advice on the industry. And for helping me to navigate my way through foreign tax forms and other lurking evils.

The Harlequin team. I am eternally grateful for the incredible support from the editorial, marketing and PR departments. I am just getting to know all of you, but recognize the hard work and talent you have each contributed in order to bring this book into the world. Special thanks to Sean Kapitain, for your gorgeous cover art. And to the wonderful Ana Luxton in the marketing department.

Patricia and Garyen. Mom and Dad, thank you for your dedication and love. For teaching me what I needed to know, for your backing and encouragement through the many years of university and through a major career change.

Johanna. I'm so appreciative of your advice and your generosity as a big sister and friend. You have always encouraged me to follow my dreams.

Friends and teachers from various university programs, yoga communities and other walks of life. Over the years, I have been blessed with the company of many kindred spirits. In particular, I thank my dear friend Jeanette, for all the positive energy you have given to this project and others.

Ed. My husband, my best friend, my real-life hero. Best daddy in the whole world to our baby pug, Dexter. Last, but certainly not least—thank you for building a life with me. For showing me the world through your eyes. For your tender heart and extraordinary compassion toward those in need. For continuing to grow with me.

The chilling Krewe of Hunters trilogy from
New York Times and *USA TODAY* bestselling author

HEATHER GRAHAM

SOME SECRETS REFUSE TO STAY BURIED...

Available wherever books are sold.

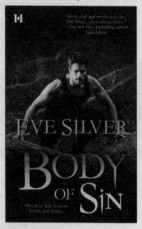

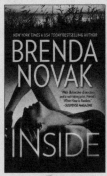
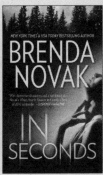

REQUEST YOUR FREE BOOKS!

2 FREE NOVELS FROM THE PARANORMAL ROMANCE COLLECTION PLUS 2 FREE GIFTS!

New York Times and *USA TODAY* bestselling author

MAGGIE SHAYNE

According to ancient prophecy, there's only one chance to avert the complete annihilation of the Undead. Twins James William and Brigit Poe, part human, part vampire, believe that they *are* that chance. In truth, the key lies with the reclusive—and mortal—scholar Lucy Lanfair.

As Armageddon approaches and anti-vampire sentiment fuels a war neither side can win, Lucy realizes that it's her destiny to not only stop a war but to save a powerful immortal's soul from his inner darkness. If she fails, his race will die—and so will her heart. Is the power of love strong enough to save the world?

Twilight Prophecy

Available wherever books are sold.

New York Times and *USA TODAY* Bestselling Author

CARLA NEGGERS

When Emma Sharpe is summoned to a convent on the Maine coast, it's partly for her art crimes work with the FBI, partly because of her past with the religious order. At issue is a mysterious painting depicting scenes of Irish lore and Viking legends, and her family's connection to the work. But when the nun who contacted her is murdered, it seems legend is becoming deadly reality.

For FBI agent Colin Donovan, the intrigue of the case is too tempting to resist. As the danger spirals closer, Colin is certain of only one thing—the very interesting Emma is at the center of it all.

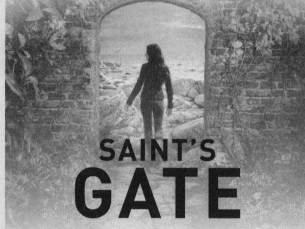

SAINT'S GATE

Available wherever books are sold.

MIRA™ | HARLEQUIN®
www.Harlequin.com

MCN1235R